THE BAZAAR
AND OTHER STORIES

ELIZABETH BOWEN

EDITED WITH AN INTRODUCTION BY
ALLAN HEPBURN

Edinburgh University Press

Edinburgh University Press Ltd
22 George Square, Edinburgh

Typeset in Weiss
by Norman Tilley Graphics Ltd, Northampton
and printed and bound in Great Britain
by Antony Rowe Ltd, Chippenham, Wilts

A CIP record for this book is available
from the British Library

ISBN 978 0 7486 3571 9 (hardback)
ISBN 978 0 7486 3572 6 (paperback)

Contents

Contents

Acknowledgements

Collecting the stories in this volume required the faith and perseverance of many people in far-flung places. Two research assistants, Robin Feenstra and Liisa Stephenson, indefatigably located materials and helped me to proofread the entire book aloud; offering astute comments on the nature of editing, they detected implausibilities where I suspected none. Phyllis Lassner and Shannon Wells-Lassagne shared their vast knowledge about Elizabeth Bowen with me on numerous occasions; I have been blessed by their insight and scholarly generosity. A month-long Mellon Fellowship at the Harry Ransom Humanities Research

Center at the University of Texas at Austin enabled completion of this book. Further research funds came from the Arts Insights program in the Faculty of Arts at McGill University and the Social Sciences and Humanities Research Council of Canada; invaluable support from these sources helped me to hire research assistants, secure permissions for this volume, and travel to the British Library, the Bodleian Library at Oxford, and Durham University Library. Jackie Jones at Edinburgh University Press, a champion of this project from beginning to end, has made every step of the process delightful. By supporting this project, Camilla Hornby at Curtis Brown in London, literary executors for the estate of Elizabeth Bowen, kindly assisted with negotiations for permissions and thereby ensured that these stories would, deservedly, come to public attention. I wish to thank Bowen's estate in particular for allowing me to proceed with this project.

Introduction

Although she wrote short stories throughout her life, Elizabeth Bowen never collected all of them into volumes. Owing to indifference or forgetfulness, she omitted at least twenty-eight tales from the books of short fiction that she assembled over the course of her career. These stories are gathered here for the first time. Two of them rank among her most accomplished: "The Lost Hope" and "Flowers Will Do." Others, especially "Salon des Dames," "The Bazaar," "Miss Jolley Has No Plans for the Future," and "Women in Love," afford insight into Bowen's technique and preoccupations. Despite the fact that some of these stories remain unfinished, they all demonstrate a command of characterisation, atmosphere, and situation that few other modernist short story writers possess. The best of these stories unfold miniature dramas in an intensely visual language.

After abandoning her studies in fine art at the London County Council School of Art – starting in 1919, she attended for two terms – Bowen devoted herself with complete absorption to writing short stories. Her first two books, *Encounters* (1923) and *Ann Lee's and Other Stories* (1926), led to a series of dazzling collections: *Joining Charles and Other Stories* (1929), *The Cat Jumps and Other Stories* (1934), *Look at All Those Roses* (1941), and *The Demon Lover and Other Stories* (1945). Her short story production peaked in the 1930s and early 1940s, then slowed after the Second World War. As her productivity as a short story writer declined, her productivity as an essayist rose. From the late 1940s onward, magazine editors solicited essays from her on diverse subjects. Despite the energy that writing essays demanded, Bowen, to satisfy publishers and readers who clamoured for her fiction, repackaged old stories with new. *Selected Stories* (1946) prepared the way for a reprint of *Early Stories* (1951), a volume that joins together all of the tales in *Encounters* and *Ann Lee's*. The anthology, *Stories by Elizabeth Bowen* (1959), included a sampling of the best stories, but no new work. The last volume published during her lifetime, *A Day in the Dark and Other Stories* (1965), mixed five relatively new stories (four had appeared in magazines) with fifteen reprinted works. Even after Bowen's death in February 1973, previously printed stories were shuffled according to thematic connections, as happened with *Irish Stories* (1978).

Bowen often published the same story in several places in order to maximise its exposure. For example, the story entitled "No. 16," about a young female poet who visits an ailing male writer, first appeared in the *Listener* in January 1939, then was reprinted in the magazine *Living Age* in September 1939. Subsequently it was collected in *Look at All Those Roses*. Thereafter, "No. 16" appeared in

INTRODUCTION

Stories by Elizabeth Bowen and *A Day in the Dark*. It was reprinted a sixth and last time in the posthumous volume, *The Collected Stories of Elizabeth Bowen* (1981). With an introduction by Angus Wilson, *The Collected Stories* slots all the works in *Encounters, Ann Lee's, Joining Charles, The Cat Jumps, Look at All Those Roses*, and *The Demon Lover* by decade. Wilson, paying homage to his friend, praises Bowen for the "instinctive formal vision" (7) and "witty" (8) representations of families and love affairs that make her stories unique. No fugitive pieces from newspapers or magazines are included in *The Collected Stories*.

Understanding that one short story could have many incarnations, Bowen also sold her stories to international markets. Business correspondence with her literary agents, Curtis Brown, indicates a brisk trade in Danish, German, Japanese, French, Greek, and other translations of her fiction. Moreover, realising that a story could achieve new vigour in another medium, she sold the rights for radio adaptations. Bowen herself reworked an early story, "The Confidante," for broadcast in 1943 (HRC 2.3). Not normally inclined to undertake the business of rewriting her own fiction, however, she granted others the right to adapt her works while holding the power to veto a script should it deviate too far from the original. In a letter dated 11 April 1953, she distances herself as much as possible from an adaptation of "Pink May" by Mary Jones: "I should like the broadcast to be announced (if it is accepted) as 'based upon the short story by Elizabeth Bowen'" (HRC 10.5). The original might inspire Jones's adaptation but Bowen does not want the adaptation to be identified as her own work. Sometimes stories were read on the air without dramatisation. Versions of "The Tommy Crans," "Reduced," "Love," "Tears, Idle Tears," "Telling," "Songs My Father Sang Me," and numerous other stories were broadcast on BBC radio in the UK and overseas. Although the radio market provided constant exposure, other stories gained public notice as adaptations for the stage and television. "Oh, Madam . . ." had a run as a play in London, and "The Inherited Clock" was broadcast on television.

In light of the extensive publication and adaptation of Bowen's stories, the omission of some works from *The Collected Stories* requires explanation. Some stories in the present volume were written for specific occasions at the request of editors; for this reason, Bowen may have viewed them as journeyman's labour not worth collecting. These commissioned stories presume widely divergent audiences. "Brigands," included in a compilation of pieces for children called *The Silver Ship* (1932), addresses a readership of ten- to twelve-year-olds. Similarly, "The Unromantic Princess" appeared in *The Princess Elizabeth Gift Book* (1935), likewise intended for children. "Brigands" and "The Unromantic Princess" are no less funny or expertly crafted because they speak to young audiences. In fact, Bowen indulges a satirical streak in these stories that she typically holds in check in adult stories. Other stories show the signs of being written to measure. Tapping the women's magazine market in the United States in the 1950s, Bowen published romances and Christmas stories in *Vogue* and *Woman's Day*, at the same time as she wrote essays on similar subjects for *Mademoiselle* and *Glamour*. The Christmas stories tend towards lovers' reunions or melodramatic terrors. Obsessed with the nativity as a central mystery of Christianity, Bowen set several stories, not all of which she completed, on Christmas Eve or Christmas Day. The cluster of Christmas stories from the 1950s promotes the holiday as a time of generosity and sentiment, if not enforced gaiety and sentimentality.

The stories in this volume bespeak multiple, distinct literary influences. When Bowen first tried her hand at writing stories in the early 1920s, she had no real idea of the challenges that the genre imposed, as she later claimed. In the preface to *Early Stories*, she states that the story was, in her youth, not

> recognized as "a form." There had appeared so far, that is to say, little constructive-critical interest in the short story's possibilities and problems . . . I had read widely, but wildly. I did not know

the stories of Hardy or Henry James; I may have heard of Chekhov; I had not read Maupassant because I imagined I could not read French. (viii)

Not educated at a university, Bowen disciplined herself by voracious reading throughout her life. As a reviewer for the *Tatler* between 1945 and 1949, and again between 1954 and 1958, she consumed, on average, three books a week. Book by book, she acquired an extensive knowledge of British, Irish, American, and European fiction, with special attention paid to advances in the short story. In a 1959 radio interview, she acknowledged that she learned fictional technique by imitating other writers:

> I can still see streaks or threads and patches of other influences of other people. I think when you get started – for my generation, my kind of writer, it was one way to teach yourself. You became aware of influences anyway – it was one pattern of one's imagination. It was rather like a palisade round a young growing tree. you knew that you felt secure in other people's work. (HRC 2.3)

To consolidate her grasp on the short story, Bowen read masterworks by her slightly older peers: James Joyce, D. H. Lawrence, Katherine Mansfield. The signs of many authors' influence, as unlikely as Isak Dinesen and Maxim Gorky, flash throughout her fiction. Several times she alludes to the fact that her first two books of stories were published by Sidgwick & Jackson, the firm that also released E. M. Forster's *The Celestial Omnibus* (1911). In the title story of Forster's collection, a boy takes enchanted coach rides; fully acquainted with Forster's book, Bowen modifies the trope of the wild ride in her celebrated story, "The Demon Lover," and, less diabolically, the bus rides that structure "The Last Bus" and "Christmas Games."

Of all influences on Bowen's short stories, none is stronger than Katherine Mansfield's. As Bowen confides in the preface to *Early Stories*, Mansfield was "not only to be the innovator but to fly the flag" (viii) when it came to short story technique. Building upon Mansfield's example, Bowen's modernism is cosmopolitan in orientation and detailed in texture. All details, however fine, count towards narrative meaning. Bowen's earliest stories, "Salon des Dames" and "Moses," both set in Europe, bear a resemblance to Mansfield's *In a German Pension* (1911) and *Bliss* (1920), although Bowen declared with chagrin that she did not yet know those stories in the early 1920s. Coincidentally, both Mansfield and Bowen revel in encounters between British and European characters as occasions for pretentiousness and misunderstanding. If the New Zealand-born writer had no impact on Bowen's earliest stories, "The Bazaar," which probably dates from the late 1920s, reveals a careful assimilation of Mansfield's ironic handling of situations and fluid narrative technique. Mansfield specialises in the juxtaposing of different temporal dimensions, as when the woman in "A Dill Pickle," accidentally crossing the path of her former lover, remembers moments from their romantic liaison six years earlier. Bowen layers time with similar finesse. In several stories narrated in the first person in this volume – "The Claimant," "I Died of Love," and "Candles in the Window" – an older woman thinks back upon her earlier experiences. Tension emerges from the split between incident and reflection. Moreover, Bowen, like Mansfield, achieves narrative economy in dialogue, characterisation, and action. Gestures reveal hidden meanings; spoken words convey unspoken treacheries. In a long preface to a selection of Mansfield's stories, Bowen praises the older writer's art for being "tentative, responsive, exploratory" (*Mulberry Tree* 72). Guided to some degree by her predecessor's example, Bowen developed an acute consciousness of the short story as a way to convey the partial, the interrupted, and the disconnected aspects of contemporary life.

By the late 1930s, Bowen was an acknowledged master of the short story. Because of her success as a fiction writer, she was asked to edit and introduce *The Faber Book of Modern Short Stories* (1937). In addition to providing forewords to volumes published by friends and acquaintances, she wrote introductions to *The Observer Prize Stories* (1952) and the first number of the literary journal *Chance* (1952). Bowen's extensive commentary on the short story, including incidental comments in prefaces and reviews, sheds light on the care that she took to perfect her own fiction. In a brief introduction to Guy de Maupassant's "The Little Soldier," she singles out "sharp actuality" and "direct emotions" as hallmarks of the French author's style ("Guy de Maupassant" 26). The short story permits immediacy, whereas the novel exploits elaboration and indirection. In her short stories, Bowen aims for sharpness and directness without neglecting the atmosphere that envelops characters in conflict. About Anton Chekhov, Bowen recalls that "no sooner were his stories translated into English than he began to be felt as an influence. Why? Because the Chekhov stories deal more with mood than with action. To us in England that was something quite new; and it opened infinite possibilities" ("Short Story in England" 39–40). The short story evokes an atmosphere, a particular climate in relation to which characters take on a face and a function.

Retaining traces of its Russian, French, and American lineage, the short story hybridises with the English language in Britain and Ireland. In "The Short Story in England," Bowen names six English short story writers whom she considers exemplary: D. H. Lawrence, Rudyard Kipling, Somerset Maugham, Aldous Huxley, William Plomer, and Katherine Mansfield (41). She refers also to James Joyce, Frank O'Connor, Liam O'Flaherty, and Seán O'Faoláin as the best Irish contributors to the genre. Plomer and O'Faoláin figured in Bowen's circle of intimate friends, which accounts for their flattering, if not entirely justified, inclusion on these lists. Kipling's name, too, comes as something of a surprise, but Bowen insists that

"Kipling the artist tended to be obscured by Kipling the national institution," which caused a delayed appreciation of his craftsmanship ("Short Story in England" 39). In "Flavia," Bernard and Flavia receive a set of Kipling's works as a wedding present, a detail partly explained by Bowen's reverence for Kipling's mastery of the short story.

According to Bowen, the dimensions of the short story impose constraints, and these constraints create the inevitability of a single mood and a compression of effect, even to the point of "emotional narrowness" (*Collected Impressions* 154). In a review of Gorky's tales translated into English, Bowen incidentally provides a concise definition of the short story:

> Short story writers form a sort of democracy: when a man engages himself in this special field his stories stand to be judged first of all on their merits *as* stories, only later in their relation to the rest of his work. The more imposing the signature, the more this applies. The craft (it may be no more) of the short story has special criteria; its limitations are narrow and definite. It is in the building-up of the short story that the craftsman side of the artist has to appear. Very close demands on the writer's judgement are made; the short story is not a mere case for the passing fancy; it offers no place for the unobjectified sentiment, for the impulsive start that could not be followed through. It must have implications which will continue when the story is done. (*Collected Impressions* 153)

Short story writers comprise a democracy insofar as no single author towers above another; the genre exacts submission from all writers, converting them into equals before the onerous obligations of art. Even if the limits of the story cause "a necessary over-simplification of characters, and a rather theatrical tensing-up of the dialogue" (*Collected Impressions* 154), the same limits contribute to unity of action. For this reason, the story requires craft – a knowledge of how to sustain pace and how to find the exact objective equivalent for sentiments. Bowen further specifies that the short story, unlike the novel, does not aim at comprehensiveness or verisimilitude. A certain trickery, out of step with mimesis, brings a short story to its conclusion, a conclusion that may seem brusque because of the a priori terseness of the form.

Yet the short story appeals to Bowen because of its brevity. Shortness borders on incompleteness and enhances the atmospheric unseizableness of situations and characters. Character, in Bowen's estimation, always takes second place to action in narrative. In "Notes on Writing a Novel," she denies the commonplace idea "that the function of action is to *express* the characters"; in her opinion, "characters are there to provide the action" (*Collected Impressions* 249). This novelistic principle holds true also for the short story, in which character is elaborated in very few scenes. The form of the short story prevents prolonged analysis of individual characters in terms of their motives, pasts, or feelings. In the preface to *Stories by Elizabeth Bowen*, she comments, "I do not feel that the short story can be, or should be, used for the analysis or development of character. The full, full-length portrait is fitter work for the novelist; in the short story, treatment must be dramatic – we are dealing with man, or woman or child, in relation to a particular crisis or mood or moment, and to that only" (*Mulberry Tree* 129). Notwithstanding the compression of character, the details that constitute their fictional being are metonyms for other forces. As Phyllis Lassner explains, "This technique reflects Bowen's theory of character as shaped by historical processes" (75).

The short story requires compression in dialogue and dramatic situation. In Bowen's stories, people talk at cross-purposes or do not express themselves fully in conversation, which exacerbates tensions. Drama arises from misunderstanding and withheld meaning, as happens between Tom and Antonia in "The Man and the

Boy." Dialogue, even when mined with misapprehensions, displays character. Any recourse to description would merely add to the length of the story. The "full-length portrait" of character suits the novel, where motive and feeling can be explained in the *longueurs* of exposition. The short story, by contrast, "confers importance: characters in it are given stature, and are moreover spotlit, so that their gestures are not only clearly seen but cast meaningful shadows" ("Rx for a Story Worth the Telling" 14). The embodiment of actions, characters do not explain their every motive, nor need they. Action unfolds in a series of spotlit manoeuvres, but the glare of the spotlight elongates the shadows thrown by characters. Characters act according to the dictates of plot, which their own volition distorts.

Bowen invariably conceives of fiction as a coincidence of pressures:

> There is the plot: that is, the author's intention. And inside that plot (or, situation) and in it only can the characters operate. And, that they may operate the better, the novelist subjects them to an inhuman pressure – keeping them at the alert, and extracting the utmost from them, forcing them along. He exposes them, night and day, to a relentless daylight in which nothing is hid. No human being, other than a fiend, would treat with his fellow humans, in daily life, in so ruthless, uncompromising a manner. ("Novelist and his Characters" 22)

The author's handling of characters borders on sadism. Plot moves along a chain of cause and effect, or event and consequence. Character, auxiliary to sequence, is gripped as if in a vice. In her introduction to *The Observer Prize Stories*, Bowen calls this "inner inevitability" a merit in any narrative (viii). The situation lays hold of the characters, rather than the characters laying hold of the situation. Whether they make the situation or not, characters have to respond to the force of circumstance. They act under the burden of necessity.

Bowen responded to a different kind of necessity by writing stories for collaborative volumes. In addition to "The Unromantic Princess" and "Brigands," three stories – "She Gave Him," "Flavia," and "The Good Earl" – initially appeared in books by several hands. "The Good Earl," a political allegory masquerading as an Irish folk tale, was written for *Diversion* (1946), a book sold to raise money for the Yugoslav Relief Fund. Proceeds from *The Princess Elizabeth Gift Book*, in which "The Unromantic Princess" appeared, supported the Princess of York Hospital for Children. On the other hand, "Flavia," written for *The Fothergill Omnibus* (1931), had no specifically charitable aim. As editor, John Fothergill invited several authors to write a story on a given plot: a correspondence between a man and woman is curtailed when the man marries; when he resumes the correspondence after his marriage, he learns that his wife and his correspondent are one and the same person. Whether *Diversion, The Fothergill Omnibus*, or *The Princess Elizabeth Gift Book*, the collaborative book either demonstrates public-mindedness or endorses public causes. The story need have no direct connection to the cause it ostensibly supports. In terms of content, 'The Good Earl" has no link at all to Yugoslavia. By contrast, "The Unromantic Princess" does offer sly advice about governance to Princess Elizabeth; although only nine years old when the book bearing her name was published, she was in a direct line to ascend the British throne.

Bowen's exuberance for collaboration grew out of her fondness for games of all sorts. After-dinner games regularly occurred at Bowen's Court, the country house in Ireland that Bowen inherited from her father in 1930. An avid player of "paper games, card games, parlour games," she also invented new games to amuse house-guests (Glendinning 87). Party games extended to book culture. "She Gave Him" forms one chapter in *Consequences*, a book that takes its inspiration from a parlour game of the same name. In turn, nine participants add a chapter to the manuscript before passing it on to the next person. Rushing to submit her chapter, Bowen felt that she botched "She Gave Him," as she told A. E. Coppard, editor of the book, in a letter dated 16 August 1932:

> I found what I had written was too long and talky, & cut it – *now*, I find much too vigorously, so that I find it is now underweight. I'm so sorry: this wasn't meant to be. Please dock my percentage accordingly.
>
> To tell you the truth, I liked the scene (your's [sic]) but disliked the characters, so made heavy weather of it: there's something about exposing the poseur I find very unrewarding: I could wish the He & She had been more straightforward and picaresque. I very much wish that my part were better. (HRC Coppard Archive)

Other writers' contributions not only create intractable problems in the plot, but also impose challenges to maintaining consistency of style and quality. The collaborative book ultimately exposes the incommensurability of talent and imagination among several authors.

Notwithstanding her unhappiness about "She Gave Him," Bowen entertained the possibility of writing for other omnibus editions. In the postscript to a letter dated 15 October 1932, she proposed a novelty book to Robert Gibbings, who published *Consequences* at the Cockerel Press:

> I've for some time been thinking over a project of getting 7 (fairly able) writers to write one story a piece to the heading of each one of "The Seven Deadly Sins." Some people in France did this – I don't know if you came across the book? – de Lacretelle, Cocteau, Morand (in his good days) and four others. The result was interesting. I discussed this with Mr. Coppard some time ago

& he said he'd do one, and I expect Mr. Strong would too. Would
the idea be of any interest to you? It's only just an idea, as I say,
and may not be worth pursuing. I think the selection of writers
would be very important, as the stories should be neither
mawkish or sensational, nor over-heavy. (HRC 10.4)

Gibbings volleyed back two further ideas for jointly written books.
In a letter to Bowen on 19 October 1932, he suggested "Excuses," in
which "four or five women writers create compromising situations
for the husbands of their heroines," or "Volume," in which "half a
dozen authors" narrate the fulfilment of a "fortune told by some
profess onal" (HRC 11.5). Even though none of these collaborative
projects came to fruition, they attest to the high spirits and
camaraderie of the 1930s. Bowen views joint efforts as occasions for
drollery. By the same token, the short stories that she writes for
collaborative books impose constraints of length, content, and tone.
The stories written for such joint ventures reveal how Bowen rises to
the challenge, or not.

Some of Bowen's best stories – "Summer Night," "Ivy Gripped
the Steps," "Mysterious Kôr" – were written in direct or indirect
response to the Second World War. During the 1950s she wrote few
stories and none at all in the 1960s, yet during this period her
critical analysis of the genre sharpened. Between February and May
1960, she taught a course on the short story at Vassar College in
Poughkeepsie, New York. In two extant spiral-bound notebooks that
contain her syllabus and lecture notes, she lays down some precepts
for the short story. The lecture notes project information tele-
graphically, for they are intended to be pedagogical aids rather than
extensively worked out arguments. None the less, Bowen extracted
the essentials of this teaching experience for an article called
"Advice," published in the July 1960 issue of *Mademoiselle*. In
"Advice," Bowen, still pronouncing in a professorial voice, claims
that "Language can not only register but heighten, by its speed, its

emphasis and its rhythm, the emotional pressure we put behind it" (*Afterthought* 214). She cautions against repetition in subject or expression that rigidifies into convention. On the other hand, the pursuit of novelty in language – ornamentation for its own sake – distracts the reader. "There is a dramatic element in language, which is latent even while held in check," she concludes (*Afterthought* 213). Despite being the place where "emotional pressure" and a "dramatic element" combine, language clamps down on those pressures like a lid on a pot.

The Vassar notebooks disclose Bowen's thinking over the genealogy of the short story in relation to her own accomplishments in the genre. In a class devoted to the short story as "unique expression," by which she means the tell-tale personality of an author stamped into the fabric of a story, Bowen considered talking about her own fiction. In the end, she refrained, or so the lecture notes suggest. Instead she discussed stories that she particularly cherished: Chekhov's "The Kiss," Mansfield's "Prelude" and "In a German Pension," Maupassant's "The Necklace," Joyce's "The Dead," Lawrence's "The Rocking Horse Winner," Maugham's "The Colonel's Lady," Welty's "The Shower of Gold," James's "The Beast in the Jungle," Faulkner's "A Rose for Emily," and a smattering of stories by Edgar Allan Poe, Wallace Stegner, Dorothy Parker, J. D. Salinger, Seán O'Faoláin, O. Henry, and others. The syllabus lists canonical tales and an exuberant dose of contemporary American works tailored to the Vassar students.

Bowen elaborates on the common ground between drama and short stories in the Vassar notebooks. Dramatic tension, she claims, coils within the short story. Drama and short fiction share "*a concentration of Forces [Tautness]* a presentation of things in terms of effect (Play must not *sag*: S.S. must not do so either" (HRC 7.3; Bowen's punctuation and emphasis). Both drama and the short story present scenes without narrative "rambling"; action unfolds with "a sense of pressure – of immediacy – of something happening within the grip of *our* senses – under our eyes" (HRC 7.3). For maximum effect, character, simplified and unified, emerges through confrontation with other characters. Dialogue in both the short story and drama can occur without being spoken. As Bowen emphasises, "The Short Story is – thus – the right – indeed the inevitable – form for the treatment *of an* incident, crisis, or, situation which the writer feels to be of greater importance than its *apparent* triviality might show" (HRC 7.3; Bowen's punctuation). The statement implies that the modern short story heightens the significance of a seemingly trivial event. The story does not take inspiration from heroic or grandiose action; its shape and length derive from its implication in ordinariness. As Bowen comments in her preface to *The Faber Book of Modern Short Stories*, the short story, as a product of the twentieth century for the most part, is not "sponsored by a tradition" (*Collected Impressions* 38). The story does not aim at synthesis, but demonstrates susceptibilities and irrationalities.

The Vassar notebooks detail Bowen's understanding of the short story as a vehicle for supernatural or uncanny events. She advises that the "'atmosphere' necessary for MAGIC *would be difficult to sustain throughout a novel*[.] Hence, suitability – for Magic – of the S.S." (HRC 7.3). The macabre stories of Edgar Allan Poe confirm such a claim, as do the ghost stories of Henry James. In Bowen's view, the story has a mandate to explore mysterious or uncanny events. The quick pace of short narratives limits rational conjecture, which allows the author to perpetrate irrational actions and activate primitive emotions such as fear. In her Vassar notes, Bowen insists that irrationality inheres in the short story form:

> The UNCANNY means – I think? – the unknowable – something beyond the bounds of *rational* knowledge –
> In this, I include the GHOST STORY – with its content of *fear*
> With *Fear*, we return to *Primitive Feeling*
> The S.S. can *depict* or *evoke fear*

The extent to which it involves *us* in the *primitive sense of fear* is the measure of the "Success" of the Ghost STORY. (HRC 7.3; Bowen's lineation and emphasis)

Having previously discussed the primitive aesthetic of modernist writers such as Lawrence in her lectures, Bowen equates the success of a ghost story with the ability to stir fear in readers or characters within the narrative. In "Just Imagine . . ." Noel and Nancy indulge their craving for fear by telling and listening to ghastly stories; as much as Noel wants to terrorise Nancy, Nancy longs to be terrorised. Pointing out the allegiance between the uncanny and the short story, "Just Imagine . . ." administers placebo doses of fear to Nancy, if not to the reader. Because the short story condenses action, connections between events or people remain unspoken. The uncanny lodges in the recesses of such unspoken connections, or what Bowen calls the "unknowable"; where information is incomplete, irrational explanation or primitive feeling springs up.

Bowen's identification of the story with uncanniness explains the preponderance of stories in this volume that have a supernatural bent or a fairy-tale quality. Unannounced, fairy godmothers fly in from nowhere to attend christenings. Wicked older women start covens and prey upon vulnerable youths. Ordinary houses turn out to be haunted by ghosts claiming to be rightful heirs. Although these traits and characters belong to the fairy tale, Bowen domesticates them into Christmas narratives or adapts them to fables. She treats the fairy tale as a flexible form that need not adhere to the enchanted conclusions of Goldilocks or Cinderella. Praising the Brothers Grimm for rescuing oral tales from oblivion, Bowen comments that the Grimm stories "are tales for all. For children, they have the particular virtue of making sense. Everything that a child feels should happen *does* happen" ("Enchanted Centenary" 113). The fairy tale appeals to her for two particular reasons: first, it embodies wish-fulfilling potentiality; second, by keeping alive oral narration, it stresses the bond between narrator and audience. As Bowen claims in "The Comeback of Goldilocks et al.," "the fairy tale, in its extreme simplicity, is a supreme test of the narrator's art" (74). In terms of its dimensions, the fairy tale roughly corresponds to the short story. Although the fairy tale depends on some recognisable formulae, it is subject to the dual pressures of representing conflict and finding a conclusion to conflict within limited temporal dimensions, as does the short story.

However unacknowledged, the fairy tale has a vibrant presence within modernism, especially but not exclusively among Irish writers. Oscar Wilde's fairy tales promote charity and urbanity as aspects of modern temperament. William Butler Yeats admires the simplicity that Wilde achieved in his fairy tales: "Only when he spoke, or when his writing was the mirror of his speech, or in some simple fairy tale, had he words exact enough to hold a subtle ear" (*Autobiography* 90). Yeats may be no judge of fit language in fairy tales, for he miscalculates their effect on the young: "Wilde asked me to tell his little boy a fairy story, and I had but got as far as 'Once upon a time there was a giant' when the little boy screamed and ran out of the room" (*Autobiography* 91). The fairy tale has calmer effects in other modern texts. James Joyce's *A Portrait of the Artist as a Young Man* (1916) evokes a mythic realm of childhood by reciting the formulaic opening of the fairy tale, albeit with a twist: "Once upon a time and a very good time it was . . ." (7). In the same spirit, Henry Green's novel *Loving* (1945) begins, "Once upon a day," and ends, "happily ever after" (1, 225).

Joyce, Green, and Bowen take up the fairy tale ironically. In *Loving*, the goings-on in an Irish country house during the Second World War defy belief. As Marina MacKay points out about Green's novel, "the neutral Republic of Ireland was something of a fantastical never-never land during what its politicians euphemised as 'The Emergency'" (103). Like Joyce and Green, Bowen responds to the myths foisted on children or countries with the evocation of tales that disconcert expectations. "The Good Earl," with its blend of a collective Irish "we" narrator and late Victorian setting, converts the folk tale into a political allegory. The earl builds a hotel and buys a steamboat at the expense of commonsense and the common good. Forests have been denuded and the castle has become dilapidated because of the earl's overweening ambition. The mythic quality of "The Good Earl" – its shifting from past to present tense, its abridging of decades – makes the story a fable of aristocratic folly. A fairy tale for adults, the story stretches the boundaries of the form.

The fairy tale is not morally static or constricted by formulae in Bowen's view. In an introduction to *The King of the Golden River*, she points out that Ruskin's fairy tale has three brothers but no princess, and a "decidedly comic" person, the bedraggled South-West Wind, who practises magic (iii). Ruskin's tale thus contradicts the conventions of the genre. No matter how earnestly she praises traditional tales, Bowen uses the fairy tale, with its provenance in housewives' stories, to revise conventions of gender and morality. She resists stereotypes of helpless girls and helpful godmothers. Cast as an orally transmitted seamstress's tale, "I Died of Love" takes place between the last years of Victoria's reign and some unspecified later time. Magical elements, such as Miss Mettishaw's sewing skill and her coming and going at the busiest times for the shop, mingle with a cautionary story of love and folly. Neither Bowen nor Miss Mettishaw promises a happy ending. Indeed, the destruction of Miss Mettishaw's millinery establishment reconfigures the "happily ever after" of the fairy tale. In a less anxious register, "The Unromantic Princess" does not deny the virtues of commonsense and punctuality, but those virtues succeed better when combined with tolerance and a human capacity to love. The princess dispenses with fairy godmothers because wizardry has no place in the proper governance of a country, which henceforth will operate along "modern lines." Many of the children in Bowen's stories show practical intelligence. In "Brigands," precocious children outstrip adults in their understanding of thieves. Whereas the adults prove incapable of thinking of anyone but themselves, Oliver and Maria act more or less out of curiosity and selflessness. They do not believe in supernatural explanations. As "The Claimant" and "Christmas Games" demonstrate, sorcery and magic are best left to adults.

The majority of stories in this volume are indeed written for and about adults. In a realist rather than a fairy-tale mode, they depict a tangle of unhappy love affairs and marriages. More often than not, Bowen trains her sights on the crisis of sundered love brought about by an accumulation of misunderstandings, disappointments, and betrayals. Lovers in these stories are rarely romanticised, let alone romantic; modern love forbids the celebration of grandiose passions in and of themselves. Lady Cuckoo comically ignores Uncle Theodore's marriage proposals in "Emergency in the Gothic Wing," which does not dissuade him from asking again. Lovers, such as the irascible pair in "Moses" or the tetchy couple in "Flavia," are subjected to ironic diagnoses, either by each other or by the narrator. Many of these stories tabulate the costs of love. An extra-marital affair painfully ends a marriage in "Story Scene." In "So Much Depends," the carelessness of a young woman in love contrasts with the anguish of a mature woman unsure of how to be in love: Ellen spreads discontent wherever she goes because she feels wronged, whereas Miss Kerry manages her more passionate feelings without ostentation.

Unhappiness is one of the steepest costs of love. Accordingly, broken engagements preoccupy Bowen. In "Comfort and Joy," "So Much Depends," and "Happiness," lovers manage their break-ups with varying degrees of success. Some lovers call a truce to their unhappiness; others remain permanently suspended in despair. A broken engagement is surely in the offing in "Flowers Will Do," but the uncertainty of that outcome reflects Sydney and Doris's uncertainty about why they are engaged in the first place. As Bowen demonstrates in her novels *To the North* (1932) and *The Death of the*

Heart (1938), a love affair is most modern when it frays and unravels under the force of mobile circumstances. "Flavia" proves the incompatibility of being a wife and a lover at the same time. The story also stakes a claim for the husband's inability to recognise his own wife in the guise of his epistolary lover. He wants some mystery to occlude his knowledge of the woman he loves. Perhaps some stories in this volume remain unfinished because Bowen did not know how to reckon the costs of unhappiness brought about by love and its ending.

Editorial Practices

I first began to gather Bowen's uncollected stories and essays with a view to writing a critical book about her novels. J'nan M. Sellery and William O. Harris's *Elizabeth Bowen: A Bibliography*, listing both published and archival materials, proved indispensable for locating obscure pieces. As thorough as Sellery and Harris's bibliography is, it does not record all of Bowen's publications. By good luck and a scrupulous reading of Bowen's correspondence, I discovered "The Lost Hope" in the *Sunday Times*. It is possible that some of the stories included in this volume as "unpublished and unfinished" did appear in magazines in the United Kingdom or the United States, but I have not been able to find them. Other stories, as yet unknown, may come to light. As I accumulated documents in order to obtain a better-rounded sense of Bowen's fictional output, I realised that other scholars would probably have to retrace the process of photocopying and visiting archives to access these same stories. This volume, therefore, is intended to widen the frame of understanding of Bowen's short stories for lay readers and scholars alike. Although some stories in this volume were published in magazines or books, others exist only in handwritten or typescript drafts. Published stories automatically have a base text against which variants can be compared, should manuscripts or drafts be extant. A manuscript for

INTRODUCTION

"The Unromantic Princess," located in the Columbia University archives, shows few variants from the published text. The typescript for "The Good Earl," held at the Harry Ransom Center at the University of Texas at Austin, deviates in minor details from the published text. Unpublished stories create a different set of problems. Although she has rounded, legible handwriting, Bowen's manuscripts occasionally defy decoding. From about 1935 onward, she wrote directly on to the typewriter, which makes decipherment easier. She edited typed copy either by using carets to insert text with a pen or by typing words between lines. Her crossings-out sometimes create confusion because parts of two formulations contradict each other. Whenever significant variants occur that might reveal something about the content of the story I have noted them.

In Bowen's complicated and sometimes inverted syntax, punctuation carries the burden of hesitation, silence, and emphasis. Bowen applies colons and semi-colons, sometimes several per sentence, where other writers would place a full stop. Writing quickly in drafts, she leaves out quotation marks and commas around quoted speech. When necessary, I have added missing punctuation without drawing attention to these changes; they are oversights rather than artistic decisions, as I surmise from Bowen's regular practice. Yet punctuation affects meaning. For instance, in the handwritten version of "The Bazaar," dashes accumulate wantonly: "With a sense of delicious guilt she touched their petals – she knew now, but could not explain, why women went wrong – 'They're so sweet, they're so dark,' she said – no, they were pale too: it was not that. She thought, 'I should make quite a florist,' dipping her face into the sweet-pea." The full stop after "that" is not clear in the manuscript because the word "dipping" rises below as an insertion and may have been written over the top of the full stop. No comma follows "thought" in the manuscript either. Bowen might therefore have meant to write "it was not that she thought" as a single clause, which would create an unusual subsequent sentence. In such cases, I have opted for plausible punctuation that renders syntax coherent.

In manuscripts and typescripts, and occasionally in published stories, dialogue bunches together in a single paragraph; two or more speakers are quoted without any paragraph breaks. In almost every instance that such bunching occurs, I have taken the liberty of separating dialogue into paragraphs to distinguish one speaker from another. In this regard, "The Last Bus" represents a particular challenge, for the accumulation of diverse voices all talking at once might deliberately create cacophony. Notwithstanding such a possible authorial intention, Bowen distinguishes individuals on the bus and their voices are, in my opinion, better served by being kept distinct from each other with a view to producing a clear reading text. In most cases, I signal paragraph breaks that have been added.

In a related matter of textual layout, typesetters often introduce a space break to distribute text across the page. In newspapers and magazines, the text has to fit into so many inches of space. Therefore editors laying out the text insert space breaks to stretch out the text. These space breaks sometimes fall in unlikely places and in all probability do not coincide with Bowen's intentions. Not having access to typescripts or manuscripts of all of the published stories, I can only deduce what Bowen's intentions might have been. In some cases, such as "Emergency in the Gothic Wing," "So Much Depends," and "Happiness," I omit typesetters' space breaks to prevent choppiness. Some breaks fall in the middle of dialogue and interrupt the continuity of the story. Bowen typically uses a space break to indicate a shift in space or time, but she does so sparingly. As a general principle, the more polished a story, the fewer space breaks that she inserts.

In drafts and revisions, Bowen maintains a conscientious regard for details. She tends not to repeat herself or forget the thread of the story. None the less, she makes occasional spelling errors, the result of hunting and pecking on the keyboard – she was not a fast typist

– or, less often, not having revised. I have silently corrected obvious spelling errors. French gave Bowen minor problems. As she recounts in the essay "The Idea of France," she glimpsed the mauve contours of the French coast across the English Channel when she was a child and yearned to go there. Go there she did. With her husband, Alan Cameron, Bowen visited out-of-the-way destinations in France in the 1920s and 1930s, and she resumed her romance with the country after the war. To improve her French, she translated sections of Proust's *À la recherche du temps perdu* and Flaubert's *L'Éducation sentimentale* into English, as documents in the Harry Ransom Center prove (HRC 9.7–9). A long quotation – so long as to be show-offy – from Stendhal's *De l'Amour* appears in *To the North*. Despite immersion in the French language, Bowen consistently makes errors with accents. Perhaps under the influence of Italian, she does not hear the phonetic difference between an *accent grave* and an *accent aigu*. She has an unaccountable preference for the *grave*, so that, for example, *necessité* becomes *necessitè* and *négligée* turns into *negligèe*.

As far as possible, editorial emendations have been kept to a minimum. Where variants reveal something about the text, I have recorded them. Because these stories were written over four decades, from approximately 1920 to 1960, spelling and hyphenation change. Early stories show a preference for keeping "for ever" as two words, whereas "forever" becomes the norm in later stories. Bowen also makes distinctions between "on to" and "onto," with the latter preferred in phrases concerning contact with a surface. Both "on to" and "onto" appear in the opening paragraph of "Happiness" to indicate distinct prepositional properties. Some of these stories, having appeared in the United States, adopt American spellings, which I alter to standard British spellings for consistency. On the other hand, neologisms, such as "multitudinies" in "Moses," stand on their own, without alteration or gloss; such invented words are part of Bowen's resourcefulness, which never ceases to surprise for its aptness and its freshness.

Capitalisation has been regularised, as has the spelling of certain recurring words ("earring" and "drawing-room"). In fact, the hyphenation practices of the 1920s and 1930s tell a story about the evolution of compound words in the English language. Some hyphenated words have been preserved because they attest to the decades in which the stories were written: "tip-toe" and "trap-door." Other hyphenations have been regularised to contemporary usage: "to-day," "to-morrow," and "week-end" lose no significance when spelled "today," "tomorrow," and "weekend." Over the years, hyphenated compounds tend to lose their hyphens. Whereas "drawing-room" usually appears with a hyphen in stories from the 1920s and 1930s, later compound nouns dealing with rooms seldom have hyphens: "schoolroom," "classroom," "diningroom," "livingroom." And, by the same token, the disappearance of the drawing-room from postwar households causes the word to retain its hyphen as a vestige of another era.

Although this volume aspires to create a fuller sense of Bowen's short story œuvre, not all unpublished fragments have been included. After deliberation, I decided to exclude seven story fragments that are housed at the Harry Ransom Center. In their unfinished state, these sketches seldom exceed a few pages in length and are uneven in quality. "Amy Ticer" and "Ellen Nevin" are short character sketches (HRC 1.1). "A Thing of the Past" concerns celebrity (HRC 9.1). Although Sellery and Harris claim that the fragmentary "A Thing of the Past" is a sketch for "The Last Bus" (234), the two stories – one set on a hot summer day near the sea and the other set two days before Christmas – have nothing to do with each other. "Beginning of this Day," a brief start to a story, plunges immediately into dramatic conflict: a girl, orphaned during the war, behaves awkwardly in front of her adoptive mother's friends (HRC 1.5). The five-page fragment called "Now the Day is Over" bears some resemblances to "Christmas Games": a young woman flees a weird consistory in a country house (HRC 8.7). The trope of the young woman out of her depth or out of familiar surroundings appears in other fragments. In "Only Young Once," a young woman's engagement does not sit well with her family, especially her mother, and she walks the countryside with her *fiancé* to avoid the scrutiny of her siblings and parents (HRC 8.7). In "Still the Moon," a young woman named Nona is hired to write the "autobiography" of Mrs. Du Picq based on her diaries and other personal papers; Nona travels to an isolated house to perform this task (HRC 8.16). Another fragment, mistakenly catalogued as a fragment of an untitled story (HRC 1.1), is, in fact, Bowen's translation of part of a letter by Gustave Flaubert. Other copies of the letter can be found among her translations (HRC 9.8). Each of these stories begins with intensity, but that intensity is brought up short by the unfinished state of these works. Of all the fragments that have been omitted from this volume, "Beginning of this Day" is notable for the quality of its writing, yet, living up to its title, it remains a mere beginning.

By contrast, I have included longer stories that are nearly complete, but not quite: "The Bazaar," "The Man and the Boy," "Story Scene," and "Ghost Story." Other stories in this volume remain unfinished, although in certain cases – notably, "Flowers Will Do," "Christmas Games," and "Women in Love" – the end is clearly in sight. The value of these unfinished stories lies in their manifest "pressure," to recall Bowen's term. Characters and events coalesce with inevitability. At the end of "Flowers Will Do," the wordless meeting between Mrs. Simonez and Sydney leaves the impression that everyone has lost something, but the story is tantalisingly inconclusive. Not liking each other, Mrs. Simonez and Sydney will meet again, awkwardly, because their troubled relations are filtered entirely through Doris. Bowen does say that a story "must have implications which will continue when the story is done" (*Collected Impressions* 153). The scale of the short story in general makes any conclusion seem sudden. Rather than ending, a story rounds off, then continues to reverberate after it stops. In this sense, a short story always implies more than it says and suggests more than it shows.

In this volume, finished and unfinished stories alike display Bowen's fierce control over materials. Authorial control does not preclude the disarray into which a story can throw a reader's expectations. In "Rx for a Short Story," Bowen describes the detonating force of the story:

> We have within us a capacity, a desire, to respond. One of the insufficiencies of routine existence is the triviality of the demands it makes on us. Largely unused remain our funds of pity, spontaneous love, unenvious admiration or selfless anger. Into these, a story may drop a depth-charge. (1)

Pity, love, admiration, and anger find expression once they have been sounded by the depth-charge of fiction. Stories continue to resonate after they end because they locate funds of unexpended feeling within the reader. The metaphor of a ship dropping charges to locate an enemy submarine heralds an encounter between the story as a work of art and the unknown, even antagonistic, reader. The stories in this volume drop a series of charges at different depths to flush the reader's hidden funds of feeling from their hiding place. Whether the depth-charges find their target depends entirely on the reader's capacity to respond and to move, either by diving for deeper cover or by taking a direct hit.

UNCOLLECTED
SHORT STORIES

Salon des Dames

It was a wet summer season, the second for which the hotel had opened since the war. The fine rain made a desolate, even sound like breathing in the pinewoods, and below, milky layers of mist covered the lake, and were stained here and there by the darkness of the water beneath. Sometimes, for an hour or two, the sun would show his face tremulously, and the ladies, picking their way up and down the wet gravel of the terrace, would say that Switzerland must be sometimes very nice.

For the last week there had been no arrivals. In the enormous *salle-à-manger* many tables made a brave and glittering show of expectancy, but their number diminished; the visitors dined together in a group by one window, inevitably huddled, starting at the echoes of their voices in the spectral void. The third and second floors were closed, not a slit from any doorway lightened the long perspective of the corridors. Each of the hundred bedrooms with their shuttered windows might have held a corpse, rotting in humidity beneath the glacial swathings of the bed. In the lounge, a mist perpetually filmed the mirrors; the wicker armchairs gathering sociably around the glass-topped tables creaked at one another in the silence, so that now and then an apprehensive human head would bob up from over a writing table or the back of a settee. The rain was always audible on the glass roof of the verandah.

It is terrible to be alone in the darkness of rain, swept aside by one's world's indifference into a corner of a house. It is still more terrible to be swept aside into a corner of a continent. M. Grigoroff was staying at Seestein indefinitely, because he could think of no specific reason for going anywhere else. Travelling was expensive, and besides, he knew the manager. He really knew the manager quite well, though his diffident inspection of Herr Müller's eyebrows, seen above the office roll-top through the glass panels of the office door, did not encourage him to enter and improve the acquaintanceship. There was something sinister, this afternoon, about Herr Müller's eyebrows.

The war had caused M. Grigoroff considerable inconvenience. He had spent the greater part of it in Switzerland, and was not at all sure that he really liked the country. It is true that he had dallied away the summer before the war very pleasantly here at Seestein. The place was different then; a band at nights and amorous pink lights along the terrace. He had met and loved an English lady called Connie. He was wondering now, as he patrolled the corridor outside the office in his greatcoat (the heating was not satisfactory), what had become of her, and whether she was married. *C'était une jeune fille superbe.*[1]

Every time he reached the end of the corridor he hesitated, in turning, before a door. The panels were all wooden and impenetrable; to the centre one was screwed a small enamelled plate, announcing: *Salon des Dames*. M. Grigoroff yearned to enter.

He did not like men, especially English husbands. Of these, there was an unusually large percentage among the visitors. They roared at him, making observations about the weather, to which M. Grigoroff responded vaguely, sympathetically, "*Oh, mon Dieu*." If he entered the salon there would be ladies; too many ladies perhaps, or there might, infinitely more desirably, be a few. There would be the warmth of radiators and draped curtains. M. Grigoroff found great comfort in the society of women. He entered.

The click of knitting-needles was suspended as the three women turned their faces to the door. They were sitting close together by the big window, looking out into the wet, black pinewoods, with their knees pressed against the radiator under the window-sill. Mrs. Hobson was knitting, Miss Pym[2] was mending something which she rolled into a ball and sat on as M. Grigoroff entered, and Miss Villars was, with some difficulty, re-translating into her mother tongue a German translation of *King Lear*.

"Come right in, M. Grigoroff," said Miss Villars, as the Romanian gentleman entered.

His pince-nez shimmered in the light as he made them an inclusive bow, and a smile tucked up his upper lip under his nose. He made gestures and little noises of diffidence and gratitude. "Do sit down," said Mrs. Hobson, and Miss Pym inspected her fingernails and fluttered her eyelids.[3]

"I expect M. Grigoroff would like to put his feet near the radiator," said Miss Villars understandingly. Leaning forward, she repeated the remark in French. Miss Villars came from Boston. So they made room for him, and he sat down, beaming at them and rubbing his knees.

Mrs. Hobson's nose had a fine edge to it, as though it were an axe, but the rest of her was comfortably rotund. She bent forward and plucked some strands of mauve wool off her skirt, and arranged the front of her blouse. "This is another muffler," she said, shaking out her work. "I finished the grey one I was beginning on Friday."

"Oh ye-es?" said M. Grigoroff, admiringly.

"Now, M. Grigoroff, do you know German? *Savez-vous parler –* "

"Oh no-o, a leetle."

"I guess that means a lot," said Miss Villars firmly. She felt that she had a great deal in common with M. Grigoroff, they were both such cosmopolitans. She did not wish to exclude the others, but how much easier it would have been to talk in French! "You speak well, German?"

"Oh ye-es, a leetle."

"I'm afraid M. Grigoroff's feeling the cold," said Miss Pym obliquely. She never made advances to men. The colour spread softly from her pretty pink cheeks to her ears, peeping through her fluffy hair, and down to the tip of her nose. She looked round under her lashes, and caught M. Grigoroff's eye, and the pink deepened. M. Grigoroff decided that she might not be as old as she had looked. It was a pity English ladies did not seem to marry. "Are you cold?" she inquired, boldly.

"Oh, ye-es," said M. Grigoroff, nodding and smiling.

"M. Grigoroff knows quite a lot about knitting, don't you?" said Mrs. Hobson, evidently referring back. "He was telling me about the shawls his mother used to make in Romania, weren't you?"

"Ye-es?"

"*Shawl*," she raised her voice and made an expansive movement of wrapping something round her shoulders. "Shawl!" she shouted.

Miss Villars did not knit. "When I was in Rome," she said – "*une fois, pendant que je suis restée à Rome*[4] . . . I used to know two or three Romanians. A charming Baroness. *Connaissez-vous – ?*"

"Oh ye-es. But it is so *triste –* "

"Oh, not *triste*, M. Grigoroff. Antique – the dolours of antiquity.

Have you read – *est-ce que vous avez lu*[5] – Do forgive me," she said aside to the others, and continued the conversation rapidly in French.

It became evident that Miss Pym did not like Miss Villars. She raised her eyebrows expressively at Mrs. Hobson, moved her knees pettishly, and dropped her scissors. M. Grigoroff swooped sideways after them, it was like a dive.

"Oh, how kind! No, over there . . . under the radiator . . . No, more to the right . . . let me . . . oh well . . . *Thank you!*"

He straightened his pince-nez and looked at her intensely through them, handing her the scissors. "Thank you," she repeated, taking the scissors, and meditatively snipping with them at the air. "I hope you're not cold any more now?"

"Oh ye-es," he smiled.

Miss Villars cleared her throat. *"Et quand je serai revenue de Florence..."* she continued.[6]

"Would you mind, would you mind very much if I were to try this muffler on you, just to try? Yes, *muffler!*" She shook it out. "I want to see if it will go round twice and tie in a knot." While he was still looking wonderingly at her, she had lassoed him; the folds of the muffler, warm and scratchy, pleasantly titivated the soft flesh under his chin.

"I think that looks very nice," said Miss Pym, generously.

"Puis, je vais aller jusqu'à Naples . . ."[7]

Mrs. Hobson adjusted and tweaked the muffler, her sleeve brushed against his cheek. Outside, they heard the breathy sound of the rain, and, indoors, the film of mist thickened on the mirrors. The smell of their woollen clothes against the radiator was warm and comforting. Soon, as evening fell, the lamps would be lighted, and Herr Müller would turn on the other radiators. Perhaps somebody would ask him to tea in their bedroom. Then there would be dinner. After dinner, he would seek out Miss Pym, *tête-à-tête* on a settee in the lounge, and show her his album with the views of other parts of

Switzerland.

In this quiet island in the centre of Europe, the dusk gathered and the rain drifted down. Deep in the hotel the chef prepared another dinner for those forty useless mouths, and in the office at the back of the empty lounge Herr Müller lurked like a spider.

M. Grigoroff, while they unwound the muffler from his throat, leaned back smiling. He found great comfort in the society of women.

Moses

She had a way of dawdling, and though Mr. Thomson had timed his appearance for ten minutes later than the hour of the rendezvous, he had still, he discovered, an unanticipated quarter of an hour's wait. Why, indeed, put it at even a quarter of an hour? Standing at the foot of the Scala di Spagna, he lashed his walking-stick angrily to and fro behind him. He looked – and felt – a little of the Lion; legs apart, staring indignantly up the Scala under his tilted hat-brim. The hot steps curved up, their whiteness blistering his eyes. They curved up and up till Mr. Thomson sweated at the thought of them; till his kindly brim came down upon them, cut them off. Behind him, in the piazza, Roman trams slid and clanged; there were ascending triplets, multitudinies of hoots. The fountain spattered, feathery and faint.

In her hotel at the top of the Scala she was inaccessible to him. God forbid that he should go up to meet her! Whichever fork of the staircase he went up by, she would come down the other; balancing her parasol on her shoulder, perhaps even twirling it; smiling at the further distances of Rome, with the possibility, the even imminent possibility, of a Mr. Thomson utterly out of focus. When they were married, he would stand behind her, always, while she put her hat on, breathing audibly and clicking the lid of his watch. Meanwhile, the proprieties ordained for them hotels sundered by the breadth of several piazze, and she was free, up there, to dawdle with her hat.

A flower-seller wondered loudly why the beautiful gentleman would buy no flowers. These dark-skinned peoples never showed the heat, and she was cool as bronze as she turned the whites of her eyes at him from under her awning, under her awning where the banked-up flowers were sultry and dim. Her swinging earrings glittered in the dusk. He thought how delighted Fenella would be if he gave her irises, and those tawny carnations, cinnamon-scented. How aloofly she would trail round Rome, carrying sheafs and sheafs of them that wilted in the heat, in and out of the churches. She would not have so much as a finger free to hold the other guide-books, from which he was not reading aloud. He resolved never to buy Fenella irises or carnations while they were in Rome.

Somewhere, in a cool church, black and clammily fragrant after the sunshine, the Moses of Michelangelo, he knew, sat looking out across the ages.[1] He gathers the destinies of peoples under his knotted hands. He hears the thunders of God in his ears, and sits tense. His lips may even now be loud with the thunders of Sinai. Mr. Thomson, familiar with many guide-books, knew exactly how he sat, but all the same, he wanted to see for himself. The guide-books were (for once) unanimous in urging him to go and see the Moses.

It – he – was one of the reasons why one came to Rome; and, having seen it, one staggered away from Rome with a sense of the greater repleteness. The wrist-bones and sinews, they said, were particularly to be observed as the characteristic of the work of this great artist. The wrist-bones and sinews . . . "O-oh," whinnied Mr. Thomson, stamping his feet, mopping the back of his neck. They had only three days more. Was he never to see anything but blazing steps, and these myriads of burning, whirling, infinitesimal particles of sound and colour around him that he doubted to be Rome?

"Never to see anything? We are *sore* let and hindered," he murmured. "Sore, sore, *sore* let – "

"Well, you're very late," said Fenella.

She stood two or three steps above him, a little pink but tolerably cool.

"*Late* . . .?"

"I've been waiting up there nearly five minutes."

"*Up* there?"

"*Oh*, but you are too impossible!" she cried. "You do waste my time. You know it was *ages* ago you were to meet me, up at the top of the Scala. We might have been half-way to the what's-his-name by now!"

Indeed, they might have been further than half-way. How cool the church would be, how black and dusky-pale the arches. How reverently would he observe the wrist-bones and the sinews of the Moses, and sense the gathered imminence of thunder by that altar of the quiet church!

She descended a step and stooped to peer under the brim of his hat.

"Hot? But you *must* try, darling, you must try and remember."

He mopped his neck all the way round.

She looked round her. "It doesn't matter really," she said quickly. "But I would love some irises . . . I *could* do without carnations, though they're not very expensive. Then we'll have an ice. Waiting about has made me hot, you see. I'm sorry I was cross," she added, leading him towards the flower-stall. "You are nice, and one can't expect you to be perfect."

The flower-woman charged exorbitantly for the irises and carnations. Compound interest, thought Mr. Thomson, for the time he had made her wait. They had been, in fact, these three, for the last five minutes, an angry and attentive triangle. "Who's going to carry all these things?"

"Oh," she said, generously, "I will. You need only carry the guide-books."[2]

When their spoons were beginning to tinkle at the bottoms of their second ices, she said, licking her lips, "Now then. Come on. What about the what's-his-name – the Moses?"

He sucked the ends of his moustache. "Those flowers look awfully nice against your dress," he said absently. "Topping. The Moses? Oh, confound the Moses! Let's sit here a little longer. It's so *hot*."

"Just Imagine . . ."

---

oel and Nancy had a childhood in common, at Wimbedon, in the midst of the most frightful dangers and insecurity. Noel read too much and Nancy was too credulous; there came, successively, as their capacity for fear sophisticated, to be tigers under the back stairs, Indians down in the shrubbery that gathered together with tomahawks and crept out punctually at the approach of dusk, and, at last, a clammy-faced Thing on the top landing that reached out for them through the banisters as they went up. Imagination can build palaces, too, and there were excursions into a high-pitched happiness, but these occurred less regularly and were less memorable. Nancy came from South America, where she had been born, Noel assured her, under some kind of curse. "It mayn't get you here," he said comfortingly, "but if you ever go back . . ."

Nancy was a rather curd-faced child, with hair skinned back so tightly into a pigtail that her eyes seemed stretched open wider than ever. She was prettily mannered, slyish but deeply affectionate, and she loved Noel embarrassingly, with an attention to detail gratifying to his elderly parents. Her aunt and uncle had given Nancy a home; she had been asked over to be a companion to Noel and they played and did lessons together and later on were sent to a little day-school. Nancy was lazy and not clever at all; she cribbed whenever possible and kept what brains she had for the service of Noel. She was tactless, yet deeply responsive; she interrupted Noel perpetually when he was reading and bored him so much by her tenderness and her habit of drinking him in that he could hardly be blamed for beginning to frighten her. Having begun he continued, and the more her terror reflected back on himself and was split into rays against the facets of his personality, the sharper his pleasure became. He was a fair, gentle, rather "unmanly" boy and was not ever tempted to twist her wrist round, kick her shins or tweak the heavy plait that walloped so teasingly between her shoulders. The absorbed companionship of Noel and Nancy, never romping together, never quarrelling, flitting round the garden and the comfortable sedate house, was a matter of self-congratulation and delight to the parents of Noel. When little Nancy cried at night, they would recount, as she sometimes did unreasonably and loudly, Noel would be the first to creep in to her and whisper into her ear something that made her curl up without a sound, draw up the sheets round her ears, and lie thus for the rest of the night, scarcely seeming to breathe, she was so still.

When she was sixteen Nancy did go back to South America, but long before this she and Noel had lost sight of one another. Noel was sent to a preparatory and Nancy to a school abroad; she spent her holidays with other relations because Noel was growing into quite a man now and could not be expected to play with girls any longer. When they did meet their interests were apart and they had little to say to each other; Nancy had left Wimbledon behind for ever. Yet for years Noel did not feel comfortable about the top landing and would make a detour after dark to avoid the shrubbery; the fears sloughed by Nancy's freer spirit still lay in wait for him.

News came from time to time of Nancy in the Argentine. While Noel was at Oxford his father died; later his mother sold the London house and moved to Kent. Noel, who had made up his mind to be an architect and was already articled, beautifully decorated and furnished a small flat and established himself in Bloomsbury. About this time he heard from his mother of Nancy's engagement. "An Englishman after all, I am relieved to hear, and so well off. It sounds ideal; dear little Nancy. Yet it seems like yesterday, doesn't it, one can hardly believe . . . Do remember to write, Noel. And do try to think of some wedding present."

Noel put the letter down with a sense of distinct surprise that anybody should think of marrying his cousin Nancy. The child of nine had elongated in his imagination but not matured. He was in love himself in a pictorial, rather unprogressive way with a beautiful fair girl called Daphne. Noel had grown up into a whimsical vague young man, kindly disposed to the world in a general way but with a charming touch of the feline. He was noted for doing strange things by himself, such as going alone to the Zoo, walking all night, or exploring the bus-routes of London. He was considered rare, and admired and loved as such by his friends in Bloomsbury. He was affectionate, naïve and a little lonely, and though most of the things he did were done for effect he often speculated as to the nature of true happiness. He did not think that he would ever be much of an architect.

A dutiful cousin, he spent some bewildered afternoons among

prints and lacquer, and finally selected for Nancy the sort of present his Daphne would have appreciated, and had it sent off. "Funny, skinny, little pop-eyed thing!" he said thoughtfully, sitting down to indite his congratulatory letter. He glanced towards Daphne's photograph for inspiration, bit his pen and had soon begun writing in his own inimitable way.

"Dear little Noel," wrote back Nancy – Really! – "Charming of you to write such a letter. Yes, isn't this absurd? I am quite *too* much in love with Ripon – whom you must certainly meet. I hope we shall be home for a bit in a year or two. Did you ever get a photograph I sent you two years ago? Perhaps you hated it, you passed it over in silence. I have improved since then; your Nancy is now rather beautiful. It would be absurd of me, wouldn't it, to contradict Ripon, not to speak of various other authorities? I should love to know what you look like – as young as you sound? Twenty-three sounds an age, but as a matter of fact we are rather children, aren't we? I feel a babe beside Ripon and I glory in it. Ripon . . ." and so on for two or three pages more.

Noel destroyed the letter at once with a feeling of shame on Nancy's behalf and of outrage on his own. What had he done to incur it, this forced letter, impossible for the child he knew to have written? In revulsion he felt pity for Nancy; whatever she'd grown into, she couldn't have grown into *this*. "Confidences . . ." thought Noel, "they're not *decent*. And, anyway, they're over-sophisticated." He had a good many girl friends and thus a fairish standard for judging women. "Perhaps she's unhappy," he thought, and it cheered him wonderfully. "After all, a rich middle-aged Argentine, probably fat . . . Poor *child*! He softened and felt some emotion. For Nancy was part of his childhood, that was what made her letter a sacrilege; she was woven in preciously among the Wimbledon memories with nightly terrors (delightful in retrospect), nursery firelight, his father's leather armchair, the smell of toast from the kitchen. Noel had never ceased to feel home-sick; the feeling was increased with the disappearance of home. He leant his head on his arms a minute or two over the scraps of Nancy's letter and felt wretched. He thought of the nursery fire for ever put out, and of how one went on through the world growing colder and colder.

For some time after he thought of Nancy now and again. She would reappear in his thoughts like a little ghost when he was melancholy; but when two years later he came home one night to find her telephone message, he had once more forgotten her. Affairs with Daphne had meanwhile come to a crisis; after an interval of distraction they had, he believed both unwillingly, become engaged. An uneasy, rather constrained feeling wore off or became familiar; he was in love with Daphne more than ever, quite intoxicated by being so much in love. He lived intensely but fluidly, futurelessly, in a kind of dream. When he picked up Nancy's telephone message it was as though something snapped. Nancy and her husband were back in England; they had taken a flat in Knightsbridge. She asked him to come round and see her the next afternoon. Noel felt really angry at being thus interrupted; his instinct was to ring up, or better still write, and tell Nancy that this was impossible, would be impossible for weeks ahead. He wondered what she and Daphne would think of each other. Falling asleep, he became the prey of a dream that Daphne had married an Argentine and was keeping Nancy, a kind of unhappy monkey, shut up in a cage. He put a finger between the bars and Nancy bit him; this made him angry with Daphne, who sat looking on ironically and coldly.

At half-past four Noel entered a lift, still doubtfully, was shot up a floor and shown through a chain of apartments into a drawing-room overhanging the Park.[2] In an air blue and semi-opaque with cigarette smoke, and sharp with geranium scent, two clocks followed each other, a taffeta curtain rustled. A synthetic fire sent out a crimson pulse; beyond the window-draperies and clouded pane dusk crept like smoke from under the trees of the Park. A handsome Spanish woman, uncrossing her legs, sprang up with an exclamation;

dark, poised, imperious, she looked at him piercingly.

"Noel!" cried Nancy.

"My dear Nancy!" said Noel in a tone of expostulation, taking the hands held out to him. He felt deceived and a little angry, and still half believed he had come to the wrong flat. A pair of barbaric earrings swung from his cousin's small ears; they fascinated him by their glitter. Her cropped hair rippled against her head with a familiar smoothness. Supple and dark, independent of lines he knew, her frock said Paris.

"Aren't you *too* picturesque?" said Nancy, holding him at arm's length. "Aren't you lovely?" She had a deep voice and pronounced every syllable distinctly. Her dark, rather wild boy's eyes travelled over him. Noel glanced at himself in a mirror behind her shoulder to reassure himself that he *had* that indefinable something. Diffident, anxious to please, he sat down in a black velvet chair and stared at the fire. "Awfully cute, these electric fires . . ." said Noel.

Nancy, taking him in, said nothing. She seemed unaware of a tension. "Now begin and tell me everything," said she, with most fearful directness.

This was not Noel's way. He began to look round the room obliquely but deliberately; he always began with a room. Nancy, as he had expected, did not speak his language at all; on the other hand, everything he had prepared to say to her had rather lost point. He was used to converse in allusions, to what the other person had read, or had once said, or must obviously feel; he lived in an intimate circle, a clique, and too seldom emerged. He longed to talk speculatively about South America (without reference to Nancy) or epigrammatically about London (without reference to himself) or best of all, about clothes. He felt nervous, as though he were shut in a room with a panther.

Nancy offered him a cigarette of a kind he did not care for, and lighting one of her own in a long holder, leant sideways among her cushions. "So I hear you are engaged," said she. "You are fearfully happy?"

Noel nodded whimsically.

"I do so hope," Nancy said maternally, "she's a really nice girl."

"Ra-ather a dear."

"What an extraordinary way to describe her," said Nancy with some contempt, and Noel felt furious with himself for not having done Daphne justice.

"As a matter of fact, she's so lovely one hardly likes to mention it."

Nancy turned up a lamp at her elbow, a lamp in a painted shade that cast arabesques and eyes over the wall. Leaning back she watched her smoke drift up to the ceiling. "Marriage," she said, "is wonderful." Her tone was Latin and sophisticated; very much a woman of the world's.

"My dear Nancy," Noel said, groaning, "must we discuss marriage? It is so overdone."

"I'm a barbarian," smiled Nancy. "I don't know what's overdone; I'm afraid I discuss what interests me. Marriage does. When shall I meet Daphne?"

"Mm," said Noel, "Mm, mm-mm."

"I know," said Nancy, "every one in London's so full up. Well" – her voice changed – "I rather wish you hadn t got a Daphne. I'm so lonely. I do want somebody to talk to."

"My dear Nancy?"

"I'm not a bit happy, Noel," Nancy said, looking at him seriously and simply. She blinked and touched the corner of one eye, quite naïvely with the tip of a long finger as though there was a tear there.

Noel felt outraged. He looked at her incredulously for a moment, then got up and looked out of the window. He could not bear that sort of thing, it made him feel sick; Nancy would have to control herself. He clasped his hands behind his back nervously and said, after a wounding pause, "I'm sorry to hear that," with cold formality.

Nancy, getting up also, came and stood behind him, a hand on his shoulder. It was hard to realise that this hand, smooth, pointed and adorned with square-cut jewels, had been used to clutch him feverishly when a little girl was afraid in the dark. He had never done much to comfort Nancy . . . It was as though this reflection transmitted itself, for Nancy said, half laughing, "You don't care. You always were cold-blooded, Noel. How you used to torture me!"

"Torture you?" said Noel. "How?"

"Fear," said Nancy. "I didn't mind pain. '*Just imagine*,' you used to say; you had froggy hands and queer pale eyes. You seemed to *see* the things; my flesh crept, it did really; I was in a perpetual state of shivers."

Noel wheeled round on her, interested. "Really, Nancy, really?" he said eagerly. It made a great man of him all at once to have bullied this Nancy of the dark and brilliant smile. Nothing Daphne ever said had so moved him.

"Mmm," said Nancy; her eyes grew narrow with retrospect. "Weren't you a little devil?"

"Was I a devil?" mused Noel, hugging this.

"I can't think why I ever put up with it. I suppose I *had* to be fond of somebody even then. But I almost think I pity Daphne."

"But I don't ever – " he began and broke off, reminded too sharply that there had been lacking in his intercourse with Daphne just this subtle and secret pleasure.

Nancy's laughter was melancholy and indifferent. She threw herself down among her cushions again and brooded, the firelight crimson in her eyes. "You couldn't frighten me now," she said. "It's only myself I'm frightened of. I'm terribly passionate."

"Are you?" he said confusedly.

"You and your Daphne," said she with friendly contempt. "You're so smug, I expect it does you good to hold hands in the dark and tell each other ghost stories . . . Wait till you've lived," she added, in a changed voice. "But you won't live – luckily for you."

"I bet," Noel said, stirred, angry and rather excited, "I could still frighten you."

She did not hear him. "You wait," she went on, "till you love someone – sickeningly. You won't till you don't trust them. You wait till you're hated and watched every hour of the day and hate and watch back again."

Noel thought they must all be very passionate out in the Argentine. He looked at Nancy with awe and a faint inferiority, and yet with tolerance, as though she belonged in the Zoo. "It's a good thing, at least," he said innocently, "that you feel all this about Ripon."

"But I don't," said Nancy, and turned on him her impatient dark eyes.

"O-oh," said Noel. "Didn't you once?"

"I wrote to you, didn't I?" Nancy said with a flicker of remembrance. "I suppose I didn't know then what I could feel. I suppose," she said to the fire, while her fingers unclenched themselves slowly along the arms of her chair, "one learns . . ."

They sat silently opposite one another in the smothered light. Her black figure melted into the black chair, and Noel, straining his eyes to distinguish her, felt that she and she only mattered, and mattered to him burningly. He was in a tumult for a moment or two, then this ebbed and left him with a cold and frightful feeling of insecurity. Fear! He was so afraid that he wanted to brandish something at Nancy, to shake her, or violently to kiss the pale cheek leaning in an attitude of abandon against her gold, preposterous cushions. The tick of the two clocks, never quite synchronising, pattering after each other, maddened him. Since the night fears of his childhood he had never felt so menaced.

"You've no business to talk like that," he said, cold with anger. "If you'll forgive my saying so, it rather shocks me. After all, however much we played as children, I am to all intents and purposes a stranger now, and I don't want to hear about your husband – it

makes me feel quite sick. I needn't say how sorry I am that you're
. . . not happy, but after all that must be between you and him. At
least, over here we think so. Perhaps things may be different in the
Argentine."

Nancy, turning her head slowly, looked at him from a long way
away. "What a boy you are . . ."

He was silent, stung intolerably, and made a movement to go.
She stretched out her two friendly hands to him. "Oh, stay! You dear
Noel, you comfort me just by sitting there. You're like something in
an English book, an old lady, a kettle or a cat. You don't know what
a life I've led – you're like an afternoon in Wimbledon . . ."

"Ah," said Noel, and looked at his cousin Nancy with dangerous
eyes. "Are you quite sure I couldn't make you afraid again?"

"I wish you could . . ." said Nancy wistfully. She stirred and
laughed in her chair. "Oh, Noel, do try . . ."[3]

A remote, inaccessible Spanish lady, veiled in tragic experience,
was laughing at the young man from Bloomsbury. He almost prayed
to be made cruel enough. "Very well," said Noel. "Look out!"

He put a hand in front of his eyes and began to grope back, back.
The paths he had trod were lonely as death, clammy, forgotten but
now once more his familiar. He shut out the rich warm room, the
stir and scent of Nancy, they fell away from him; Bloomsbury, life,
hope, dreams, ambition and Daphne fell away from him, too; he ran
on alone to the edge of the Pit. Within him there was an absolute
silence, a blank across which shadows doubtfully shivered and fled.
Nancy laughed and turned out the lamp at her elbow; the room was
dark except for the firelight and the lights coming up from the Park,
silent except for the clocks and the rushing past of the cars. These
sounds swelled up and filled the room, then died down, leaving it
empty. From the forgotten source, deep in Noel, terror began to
well up.

He knelt, half crouched, beside Nancy's chair, and, reaching out,
caught her hand, smooth and firm, in his own, which was very cold.

He felt her pulse jumping. Motionless as beneath some compulsion she waited, while his intense consciousness of her there beside him fought with his icy flood of overmastering fear. He had opened the floodgates for her, so he felt it right to press himself against the side of her chair and lean his head on her arm as they had done in childhood.

"Just imagine . . ." Noel whispered against her ear. Starting violently, he pointed into the dark. Her hand leapt in his, she laughed on an intake of breath as though she were stepping into cold water.

"We're not alone! Cover your face and don't look, my dear, for we're . . . we're Not Quite Alone . . . A-ah! – Oh, my God, IT'S *there* on the sofa . . . Don't be, don't be too much afraid; shall I tell you? – It's turning Its head . . . But It can't, Nancy. It can't possibly turn Its head . . . Because It – hasn't – got – a neck. No, not a neck. Only a . . . strip of skin. And that's, that's, that's – ALL ROTTING AWAY."

Nancy, between a laugh and a shudder, as though cold water were rising round her, taunted, "Go *on*, Noel . . ." She turned out the electric fire; they watched the red square fade and all that they could see of each other fade with it. Nancy made a movement, he clutched her in terror, afraid to be left. She got up, drew the heavy curtains across the window and turned out the light in the vestibule so that not so much as a crack came in from under the door. So soft were her movements, so quiet her step, that he only guessed at her whereabouts and shrieked when, groping back to her chair, she put a hand on his face.

"*Noel!*" cried she, appalled by his moments of silence.

"Hush – I am listening. Listen, too; do you hear? Some blood's dripping – tip, tap, tip, tap. Don't *move!* It's all over the floor. A-ach, it's all over my hands. It's all sticky and cold. *Cold* blood, Nancy . . . where shall I wipe it off? But you mustn't stir. It will hear. You forget: WE ARE NOT ALONE."

At this moment the sofa creaked, a cushion slid off and fell to the floor.

Noel, pressing his cheek against Nancy's arm, felt the muscles contract. A crack by the door and the sound of a heavy stirring answered the creak of the sofa. There began, interrupted by silences, the sound of something slithering, dragging itself along the wall.

"Noel!"

A shudder beside her.

"Noel, stop it now. It's too real, I can't bear it. Stop . . . You've won! Oh, STOP it!"

"But, my God," whispered Noel. *"I don't know what it is . . ."*

"What have you done?" Nancy laughed with horror. "There *is* something in here?"

"Yes . . ."

Noel felt he must crouch till he died in the silent blackness, counting the thuds of his heart. This horror had taken life from himself, had been born of his mind and was creeping about the room. When a fumbling began not far away and a hand seemed to be feeling its way towards them over the furniture, he reached out an arm for Nancy and held her against him. The delusion of life showed its falseness, of action, security, manly and womanly freedom from fear; they were plumbing together once more as in childhood the terrible deep. They were very close.

"Oh, fool," shivered Nancy. "Oh, fool; oh, you fool!" Her breath ran through his hair.

"Be quiet," he cried, putting up a hand and crushing her lips to silence. A yard away, a chair slid forward softly over the parquet. "Find the light!"

"Oh, I can't, I daren't put my hand out. Oh, Noel . . ."

Kneeling up, scarcely breathing, an arm still round Nancy, Noel felt along the back of her chair for the lamp at her other elbow. He touched the base of the lamp, heard it rattle, and his fingers crept up to the switch. At this moment a cold hand, shaking a little,

closed on his own. "Now," thought Noel, "I am finished." Holding
Nancy against him, his cheek against hers, he waited while the grip
on his fingers, compelling them, wrenched round the switch.

The light sprang up.

Very tall, going on up indefinitely towards the ceiling and
spangled over with arabesques from the shade, the grey figure of
Ripon loomed over them. With the revelation of his material
presence, his identity flashed upon Noel. A shoe was tucked beneath
either of Ripon's armpits: Noel looked at his silver-grey huge feet
planted squarely apart on the parquet.

"I thought I heard you in here," said Ripon. "Am I in the way?"

Nancy, pale and insolent, stared up with dilated eyes.

"Is that the way one usually comes into one's drawing-room?" she
asked in a voice over which she had not recovered control.

"Is this the way one usually entertains one's visitors?" asked Ripon,
staring back.

Nancy shrugged, a gesture of disdain and helplessness. "A game,"
she said, "a favourite game of Noel's. This is Noel – Ripon. Ripon –
Noel."

Ripon turned, half bowed, and for the first time bent his dark,
intent and heavy gaze on Noel. Noel's eyes, running agitatedly over
that immense and too-well-tailored person, focused themselves
under the chin, upon a flashing tie-pin. "Bounder!" he thought – the
word was balm to him – "Rotten cad!"

"I'm afraid," he said at last uneasily, "you'll think me pretty mad.
We were playing ghosts; I frightened Nancy. I didn't know we had
an audience. An audience generally . . . declares itself."

He glanced down and dusted the knees of his trousers: a gesture
purely, for Ripon's parquet had been immaculate.

Then he realised that the big man was looking no longer at
himself but back again at Nancy. He had been brushed clear of
Ripon's thoughts like a fly. Ripon's eyes beneath his beetle brows

had an uneasy, tortured look, like some large dog's whose trust in life has been destroyed. He was looking towards Nancy dubiously, bitterly, imploringly, asking for his cue. Nancy sat indifferent, a smile for both of them, stroking back her smooth hair against her head. A glance, a word from her, directed by an intention, could have made Ripon either break the young cousin to pieces, or else shake his hand, apologise to both of them, or even (inconceivable as the thing seemed) cringe. Deep-set in the impressive face, the eyes of Ripon held a torturing uncertainty. And Nancy, non-committal, smiled on, made no sign.

Shame-faced, Noel quickly turned away, and, until that terrible look ceased, could look at Ripon no more. There was an abyss here he could not fathom.

The Pink Biscuit

Sibella spent her Easter holidays at Folkestone, with her aunt by marriage, Mrs. Willyard-Lester. Her aunt lived in a maisonette on the Leas, with balconies, and Sibella occupied a spare bedroom overlooking the sea. When, waking up in the mornings, she saw this blue or grey line drawn across her window, saw the dipping wings and heard the cries of sea-birds, Sibella was always glad that she had come, and though sometimes during the day this gladness might be clouded over a little, it never entirely left her. When one's mother is dead, one's father in India, the laying-out of holidays becomes a problem seriously to be considered. School friends' homes are not always open; two days after the end of term Nancy wrote with the staggering pen of desolation that her mother had asked, after all, two dreadful women to stay. Sibella, likely to be stranded at school, was forced to accept Mrs. Willyard-Lester's long-proffered hospitality. This was the least disagreeable of several alternatives; there are aunts and aunts.

She had not seen Aunt Marjory for eight years, since an afternoon when she slipped a finger up Sibella's ringlets and said she was charmingly pretty. Mrs. Willyard-Lester was one of those childless people with no idea at what years of a child's age these irreticences should be avoided. The alert child of seven, un-accustomed to comment, had glowered at[1] her aunt, despised her, and followed her round, with gratitude. Possibly it was remem-brance of this that led Sibella to honour, on this occasion, Mrs. Willyard-Lester: her instinct had not been at fault. Mrs. Willyard-Lester treated her like a bride; praised her hair, gave her early tea in the morning and coffee at night, and exclaimed that this was real, *real* pleasure. Sibella wore her Sunday blouses every day and her two school dance frocks turn-abouts for dinner. The food was delicious, though perhaps there was not quite enough; Aunt Marjory even offered Sibella burgundy, a nasty-smelling drink which made Aunt Marjory flush.

Certainly it was not exciting, though she had been taken twice to matinees and several times to concerts on the Leas. Her aunt deplored the absence of young folk – young men, she meant, she never thought of girls. "Those *nice* Jefferson boys," she said, "in Westcliffe Gardens; one's always away and the other's just gone back to Woolwich. Then there was a young Captain Somerly I used to meet at bridge; *he* would have admired you, but he's gone too. Even Jacob Laurence is away, though he does squint rather: it's too bad."[2]

Sibella said, "Oh, thanks very much, but I really don't care for men," in the tone in which she would have refused oysters.

Aunt Marjory did her hair elaborately, wore remarkable rings, and seemed to have been poured into her tailor-mades. She played bridge every afternoon and most evenings, and was an irreproachable mother to her little dog, Boniface. In the mornings, the three would stroll up and down the Leas; every second morning one went to the library to renew Aunt Marjory's novels. Sometimes she took Sibella to tea where she went for bridge; Sibella sat by the windows of the tight, hushed rooms, not liking to turn the pages of papers she had been given. At tea, everyone would be charming to her and say they feared it must be dull; ask her whether she liked her school, when she went back there, and whether she often danced. A colonel once said he would teach her to play bridge; an even older colonel promised to take her on the pier; but she never saw either of them again. The disappearance of the colonels was a relief to Sibella who, much as she disliked women, disliked men more.

She went for longer walks alone with Boniface, though her aunt complained that there were funny people about, and that Boniface, though so brave, had a small bite. A girl of Sibella's appearance . . . Once she went to Hythe in a charabanc with Elizabeth Eldon, the middle-aged maid who saw to the maisonette, Aunt Marjory's clothes and the household shopping. Elizabeth, decent and invincibly unsmiling, went most reluctantly into Hythe Crypt with Sibella to be grinned upon by the skulls. She cried, "Good Lord, have mercy!" as the verger clanked the door shut; and declared, throughout tea at the Oriental Café, that she could not eat anything, she felt that queer. She did relent to the extent of one plain cake. Sibella decided in future to go less far but alone. Alone she was very happy.

She was always happy alone; her thoughts were like an orchestra. She peeped at life this way and that way, down all the queer perspectives. She was glad she had fifty-five more years of it to live. She had read several novels since she came to Folkestone and didn't think they were so bad. She supposed they must be calculated to make one take an interest in men, and were perhaps necessary. Though she and Nancy were not anxious to marry, their lives were to be romantic. They would have two or three tragedies each. Husbands, they thought, were so permanent. As for keeping house – but too soon was Sibella to suffer the cares of a house, for Elizabeth Eldon fell ill.

Elizabeth lay in bed, her head wrapped up in a wan pink shawl, moaning; Aunt Marjory, tapping her penholder on her teeth, frowned at the sea. She said that it was most annoying. Nobody could be sorrier for Elizabeth, but really this did make things difficult. "If one were only not such a busy woman oneself . . . First, you see, there are all my letters to answer, generally cheques to sign; then I have to exercise my little Bonnie. No, it's so sweet of you, Sibella, but nothing is quite the same as going out with his Mummy; I couldn't look him in his little face. Then one must keep up one's reading; that means the library almost every day. That's the morning gone. Then lunch and one's lie-down, then before you know where you are it's time for bridge. Don't you notice, it is always the busy people who are still further put upon? I've got that dreadful 'temporary' woman to come in, though I feel sure she's a Socialist. But it's the *shopping*, Sibella. You see, Markham doesn't send for orders every day for my small custom, and even the butcher only three days a week. Elizabeth goes down town and brings up the things herself. Now I do wonder . . ."

Sibella, who had drawn a large breath for this purpose, brought out with a burst: "But, Aunt Marjory, *I* could shop!"

Mrs. Willyard-Lester had thought of this, but the suggestion distracted her. She twisted her rings round and sighed; it was too bad, it was really. If Sibella *would* . . . She should take Aunt Marjory's stamped suede satchel, used for the library books, so as not to be seen with that nasty basket; also she must be *sure* to make them send anything at all heavy. And she must really have coffee and a biscuit before going out – here Mrs. Willyard-Lester boldly rang for the temporary who had obliged her. The temporary glared at them from the doorway, very unofficial and large in a flowered blouse; Boniface fled shivering to his mistress.

One blessing was, Aunt Marjory said. they did nearly all the shopping at one good grocer's, Markham. It was universally conceded to be the best grocer's; except for things like veal and cauliflowers, and, of course, bread. To Markham's, therefore, Sibella, half an hour later, made an awed approach.

On her left arm, carefully crooked, she carried Aunt Marjory's stamped suede satchel; she would have preferred, secretly, the nasty basket. Into her right glove were slipped Aunt Marjory's card and a list of requisites dictated between the groans of Elizabeth. She did not ever remember having bought much at a shop except sweets, stamps, postcards, diaries – and hair-ribbon in the days when one had hair; she stood for some time in the mosaic entrance-porch, feet sunk deep in a resilient mat. China's self must have laboured to perfect those dragoned crocks of ginger, white and blue, of which a pyramid on her left tottered up to singleness. In glittering films of crystal the citrons, oranges of Italy and Spain were staked as for a banquet, triumphant from their syrupy ordeal. There was a something of triumph, too, in the repose of that whole side of a split pig, reclined voluptuously on a bank of moss; a stuffed Oriental bowed above a lacquer bowl of tea.

Sibella placed one finger on the plate-glass door; the door receded cavernously, drawing Sibella after it by the finger. She advanced quite soundlessly as after death over the soft cork floor; one must be silent here though one might stamp and stamp. The shop was full; at once Sibella felt herself a magnet to all eyes – sensation not uncommon to Sibella. "So young a girl" – perhaps they thought – "entering so large a shop with such complete assurance!" or "What a capable-looking girl; what lovely hair!" Or did they perhaps think she was married; married very, very young? Sibella drew the list out of her glove to study it, all eyebrows, as she had seen them study hands at bridge. Then she crossed the shop diagonally to the furthest counter, leant her stomach against it, propped the satchel upon a chair, and looked to left and right, drawing a long breath. A white young man in an apron looked at her through an archway of potted meat, crackled towards her, arranged the tips of his fingers on the counter, and bowed across it.

"Madam?" She still saw the crown of his head, and it smelt delicious. The air smelt also of apricots, rind and sugar. He had an austere male beauty; the shop rose over them, very high and pure: marble. "*What* may we – ?" he began.

"Small packet curry powder one two and threepenny bottled anchovies quarter of a pound almonds best quality large packet Quaker oats quarter of a pound coffee fresh roasted half a dozen matches usual make – " Sibella herself was surprised at all this; the young man's pencil flew.

She resumed: "Large size galantine chicken Poulton and Noels or other good make small pot Yarmouth bloater pound and a half two and threepenny bacon – "

The young man, pencil arrested, looked up in reproach. "That would be at the Cheese and Bacon, Madam. If I might direct you?" He looked inspiringly into the eyes of Sibella; she looked back at him trustfully. He let himself out by lifting a kind of portcullis, and she followed him across the shop.

The young men at the Cheese and Bacon were very, very deft. They set whirling great steel wheels; knives rushed and rashers curled away from the knives as delicately as petals. They bowled great cheeses along the marble, and tossed them to one another in titan frolic. They went effortlessly through great waxen slabs with a taut wire. Ladies, apparently fascinated, thronged before the counter; Sibella had to stand on tip-toe to see what was going on. There was a hum of conversation; the young men were prepared to talk to you – disengagedly – and the ladies seemed to like talking; they lingered, comparing the streaks on different bits of bacon, while anxious others murmured and surged behind them.

It did not take long to choose Sibella's bacon, because her young man, though gentle, was quite inexorable. He said that all the two-and-threepenny was of the same quality, similar in streak and of superlative excellence. He remarked with a shade of reproof, when Sibella implored him to cut the rashers fine, that they *always* cut rashers fine unless requested not to.

He took Mrs. Willyard-Lester's name perfunctorily; he did not seem to wonder who Sibella could be, or how so young a girl came to be buying bacon so efficiently. Sibella went gratefully back to the other young man. On the way she came to the fancy biscuits.

The fancy biscuits, occupying a table like an altar, vomited opulently out on to plates from a cornucopia. They first became[3] noticeable to Sibella by their fragrance, sweet and nutty. They seemed a whole mint of sugar coinage, lemon, chocolate, mauve and pink, auburn scalloped edges of the biscuit showed around the margin of the sugar. Sibella was hungry: the breakfast provided by the temporary had been slighter and less appetising than Elizabeth's. As she approached, some vibration made a pink biscuit, balanced at the apex, clear a plate's rim and quiver to stillness at the very edge of the table. Sibella, scarcely pausing, brushed the biscuit into her jersey pocket.

The first young man, throughout so sympathetic, helped her pack parcels into her satchel: they just fitted. She was so much overcome, she forgot to give him the account address: he asked for it with infinite delicacy. He bowed even lower as he said "Good morning," and when she turned again and caught his eye, he bowed again. She passed out; the plate-glass door sighed gently as it swung behind her. Her feet were sucked once more into the mat. Sibella, detaching herself, came to a full stop of contemplation before the swooning pig. Here, shifting the now weighty satchel, she ate the biscuit. She alternately licked the sugar and nibbled the biscuity part underneath. The surface was delectable to the tongue; its glaze was dimming; it became gradually moist and porous. The biscuity part had a flavour caramels missed. Sibella had never found a biscuit half so good; she only wished she had been able to take another.

Suddenly Conscience woke, flinched, stared and veered gigantically round upon Sibella . . . *How* had Sibella come by the biscuit? It was STOLEN.

Sibella had never met a thief; Nancy had once spoken to a housemaid who had been later arrested. A captured thief was dragged off, horribly resistant. A thief was less outrageous than a murderer, but more dowdy; a person quite unclean and scabrous, like a rat. One had only to cry "Stop, thief!" and the jolly world was after him. He wasn't killed, he didn't die – he ended. And people, munching over morning papers, said "How dreadful!" Sibella stared at the split pig in Markham's window with eyes that might have scorched a brand upon its flank. Then she thought that she must fly – soon, now – before they came out after her.

The satchel swung against her thigh at every step; the little crocks and bottles in it rattled. In the pale social stare of April sunshine she darted down the verdant avenues of Folkestone. When she came out on the Leas she walked more slowly: people must not notice. She looked straight ahead, her eyes were caverns, her parched palate echoed with the biscuit. Her tongue, investigating fearfully, dislodged some crumbs. She increased her pace, the satchel whirled, the handle-strap cut deep into her arm. When she reached her aunt's house she stood looking up. In the first floor window, between looped-up curtains, Mrs. Willyard-Lester sat in profile at her writing table in the sunshine, by a vase of daffodils. She was still immune, ignorant. She should be spared, she loved Sibella . . . Sibella realised it would not be fair to go into her aunt's flat and be there arrested. Homeless she sat down on an iron seat, stared out across the sea, and tried to reach, from her despair, its calmness.

She *was* calmer when, panic having subsided, she perceived that the profound moral indignation of Mr. Markham was unlikely to pass over into legal action. She had a notion that a prosecution was expensive; and she could not, either, visualise a Markham vehement and implacable behind battalions of those kind young men. *Would* Mr. Markham even be so avaricious, so distrustful as to order those exposed biscuits to be daily counted? Any distrust of Mr. Markham's would, as things were, have been tragically justified. But would he readily expose, by her exposure, his avarice to the world? Actually, the defection of the biscuit might be overlooked. But fear and horror, having ceased to bludgeon her, assumed a needle point and drove deep in. She had devoured furtively a stolen biscuit; her stomach even now digested it. She was a thief.

Nancy would never do a thing like that, she was blisteringly, probity's very soul – besides, she wouldn't have been smart enough . . . For a minute, Sibella's mind sweetened; she saw herself telling Nancy about the biscuit, on a walk. She saw Nancy's eyebrows shoot up with amazement and horrified – admiration? "My dear, you *didn't!* . . . My de-ar, how you could! . . . Tell about it, Sibella; go on!" Then an arm crooked tight through her own, ecstatic; excited Nancy pressing against her side. Then Nancy asking the others: "*Do* you know what Sibella did last holidays? Won't tell, *swear?*" And Nancy telling, proud raconteuse . . . But that was, alas, knowing Nancy, not an aspect that long prevailed. Sibella now felt cold in her stomach, seeing a lip curl, feeling an arm withdrawn. "*Stole* the thing?" Oh, oh, oh, how Nancy would be bitter! She would lash Sibella, always with slight restraint, then go off and write her a letter. Then there would be nothing left in Sibella's world; it would be quite empty.

Aunt Marjory, though so confused and foolish, must be an honest woman. She was always writing cheques in payment, she had a clear round eye. Sibella had not yet fully gauged her aunt, she could not be certain; but she imagined that, enlightened, she would with flushed face and protruding eye at once return Sibella to her head mistress, to be, on the first day of term, expelled. Aunt Marjory had believed her young visitor to be beautiful and distinguished. When she found that she had cherished, harboured this greedy thief . . . Elizabeth Eldon would wince colourlessly, as among the skulls, and Boniface fly trembling with repudiation to his mistress. Sibella felt so naked, her very soul squirmed.

A clock struck one; Sibella realised that she had not yet delivered the groceries. She went in reluctantly and gave the satchel to the temporary. Mrs. Willyard-Lester had spent the morning trying to darn a stocking; she was flushed (though not yet with anger), she blinked; she said her eyes were tired. She said that she didn't know how she was to face that afternoon's bridge; she kept bracing herself heroically. Life was difficult sometimes, said Mrs. Willyard-Lester. The room stared; sun streamed in through the curtains. Sibella at lunch could hardly eat anything. This Aunt Marjory was too much tired to notice; she did not notice, either, how humpily Sibella sat.

Later, the outcast crept down the Lower Sandgate Road, through the pines, in an agony of spirit. Girls of her age went past her, arms linked, as herself and Nancy were not to walk again. Elderly couples turned, and Sibella knew how her desolation intrigued them. She was, however, as nearly as possible unconscious of Sibella's appearance.[4] She climbed up a bank to be out of everyone's way and sat leaning sideways against a pine tree, arm crocked round the trunk, cheek pressed to the scaly bark. It appeared that her spiritual life had ended in this pit of deadness; she ground her heels into the sandy soil. Even God seemed perplexed; she strained closer against the tree. One companion alone was left her – this unshrinking pine. She saw the green beneficent sweep of the branches, where wind, lingering like a memory, faintly hummed. Thin spring dusk now deepened between the pine trunks; she discovered with awe that it was six and she did not want any tea: it might be better to stay here, then to be found next morning clinging to the tree trunk – dead.

Then she had shot down the bank and in the middle of the path stood as though she had sprung from the earth, with arms outspread. For the future had blazed suddenly with amazement and hope. For by reparation she could return – it was biblical – to a positive innocence. What an immense vocation: to retrieve sin. She tugged out her purse and, inaccurately, counted the contents twice over. Of the pound of holiday pocket-money she had still, with a fortnight to expire, seven and sixpence left. Seven and sixpence – all she had in the world for her pier money, crêpe de Chine handkerchiefs, sweets, that daily stamp destined for Nancy. A great light shone above the sacrifice. Thumping internally, she fled like a hare down the Lower Sandgate Road, and breasted the first flight of steps that zigzagged up the sheer face of the Leas to Folkestone.

The sun set, the sophisticated faces of houses shone in the after-glow. Blue watery dusk flowed down the avenues; gardens, metallic, softened. In a hotel drawing-room, a girl behind a foam of geraniums sang to a violin accompaniment: under the open window Sibella paused, noting a strange prick: tears of happiness. Rooms were everywhere, orange or lemon with electricity: as Sibella approached Markham's (which, by intention, stayed open on Fridays till half-past six) the shop front suddenly gorgeously blazed. Sibella did feel there was joy in Heaven. She advanced exaltedly into the beaming shop. A young man like St. Michael, grave and beautiful, came to meet her.

"Madam?"

"Rejoice with me!" sang Sibella's heart wildly. Aloud, she asked: "How much are those coloured biscuits?"

"*Coloured* biscuits, madam?" said the young man, surprised.

"The ones with the plain, smooth tops," she said. They approached the table.

"Ah," said he, smiling with infinite comprehension. "Yes, madam. Three shillings a pound."

She calculated. "I should like two pounds and a half."

He brought a small shovel and very big bag. "If you don't mind," said Sibella, "I'd like them all pink."

"All pink, madam? . . . You would find the lemon and chocolate flavours highly satisfactory . . ."

"I would rather they were all pink," said Sibella, firmly. The young man bowed and sighed, "Certainly, madam." He shovelled pink biscuits one by one into the paper bag. There were not many pink in evidence, and the search for more took rather a long time. Once or twice the young man paused to straighten his back for a moment, sigh, and glance a shade restively round the shop. Then he returned to his labours, raking the biscuits over and over again. Finally, straightening himself, he with flushed face carried the bag across the shop, weighed it, and delivered it into the hands of Sibella, who received it reverently. It was a large tight bag, highly glazed. Having given up her three half-crowns, she pinched her purse to assure herself that it was quite empty. Then she walked slowly across to the Cheese and Bacon.

Here the young men lounged god-like against the marbled shelves. The swift steel wheels were silent; only one old lady broke in on the hush. Sibella, assuming a very great abstraction, slowly walked down along the counter, awaited her moment. She paused, eyed the young men, then stealthily put down the bag of biscuits, forcing it between two enormous cheeses. Then, like the thief she no longer was, she turned and fled over to the door. Not a young man stirred.

Towards the Leas homewards went Sibella; melted into the evening itself with peace. Innocence was an ecstasy. Light from the windows followed her with halos; her shadow looked thin with asceticism.[5] Tonight she would go early to bed, open her window on the sea, and write a long, long letter telling Nancy everything. She would borrow a stamp next day from Elizabeth Eldon.

There came the scuff-scuff-scuff of someone running tidily on the pavement. Someone was now hard upon her heels.

"Madam!" a voice gasped, "Madam!"

The young man like St. Michael was still running; his white apron writhed round his legs, his coat flew behind him. Panting, he stretched out the bag of biscuits towards Sibella, "Madam, you left these behind."

She stood, silent with despair, looking at him.

"Your biscuits, madam."

"No yours – Mr. Markham's – I *owe* them to him."

"There is no Mr. Markham, madam: we are a company."

Then became indeed, at the dissolution of Mr. Markham, a kind of chimera. Sibella, backing away, said wildly: "It was atonement."

"But you selected them specially, madam," said the young man, unintelligent as any saint.

"I ate one this morning," said Sibella in a deadly voice.

"We are delighted that customers should sample our biscuits at any time . . . If you would be so kind; it's just on closing time."

Her hands, passive as though under the force of mesmerism, were drawn towards him. Placing the bag in them firmly, St. Michael turned and ran, scuff-scuff, back to the shop. He vanished with a flash of door.

Sibella stood quite still, holding her bag of pink biscuits.

Flavia

F lavia set up in Bernard a charming susceptibility; the everyday took on a quality of its own: there was no doubt she educated him. The very mornings her letters arrived had character, freshness – he was a poor waker, and meeting any day for the first time under his eyelids would gladly have cut it dead. But the sun might be said to rise, the wintry firelight to expand a Dickensian nature, when he perceived her violet typescript on the blue Palm Bond envelope by his coffee pot. *Très gourmet* also, she brought out the faint exquisite smokiness in his Wiltshire bacon; her smile, remotely intimate as the hour, was in the visibly mounting fragrance above his coffee cup. Bernard was "well looked after," fortunate in his landlady; he liked intermissions of solitude and did not wish to marry even Flavia.

On such mornings you could not have avoided noticing Bernard; he noticed himself: his gait, his look, his manner had quite a new consciousness. Caroline noticed him immediately.

He arrived for lunch at the Dobsons' a little early, and was announced while Caroline was alone in the drawing-room looking out at Regent's Park and wondering whether the Dobsons would keep her till Tuesday. She was aware that the Dobsons expected a Mr. Someone-or-other for lunch, not in any way outstanding. They might not have asked him to lunch at all if Caroline had not been with them. Helen Dobson thought he might entertain Caroline, might pass for the kind of young man she expected to meet at their house; the girl was not critical. Caroline recognised the kindness of Helen's intention, and accepted some qualification on the unknown Bernard's behalf. She knew she could not hope to attract a distinguished man. Helen plainly thought she and Bernard might do for each other — at least for lunch. Caroline had not caught the name of Helen's guest beforehand (she did not like to ask again in case this appeared eager). She once more did not catch the name when he was announced.

They had to introduce themselves, and effected the introduction.

"Oh," said Caroline, surprised, "are *you* Mr. McArthur?"

"Yes," said Bernard, pleased that she must have heard of him. She was certainly very naïve. And though his taste was at present all for Flavia's type (what would be certainly Flavia's type: thin, dark, ironical, perhaps myopic for all her clear perception, for she had a delightful habit of narrowing the eyes), he could not help liking Caroline's round pink face, turned so expectantly from the window. He made a study of her for Flavia — she *was* quite a little study: "the sort of girl one meets." Her rather "general" quality, the rather appealing obviousness of her remarks, remained engaging, then and throughout lunch. Though he could not help resenting Mrs. Dobson's plain implication that Caroline was the sort of girl one expected Bernard to like. He was annoyed by Helen's benevolence, by the way she and her husband withdrew from the conversation; he was annoyed with them altogether, for Regent's Park was a long way from his office and they did not give him a good lunch. So inevitably he smiled more and more at Caroline, and the Dobsons "placed him" more and more fatally.

What Caroline thought of Bernard it would be impossible to say. She was a nice girl, modest; she lit up under any kind of appreciation. She was pleased to be such a success with the Dobsons' friend, for she had begun to fear she bored them and was hanging heavily on them from having fewer engagements in London than they expected. At a quarter to three Helen Dobson raised her eyebrows at the clock, and said poor Caroline must not be late for her wretched dentist. Bernard, declaring himself alarmed by the hour, asked for a taxi, and Helen suggested that he should drop Caroline at Park Crescent. Neither Bernard nor Caroline was[1] pleased at having the matter taken out of their hands. In the taxi he said to her that the arrangement had been delightful, and she replied that he must encourage her: she was a coward, she said, she did dread the dentist. Bernard was interested, for last week he and Flavia had written each other some pages about their own apprehensions, and now he thought he would tell Flavia what kind of apprehension these girls one met, like Caroline, had. Caroline said he was so sympathetic. She told him that next month she was going to Wengen[2] for winter sports; it was obvious she would have liked to ask him to join their party. He rather trifled with the idea; he did not mind letting Flavia guess that he was much in demand. Caroline, from the portico in Park Crescent, smiled back a brave little smile at him.

Later, he did not mind letting Flavia guess that Caroline quite attracted him. For really Flavia was perverse, she refused to appear. She refused to allow him to see her handwriting; she refused to write from anywhere but a *poste restante*. "And this," she added, "is nowhere near where I live." (She must be at some pains to fetch his letters.) From the moment she first wrote direct to him, with reference to a letter of his in *The Athenaeum*,[3] she had established himself and herself as superior people who could not wish to meet except in the spirit. "Those imminences," she had been writing after a week or two, "those perplexities . . ." She cited quite a large number of correspondents in this manner. "Nothing," she wrote, "is more perishable, nothing lovelier than a distance." But really it was annoying. He would have liked, for instance, to have confronted the Dobsons with Flavia. *Caroline*, forsooth! And if ever a woman had been provocative – "My tall shadow," she wrote, "My absurd voice that will not pitch high," and "He could not see me, my head was against a dark cushion . . ." She knew altogether too many men. It was this, of course, that made Bernard so special. But he did feel at times too special. When that letter of hers arrived by the evening post, the emptiness of his room became intolerable. She probably lived in Westminster. Her clothes, "my absurd preoccupation," must be delicious. "I laughed inside with you all through the dinner party."

This was all very well.

Caroline did ask him to join their party for Switzerland; Bernard did go out with her. In that bright air she flowered, all pink and gold. In every letter he sketched some movement of hers for Flavia. He could not help speaking to Caroline of Flavia; she wished *she* had such a wonderful, wonderful friendship, too.

"Is she very beautiful?"

"You'll think us absurd," said Bernard, "we don't meet."

"How *clever* of you," breathed the young thing. Her relief was obvious. That night he wrote Flavia a letter about a kiss: did she know, did she ever feel . . .? Caroline waltzed divinely. Flavia's letters became a little less interesting; he suspected she did not care for dancing, just possibly she might not dance very well. After a silence of ten days, she wrote: "Of course, you are in love with her."

Very much startled, Bernard proposed that night to Caroline.

Caroline from the first said she feared that after Flavia Bernard would find her dull. But the letter Flavia wrote him about his engagement had not been intelligent: she was, after all, a woman, and she had certainly lost interest. Now there was no doubt that Caroline found him interesting. Their engagement was brief and very demonstrative. Towards the end of the honeymoon there was more time to talk; he found himself, while dropping Flavia's name right out of their conversation, pointing out to Caroline several things Flavia had noticed. On several occasions some remark of Flavia's would become apposite. "What marvellous ideas you do have," said Caroline, twinkling all over with an appreciation which, if not subtle, certainly had a charm of its own, a quality. She was a curious little thing; she lacked humour in the usual sense – his and Flavia's humour – but at some quite slight allusion, some accident of the day, her laughter would come on quite almost unaccountably, as uncontrollably as bleeding from the nose; you would say it was almost hysterical.

Bernard found for himself and Caroline a delightful flat. As she said she had not much taste and, anyhow, did not mind, it was he who decorated the flat. He sighed; this would have been the perfect setting for Flavia. Bernard, who had a little money, had recently set up as a publisher: he had an office in Soho, a sympathetic staff, not much to do at present. He was a good deal at home; perhaps at home a little too much. The Dobsons, who had sent them a beautiful set of Kipling, were among their first visitors.

At dinner he could not help quoting Flavia to Helen Dobson. Afterwards Caroline asked: "You do miss her, don't you?" The dinner Caroline had given the Dobsons had not been much nicer than the lunch the Dobsons had once given Bernard and Caroline; Bernard, who had wanted it all done with crushing perfection, said: "Well, you could hardly expect me not to."

Caroline pulled out a pink-and-white check handkerchief and

began to weep. "I thought I was enough," she said. "Can't you ever love a *real* woman, Bernard?"

Unfortunately, Caroline had a most infantile taste in handkerchiefs. These had elephants round the borders, or Mickey Mice, were pink, blue, or lemon (never Flavia's green or plain mannish lawn), and seemed to be always appearing. She was for ever wiping her fingers or dabbing her pretty, pink little nose; besides this, she wept a good deal. She wept now. "It's not *my* fault I'm not d-d-d-dark, Bernard."

"My dear, we can't all be the same."

"You didn't like the dinner," she sobbed.

"Perhaps roast chicken wasn't very original."

"But everybody *l-l-likes* roast chicken."

(What dinners he might have given the knowing Flavia! What dinners she might have ordered him!) "You don't love me," wept Caroline. Having exhausted her pink check handkerchief, she thrust it behind a cushion and brought out a Mickey Mouse one.

"If I hadn't loved you," said Bernard, shutting his eyes, "should I have given up Flavia?"

"She might have b-b-bored you," sobbed Caroline. She became most annoying, and he advised her to go to bed. She left him, and the distinguished little room looked flat and empty, as though it had never been inhabited. No tall shadow had ever moved on its walls, no low voice enlightened it; against the dark divan cushions no dark head had ever been invisible. Days came and went, he perceived no longer the Wednesdayness of a Wednesday, the uniqueness of ten o'clock- the sun became a mere busy planet, odious, jumping the skies like a Kruschen[4] grandfather; the fire was genial without intimacy. He suspected Caroline's husband, the Dobsons' acquaintance Bernard McArthur, to be an ordinary little man. It was now past midnight; Bernard drank a whisky-and-soda and went to bed.

Two days later there was a letter from Flavia.

"So now you are married," she wrote. It was a charming, ironic letter of speculation. Not speculation entirely – was she then married herself? It was possible – it was improbable . . . It was unthinkable: Bernard, he knew, possessed her. Dear Flavia, lonely, lovely. "We would not meet once," he wrote back, "we must not meet now." "Oh, why, why, why?" cried every sentence of Flavia's.

Bernard was annoyed, but not quite annoyed, when he looked up once to find Caroline examining Flavia's blue envelope across the breakfast-table. She had a little cold that morning, her eyes watered; she said nothing. He said nothing. "Poor little Caroline," Flavia had written. "I can't help wondering if you're nice to her."

"Caroline," said Bernard, "I wish you would take that zoological handkerchief off the breakfast-table. As you have such a cold, my dear, it's not even hygienic."

"Yes, Bernard . . . No, Bernard," said Caroline. She suddenly burst out laughing. "How f-f-funny you are," she tittered. "Zoological handkerchief! Oh, Bernard, how funny you can be! Oh . . ." She had her laugh out. Bernard thought perhaps she was running a temperature.

"She's like a child," he could not help writing (though they had sworn not to discuss her). "You said once all women[5] were children. But I don't think you are, Flavia." He could not resist another study of Caroline, the sort of woman one marries. He went perhaps a little too far; Flavia took a rather unpleasant licence; her subsequent letter displeased him. Perhaps she was rather hard? Poor Caroline was charming that morning. She did not glance at the envelope or refer at all to it, but sighed (sitting there rather pleasantly in the sunshine) and said she wished *she* had a friend. "An interesting friend," she added, "but, of course, I am not interesting."

"Yes, you are, darling," said Bernard amiably. "You're interesting in a different way."

"Am I, Bernard? How?"

"Well, you've got a delicious little personality."

"Have I, Bernard?"

"You have ideas that you can't express."

"Oh, do you think I have? Would you like me to express my ideas, Bernard?"

"No, darling; they're perfect the way they are."

"When you first saw me, did you think I was interesting?"

"Yes," said Bernard. He did not tell her that that day he had found everything interesting – the cat, the taximan, the advertisements on a bus, the colour of the Dobsons' front door. (It was the day he had got that wonderful letter from Flavia about himself.) "Did you think I was interesting?" he added, humouring her.

"No," said Caroline thoughtfully.

Bernard put down his coffee-cup.

"You were nicer than I expected," said Caroline. "Less nonsense about you. For instance, when I talked to you about winter sports, I quite expected you might be superior."

"Because the Dobsons' friends are superior?"

"Oh, but the Dobsons said you were rather dull. But I thought you had a nice sense of humour. Generally when I am talking to men I wish I were dark and thin, but you were so nice and homely, you made me feel comfortable. And I thought you might be nice to be married to, because, though you might not know much about food (even I could see that the Dobsons' lunch was horrible), you had quite a large appetite. I knew I shouldn't like to marry a clever man, but I shouldn't have liked to have married a dull man either, and I thought you were good at using other people's ideas in your talk. I thought you were rather pathetic, too. I suppose I do like men to be rather pathetic. And when you talked to me about Flavia in Switzerland I thought you were still more pathetic. I really did fall in love with you. I thought to myself, 'Fancy swallowing all *that* stuff.' I thought what a lamb you were."

"Thank you, Caroline."

"Well, really, Bernard, it made me feel quite embarrassed. I thought, 'What a good thing he is talking like this to someone as stupid as me.' You see, I did love you."

"Thank you," said Bernard again.

"You know, Bernard, she *is* pretty awful. Even a girl like me could see that, you know. She gets it all out of novels. I thought, 'She must be a typist.' I mean, she types and everything, doesn't she? And all that about food you told me was pages out of 'Marcel Boulestin.'"[6]

"It was *not* pages out of 'Marcel Boulestin.'"

"It was, Bernard: *I* read 'Marcel Boulestin.'"

Bernard let this pass. He pushed back his chair from the table and stared at Caroline, at her pink-and-white innocent, wise face, like a child's over the round, white silk shirt-collar and neat red tie. She sat up to the table, her hands folded. She looked pleased; no doubt because she was married, could speak home truths to a husband, and had thought, for once, of something to say. He thought of saying, "You do not even annoy me," but hesitated, not because this was untrue, but because he doubted if he could bring this off. Flavia's letter lay his side of the coffee pot.

"I expect now," said Caroline, "she writes to tell you you ought to be nice to me. 'Poor little Caroline,' I dare say she says. I dare say she expects I am a good little thing?"

"You are remarkably clever," said Bernard sarcastically.

"Not clever the way I seem," said Caroline. "Clever in a much more obvious way. You see, I do read a lot of novels – I hope I'm not being unkind, Bernard?"

"Oh no! You interest me."

"*Do* I interest you, Bernard?" said Caroline wistfully. "I do want to; I love you so much."

This seemed to Bernard beside the point, he was by now really angry. "The fact is, you're jealous."

"Of Flavia? Oh no, not *now*. I was at one time. At one time I got rather carried away by her myself. She seemed to have everything in her favour. You see, in those days I had no confidence. No one had ever told me how nice I was myself," said Caroline, dimpling. (He remembered with fury how well he had spoken of her dimples to Flavia.) "She had lovely clothes; she went to so many parties; she knew so many men. She could remember all the clever stuff she had read. She would have impressed the Dobsons. She could be certain to marry, only she was too grand. She could make any interesting friend she wanted. When I read that letter of yours in *The Athenaeum* about Turkish women, I thought to myself, 'Now that is exactly the sort of man Flavia would get to know' – only I didn't know at the time her name was Flavia."

"Oh, so *you* saw the letter of mine? I didn't know you ever saw *The Athenaeum*."

"I don't generally; someone had left it at my dentist's. I was going to the dentist's a lot at that time, do you remember? I longed to know you, Bernard . . . When you introduced yourself to me at the Dobsons that day I said to myself, slowly, 'This is Bernard McArthur.' Then I said to myself that I expected *Flavia*, too, would be surprised if *she* met you, too. Then when you seemed so pleased with me but so sort of doubtful I expected you'd write to Flavia and say I was the sort of girl one did meet, and smile a good deal about me in your letter, then wish you hadn't. I wondered if Flavia really was a nice friend for you, then the more I could see how nice you were the more I could see she wasn't. I began to worry; I thought up to a point she had been nice for you, but now she was doing you harm. But by the time you told me about her in Switzerland she was simply a joke. Then I wondered how anybody like Flavia would take it if you were to marry. I thought it would be interesting to see – "

"You've talked for some time," said Bernard, "but I think this is enough. Will you please leave Flavia alone? She's not your type; you can't possibly understand her. She's been magnificent – "

"All the same, she did sulk, didn't she? I mean, she stopped writing."

"If that's all you're generous enough to see – "

"Oh, all right then; she stopped writing because she bored you.

She did, Bernard; she did bore you when we were engaged. And on our honeymoon you didn't like to think of her much; she made you feel rather ordinary. All the same, I do think it was mean of you to use up all her remarks. They were wasted on me – "

"A good deal seems to be wasted on you," said Bernard. Vague phrases from a possible letter to Flavia swam through his head . . . "We have reached the turning-point" . . . "Do you understand now why my marriage has been a failure?" . . .

"If you really must know," he continued, "Flavia warned me – "

"I know she did. She did everything right. Oh, Bernard; oh, darling, I was in despair; I thought you'd never propose to me. I had just to make her tip you over the edge. But, oh, how I cursed her! Oh, Bernard, are you going to divorce me, or anything? I wish I'd never begun it."

"Caroline, if you weep again I shall hit you. Begun what? – Pull yourself together! – Never begun what?"

"*Flavia, you idiot!*" Caroline fumbled in her neat shirt-pocket for her handkerchief, then up one cuff, then up the other. "Oh, Bernard," she sobbed, "it was such a sweat, I did think her out so, and directly we met I saw it was all unnecessary. Oh, Bernard, if you won't forgive me I think I shall divorce you. I've got all your letters . . ."

And at last she brought out her handkerchief, which was blue check in the middle today, with elephants round it. For this occasion it was more than inadequate. Bernard was doubtful whether to lend her his own or not.

She Gave Him

The look – upon which Henry's eyelids had come down almost at once so oddly, with such a disturbing suggestion of smug finality – followed Magdalen for the next hour, and not too pleasantly.[1] She did not care for the look. Nobody, either before or since she became a Woman,[2] had looked at her quite like *that*. It had held worse than repudiation: a nasty kind of complicity. Her reflections upon it, however, were jolted about, perhaps not unkindly: in this next hour there was a good deal of that "business" with which life, just as well as the stage, can fill in an emotional standstill – more onlookers trailing up, gathering, somebody taking command; Henry's being removed to the cottage of young Henry's not at all grateful mother; the doctor's arrival and rather too brisk pronouncement; a general conviction of onlookers that they'd been rather let down. Death was not likely and there was no visible blood.

During this interval Magdalen, shattered and not very notably useful, kept darting this way and that way, or stood wringing together her fingers with a distressful diligence. She had been given the head of the cortège behind Henry's limp and distinctly forbidding body into the dark cottage lamplight, as though she had been his widow. But of what should have been this most impressive of moments the unfortunate Magdalen savoured little.

This fuss, with its grateful distraction, was too soon over. Henry gave every sign of disliking the cottage: the doctor could find no reason why he should not be moved. So removed Henry was, in the farm car that had been rushed to the scene tooting, with jolting headlights. He departed, propped in the back with his head just in swooning-distance of Mrs. Linaker's bosom – not Magdalen's. Magdalen, silent and lowering, got in beside the pink boy: bumping wonderfully little they drove back to Linaker's farm.

"Knocked silly, that's what he was, the poor fellow," said Mrs. Linaker.

"He was," agreed Magdalen with unusual eagerness. "Knocked *quite* silly."

Mrs. Linaker's manner with Henry remained rather ruefully matter-of-fact, as though he were a damaged chicken: she put him out on the parlour sofa (as though into a box with flannel) and said he'd be better shortly. Magdalen's view of Henry, hair all disordered into a palish fluff, was as not unlike a chicken. Mrs. Linaker went to heat milk, Magdalen slipped upstairs, lit those candles and snatched from the mirror between them what was not much more than a disconcerted glance at herself. She patted her hair into place with unusual briskness and shut with rare violence – for she was not as a rule unkind to inanimate objects – two or three boxes and drawers. Puffing face-powder from the mirror she was unable to rid herself of that unnerving sensation of having caught, for the moment, *not* Henry Mayburg's or Maybird's eye but her own.

"There's no doubt," she kept thinking angrily, "he's been heroic."

Smoothing her dress on her fine hips, drawing a strand of hair clear of an earring and tightening her belt by one hole she went down to meet the hero. A rather lugubrious silence pervaded the parlour, in which a glazed cotton blind was pulled down decisively over the night in the window and Henry, shading his eyes from the lamplight, stared at his own small feet as though they did not belong to him but were a pair of belongings of Mrs. Linaker's, placed by her on a newspaper at the far end of the tight red couch.

"Well . . ." began Magdalen, sitting down.

Henry turned her way one weary glance, in reply.

"We all," she continued, "feel very proud of you, Mr. Maybird." She could not help stressing the second syllable ever so little.

"Oh, well . . ." said Henry, and watched his feet wriggle ruefully.

His embarrassment was quite likeable, even a shade affecting. Even Magdalen – on whom any impact of anyone else's feelings was but as the bump of a moth, outside, on a tightly shut window – even Magdalen realised that Henry was not himself. But what Henry's self could be she did not enquire. She sat down, beyond the round table, sending into the lamplight between them a voluminous weighty look that meant nothing in particular.

"I suppose," she said anxiously, "this – I mean all *that*, is mostly a blank to you now?"

"Well, more or less," he agreed. He spoke slowly and leaned on his words, as though his thought was on crutches. She was more than half reassured. But his feet, at which Henry kept staring so hard that she had to look at them too, cocked their toes up at the two of them with an intelligence that was most disconcerting.

"It's so odd," she said, ploughing ahead, "how one little thing changes everything."

"Do you refer," Henry said, "to my accident?"

"Oh dear no – I didn't mean *that*. I should have said really, something, *not* little, that happens all in a flash."

"Yes," he agreed, "in a flash."

"But changing everything. *Before*, we'd been talking so trivially . . . Hadn't we?"

"I don't," he said primly, "remember."

Oh, didn't he? Could one be certain? "We were," she said firmly. "Because I remember thinking how trivially we were talking in this mysterious night."

"Then there," said Henry, "you have the advantage of me."

She opened her mouth, but his manner inspired mistrust, so she said nothing more. For this one relief, Henry thanked her. He was, naturally, very much taken up with himself. He had recently nodded at death, and still had a sense of importance as though he had met royalty. And here *she* sat, persistently chatting about herself and her thoughts. Meanwhile he looked at his hands and felt over, mentally, his restored body, thinking: "*So* nearly finished; so nearly not any more!" He would be a hero tomorrow: he kept this fact tucked in beside him like an unopened letter too full of promise to read.

Nothing, however, would keep her silent for long. Too soon she came out with: "Night always seems to me very mysterious. So full of echoes. So full of echoes of other nights. Has that occurred to you?"

"Well, yes, it did once," said Henry. "But I don't think it will again."

In fact, he had graduated in experience: his air was decidedly lordly as he leaned back further and clasped his hands carefully under his head. Her presence was like being wrapped to the chin in an eiderdown he was too weak to throw off: he felt a vindictive and ingrowing wish to offend Magdalen mortally. As from thoughts of the mayonnaise and the trifles of which he partook too heartily coming back in their eggy stickiness to afflict the bilious sufferer, Henry was in revolt, with a violent queasiness, from much that he and Magdalen had in common. Swinburne, for instance, dripped thickly over his nerves like an upset custard. It seemed hopeless to try to escape from Magdalen in this new attitude of the woman ministrant, with her white cuffs and her hands crossed in the lamp-light a touch of the nursing nun chastened her manner but did not disinfect it of what he most disliked. If his sick head yearned for a bosom, it was not Magdalen's. He examined – but with a surprising dryness – his lack of his mother, but could think of his mother not as an inclined bosom but as someone tearing arpeggios from the pianoforte in powerful Kilburn gaslight,[3] against yellow curtains. The very thought was arduous – with a qualm, as though he had questioned his mother's honour, Henry did ask for a moment if women were all alike. Though he shut his eyes, and kept his eyes shut firmly, Magdalen's presence came at him like a continuous pressure of hot air.

"She's very possessive," he thought. "It wasn't her fault she wasn't in at the death. You'd think she thought she'd a right here" – Then: "Oh, my God, *was I making love to her?*"

He had only her own assurance – and that put forward with a provoking arch air, as though to invite contradiction – that their talk had really been trivial. His oblivion became full of pitfalls, and frayed at the edges with horrid tremors. *What* had one been saying the moment before little Henry ran under the car? And what had she been replying as he, Henry major, lay prostrate? He found a bruise on his memory, as though during numbness he had sustained some violent collision: at one or another moment this woman *had* had a tight hold on him.

With a sinking sense of fatality, with an immeasurable apprehension Henry eyed Magdalen, as though he had been delivered over to her and his future were in her hands. She sat looking down at her cuffs: her fine, full, too mobile mouth was in threatening repose.

"Yes?" she said, lifting her eyes, for his horrified look had been urgent.

"Do you know," he said, shading his eyes from the lamplight and looking owlishly at her from under his hand, "I am quite often not quite myself. It's been my trouble from childhood. I wouldn't mention it now, but this evening has been unusual."

"Yes," she agreed, with a kind of Olympian primness, as though he were exchanging small-talk with Venus herself. Very much attached to her prey[4] – oh yes, he thought, very.

"I often say things I don't mean."

"Yes," she said, "yes, I thought so."

"What do you mean?" he said, starting with natural annoyance.

"Naturally," remarked Magdalen, "I have some knowledge of men."

She was round him in coils: he made a restless, despairing gesture, rolling his head on the cushion in sick anger: the cushion slipped from under it to the floor. She came round the table, stooped, and picked up the cushion. He raised his head, she put the cushion back; then she remained by his side looking always down. "You must be quiet," she said with magnetic gentleness: shutting his eyes, he felt something descend: she had placed a hand on his forehead. He lay helpless under that cool and unmoving pressure. She gave him the cold shivers.

Brigands

O liver's uncle's house seemed so odd that Oliver
pinched himself when he woke up in the mornings for several days
after he came to stay.

He had been sent to stay with his uncle, who having made an
enormous amount of money in South Africa had come home to buy
a house as large as his fortune and settle down He had brought back
with him his wife, Aunt Alice, and his daughter, Priscilla, a very fat
girl of fourteen. The castle Aunt Alice wanted had not been hard to
find, in fact she had had several to choose from, as people do not
want that sort of thing nowadays.[1] Oliver liked his uncle, who had

tipped him two pounds when first they met, and whenever they met again pulled his ear kindly and asked him how he was getting on. He was a nervous man, chiefly on account of Aunt Alice, but full of kindness. Oliver had been sent here to stay because his father had been ill and these Easter holidays had gone abroad with his mother to get well again. They hated to miss Oliver, but it could not be helped.

His uncle's enormous house looked like a castle, with turrets and battlements, but it was really quite modern and shiny inside, not at all dark; it was filled with bathrooms, and footmen to please Aunt Alice, and family portraits she had had the trouble of buying at auctions, because, she said, they had left their own family portraits in South Africa. The house (or castle) was built at the head of a steep, craggy valley in the north of England; a flag was kept flying and it looked very grand as you drove up. You drove in over a drawbridge, but this was a practical joke as the drawbridge did not pull up. All the country round was full of these craggy valleys, with limestone cliffs and rivers that flowed underground; it was said to be full of caves, but no one in the castle could tell where the caves were. If it had not been for Aunt Alice, Priscilla, the footmen and a few other drawbacks, you could not imagine a better place to be staying.

Oliver would not have blamed Priscilla for being fat if she had not been so haughty. She was not intelligent and could tell him nothing about South Africa except that it had been hot, which he knew for himself. She did not have much of a time, poor girl, as when she was not at lessons with her French governess (she seemed to have no holidays) she was doing exercises on a back-board or walking round and round with a book on her head, in order that she might be beautiful when she grew up. This did not seem to Oliver likely. Every day, Priscilla bumped round and round a field on a pony, looking miserable, as her mother thought this might make her thin. The food in the schoolroom[2] was terribly plain, for the same reason, but the children came down to lunch in the diningroom and on these occasions Priscilla ate all she could. Her mother adored her and could not bear to say "No" (which was why they kept the French governess) and it was with great distress that Aunt Alice watched Priscilla stuffing herself with cream puddings.[3] Oliver also ate all he could, but no one minded about his figure.

The chauffeur was nice, and Oliver spent a good deal of time in the yard, watching the cars being washed and looking into their engines. There were six cars. The third morning after he came, he saw a girl in a red jersey, also hanging about the yard. She looked about his own age, which was ten, but she scowled when he looked her way and he thought she might be as haughty as Priscilla. The chauffeur said her name was Maria Pelley, and that she lived with her uncle who was Oliver's uncle's agent in the house near the lower gate.

However, Oliver made friends with Maria the same afternoon, when the groom took them both out ratting She was sensible, did not scream, and when she found out he had not much use for Priscilla she got quite friendly. He asked Maria about the caves, she said she knew of one, about three miles away, that she promised to take him to, but she saw no reason why there should not be others, and they decided to look for them. She also told him this house was supposed to be built where a brigands' castle had been. Oliver felt quite certain the caves should be easy to find.

The next morning, when Oliver, waiting about for Maria, was bouncing a ball on the terrace, he happened to knock the heads off three pink hyacinths by sending the ball among them, and to tread on a few more while getting the ball out. He heard an awful roar from behind him, and turned to see the head gardener, Perkins, shaking his fist at him, shouting and making a face: he looked furious. If Perkins had not been nasty, Oliver would have apologised: as it was he walked off with great dignity. He was sorry about the hyacinths, but did not see that it much mattered. The hyacinths had been planted in thick pink rows down the terrace and looked like something to eat. Whenever they met after this, Perkins scowled and Oliver knew he had made an enemy. He was an ugly man, who wore bulgy spectacles. Oliver noticed how different Perkins's manner was to his uncle, his aunt, and Priscilla. Head gardeners are supposed to be fierce, but Perkins was quite oily and lost no opportunity of telling Aunt Alice what a fine young lady Priscilla was. All this seemed to Oliver rather fishy. He apologised to his uncle about the hyacinths and his uncle said it was all right. His Aunt Alice said nothing.

Oliver told Maria about Perkins, and she suggested that they should have a vendetta,[4] which is the way Sicilians keep on paying each other out. She had read a good deal and was full of ideas: this plan seemed to Oliver excellent.

That evening, the schoolroom supper was intended to make Priscilla slimmer than usual: when it was over Oliver still felt hungry. His aunt was giving a dinner party and extra good smells came up the kitchen stairs to the schoolroom wing. It is a shocking thing to steal food, but Oliver happened to be about in the back hall, near the service door of the diningroom, at a place where the footmen put down the trays when they left the diningroom. So he got two quails in aspic, later on some very good rich pudding, and finished up with several bits of a savoury made of crab. This is the darker side of his character, and is only mentioned because of its exciting results.

His inside, combined with a very good book Maria had lent him about vendettas, kept Oliver from sleeping as usual that night. Also, it was a full moon. He went to sleep but had queer dreams and kept waking up again. He felt excited and restless, and certain that something was going on. He heard one o'clock strike from the stable belfry.

He lay with his eyes wide open and his ears drumming as though there were a clock under his pillow. Then he did really hear something. The creak, creak, creak of a wheel going round, and a faint scrunch of gravel outside, like somebody walking on tip-toes. He jumped out of bed and ran stealthily to the window. His room looked out on a less ornamental part of the garden, the same side as the kitchens; there were sheds there, always kept locked up. He peered down – the moonlight was very bright, almost dazzling – and saw a man wheeling a wheelbarrow,[5] trying to keep at once well in the shadow, but not too near the windows. The wheelbarrow seemed very heavy, for the man kept stopping and straightening his back. As he did this just under Oliver's window, the moonlight gleamed on his spectacles: it was Perkins. The whole thing seemed very suspicious. Perkins picked up the wheelbarrow and disappeared with it round the corner.

Next day, Oliver said at luncheon: "Why does Perkins wheel wheelbarrows in the middle of the night?" His uncle looked gloomy and said Perkins was a good gardener and had his own way of doing things. His aunt said sharply that this was impossible. Oliver must have been dreaming. Priscilla turned up her nose and said: "Our head gardener doesn't wheel wheelbarrows: he has twelve under-gardeners to do it for him." In fact, what Oliver said was not a success.

So directly after luncheon he told Maria, whom he had not been able to find that morning. She said at once that this *was* very suspicious, and that they had better conceal themselves that night in order to shadow Perkins. So that night Oliver slipped out of the house by the back stairs, when he was supposed to be sound asleep, carrying an electric torch he had got from the bedside of the French governess. Maria was waiting for him round the corner of the house, near the yard gates: her uncle gave no trouble. She wore a mackintosh, in the pockets of which she had another electric torch, a water-pistol and a pea-shooter, besides some biscuits and a bit of rope. She gave Oliver the pea-shooter, as he was the better shot. So they were heavily armed.

Time went by very slowly, they told each other long stories in whispers to keep awake: when their imaginations gave out they pinched each other. There was so long between the hours they thought the stable clock must have stopped. Nothing seemed to be happening.

But at last something did. They heard a faint sound and flattened themselves into the doorway where they stood: there were clouds over the moon tonight, fortunately, and it was not nearly so light. Scrunch, scrunch, softly over the gravel came Perkins with his wheelbarrow; now and then the wheel creaked. Each time the wheel creaked he stopped dead. Then he went by them, puffing and blowing, with his spectacles glittering like a witch's eyes. They gave him time to get past, then in their rubber-soled shoes crept after him, ever so softly, round the corner of the house. They were just in time to see him unlock a shed, glare round cautiously, wheel the wheelbarrow into it and disappear.

Very cautiously, Oliver and Maria crept up to the shed, to listen. Utter, complete silence. But that the door was a little ajar you would have thought they had come to the wrong shed. Pressed flat to the outside wall of the shed, they waited and waited. But no one came out again. It stayed perfectly silent inside the shed.

At last they did a very bold thing, they opened the door by inches. Then they drew a deep breath and turned their electric torches full into the shed. It was *empty*, as though Perkins had melted. But here was the wheelbarrow, its load tipped out of it, lying face down on the floor. They went into the shed: it had a board floor, which seemed odd for a shed of that kind.

Maria and Oliver were quite staggered. For a moment, they accused each other of having gone to sleep. But they knew this was not so. Not quite knowing why he was doing this, Oliver stamped carefully over the floor of the shed. And suddenly, a whole part of the board floor gave a little, and creaked.

"A trap-door!" exclaimed Maria. They knelt down and pulled at the floor – and, behold, it was. A great square of floor came up, and they looked down a square black shaft cut in the rock. A cold, damp breath came up, and though they flashed their torches into it they could see no bottom. They saw, however, a ladder. Down this Perkins had disappeared.

They looked at each other. "*Well*," said Oliver. "Look – "

"Come on!" said Maria.

However, he would not let her go first.

They climbed down very cautiously, their torches were in their pockets, in case they should suddenly be attacked. Oliver carried the pea-shooter between his teeth, Maria carried the water-pistol the same way. In the darkness Maria, in too much of a hurry, kept stepping on Oliver's head. The ladder was very slimy.

After what seemed hours, Oliver reached the bottom; he stood clear of the ladder, Maria kicked his face for the last time and came down also. They got out their torches and saw, straight ahead of them, a low passage winding away through the rock. Its sides were shiny with damp, which ran down in trickles. Oliver and Maria ducked their heads and holding their torches firmly crept down the passage. Perkins, who was quite tall, must have crawled.

When they had followed several turns of the passage Oliver said: "*Hist!*"

"What?" said Maria.

"*Hist* – lights!"

And sure enough, a faint jiggly red light, like firelight, began to play over the wet passage walls. Once more they were very cautious; they went along inch by inch, with their torches out, prepared to stop dead in a moment, holding their breaths. They began to hear voices. The red light grew stronger and brighter. One more turn of the passage and they pulled up, in sight of a scene that was most amazing.

In fact, they could hardly believe it was true. The passage broadened out suddenly into a high and enormous cave. Its walls, all scaly with damp, shone red in the light of what was not a fire but a dozen flaring and smoking torches. Enormous stalactites, shaped like cocoanut cones, hung from the roof of the cave; now and then a drop fell from the tip of a stalactite on to a torch, which would fizz horribly. There were pools between ribs of rock on the floor of the cave. The torches were held by twelve men of most dangerous appearance, who sat on the rocks in a circle, and in the centre, on the highest of all the rocks, sat Perkins. Perkins did not hold a torch, he was too important, but something shone in the torchlight; he had a gun over his knees. He looked absolutely different, as unpleasant as ever but terribly fierce and menacing as he addressed his followers; his oily manner had disappeared.

One great thought: *"Brigands!"* flashed through Oliver's and Maria's minds. They stared at each other, but dared not speak.

"And *that*," they heard Perkins say in an awful voice, "is the lot."

At these words, a murmur of admiration ran through the brigands; they lowered their torches and scrambled together to look at something at Perkins's feet. In the lowered torchlight the children saw, as the brigands' excited bodies closed in, a great gleam and flashing. Gold plates and goblets and silver statues, with diamond tiaras amid emerald chains straggling over them were piled up in a heap. The diamonds and emeralds Oliver already had seen on Aunt Alice's chest. The statues came out of the drawing-room cabinets. The goblets, his uncle had won for shooting. The gold plates must always have been locked up, till Aunt Alice could entertain royalty. All this was Perkins's booty. Oliver gasped.

Maria gasped also, for as the brigands' faces came more clearly into the light she recognised three of the gardeners and four of the footmen. The other gardeners and footmen who, as they were not here, must be quite respectable, these brigands must have been ready to murder at any moment. It is extraordinary how unlike gardeners and footmen brigands can look when they return to their true characters. Though they had not grown beards, their faces looked quite wolf-like; their teeth flashed, their eyes glittered and it was clear they would stop at nothing.

Perkins, looking very pleased with himself, watched his brigands examine the booty, though he kept his gun ready in case they should help themselves. When they had done, he said: "Order!" and thumped his gun on the rock. The brigands obediently scrambled back to their places and Oliver saw what a strong will Perkins must have.

"And what," Perkins said, "shall we ask for the girl?"

"Ten thousand pounds," shouted one of the brigands.

"Twenty!" exclaimed another.

"Thirty!"

"Fifty!"

"A hundred!"

It became rather like an auction. Perkins, looking scornfully at them, said: "I say two hundred thousand, or she's not worth taking at all."

There was another murmur of admiration, then a pause, while the brigands, doing arithmetic, worked out how much they would each get. "Are you sure they've got all that?" said one of the brigands, cautiously.

"*D'you mean*," shouted Perkins, with a frightful expression, "that *I* don't know what I'm talking about?"

"Oh, no," said the brigand, so much alarmed that he dropped his torch into the puddle and could not light it again. He was quite young and had only just joined.

In this roaring confusion, Maria put her mouth close to Oliver's ear and whispered: "They're going to kidnap Priscilla."

This became quite clear, for Perkins went on to speak of his plans in a cold-blooded voice. There was no doubt, he said, that the robbery of the gold plates, silver statues and jewellery would be discovered tomorrow – in fact, he said, grinning horribly at his watch, *today* – for though the things taken the night before had come out of the safe, which no one had since had occasion to open, the silver statues out of the drawing-room had left such gaps that even people so stupid as Aunt Alice and the respectable servants could never fail to notice. So Perkins was going to go back and leave false tracks, such as broken shutters and wrenched-open locks and footmarks, that would look as though ordinary burglars had been there – at the name of ordinary *burglars*, all the brigands sneered – so tomorrow the whole house would be in confusion, with everyone telephoning to the police, trying to get bloodhounds and running about talking. So, while everybody was busy, Perkins would put wire out in the field where she rode to trip up Priscilla's pony. He would then spring out and knock Priscilla on the head as she fell, drag her off into hiding and, after midnight, drop her gagged and bound down the rock-shaft into the shed into the hands of the waiting brigands. Then they would send off letters asking for ransom to her distracted father and mother.

"And don't give her anything to eat," Perkins said, "it's a waste of money, and she is too fat already."

He then went on to say things about Priscilla's appearance and character that would have surprised and horrified Aunt Alice. Though Oliver partly agreed, he felt Perkins had no right to talk like this – even if he were the Chief Brigand. Maria giggled and stuffed her handkerchief into her mouth.

"Well," said Perkins, "I think that concludes the evening."

All the other brigands, raising their torches higher, stood up, drew a deep breath and sang: "For he's a jolly good fellow." They paraded round and round Perkins in a circle, waving their torches and stumbling over the rocks. The cave echoed. Perkins, looking extremely pleased with himself, sat there holding his gun.

"Look *out!*" said Maria. "They're coming!" And sure enough, the whole file of brigands began to come winding this way, prepared to march Perkins in triumph to the foot of the ladder. How they could march in triumph along a passage too low for even Maria and

Oliver, it was hard to imagine. However, no doubt they would crawl.

Rushing for dear life Oliver and Maria fled back down the passage, not daring to use their electric torches till they were well away. They thought they would never get back, but they just did. As Oliver reached the top of the ladder, pushing Maria before him as hard as he could, he heard the puffing and scrambling of the first brigand, still some way down the passage. They slammed the trap-door and both raced out of the shed in different directions, not daring to talk. Oliver heard a cock crow and knew it would soon be morning.

The servants cannot have dusted the drawing-room early, for by nine o'clock that morning no word of the burglary had reached the schoolroom. Directly breakfast was over, Oliver ran to look for his uncle. He found him walking up and down on the terrace beside the hyacinths, looking gloomy, as though he wished he were back in South Africa.

"Uncle *Arthur*," said Oliver, "there are *brigands* under the house!"

His uncle stopped and looked at him absent-mindedly. "Yes, yes," he said, "that is very nice."

"Uncle Arthur, *Perkins* is the Chief Brigand!"

"Dear me," said his uncle, "he's a bit short-tempered, I know. But you mustn't mind that."

"Oh, *listen*: they've robbed the whole house; they're going to kidnap Priscilla!"

"Priscilla?" said his uncle, "I expect she's doing her exercises. Run away now, Oliver, there's a good chap; I'm busy."

"*Uncle Arthur, listen —* "

But Uncle Arthur, clasping his hands behind his back again, walked away. He always did this when anyone talked excitedly, because he was accustomed to Aunt Alice.

In despair, and knowing that there was not a moment to lose, Oliver rushed off to find Aunt Alice, who was quietly reading her letters beside her boudoir fire.

"Aunt *Alice*," he said, "there are brigands under the house."

"Hush," said Aunt Alice, "you must not make so much noise."

"*Perkins* is the Chief Brigand!"

"Hush," said Aunt Alice, "I cannot allow you to shout in here."

"They've robbed the whole house; they're going to kidnap Priscilla!"

"If you want to play brigands," said Aunt Alice, trying hard to be patient because he was somebody else's child, "you must go into the garden. And don't disturb Priscilla; she's doing her flat-foot exercises till eleven o'clock."

"If Priscilla rides today, she'll be hit on the head!"

"Really," said Aunt Alice, "you *are* an inconsiderate little boy." And not knowing what to do she rang for the butler.

By this time, Maria had turned up. They held a council of war. It was really desperate. They went to the French governess and told her; she went into hysterics. But when she recovered it turned out that this was because she had a brother-in-law who was a brigand in Corsica, so she considered the subject personal. She was very angry and told them to go away. So they found Priscilla, who was doing knee-bending-and-stretching exercises, bobbing up and down in the middle of the schoolroom with two books on her head; she looked very cross.

"Priscilla," Oliver shouted, "*don't* ride your pony today."

"You'll be hit on the head and kidnapped!" shouted Maria.

"Go away," said Priscilla, who did not like to be looked at. The two books fell off her head.

"How would you like," said Oliver, "to be bound and gagged and dropped down a slimy black hole?"

"How would you like," said Maria, "to be starved by brigands with torches?"

"Go *away*," said Priscilla, "I'll tell mother." She burst into tears.

"Oh, really!" exclaimed Maria. "I think we'd better let Perkins have her."

"No we won't," said Oliver, "it would be such a score for Perkins. I despise Priscilla, but I loathe him!"

When Priscilla heard she was despised she sobbed louder and louder. In fact, she went into hysterics, which she had learnt to do from her French governess. She lay down and banged her heels on the floor. This made such a noise that a housemaid came in to see what was the matter.

"Dear me!" she said. "What have you two been doing to Miss Priscilla?"

"The silver statues are gone from the drawing-room!" Maria and Oliver shouted.

"Sakes!" said the housemaid, and rushed off. After this, of course, the robbery was discovered. Aunt Alice's maid missed the jewels, the butler looked into the safe and found the gold plates gone. The whole house (as the wicked Perkins expected) was in an uproar. They found the false burglar-tracks and believed them; everyone started screaming for the police, telephoning for bloodhounds and running about talking. Aunt Alice went to bed and took sal volatile,[6] Uncle Arthur discovered that they had taken a small silver mug he had won for shooting, which he valued more than anything else, and went about stamping and saying that this came of buying a castle. Two policemen came in and took notes. Nobody, least of all the policemen,[7] would listen to one word from Oliver and Maria. Meanwhile Priscilla stolidly went out to mount her pony. She rather wanted to ride this morning, because Oliver and Maria had asked her not to. That is always the way.

And meanwhile Perkins, looking perfectly calm, walked about on the terrace, tying up the pink hyacinths Oliver had broken. Whenever anyone passed he stood up and touched his cap and said it was a pity about the burglary.

Maria said: "There is only one thing to do." They went round to the stable yard, and just as Priscilla climbed heavily from the mounting-block to the saddle, with the groom respectfully holding the pony's head, Maria opened her long, sharp penknife, stooped down and cut the girths. The saddle swung round, Priscilla fell off with a flump, on her ear. The pony snorted and bolted across the yard.

"That," said Maria, "will teach you."

When Uncle Arthur who was walking about out of doors to avoid the police saw his daughter being carried into the house, he thought at first she was unconscious, until he came nearer and heard her screaming and roaring. "Oh, oh!" she said, "Maria has killed me!"

"Maria," said Uncle Arthur, feeling that this was really the limit, "what have you done?"

"It was for her own good," said Maria. "There are brigands under the house."

"Perkins is the Chief Brigand," said Oliver, slowly and distinctly, trying to make Uncle Arthur collect himself.

"Don't talk to me about brigands," said Uncle Arthur, "when we're overrun with burglars. They've taken that silver mug I won in 1895. It's been with me everywhere. I think everything of that mug."

"The burglars are brigands. Perkins is their chief. They have got your mug. They were going to kidnap Priscilla."

"Do you mean," said Uncle Arthur, pulling himself together and staring at Oliver, "you really know where that mug *is*?"

He forgot all about the gold plates, he forgot Priscilla; at this good news of his mug he became quite docile and listened carefully to what Oliver and Maria told him. Rich men are often like this. They led him round to the shed, which Perkins had locked, of course; Uncle Arthur was so impatient that he sent for the groom and the chauffeur to break the door open. Then they rushed in and pulled up the trap-door. There was the deep, dark hole in the rock, with cold air coming up, and the top of the slimy ladder. Uncle Arthur took one look down and disappeared down the ladder, to find his mug. The groom and the chauffeur went after him, striking matches and filled with respectful curiosity.

"Do you think," said Maria, "the brigands are still down there?"

But before they had time to wonder, they heard a step on the gravel.

There was Perkins, a pink hyacinth in one hand, a bit of bass[8] in the other, looking in at the door of the shed. When he saw the trap-door open, he knew everything was discovered. He gave one awful oath and bolted. Like a pair of greyhounds, Oliver and Maria went after him.

"Police, police!" yelled Maria. But the police were looking for clues in the kitchen and being given beer by the cook. They did not hear; no one came out.

As they ran, Oliver pulled the pea-shooter out of his pocket; Maria held the water-pistol ready to aim. Perkins dodged round the house and doubled; panting and cursing he sprinted over the lawn. His spectacles fell off. Like many other brigands, he was extremely short-sighted; he went quite blind and rushed head-on into a tree. He rebounded against the tree, but at this point Maria, with great presence of mind, flung herself right on the ground just under his feet; Perkins tripped over Maria and went crash down. At the same time, Oliver let off the pea-shooter, picked up the water-pistol Maria had dropped and fired this down Perkins's neck. Maria crawled from underneath Perkins and sat on his head. Oliver seized one of his legs and, though Perkins lashed about, kicking wildly, Oliver tightly held on. They all yelled. A great many people rushed out of the house, and the police came after them.

The rest was quite simple. When the footmen-brigands saw that all was discovered, they were too mean to come to Perkins's rescue, they rushed away through the house and across the drawbridge, but the bloodhounds, which had just arrived in a van, were sent after them. The gardener-brigands, who had left their guns in the cave, locked themselves into a greenhouse, but were soon captured. Perkins, tightly bound up with ropes and swearing horribly, was taken by the policemen into the shed and forced, by having real pistols held to his head, to lean down the hold and shout the Brigands' Countersign. Five or six brigands *had* been down in the cave; when they heard the Countersign they stopped knocking Uncle Arthur, the groom and the chauffeur about and rushed faithfully up the ladder, thinking there was going to be a raid. The police hit them on the head, one by one as they came up, and arrested them. They were all very much surprised. The police were only prevented from hitting Uncle Arthur over the head by the fact that he came up shouting, waving the silver mug.

When the whole plot, and the awful wickedness of Perkins, had been discovered, Uncle Arthur and Aunt Alice could not be grateful enough to Oliver and Maria. They gave a large party in their honour, at which all the gold plates were put out. They gave Maria Priscilla's pony which Priscilla was told she need not ride any more, promised to send Maria to Switzerland for the summer holidays and even offered to buy her a small island to live in when she was grown up: Aunt Alice also gave her a pearl necklace to wear when she was eighteen and went to balls. They gave Oliver a gun and a new bicycle and promised him a car when he was eighteen; they also opened an account for him at Fortnum and Mason's, so that he could order whatever food he liked to take back to school. They gave them both silver mugs with inscriptions, like Uncle Arthur's. Even Priscilla thanked them, and the thought of what she had escaped made her quite thin.

After this, Aunt Alice would have nothing but lady gardeners; she also gave up footmen and had nice parlour-maids. They dismissed the French governess, because they did not like to keep anyone who was even related to brigands. Aunt Alice persuaded Uncle Arthur to have machine-guns mounted on all the turrets, but these were not needed, as life in the castle remained quite peaceful after this.

The evening before they went back to school, Oliver and Maria had a party all to themselves in the brigands' cave and danced round each other with torches.

The Unromantic Princess

When the Princess was born the Queen, who knew what was usual, invited two Fairy Godmothers to her christening. Unfortunately, they arrived in a workaday mood, and full of modern ideas about girls. So that the gifts they gave the Princess were as follows: one gave her Punctuality; the other, Commonsense. This had not been the Queen's idea at all, and she was grievously disappointed. Besides being so dull, the two Fairy Godmothers were a nuisance throughout the christening party. They would not sit down to lunch, but moved about restlessly, nibbling moth-wing sandwiches out of their reticules. They cast a gloom on the party, where all the other guests were in gold, silver or mother o' pearl brocade, with their severe poke bonnets[1] tied under their chins and sensible boots that had tramped miles in Fairyland. Their motto was: "one should never fly when one could walk." They gave the guests several quite unasked-for home truths, and everyone found them tiresome old bodies. Everyone blamed the Queen for not being more exclusive. She felt wretched, and stole away to her baby's cradle. "My poor darling, you *shall* be lovely," she said. The Princess gurgled and blinked, but did not look quite happy.

At the ceremony, the Princess had been christened Angelica. She had a whole string of other names, but they did not count; she was *called* Princess Angelica – this had seemed to the Queen a safe name: if she grew up beautiful it would suit her beautifully; if she were simply good it should do as well. After the christening, the poor Queen began to watch her daughter anxiously. "When I have another baby, I shall pointedly *not* ask those wretched Fairies," she said. But she had no other baby, so Princess Angelica grew very important. Before she could walk, her terrible Punctuality began to make itself felt throughout the palace. If anyone were late anywhere she would yell: as for her Commonsense, it was impossible to appease her with rattles or fluffy jumping toys.

Unhappily for the Princess, these two gifts she had been given did not take up the whole of her character. She had a soft heart, was dreamy and loved beautiful things. When her Commonsense eye drove her mother away from her cradle, she would be found weeping because her mother had gone. The third time she ever walked, she tottered up to a mirror, and the royal nurse saw her taking a good look at herself. But what she saw in the mirror made her crinkle her face up. She was a fine baby, chubby and rosy, a model to all the baby girls in the land. But what the poor Princess had been looking for had been curls.

Her hair never would curl. It was soft and fine, but nothing would make it anything but straight. The first time she drove out in the royal coach with the Queen, all the mothers in the crowd nudged their pretty, curly children and said: "You learn to be good, like Princess Angelica!" The Princess heard, and tears rolled down her face. "There," said the mothers, "she's crying because you are so naughty!" The first two inventions to be called after her were *The Princess Angelica Alarm Clock*, and *The Princess Angelica Children's Self-Help Guild*. The Queen's heart bled for her poor little girl.

When the Princess was seven the Queen died of a fever, and the King became very melancholy and old. He relied more and more on Princess Angelica's advice, and used to talk to her about matters of state. He used to send for her to sit with him in the evenings, so that she often sat up far too late. Punctuality told her this was long after bed-time, and Commonsense that she would be pasty and cross-feeling next day. But she sat patiently on in her black frock, doing what she could for her beautiful mother's sake.

The Princess read geography, history and natural history to satisfy her Commonsense. But to please her dreamy side she read fairy tales. She read fairy tales, but these were very discouraging. They were nearly always about princesses of dazzling beauty, who though shut up in towers, transformed into cats or swooped off with by dragons were always rescued by a beautiful Third Son. The Third Son always turned out to be somebody they could marry, but they fell in love as soon as their eyes met. He had generally loved her first, or heard of her dazzling beauty, though, disguised as a miller, a bear or a minstrel, he had had no opportunity of speaking to her. The Princess saw that it should be very romantic to be a Princess at all. But then she went back to look at her own face in the mirror: a nice little good snub face, edged with straight brown hair. "Will anyone marry me?" she said to her nurse one day. "Oh, yes, indeed," said her nurse, "someone will have to. And much honoured they'll be."

When the year of mourning for the Queen's death was over, the King thought he would give a party to cheer up the Princess. He asked all the children of all the important people, and kindly had galleries built round the walls of the royal garden so that the children of unimportant people could come and look on. The day was very fine: the sun shone, the birds sang, the fountains flung rainbows into the air, even the royal goldfish swam more merrily in the marble-edged pools. The rose-trees had been kept for a week under large glass shades, so as to bring all the roses out at once. Princess Angelica, in a white satin dress, stood by the centre fountain receiving her guests. A small pearl crown was fastened with tight elastic underneath her slippery brown hair. All the children of the important people were very proper and shy: they shook hands, curtsied, then stood round in a circle staring at her. Yes, the scene was gay, but the party was not.[2] As this was the Princess's first party, she did not realise how dull it was being till she looked up at the galleries and saw the merry faces of the unimportant children, who were having a good deal of fun, licking ice-cream out of cones and pointing at what they saw in a rude but natural way. She noticed, particularly, one little boy with red curls, in a yellow shirt. He had finished not only his own cone of ice-cream but one he had pinched from the little boy on his right: now he was leaning his elbows on the rail of the gallery and looking down in a serious, dreamy way. He looked about twelve. The Princess thought at once: "He must be a Third Son."

But, oh dear! Down here, the important children danced a quadrille rather creakily on the lawn.[3] Then they played catch with hollow golden balls. When the Princess missed a catch, which she did once or twice from nervousness, they murmured "Too bad." They were so much afraid of not doing everything up to time that they had all borrowed their mother's or father's wrist-watches, which they kept looking at. They were all so afraid of saying something not sensible that they could not speak at all. The Princess's heart sank. She *saw* this was very dull, and felt all the children up there must be pitying her. She did not know that they only saw the fountains, the roses and the flashing gold balls, heard the loud tunes the band played with great pleasure and envied the Princess's pearl crown and quilted satin dress. She glanced up again and again at the proud, dreamy, red-haired boy with his elbow sticking out through a hole in his shirt. "He *knows* he is in disguise," thought Princess Angelica.

Suddenly, the important children all gaped. The Princess, who had been holding a golden ball in her hands, stopped, smiled up, and suddenly threw the ball at a gallery. The red-haired boy, unfolding his arms in a flash, caught the ball with one hand. All the children in the galleries shot up with excitement. The boy held the ball, looking down at the garden and smiling. Then he threw it back. But not, oh, not to the Princess! He threw it to one important little girl whose long flaxen curls bobbed beautifully on her emerald velvet dress. The Princess's heart broke. She pushed her crown back, pretending not to notice. She thought: "I have behaved with absolute commonsense. If one recognises a Third Son in disguise, one should do something about him. I was quite right."

The important girl with flaxen curls missed the ball disdainfully and let it roll on to an important boy.

But the palace guards, who had been watching the galleries carefully to see the unimportant children did not misbehave, noticed the incident. What the red-haired boy had done was a shocking breach of manners. To have a gold ball thrown to you by a princess is an honour: you should throw it back to *her*, having first bowed three times. To throw the ball to anyone else is treason. The captain of the guard said: "He has insulted the Princess." So the guard went quietly round the gallery and arrested the red-haired boy. The Princess saw him being dragged out. Soon after, the trumpets sounded for tea.

Next day the red-haired boy was brought for trial into the palace courtyard. The King said he was sorry but the Princess would have to be there. He would have been glad to have let the matter drop, but all the courtiers were furious and kept him up to it. The flaxen-haired important little girl had to be there as a witness. The poor Princess could not fail to be up to time: as it happened the King's procession was late, so she sat on her small throne looking round the empty court till the trumpets sounded and the procession appeared: the prisoner was then brought in by another door. The flaxen-haired girl looked down her nose disdainfully.[4] The boy with the red curls looked scornful, indifferent. Standing between his two guards he gazed round at the courtyard and all the people in it: his eyes once met the Princess's without a flicker.

The heralds sounded their trumpets and the trial began. To two long rolling speeches made by people in wigs the poor Princess was far too anxious to listen. The boy was being accused of treason, but he did not seem to be listening either. The King sat listening sadly; he had never thought the party he gave for his daughter could end in such a way: his wish all along had been to make the Princess and everyone else happy. He suddenly put up his hand to make the long speech stop, leaned forward and said to the boy kindly:

"Didn't you *know* you were rude to the Princess?"

The boy, looking up at the King, said: "No, Your Majesty."

"But didn't you think?"

"No, Your Majesty. Why should I?"

The King, who always thought for rather too long before he could do anything, looked perplexed.

"I didn't think," said the boy. "I just threw the ball."

The King cleared his throat and said: "But why do you think the Princess threw the ball to you?"

"I don't know," said the boy. "I suppose she wanted to."

"Did you not see she was doing you an honour?"

"Well, no," said the boy. "I thought it was just fun."

"Fun or no fun," said the King, "why didn't you throw it back to her?"

The boy looked puzzled. "I couldn't," he said; "I had thrown it back to that girl." He glanced at the blonde little girl, who was looking less pretty today in plain grey cloth.

"Now listen," went on the King. "By the law of the land you are threatened with a very serious punishment. People have been beheaded for treason, you know. Your only chance is to tell us why you did what you did. Why did you throw the ball to that young lady instead of to the Princess?"

The boy looked amazed – perhaps that such a long question should have such a simple answer as he was going to give.

"Because her dress was so pretty."

There was a sensation in the court. The ladies present could not help being pleased by the reply: they whispered among themselves and said how poetic the boy was. A man in a wig got up and, shaking his finger sternly, said: "But the Princess's dress was exceedingly beautiful."

"But I like emerald green better than white."

There was another buzz. The King, holding up his hand for silence, said: "You seem to be speaking the truth; nobody could invent this. I have one other question to ask: are you sorry for what you have done?"

"Yes, I was at once," said the boy, "because the Princess looked so fearfully disappointed. If I could have had the ball back I would have thrown it to her. She had a nicer face than anyone else there. The young lady in green has a dull face. When I saw how she opens her mouth when she's trying to catch things, and how butter-fingered she was, I was sorry at once. Then the guard arrested me. But I am sorry still."

The blonde little girl went into hysterics, and had to be carried screaming out of the court. (What the boy said about her having a dull face stuck to her all her life and she never married.)

The King said: "Will you tell the Princess you are sorry?"

The boy turned to the Princess's throne. Bowing, he said in a cold voice: "I am sorry I hurt Your Royal Highness's feelings."

Everyone who was present turned to look at the Princess. She said in a small sad voice: "Oh, that is quite all right."

The King announced: "I command that this charge of treason be withdrawn."

The guards took their hands from the boy's shoulders: he bowed to both thrones, turned, and walked out of the court.

The next dress the Princess had made was emerald green, and everybody pretended not to know why. On her small white pony, followed by her governess on a black mare and four palace guards on chargers, she rode through the streets every day. People used to set their clocks by her, for she always followed the same route, through the poorer parts of the town where she thought she was most likely to meet the boy. She bowed to right and left, trying not to look anxious. For weeks she was unlucky; she thought he must have left town. Then one day she saw him lying on the steps of a fountain, quite idle, sunning himself like a dog. She pulled up her pony, her governess reined in her mare, the four chargers were pulled back on their haunches.

The boy stood up and bowed.

"Thank you," she said, "for what you so kindly said about my face."

"Oh, it's quite true," said the boy; "I have often thought about you."

"Have you?" said the Princess.

"Yes; so many people have so much nonsense about them, but there seems to be no nonsense about you."

"Oh," said the Princess.

"Yes," said the boy warmly, "I have written a poem." He fished about in his pocket and brought out a piece of paper, very crumpled and grey.

The Princess read: –

"Dear kind Princess in white
I did not mean, indeed, to ruin your delight.
The roses were so red, the fountains were so bright
That when you threw the ball
I did not think at all.

"You did not understand
What made me lose my head. The goldfish and the band.
The sunshine was so bright, the trumpets were so grand
That when you looked at me
I did not even see.

"When you stood still in white
She ran about in green, the green was oh so bright,
But she was oh so wrong and you were oh so right.
I did not see you till,
Too late, you stood so still.

"You must not be so sad.
I cannot bear to see the sorry smile you had.
The fountains are so small, the music is so bad,
The roses wither, when
I think I hurt you then."

"May I keep it?" said the Princess.

The boy looked doubtful. "Yes, all right," he said. "I think I remember it."

"I am wearing green today," said the Princess timidly.

"So I see," said the boy. "But I think white suits you better."

He bowed, and the Princess rode on, tucking the poem carefully into her pocket.

When she got back to the palace, they all saw an extraordinary thing had happened. *The Princess was ten minutes late for lunch.* When she saw the clock, something seemed to slip or come unhooked inside her character: she did not know whether she were sorry or glad. As luck would have it, her two Fairy Godmothers had arrived for lunch. They had not been back since the christening, but, both being on their way from a committee in Fairyland, had happened to find themselves in the air above the palace and, as they had forgotten their sandwiches, thought they would drop in. They may not have known how unpopular they were with the King ever since they had made his dear Queen so unhappy at the Princess's christening. If they had known it might not have stopped them: fairies are not sensitive. So here they sat in the hall with their reticules, waiting for the Princess to come home.

"I am sorry," said the Princess, "I'm afraid I am late."

"*What!*" said the Fairy who had given her Punctuality.

"I am late," repeated the Princess.

"Well, no gift I gave has *ever* not worked before!"

"It has not worked today."

"Why?" said the Fairy who had given her Commonsense.

"I stopped to talk to a boy."

"Is he a member of the Princess Angelica Children's Self-Help Guild?"

"No. He writes poetry."

"And you stopped to *talk*! Then where was your Commonsense?"

"I don't know," said the Princess with a happy smile.

"Miserable child," said the two Fairies in chorus, "you prove yourself unworthy of our two great gifts."

"Well, I didn't ask for them," said the Princess politely but firmly. "And they have stopped work of their own accord today."

The Fairies looked at each other. "We will take them away," they said in one terrible voice. "You shall have instead what has brought many Princesses to bad ends: Good Looks and a Sense of the Ridiculous. Some day you will be sorry."

The Princess tried to quail. But even before the Fairies had finished speaking, she had a curious sensation in the tips of her hair: it began violently curling. In two minutes, it was in tight little clusters, like brown silk rosebuds, all over her head. Her eyes, opened wide in surprise, turned from grey to the brightest blue, and a pair of lovely dimples appeared in her smiling cheeks. At the same time, the sight of the two Fairy Godmothers sitting side by side in the hall, looking at her triumphantly and balefully, made her burst out into fits of hysterical laughter. "There, you *see*," said the Fairies. "Your bad end is beginning." They rose, spread their musty brown wings and flew off down the hall, through the arch and away over the palace to look for lunch somewhere else The pages standing out in the courtyard saw their reticules, sensible boots and tight poke bonnets disappear in the sky, and thought they looked as ugly as a couple of crows.

The Princess did not come to a bad end. Fairy Godmothers may do much to spoil (or, if they are nicer than hers, to improve) your chances, but they cannot really interfere with the nice character you have inherited from your father and mother and the right way you are brought up. Curls, bright blue eyes and dimples did not make the Princess's face less kind and good. She exercised her Sense of the Ridiculous by making her father turn out a good many silly courtiers who had been making the palace fussy, prim and dull. She preferred amusing people, but, if you look closely at it only nice people stay amusing for long, so the new appointments she saw to worked very well. Her advice became still more valuable to the King her father, and while all the countries round them were having revolutions, he continued to reign. As for her good looks – which increased as she grew older – everybody fell in love with her: this pleased and excited her so much that for some years she, quite naturally, forgot the red-haired boy. But one day she turned up his poem in the pocket of her out-grown emerald green dress. She showed it to the King, who said: "By the way, that reminds me: we have no court poet. How would it be . . ." So they arranged a poetry competition, which the red-haired boy, who was now nearly grown-up, won. So he came to court, in discreet black clothes, and walked about, refusing to show his poetry and looking critically at the Princess: he did not dare to presume on their former meeting.

One day the Princess, who was now grown-up, passing him in a passage, said: "Why do you look so cross?"

The red-haired young man said: "The appointment leads to nothing; I want to be important. I am a Third Son, and I ought to have more luck."

The Princess started. "Third Son?" she said. "Whose?"

"I have no idea," he said. "I only know that."

"What would you like best to do?" she said.

"Marry you," said he. "I do not think curls and dimples suit you, but there is still no nonsense about you and you have the nice good face that I always liked. Marry you, yes, and then take charge of this country. The court is all very well, but everything outside it ought to be run on much more modern lines. The unpunctuality nowadays is appalling, and the laws should be overhauled from a common-sense point of view. If I have to write any more poetry, I shall go mad."

The Princess sighed. She thought of all the nice princes who came from miles away to tell her she was perfect. But, unfortunately, she always laughed at them.

"Very well," she said, "I will ask my father."

The King said: "There is nothing I should like better. Times are changing. But I thought that young man was here to write poetry. Are *you* not disappointed?"

"No," said the Princess.

The Princess's children did not have Fairy Godmothers.

Comfort and Joy

A
t school they twitted the two about their couple of Christmas-carol names. They were both new girls that autumn term; they were both twelve; they were inseparables – that is, until the end of the school day, when Joy, day-boarder only, mounted her bicycle and whizzed home, and poor Comfort, boarder who did not like boarding-school, resigned herself to an evening spaced out by bells and to the rigid classroom in which she did her prep. Comfort was a fastidious, rather exquisite child who should not have been sent to boarding-school. Not only did she miss her mother but she missed the warm, pretty side of her home life. Almost every

Saturday, every Sunday Comfort obtained leave to go out to tea with Joy. It may have been the possession of a home so near that endeared rough, intense little Joy to her friend. Joy lived the other side of the common – from the upper front windows of Helmbourne Hall School the Devises' house (low, white, with green porch and gables) was to be seen. That Joy should sleep every night in her own bed, do as she liked at weekends, be tucked up by her mother, made her, in Comfort's eyes, almost glamorous. Comfort's own home in London had been closed since the war.

And certainly Comfort had glamour, for Joy. Joy was a country child, whose awe-struck glimpses of London had been on half-day excursions with her family. Though London was only thirty miles from Helmbourne, it might have been in another world. Comfort, on the other hand, was a little Londoner to her finger-tips: she spoke with ease of theatres, she had assured, cool manners, she wore her blonde hair in a sleek, page-boy bob. Her experience was (it seemed to Joy) immense. Comfort's mother's white satin bed, the white rugs, the crystal lamps, the lilies, the harpsichord in the (now shut) flat overlooking the park made fairy-land images in Joy's mind. So much so, that she had brought Comfort home with her, on the first of those Saturday afternoons, with a certain amount of timidity. But Comfort, thrilled to be out of school, found nothing lacking in the Devises' home. She soon established her right to one deep chair. She had not Joy's ardent nature: she could take what there was.

When, towards the end of term, the bad news came that Comfort would have no home for Christmas, and so, like several more of the London boarders this year, must stay for her holidays at school, Joy's mother took pity on Joy's anguish at the idea of Comfort's vicissitudes and invited Comfort on a three-day visit. This was to start on Christmas Eve. The Devises' shabby, elastic house was, already, fuller than it could hold: there were the Warrington family, Aunt Christine and the young billeted officer. Comfort must have a camp bed in Joy's room. The two could talk for three nights – they were as happy as larks.

To crown everything, it was a white Christmas. Snow laid a gleaming blanket over the common and, around Helmbourne, powdered the brown bare woods. The wide street of the village at the foot of the common looked like a scene on a Christmas card. The soldiers billeted everywhere whistled carols, crisply trampling the snow. In the dusk of Christmas Eve afternoon the Devises' hall was wreathed with holly; firelight streamed from the open living-room door as Comfort and Joy clattered in, with Comfort's suitcase from school. On the mat they stopped to knock snow from their boots. They did not stop singing what they called their signature carol:

> "Glad tidings of Comfort and Joy, Comfort-and-Joy,
> Glad tidings of Comfort and Joy."[1]

The young officer reading a letter at the hall table looked up from the letter, looked right *through* them. His eyes were deadened and horror-struck. Then he picked up his cap and strode past the children, the letter tightly crushed in one hand.

Comfort said: "Now what *is* the matter with him? Maybe he doesn't like carols."

Joy said: "He didn't seem to like us."

Their hearts sank – they had a hero-worship for him. He was handsome, silent and twenty-four. When he did speak, they stopped their chatter to listen. Their eyes, with candid devotion, followed him round and round any room. They each had a present ready, tied up in holly paper, to give him tomorrow morning. His name was Cyril Elwin – from the way he had just crashed out they felt they might never see him again.

Nobody did see Cyril for the rest of the day: he came in soon after eleven and went straight to his room. He had to be quite alone – but he could not sleep. His room was next to the little girls': they both heard him tossing about, and he heard them chattering, through the wall. "Little blighters," he thought. And, in a painful way (tonight, any thought hurt him) he wondered what secrets girls had. Girls grew up to know the secret of being cruel, all right. For minutes together he lay in the dark, rigid, hands locked under his head – then he would fling himself over, switch on his bed-lamp, read the letter again (though he knew every word by heart). Since that afternoon, every word had blazed round and round in his brain . . . Outside, beyond the blacked-out houses, stretched the unmoved snow. And across the snow's silence, hour by hour, he heard the clock strike.

Downstairs, Mrs. Devise sat up late, tying up the last of the Christmas presents. Across the table from her sat Mrs. Warrington, helping: one lamp shed its light on their bent heads. The fire had been let die down, but the warmth of the embers still filled the big shabby livingroom. Everyone else had gone up – and once or twice Mrs. Devise stopped working, as though the silent household were in her mind. Her husband, like Mrs. Warrington's, was away this Christmas; tonight she felt like the captain of a ship.[2] Under this one roof, what a curious medley of dreams and hopes and fears. Suzanne Warrington read her thoughts (these two had been friends since their schooldays) and said: "I expect they are all asleep."

"What is the matter with that young man, Suzanne? He never looked in to say goodnight."

"I wondered, too," confessed Suzanne.

"What a pack of women we are. He is the only man in the house, and we can't help noticing what he does or he doesn't do."

"He didn't whistle," said Suzanne.

"I don't like things to go wrong," sighed Clare Devise.

The livingroom door began to open by inches: Aunt Christine came in, in her dressing-gown. Over her curlers and round her neck she had twisted a little Shetland scarf. "Oh, *here* you both are," she said nervously. "I thought I didn't hear you come up to bed."

"Aunt *Christine* – can't you sleep?"

"I did drink my glass of milk, dear, but somehow I couldn't settle. I had a feeling something was going on."

"Christmas Eve's going on," said Suzanne with her calm smile. "I thought my three were never going to sleep. But they are now; I've just had a look at them."

"Ah, your three are young," said Aunt Christine. She turned to Mrs. Devise. "You don't think that little Comfort over-excites Joy?"

Mrs. Devise said: "No – why?" just a shade too quickly. In her heart she had been wondering this herself – Aunt Christine had a way of stirring shadowy worries up. Mrs. Devise, who hoped to like everyone, blamed herself for not liking Comfort better. Could one be jealous? A dreadful thought. Up to now she had had the whole of Joy's confidence; now, Joy seemed completely possessed by her friend. Children have got to grow up, she told herself. Joy must have her illusions and find out her mistakes.

"I'm glad to have Comfort with us," she said firmly. "It's the child's first Christmas away from home."

Aunt Christine, who had sat down for just a minute, discreetly arranging her dressing-gown, said: "I am sure that's the way to look at it, dear. You make us all very happy – even that young man. By the way, where was he tonight? He didn't – "

The church clock struck midnight, across the snow. The last stroke and the first Christmas minute seemed to echo over the world: each of the three women, in that minute, felt something move in her heart.

Aunt Christine broke the silence. "About that young man," she said, "you know that khaki muffler I knitted for him? As he goes out so very early, would it be any harm if I left it outside his door on my way up? He might like to wear it tomorrow – the mornings are very cold."

Cyril Elwin, lying locked in his black thoughts, had only welcomed

Christmas in with a groan. Two or three minutes later he heard the cautious slip-slop of Aunt Christine's felt slippers along the passage. Stopping outside his door, she put something down: a board creaked: she slip-slopped away again. Had she mistaken his door for the little girls'? Restlessness got him up and across his threshold, to play a beam of torch on the passage floor; he stooped for the parcel – and read his name. "Oh *lord!*" he thought, touched and miserable. The gift made him run a hand through his hair. He stepped back into his room and began to pull at the string.

The letter had dropped unnoticed from his pyjama pocket: it stayed where it fell, in the darkness outside his door.

Comfort and Joy, wide awake in the next room, overheard the whole incident from the start. Aunt Christine's idea did not seem to them bad – they were impressed by Cyril's immediate response. Rolling round her head towards Comfort's on the adjacent pillow, Joy whispered: "Why not us do the same? Then he'll have to say *something* when he sees us tomorrow." They gave it ten minutes, then, with their offerings, made a bare-footed sortie to Cyril's door. "You can put them," breathed Joy generously – and Comfort kneeled down; the board creaked once more. Comfort's hand brushed the letter. "What's this?" she said – and she took the letter back with her to their room. Then they were busy listening – but nothing more happened: Cyril did not come out again.

Joy slept late. She opened her eyes to see on the wallpaper a pink reflection of winter sun – and to see the same pinkish burnish about the head of Comfort, who, wide awake, sat up on her pillows reading a letter. "*Happy Christmas!*" Joy mumbled.[3] "Has post come?"

"No," replied Comfort briefly – not even raising her eyes from the letter. A minute later: "This is *awful!*" she breathed.

"Show!" Joy said – still no more than half awake she stepped from one bed to the other and got in by Comfort's side. They were half way through the letter before Joy's cheeks flamed. "But Comfort –

this isn't written to *us!*"

"Thank goodness," said Comfort, turning over a page.

"Then we mustn't read it. It's horrible, anyway."

Comfort gave Joy a side-glance out of apparently quite candid blue eyes. "It *might* be to anyone," she said. "Nobody wants it, anyway; it was out in the passage. It's simply to somebody called 'My dear.'"

"Who's it from?" said Joy miserably.

"Simply from somebody called 'R.' I know I should hate her," Comfort added. "Fancy breaking off an engagement on Christmas Eve!"

"I don't care what it's about! I – "

"Oh yes you do," said Comfort. "You care what happens to Cyril. You know you do."

Something began to choke Joy: everything went ugly. She got out of Comfort's bed, went to the dressing-table, tugged a comb through her hair. "This has ruined Christmas," she said. "I feel mean."

"You're not nearly as mean as her."

"Oh, shut up, Comfort," said Joy.

Downstairs in the diningroom sausages sizzled on the hot plate. Aunt Christine was in from early church; the table was massed with Christmas cards; the three little Warringtons were already falling upon their presents. The room was bright with reflections of sunny snow. Mrs. Devise, busy making the coffee, said to Mrs. Warrington, shaking cereal from a packet, "No sign of the girls."

Aunt Christine, glancing at Cyril's place, said: "I hoped they would let him back for breakfast today."[4]

Comfort slid into the room, very trim in blue wool crepe ("As pretty as a picture," Mrs. Devise thought), kissed everyone round the table and took her place. Composedly, she began to open her presents – several had come for her by post. "Oh, *look* what Mummy has sent me!" They all looked: the pendant glittered, twirling round in the sun. While they were still distracted, Joy was among them, doggedly scrambling on to her chair. "Happy Christmas," she said in a loud but unhappy voice.

"Why, Joy," began Aunt Christine, "what *is* the – "

"Aunt Christine, you've got three more robins this morning," Suzanne Warrington put in hurriedly – and Aunt Christine, diverted, smiled at the window-sill and began to brush up the toast-crumbs round her plate. But then the eldest Warrington child said: "Oo, *Joy*, you aren't opening your presents!" So Joy began to untie knots with shaky fingers: she opened gift after gift with a wan smile.

Aunt Christine had gone to the window to feed her robins; she was easing the sash up. "Now guess who's coming!" she said. "And he's got it on!"

Cyril had decided to face things out. He came up the path with his chin sunk in Aunt Christine's muffler, inside his trench-coat collar. There was still something flattened, heavy about his step on the snow. In the crook of each arm he carried a pot of Roman hyacinths. They all saw, through the window, his figure outlined against the dazzling day and the little Warringtons, singing, beat their spoons on their plates.

"God rest you, merry gentlemen; let nothing you dismay!"[5]

Comfort turned shell-pink; she stopped twiddling the pendant and glanced at Joy sideways under her eyelashes. Joy did not look up: she turned dead white.

Cyril stood in the diningroom doorway. "Happy Christmas," he said, smiling rather too much. He looked boldly at no one particular, and they all saw the circles round his too-bright, fagged eyes. Everyone, turning round from the breakfast-table, opened their mouths to say something to him – but nobody spoke. The children put down their spoons.

"Is there – bad news?" faltered Aunt Christine.

Then Joy shot up and ran straight to him: she moved so quickly no one could see her face. She flung her arms round his neck and clasped him tightly, pulling his head down. What she said no one heard.

Then she fled. They all heard her flying across the stone hall, flying upstairs, banging her bedroom door. "Well!" smiled Mrs. Devise, while Comfort looked at her plate.

"That was most awfully nice of her," Cyril said. He took his place and began to pull in his chair.

The Good Earl

Yes, sir, that is the Castle across the water. You will meet no other any side of the Lough. The tide is under the jurisdiction of the ocean, but the two shores belong to the Good Earl. The Earl himself built the Hotel.

The Earl was our benefactor; there have been none like him before or since. From the time he succeeded into his father's place he put a halt to the wicked doings. While he was still young he became famous as an improving landlord; and in the latter days he never quitted the country, except to express his opinion among the Lords and to make his obeisance to Queen Victoria. In his young manhood, however, he had travelled the world, and there was no capital city of which he could not tell us. His conversation was of the kind to draw all to him, and he was sought out. He was in favour of science and he had a telescope mounted on the terrace of the Castle and he was an accomplished reader of books. But the Earl was not puffed up. He would greet those he perceived, and my father recalled the evening he and the Earl conversed on the Lough shore till you could have wrung the rain from their two beards. The Earl spoke to my father about a comet.

The Earl's father had been the Bad Earl, but we forgave his name for his son's sake. From the day he succeeded into[1] his father's place the Earl did not rest until he had righted injustices. It was known he could not lie easy under his coronet canopy while any tenant of his lay under an unsound roof. He advocated to us many improved methods of doing all things, in the manner in which he had witnessed them done abroad; and he would dispute with the most stubborn farmer. We listened to him in patience, while we preferred it better to keep to our fathers' ways. The Earl restored the Castle, which had been destroyed with neglect and riotous living in the preceding times; he renewed the roof and the lead piping and sealed up the cracks asunder in front and back; he stripped down the sullied brocades from the saloons and commanded their copies from France and Italy; he brought a scholar from Dublin to list the books, and he renewed the heads to the garden statues, taking away from out of it those that were unseemly. He dispelled the dead from the nether part of the Castle by raising the ancient gravestones out of the kitchen floor; and from the day the kitchen was repavemented no voice but that of the living was heard there. The Earl introduced drainage.

The piety of the Earl and his Lady was well known, and the Primate travelled from Armagh to be their guest. But the Earl and Her Lacyship did not tamper, confining their activities to the Protestants. If any further affliction came to the Earl's ears, he would make no move till he had conferred with the priest. The priest dined at the Earl's table. The Lady Mary taught the Bible on Sundays to the Protestant children in the schoolhouse adjoining on to the church. She was to be met in the Wood Walk, stepping it fearlessly to the schoolhouse, for the Earl on Sundays would not let the carriage out, with the ribbon marker fluttering from her Bible and the Little Dog[2] running beside her skirts. The Lady Mary was the Earl and Her Ladyship's one child; God sent them no other, and no son.

To announce the eighteenth birthday of Lady Mary, a ball was held. So great was the reputation of this ball that the aristocracy of the country were competing among one another to be bidden. The preparations occupied many weeks, no part of them escaping the Earl's notice. On the memorable night, the illuminations of the Castle were to be seen not only across the Lough but from every top of the mountains around here. Not a curtain was let be drawn, on account of the Earl's wish that we should freely look in upon the festivities. From noon the countryside was in motion, and by darkness we had taken up our places in the Castle woods. The lamps of the carriages and the coaches pressing upon one another in the avenues, and the sounds of beauty and laughter proceeding out of them, made the young girls with us tremble inside their shawls.

We observed the Lady Mary to be keeping modestly to her father's side. She appeared loth to be tempted into the dance by the finest of the young lords and gentlemen. Indeed no presence among them approached the presence of the Earl, with his forehead rising up above all. Her Ladyship in her diadem also shone, and the smile never left her mouth. In the confusion of the waltzes and the mazurkas the family were from time to time hidden from us; undoubtedly there were famous beauties present, revolving in the hold of the gentlemen, flashing their gems and dashing their silks and tossing their raven and golden heads. We agreed amongst us, however, that Lady Mary surpassed them all in virtue. Throughout the rejoicings her cheeks were as white and blameless as the dress on her person, and the rose in her hair. She was adorned only with the one string of pearls.

Now it was made known that the Lady Mary was marriageable, we looked for suitors, and we were confounded seeing the time pass. The grand ball had left our women with the thirst for a wedding. The Lady Mary continued to walk in the woods with the Little Dog. No doubt there were many beheld her face who were daunted from raising their eyes to her high position. But we took count that there should be, in beyonder parts of the country, some few fitted to proffer her name and lands. But the Earl, concerned with improvements and science, was without time to dally with other schemes; and Her Ladyship raised no finger without his bid. Moreover, though free with the humble and with the scholarly, the Earl consorted little with those claiming to be his equals in rank. He had no patience with them and their pursuit of fashion. The Earl held that progress bettered the world. Having completed the ball for the Lady Mary, the Earl turned his attention to other matters. He conceived the project of the Hotel.

The Earl's door stood open all day to guests, and among the many consorting around his table would be officers and young landowning gentlemen. No doubt among these numbers were some who had the Lady Mary in view. But the Earl drew and gathered all to him with his conversation. And when the table was quit the Earl conducted the gentlemen in a cortège away to view the improvements that he had made. Lady Mary remained behind him, in the rear of the telescope, with the Little Dog.

The Earl burned up with the project of the Hotel. In this as in other matters he was our benefactor; there was not one of us to whom he did not speak of it. The Earl conceived that the Hotel was to do great good to us country people by bringing foreign money into the land. He was telling us that the Lough was of grand beauty, deserving to be admired by all the world, and to elevate all who saw it. He was telling us how in the northern country of Norway the sea also enters deeply into the land, and that such spots were besought by travellers and visitors who were lodged in hotels, to the great benefit of the country people. The Earl foresaw no further distress amongst us once an hotel was erected on our Lough. The Earl was particular that the Hotel was to be of no kind seen in this country yet; it should rise direct from the water, and sustain on its front balconies on which the ladies and gentlemen should disport themselves and behold the Lough. You have seen the Hotel, sir. That is the Earl's design. In order to have the design correct the Earl journeyed to Norway in the late summer, taking with him Her Ladyship with her sketching book. He was absent from us five weeks. The Lady Mary remained behind at the Castle, under care of a widowed lady who was a cousin.

The Earl's goings from us were often attended by some disaster. In this instance it was the Little Dog fell ill. The Lady Mary could hardly be led away from the Little Dog's bedside, and there was riding to and fro through the nights to the veterinary surgeon's for the medicaments. It was Mr. Harris offered his services to Lady Mary in aid of the Little Dog. Mr. Harris was a young gentleman who had lately been accepted in the Estate Office on account of the Earl's activities and improvements being more than the Agent alone could handle. The Agent requested for an assistant, and the Earl acceded to his request. Mr. Harris was therefore procured from Belfast city, and grew to be tolerated by all. He was just and quiet and led a blameless life; he was to be encountered in the evenings about the woods, with his gun and his pot hat. For his tours round about the demesne Mr. Harris made a companion out of my brother, who was a young lad at the time.

In the end of it the Little Dog died. It was Mr. Harris gave out the orders for the small little coffin and for the gravestone, for the Lady Mary was unable to speak. She intended the burial should be in the lawn plot back from the Wood Walk, and Mr. Harris saw that it was so. It came to be known she replenished the flowers daily, but none of us saw her come or go. From that day she went to the Sunday School by another path. None of us perceived her beside the grave.

None of us perceived her beside the grave until, one certain evening after the rain, my brother was following after Mr. Harris on some employment or other about the woods. The two of them passed through the whipping branches out over into the Wood Walk, forenist[3] the lawn plot; and they were upon her before they could draw back, on account of her dark cloak matching into the trees. The Lady Mary stood above the grave like a spirit, holding her handkerchief to her mouth. The two of them were ashamed to intrude now, and they turned to retreat into the woods. But Lady Mary withdrew her handkerchief from her mouth and she motioned to Mr. Harris to remain.

He was my faithful companion, says Lady Mary.[4]

Mr. Harris stays with his head uncovered, fixed there by her sorrowful look at him. She cries, Pray God to give me resignation! and casts around her on all sides, not knowing where to go. Her knees flowed under her; she looked likely to fall. Whereupon Mr. Harris steps swiftly across the grave and extends the strength of his arm to the Lady Mary, and he conducts her away down the Wood Walk towards the vicinity of the Castle, leaving my brother to go the way he had come.

He did never seek her out, nor presume to seek her. My brother witnessed the start of it; and we who observed the Castle during the Earl's absence found Mr. Harris pure of any craft or design. It was the Lady Mary who turned to him in her loneliness after the Little Dog and her distress with her father across two seas. She was as innocent as the Earl himself; and she as yet was ignorant that she was a woman. She frequented Mr. Harris in the original start for joy of the comfort that he gave her. They instructed one another in conversation. They employed the telescope, and spied upon the birds in the woods, and my brother accompanied them in the boat to view the ancient chapel upon the island. He saw the Lady Mary behold about her at the water and hills, as though this no longer were her known and familiar home, as though she were wondering at some new scene. At this time of which I speak, she came out into flower like a thorn tree, and no beauty in the country could have defied her. Also the rains gave over, and the corn stood up gold and ripe in the fields. We were wondering would the Earl be back for the harvest.

The sinless harmony between the Lady Mary and Mr. Harris was not detected by the widowed lady cousin. The widow was timid and disposed mainly towards the fear of robbers; she was also weak in her constitution and would remain within in her own chamber, perusing romances and snuffing salts. She took no reckoning of Mr. Harris, on account of his humble employed status. We understood at this time that Mr. Harris, alone and only, carried the pain of thought; when he walked apart from the Lady Mary he walked with a dumb still face; and he was heard to groan aloud in the nights.

The Earl returned to us out of Norway carrying with him the project of the Steamer. It appeared, the hotels on the inland water in Norway have steamers plying to them out of the outside sea; and nothing would now content the Earl till we should have a Steamer also upon the Lough. The Earl was telling us of the many advantages of the Steamer; how it would carry the mail posts and fine manufactured goods for us from the cities, and carry away for us to the city markets what we might be able to raise that we should sell.[5] Moreover, the Steamer would swell the advantages of the Hotel the Earl was now[6] to erect, for without it there would be no access for the visitors other than the twenty-mile drive from the railway train around the head of the Lough in the long car. The Earl judged that the gentry visitors might shrink from the jolting and from the many hours, and from maybe the contrariness of the storms. The Earl was set to procure the Steamer.

The Earl gave a kiss to the Lady Mary's brow and spoke a compassionate word for the Little Dog. He then immediately sent for the superior Agent and Mr. Harris in order to confer with them of the Steamer; and he had the two out behind him till past sunset, pacing out the foundations of the Hotel. The Hotel was to be placed around one bend of the Lough in the inland direction from the Castle; and the Earl was informing the Lady Mary that they should be enabled to set their clocks by the Steamer's passing by of the Castle terrace. Within the week of the Earl's homecoming he had masons at work constructing the Steamer jetty, and cords pegged to show the proportions of the Hotel. Our children had great sport leaping between the cords; the girls and we young fellows could not be kept from advancing along the jetty, signing our tracks with our heels on the moist cement.

In the course of the winter that was to come, the Steamer business was having the Earl tormented: we were sorry to learn that all was not running smooth. It appeared, he could not procure or set in motion the Steamer without a company be formated first, and that none would step out to formate the company with him. The Earl from time to time paced amongst us denouncing those who obstructed Progress. He became more fractious than in the former times; the beauty of his temper was overclouded; and with his impatience his manly fullness seemed to consume away. He was known to thresh through the nights beneath his coronet canopy till Her Ladyship waned with the want of rest. For out of the many projects the Earl had had, this was the first had ever stood still upon him.

We did not know, was the Lady Mary intending to tell the Earl. It was his due to know what was in her heart. Himself and Her Ladyship were her loving parents; they had denied her nothing they saw good, and she should have lacked for nothing she could name. It might be she could not name what she lacked, and was therefore grown up silent within herself. It might be that from the hour of the

Earl and Her Ladyship's homecoming to the Castle, the Lady Mary was only biding her time to introduce the matter of Mr. Harris, but that the Steamer forbade her tongue. For how should she intrude herself on her father whilst he was undergoing this great vexation? And how should she find her way to her mother's ear whilst Her Ladyship was bent only upon alleviating the Earl? Also, from after the Earl's return, the hours of loving company were no more, and there could be no word spoken nor look exchanged between the Lady Mary and Mr. Harris. For this reason, the Earl with his present scheme now kept the Estate Office skeltering day and night.

For one morning the Earl rose up from his tossing bed to declare he'd formate the company in himself only.[7] He pulled bells and he shouted for his advisers, and he communicated with London by telegrams; and there was now to be tremendous confabulation. The Earl drew wealth from every part of the world, from the diamonds in Africa and the tea in India, from railways passing through the Canadian mountains and from the streets of houses that he possessed in London.[8] But it appeared, there were those who constrained the Earl, and who menaced him with the interests of his heirs, and who would not let him disturb or tamper with the source of his money where it was all set. This was a puzzle to us and a fret to him. You should think he should readily lay his hand on the sum of money, to formate the company and to float the Steamer. But, however, the Earl could only do so by sacrificing out of his privy purse.

He therefore cast about him, setting his eyes on all things in the Estate. At the start of it, he felled the High Wood, and a contractor purchased the timber from him. He gave over the drainage he was executing upon the bog, and he undid the orders that had gone out for the metalling of the lower road, for the stone bridge, for the observatory and for the drying barns. He sold two farms that had the tenancies fallen in, and he leased a mountain out to a sporting syndicate. Throughout all, he did not raise a single rent, but he closed up the Castle wing where the ball was held, he sacrificed three gold-framed Italian pictures of very little size but great history, which were carried away in a cart to go off to America, and he sacrificed Mr. Harris out of the Estate Office.

The felling of the High Wood could not be hid, and the putting stop to the works could be seen by all; but the Earl, it might be out of grief or shame, made no private or public mention of Mr. Harris. Mr. Harris was to continue till what he did was done. It might be through lack of chance or through lack of heart, or it might be out of respect for her confused father, but it appears Mr. Harris sent no warning nor word to the Lady Mary as to what was now come about.

Before the High Wood was stripped, my mother sent my brother to fetch down branches and twigs. It was towards the end of winter; a sweet, soft day. My brother was leading the ass cart up the ascent when he overtook Lady Mary beside the track. Around her was the bared hill and the lying trees and the stumps, and she says: There is surely a great change here!

However, my brother says, 'Tis a wonder what we can see with the trees gone.

The two looked below them upon the bends of the Lough and upon the Castle, and the demesne and upon the Protestant church with the graveyard and Bible house, and upon the island having the ancient chapel, and upon the jetty expectant of the Steamer. Why, it is like a picture, says Lady Mary, when you can see the whole!

You would wonder, says my brother, who painted it.

Lady Mary laid her hand on the ass's neck, and they continued up the ascent. There was this between herself and my brother, on account they were both companions to Mr. Harris. At the flat place, my brother commenced to glean up the twigs and branches, while the Lady Mary, into some kind of dream, leaned herself on her hand on the standing wheel of the cart. It was my brother, loading the twigs and branches, who perceived the Earl coming legging it up the slope, with Mr. Harris behind in attendance on him. It had now come into the Earl's mind to retrieve a share of timber from the contractor to furnish joists and uprights for the Hotel. The Earl looked this way, that way, pointing out with his stick, whereupon Mr. Harris chalked on the chosen trees. The Lady Mary drew up to watch the two.

The Earl draws his fingers down the length of his beard and addresses himself to his daughter, Lady Mary. Isn't it the great pity, Mary, he says, that Harris will not behold the complete hotel?

Why so? says she, gripping the ass cart wheel.

Why, Harris is going from us, the Earl says. There are[9] great opportunities for a young man to be found in the distant and future countries, and it is no longer right to have him confined here. Isn't that so, Harris? threw in the Earl.

Mr. Harris nods with his head but makes no reply, and he does not turn his eyes to the Lady Mary. I'm sure, my dear, says the father, you'll wish him fortune, for he has been very faithful with us.

The Lady Mary says only, Is this so?

It is, Lady Mary, says Mr. Harris, constrained to face her. He lifts his pot hat and he stands with his head bowed, bare, as he had stood by the Little Dog's grave. My brother continues to stack up the twigs and branches behind Lady Mary upon the cart.

Oh, father! she says.

What is it, me darlin', what is it now? says the Earl.

I don't like, she says, like a dreamer, to see the High Wood lying. And she looks from tree to tree on the ground, as though upon every one of her fallen hopes.

Only wait now; now only wait, says the Earl, till the fine day you see the Steamer come up the Lough.

It was on the eve of Mr. Harris's going that the men buoyed the channel for the Steamer. For they say the Lough has a very treacherous bed. We watched them drop the plumb lines out of the boats, and we followed up to number the buoys behind them. From then on, our children could not sleep for thinking and talking about the Steamer; and a mountainy woman prophesied it would have golden sails, and be carrying back to us all the Earls formerly driven from our shores. Meanwhile, the Castle held locked up the mystery of the saddening hearts within it. It was said Lady Mary beseeched her father, who had no ear for her, being deep in plans. It was said she beseeched Mr. Harris, in the dark of the evening, to take her to share his fortunes in American lands, but that he in his humbleness found her too lofty for this, and in his faithfulness would not betray the Earl. For Mr. Harris was carrying to America a letter of commendation in the Earl's own hand, to some ostensible person in America who should promote him up for the Earl's sake. And but and for the Earl's letter, Mr. Harris had nothing but the few pounds put by. For whatever reason, if it was truly said that the Lady Mary beseeched him there in the evening, it was equally said Mr. Harris put her away from him, tears coursing down his face as they did hers. But it was also said that she said nothing, only prayed to God to stretch out His hand. We all saw winter upon her face.

My brother was at the Castle gates when the trap came out of the avenue carrying Mr. Harris, with his possessions and gun-case strapped on behind. The horse was impatient and they had few farewells. My brother had a wish through the greater part of his life to be following Mr. Harris to America, but he never did so in the end of all. The groom let the horse go, and round the turn of the road, Mr. Harris bestowing no backward look on the Castle.

Little account was taken of Mr. Harris's going, due to the Earl himself setting out for London, for the sealing of the business about the Steamer. His going from us was attended by the usual preparation, ceremonial and skeltering. All could see the Earl about this time was consumed with all these contests into only the bones and beard; his height was bowed with his stooping[10] and calculations, and the nobility of the eye flashed out like the wick of a naked lamp.[11] He ate only what would have sustained a sparrow and he was loth to rest. We held, and Her Ladyship held, however, that the fulfilment of the Steamer should once more set him up. We shook our heads, but we foresaw nothing. It came to be known later that the mountainy woman saw the Bird in the air upon the top of the Castle the day the Earl with Her Ladyship went to London. It was given out, the Earl was to bring back the Steamer with him; we were less cast down at his going on that account.

The chill caught the Earl in London, causing him to die far from his own land. When they carried the telegram to the Castle, the rain was weeping into the Lough. They drew down the blinds of the hundred windows and bolted the white-painted shutters upon them. There was silence; and clouds rolled down upon those lamenting in the upper parts of the mountains. The Protestant clergyman and the priest went to address themselves to the Lady Mary, but they were graciously turned away. No word came out of that tomb place. On the third day, the men opened the vault and polished the silver plates on the other coffins, and swept the vault and strewed it over with ferns.[12] In the evening of that day, it became known that the Steamer was to bring back the Earl's body.

From before the grey of that dawn, we were all travelling down to the Lough side. We were in our hundreds; the aged women upon the ass carts were keeping their shawls drawn over upon their faces; and the aged men were never raising their heads bowed with the grief of time. The women held their young children speechlessly by the hand; and the men were withdrawn from them and stood apart. The girls stood leaning upon each other in the edge of the water, and we young fellows in our black decent clothes mounted some way into the stripped woods. The two shores of the Lough were white with our faces; and from each shore we faced on the other's grief, with rain all the time falling down between. The wet ran from the fringe of the women's shawls and penetrated into the men's bones. There was no wailing nor keening; the Castle forbidding us with its shut eyes. No weeping was heard louder than the Lough tide creeping upon the stones. From awaiting the Steamer this long time we were become still as the stones themselves.

The rain relented and the mist clouds withdrew slowly away from the tops of the Earl's mountains; wherefore word passed through us, he would be coming soon. Then, surely, we heard the cry of the Steamer, distantly entering down the Lough. From its nature it could be no other cry. The girls advanced further into the water and the young men mounted further up on the hills, and the aged men and women raised up their heads, and the infants cried out at this new thing. The sun could no longer withhold itself, and descended upon the water in a ray. The Steamer again cried out, and we again trembled. When she had cried the third time, she came turning towards us round the bend.

So white was she that we all smiled with sorrow. No sail bore her, only a sail of smoke which was devoured up by the sun. She advanced towards us along the buoyed passage, trembling but steady, cleaving a long wake. We now smelled her rich oil and heard the engines in her internal parts. The sun leaned on her, and from her inward trembling her brass polished ornamentation flashed. She amazed the Lough and amazed the mountains; and she knocked upon the heaviness of our hearts. But on her forepart she carried the Earl's coffin. So past and by, and cleaving between our hundreds travelled the coffin bearing the laurel wreath, and so travelled the Steamer bearing the coffin. So the Steamer entered the Lough for the first time.

She came to us, she passed by us; and as she passed we turned to pursue her upon her course. She stilled down her engines as she approached the jetty; and it was thus the Steamer stole past the Castle face. And it was the Castle now drew our eyes — for the shutters opened upon one terrace window, from which the Lady Mary stepped out alone. The height of the Castle and the wide of the water made the Lady Mary appear to us very small. She advances to the balustrade of the terrace, to come as near the

Steamer as she could come. She puts her hand to shade her eyes from the almighty whiteness striking out from its flank. We could not see her face to see did it change. She attentively, slowly turns her head, watching the Steamer proceed past her; she considers its wake and looks over the balustrade. For below in the chopping and heave of the wake's end the Castle's watery image is broken up.

There were few to perceive the Lady Mary turn around and go back and shut the window behind her, for the hundreds of us were now trampling down from the woods and speeding by on the tracks, and the shores and the stony places. We were gathered at the jetty to meet the Earl.

The Lost Hope

"Miss Mapsby – how nice that you are still here!"

Miss Mapsby, thus accosted, did not so much as start. "'Still?'" she repeated, in her most daunting manner. "We have not been away." Turning, she latched her garden gate behind her with a proprietary firmness that said much – Bertram realised that nothing short of a direct hit could have dislodged Miss Mapsby from Windy Bend. And Miss Moira probably had not been consulted.

He saw, too, that she must have found his remark either patronising or over-familiar. Decades of success had not covered his sensitiveness with more than a very thin crust: if, as a celebrity, he had come to allow himself naïve little exclamations of private feeling – flattering to the hearer, who became confident, and always flatteringly received – he had not lost his dislike of putting a foot wrong.

He had not been at Seale-on-Sea since the war: it *was* nice for him (nicer than she could know) to see Miss Mapsby come doughtily down her garden steps as though nothing had happened in the meantime. The steps zigzagged to the gate between walls of rockery neatly tufted with plants. Stoutly gloved and shod, Miss Mapsby carried her shopping basket on the crook of her elbow and her dog's leash coiled round her wrist. Windy Bend, an Edwardian villa so much embowered as to look like a cottage, was niched in its steep garden towards the top of the hill above Seale-on-Sea. This October morning of 1945 still had, to Bertram's senses, the sweet but aching quiet of a morning after a storm. For Seale, from which on clear days you could see France, had in the bad days been in the front line. Hints of what must be happening, muffled by censorship, had not ceased to prey on Bertram's imagination. It gave a focus, this little town, to his aesthetic horror of loss and change.

"Back at the Swan, as usual?" said Miss Mapsby, as they walked down the hill together. "You find it, and us, a little battered, no doubt? Soldiers, soldiers, soldiers, roaring about the place – so much noisier since they were mechanised, poor boys. They and the Germans between them gave one plenty to organise: we hardly know where we are, now they're gone."

"How much must have happened here!" Bertram said, with a mingled pang of jealousy and distaste.

"However," Miss Mapsby concluded kindly, "we are always glad to see visitors back. You, I suppose, have kept on writing away?"

She was right: Bertram was, *au fond*, the eternal visitor. His love for Seale, which reached back into his childhood, was of the wholly enjoyable, pure, illusory kind, not strained by ties, not taxed by responsibilities, not charged with serious memories of any associations more poignant than those with his own past feeling. The old town, the hill, the marsh, the curve of the bay had composed themselves long ago, and remained composed, into something that inexplicably, gently and recurrently pierced, then soothed his heart, something as unique as the relation between the features of a beloved face. Seale was, to him, timeless, but at the same time drenched in something amicable distilled from time. He loved the place, perhaps as one loves a place in art – immune. This feeling of his extended even to Seale people, and to the rhythm of their lives. It can be seen with how many apprehensions he had returned *this* time – in fact, how nearly he had not returned at all.

During the walk to town, this morning Miss Mapsby outlined for Bertram what they had been doing. *She*, of course, had always been as strong as a horse: he was more surprised to learn that delicate Miss Moira had worked long night shifts at the canteen in the church hall. This had, said her elder sister firmly, taken Moira completely out of herself.

Bertram (though only now) recollected hearing that Miss Moira had had a *fiancé* killed in the 1914 war: if *this* war had made, in however abstract a form, any restitution for *that* – good. He found it hard, however, to revise his picture of the middle-aged girl,[1] in whom hopeful youthfulness, a few unspent bright drops in a misted phial, seemed forever to have been stoppered up by grief. He had not yet, in fact, had time to revise the picture when Miss Moira herself greeted him that same day. In the afternoon silence of the scarred, battered High Street someone came up behind him in a breathless hurry: before he could turn, Miss Moira's hand was lightly upon his elbow, and her blue eyes were fixed upon his face before its abstraction was quite gone.

"Mr. Bertram – I am so sorry. I'm afraid you were thinking! But my sister told me at lunch that you had come back, and I wanted to speak to you so much. In fact, I have been to look for you at your hotel. There is something – for several years I have thought of writing to you."

"How I wish you had! Is there, was there, anything I could do?"

If there were, she did not know how to begin. Bertram said, "Let's go back to the Swan; let us have tea."

So, they were side by side in broken-springed hollows of the hotel sofa. She, pouring out, stooped intently over the tea-tray on the dwarf table. Not till the lounge was empty, till there was nobody left to keep casting glances at the shy local woman and the distinguished strange man, did Bertram say gently, "Well . . .?"[2]

She was ready. "It's that I wanted to show you – *this*." She brought out of her handbag a wad of writing: limp manuscript paper, dingy-cornered, rubbed. With one glance, with an uncontrollable inner groan, he exclaimed, "Why, Miss Moira – *you* have been writing stories?"

"No; all I did was to promise. It was a young soldier: about in the middle of the war he came in twice to the canteen, from some place out in the marsh. In those years altogether so many hundreds came in, perhaps more; they were all different when I began to know them, but he was more different, though he only came in twice. He looked round, the first time, as though he could not get the darkness out of his eyes: I could see that he did not intend to speak. He stood warming his hands round his cup, frowning to himself. But then suddenly, as if a wire had pulled at him, he pushed through the rest and joined into the conversation. That was when I said your name."

"*My* name?" Bertram exclaimed on a gay light note of gratification, as though his name had never been heard before. "In what connection?"

"The men had begun by talking about film stars; then somehow the talk passed to any kind of celebrities, famous people. They asked if I, in my life, had ever met one of those, and I said" – she coloured – "you. He stared at me and said, 'what, do you know *him*?'"

Bertram concentrated on lighting a cigarette: finally, off-hand, he said, "And so?"

"So then, of course I asked if he liked your books."

"You would spare me, I know, if he did not."

"He said, 'He's very successful, isn't he?' He waited for the others to move away with so much patience that I was sorry: in his face I saw questions coming that I could never answer. I was frightened by the importance of you to him. He seemed to me younger than the others, not because less had happened to him but because more would happen. His mouth moved, and his hand looked as if it were going to break his cup; he fixed his eyes, when I couldn't answer his questions, as though he were trying to spell out something I must know without knowing I knew. Last of all he said, 'But did you know him when he was young?'"

"Now, *that* was absurd," said Bertram, smiling, brotherly, into her unlined face.

"Why?" she said – lost, indifferent to his grace. She went on: "The second time he came in, it was in a hurry: his lot were moving out next day, though we did not know that, we never knew. He had come in only to give me this – ." She raised the manuscript from the seat between them, as though to make Bertram aware of its key presence. "He made me promise to give it to you. To read."

"I see."

She flushed, sensing at least something of what was behind the dryness of his tone. "I hope I did not do wrong? But I – I have never been asked for a promise that meant so much. And I thought perhaps you might look on it as, as an honour."

"And did your young man send any message to me?"

"He only sent you this," she said, fingering a corner of the manuscript.

"Or expect some message from me?"

"He didn't say so."

The monomania, the persistent impertinence of young would-be authors did not become less, Bertram found, when they joined the Forces. He found it hard to believe that at any age *he* had been so well able to look after himself. Generosity, born of the first pure flush of joy in his reputation, had years ago ravaged too much of his time: it became necessary for him to make a stand; and, behind the guard of a secretary, he had kept to it. Mr. Bertram now read beginners' manuscripts under no circumstances whatever. Miss Moira owed her victory (without even knowing it was a victory) to Seale, to its ambience, to her share in that, to his unguarded lover-like happiness in the place and susceptibility to its littlest events. Bertram took the story up to this room that night.[3] The bedside lamp cast a half moon on to the difficult writing; a sea wind, which had sprung up at dusk, rattled his window and made crepitations around the room.

Next morning he started uphill to Windy Bend. The wind had not dropped: the October sun blazed. He saw everything – the dishevelled petals of the michaelmas daisies, the leaves and the veins in the leaves of the red Japanese plum boughs that together swirled in the gardens, the patterns on curtains blowing out of the windows – as though he were wearing too strong spectacles. In the same way the sea, when he looked behind him, had broken up into white horses. He smelled pungent rot from the gardens and smelled the saturating and singing wind – beneath whose accompaniment he could hear everything: a sewing machine at work in one of the houses, a bluebottle on the inside of a pane. All this sensation was forced on his unwillingness like a draft. Before the ascent of the Windy Bend steps he stopped to regain his breath, to control his nervosity. At the top of the steps Miss Moira came to meet him, untying the housework handkerchief from her hair. She went in ahead of him to the living room, inconsiderable annexe of a vast bow window. She looked at him this morning as though there were something new, untoward, between them: their relation had changed.

"Well, I have brought you your story back."

"So soon? – What a strong, clean envelope: one of yours?" They sat down at opposite ends of the window seat: she plunged into the pocket of her overall what might have been betraying hands. "You've read it?"

"And you want to know if I thought it 'good'?"

She glanced at him, boxed and framed in the glare of the window: the villa faced, at its own level, nothing but the sky. "Not when you're tired," she said. "Not today."

Bertram straightened himself. "There may be a hundred uses of 'good': with me, there's only one that can pass. I would like to say, because you would like to hear, that I found something, *here*, to take away my breath. That didn't happen. The effect on me was – how shall I put it? – exasperation, strain, as though I were assisting at[4] a struggle, against my will. I felt the struggle need not have taken place – all that passion heaving against, under, that tortuous, knotted style. What is the matter with him, your young man? Let him relax, let him breathe, let him love a little – I believe all writing to be the overflow of a delight, even though it be a delight in pain. Why all this urgency? Let him take his time." He glanced at her, as it seemed, uncomprehending face. "If I cannot put this to you, how can you put it to him?"

"I can't. He's dead now. He was killed."

He said in a harsh voice. "You should have told me."

"But does that make any difference to his story?"

"You knew how much, when you did not tell me. You let me be reproached by my own words." He took back the envelope, weighing it in his hand. "If I had known that this was the end, all – ! You left me to judge this as a beginning. And I have been racked by asking the beginning of what?"

"You had been going to say, probably, that he would have improved with experience?"

"Experience!" cried out Bertram. "How am I to judge between his and mine! I was appalled by his misuse of experience – crushed in on itself, over-packed, bruised. Yes, over-packed. He was obsessed with trying to pack life – yes, the whole of life, and his whole bursting sense of it – into those dozen miserable pages. What a stupid hope! Art is not a trunk to be crammed till it will not shut. Art cannot contain all life. To become a writer – and I speak as a writer – one must discover just how much art *will* hold. Your young man has not lived to do that."

Miss Moira saw not Bertram but the young man's face. She said, "Might he have been disappointed?"

"*I* survived disappointment. The greater artists only put greater faces on disappointment. What else, what else is it that gnaws and grows inside each new victory of the accomplishment?" He rounded on her: he frowned; he stared out at the skyline behind her head; he said sharply, "You say he admired me?"

"He only said, 'Be sure to give him my story.' He only said, 'Did you know him when he was young?'"

I Died of Love

 $\mathbf{M}$ iss Mettishaw always used to tell us how she used to have an establishment of her own. She had a toneless voice she could somehow pitch above the stutter of the sewing-machine; and you had to pitch your hearing to go to meet it. Only pins in her mouth stopped her talking quite. She had to talk to anyone in the room; we only knew she did not talk to the room because as we opened the door she would newly open her mouth.[1] She was a dutiful sewing-woman, never idle; her eye would wander over the work in progress even when she was stopping to drink tea: holding the cup in her right hand, absently, inexpertly (as though she denied

---

the proper use of her fingers to anything but their craft) she would with her left hand caress or test gathers, draw up and pull out a tacking thread, or flatten inches of tuck or hem with her thumbnail. But as she was just to us she must be just to herself, and what she owed to herself was to tell us. This duty fatigued her more than anything else: we could see her flag under it – as she did not flag under the cutting, stitching and fitting that was her duty to us.

She came in to work for us by the day: in spring and autumn, the poetical seasons when clothes are being conceived, we required her on end for about a month. Also she would come at odd times if we were invited to an important party or had to go into mourning. She came in to make a trousseau, but made no comment on the excitement to be felt all over our house, in which love had arrived for the first time. She did not give a single thought to the fates she sent us out to meet in the clothes she made – she would cast one last glance, like a thread snapping, at her dresses walking away from her on us. Girls are used to interest in their fates; it took us some time to understand that her humanity had gone to the bottom with her establishment, when that foundered. Her humanity had been a whole cargo lost.[2]

She made what we wanted without comment; blamelessly[3] she carried out our mistakes in taste. Dresses seen in our dreams came to us complete from her fingers lifeless: to become happy in them took as long as the making burn up of a fire in a stone-cold grate. We were to ask one another, after her death, what could have held us to her so long. Of course, it was the establishment that had cast the spell.

Her establishment had been in a cathedral town; in a street, she said, five minutes' walk from the Close. This had been in the last years of Queen Victoria. The street had a high wall on its other side, above this appearing only a row of poplars: the establishment was thus not overlooked. The street was quiet: soon you came to recognise every step. Carriages entered only to stop at the establishment door. Miss Mettishaw built up a good connection, and could soon refuse[4] any customer she did not wish. The best ladies recommended her to the other best ladies; soon she withdrew from the window her engraved card for fear of drawing someone unknown in. The establishment was as an establishment from the day she hired her second seamstress, Rose. The first was Harriet: both were dependable. Miss Mettishaw extended her premises down to the front ground floor room of the house, though the sewing rooms remained on the second floor. At rush times, such as before a ball or wedding, she herself would take a hand with the girls: she preferred this to employing an outside person. She allowed no sewing to leave the house.

Into the front ground floor room she had introduced a gas chandelier; and from the first of October to the middle of April a coal fire had been always burning. She had divided the room in two, into back and front, by means of a red velvet curtain along a rod: this rod was kept greased, so that the rings ran smooth. In the back, behind the curtain, had stood the cheval mirror for trying on, a shamrock-shaped table for the hand mirror and pins, and a sofa on which to lay out the dresses. In the front there had been a sofa, two chairs and a circular walnut table for fashion papers: this table was beautiful, having an inlaid top which always shone like satin, and carved feet. Against the lace of the window hung a cascade fern that she always watered herself.

Talking above our machine in her toneless voice she made us vibrate in the heat of the coal fire, and hear the slippery fashion plates turn over on the waxed table-top. Light, the not bright but intense light of the past, was reflected back from the wall across the street: against the lace of the window we saw a lady under a prow-like hat sitting intensely forward on the sofa. All the clientele of Miss Mettishaw came to seem to us to have been like swans.

They were the ladies of the County and of the Close.[5] No lady was admitted to the front half while in the back another was at a

fitting. That would have never done. The discretion of the establishment was complete: you would call it now a mystery factory.
Neither Rose nor Harriet ever talked. Therefore no one of Miss
Mettishaw's ladies knew, till she confronted another at a social
occasion, what the other would wear. Miss Mettishaw knew how to
wean a lady away from a shade already selected by any other. To all
this the establishment owed its tone.

In summer there had been the garden parties and in winter there
had been the County balls. There was also always a Regiment,
which not only attended functions but itself entertained. If a dress
coming downstairs and a dress going up brushed against one
another, they did not whisper.

The establishment, ever-real to Miss Mettishaw, became, you can
see, ever-real to us. In fact it became magnetic, so we were drawn by
it across the line between now and then. Sound of pins in a tray or
smell of dress stuffs conjured it up. Diving our way up into our cold
clinging, half-made dresses, we in our senses expected to come out
near the heavy velvet red of the curtain, opposite the cheval mirror,
under the chandelier. In its timelessness the establishment had no
story: its only story was its untimely end. The idea of the fall was
necessary to the idea of the height. The height of the establishment
had been moral. To be high really means to be high or nothing. The
establishment there one day was gone the next.

Was it burned down? You could say so. But not by fire.

Mrs. P., a sister-in-law of the bishop, followed custom by bringing
her daughter to be dressed on the day of the young lady's leaving
the schoolroom. Miss Annabelle P.'s figure was quite formed: she
had a small waist and nice ballgown shoulders, and a somewhat too
short though milk white neck. Her freckles were under treatment by
lemon, and she was forbidden boating parties for fear of more. Pink
for her, of any shade, was out of the question, owing to her fine
head of hair being red. Apart from this she was unlike other young
ladies only in that at fittings she stood still: from the first she stood

like a statue or you might say a dummy, looking in her own eyes in the glass in a trance. What was draped upon her she did not care or see. They, of course, do say still waters run deep, but you do not think of everything at the time. She was the only child and would be the heiress: Mrs. P. ordered a whole outfit for Miss Annabelle. While this was still in the workroom there was an increase: Mrs. P. announced the daughter's engagement to marry Sir Peel B., which now meant the trousseau. Sir Peel B., being a neighbour of Mrs. P.'s, must have been only waiting for Miss Annabelle to mature. Just with all this pending, it had been really too bad about Rose. Rose, being as you will remember the second seamstress, had always coughed but now began spitting blood. She had been a handsome girl, but you would[6] never know: she was now all great big eyes and with a flush. She beseeched not to go, saying in that case what should she do then, and indeed she could hardly be done without. But every day now delicate dress stuff bales were coming heaping into the workroom. Rose promised she would take every care.

Sir Peel B. once or twice accompanied Mrs. P. and her daughter to the establishment door. When the ladies had entered he could be seen to step back and cast a glance up the front. He was on into years, but quite looked the baronet that he was.[7] It was understood that Sir Peel would have preferred the trousseau to wait for Paris, which was to be the scene of the honeymoon; but Mrs. P. was in a position to talk him down, herself not favouring finicking French fashions. Mrs. P. kindly let it be known that she preferred the establishment to abroad. This being so, and with all the wedding guest orders, they were kept working to midnight, six days of the week, that summer. Rose used to fancy the gas made the workroom hot.

At the height of this, everything was brought to a standstill by Miss Annabelle's becoming irregular at her fittings, on from the day after the Regimental ball. Three, no, four times she never came at all; and there was no word. Sir Peel B. was in London, and Mrs. P. had many other things on her mind. Each time, a maid called for

Miss Annabelle at the establishment, only of course to find her not there. Miss Mettishaw finally reached the point of wondering if she ought to write and ask. All the overtime sewing looked likely to go for nothing. Then, though, Miss Annabelle did come running in – no appointment, no maid, no parasol, no explanation, nothing. It was shocking how she had burned and freckled; and the flounces of her skirt were stained green with grass.[8] She sang and smiled as she prepared for the fitting.

But when she had been got in front of the mirror and the curtains drawn, she shivered, though it was a hot day. She crossed her now bare arms across her bosom.[9] She was standing like this when Rose came in through the curtain, bearing the *eau de nil* dress. Suddenly she and Miss Annabelle stared right at each other, in the mirror. It was not right, and it was noticeable. It was as though the illness made Rose forget her place. Miss Mettishaw said, "That will do, Rose." Rose dropped the curtain and went out, and Miss Annabelle was put into the dress. It was really lovely. Miss Mettishaw was just fitting the waist when Miss Annabelle stooped and plucked up a fold of the skirt in front, and cried out, "Why, who has hurt themselves?" There was a blood spot. Small, but that meant the whole front length had to come out. That settled Rose's having to go.

When told, Rose had made no remark, simply tidied her table and put her hat on. With only a quite inexperienced new girl there in Rose's place, Miss Mettishaw had to oversee every stitch herself. And at what a time, of all times! She had enough on her mind without the officer walking past the window. No sooner was Miss Annabelle in for a fitting than outside his step would again be heard. To attempt to fit a dress on her at this time was as much good as attempting to fit a dress on a puff of wind. Also each time a dress was brought through the curtain Miss Annabelle expected to see Rose. Anything to do with a young lady is so delicate, and you never know how a mother will take a thing. Should or should not Miss Mettishaw have mentioned the matter to Mrs. P.? From never knowing whether she should or should not, Miss Mettishaw became unable to sleep at night. And meanwhile the wedding was in a month.

Rose did not go to hospital where she should have gone. So unfair of her, as this upset the workroom; the two others constantly meeting her in the town. What was she hoping for? Until one day, if you please, the establishment front door bell rang, and there was Rose on the white step like a lady waiting, but with her hand to her mouth. What a joke to play! "Is she fitting now, is she?" Rose said, " – Miss Annabelle?"

"What's that to you, Rose?" said Miss Mettishaw, making to close the door.

Whereupon she cried out, "Where she is, he is!"

Of course it had been talk in the workroom some time ago, Rose and some officer; however, Miss Mettishaw always had made a point of not taking notice, provided a girl of hers did not go too far. The overtime summer work had since put a stop to that, and a good thing! But *now* what a situation, really – the same officer! How it could but lower Miss Annabelle to be succeeding Rose? Sir Peel B. should now rightly look for a bride elsewhere – but what of the wedding orders in hand? All might become a complete loss. Everything might reflect upon the establishment. Miss Mettishaw could not feel called upon to open what was so shocking to Mrs. P.

The last time Rose was seen she was at the corner, one end of the street. It was very sultry and thundery, in August. Miss Mettishaw was in the act of showing a previous lady out when she observed Rose, ever so still, waiting: the cathedral clock struck four, which was to say that Miss Annabelle was now due for the wedding dress fitting. Certain Rose meant some harm, Miss Mettishaw started off down the street to tell Rose to be off, and however dared she. But then round the corner at the other end came Mrs. P. and Miss Annabelle; moreover, accompanied by Sir Peel B. Rather than be found in the street hatless, Miss Mettishaw was compelled to hasten back to receive them, leaving Rose out there at the one street corner and the baronet, who had delivered the ladies on the doorstep, vanishing round the other. Miss Annabelle was hurried behind the curtain to prepare for the fitting, but Mrs. P. was still on the front room sofa, regretting ever so graciously that she had been unable to look in for so long, when the officer made his step heard by once again sauntering past the window.

On account of the thundercloud Miss Mettishaw sent for a taper, and was in the act of lighting the chandelier. The wedding dress entered, like a bride itself wrapped up in muslin, and Miss Annabelle was half way into the dress when the scream came from Rose there in the street. Rose who had used to seem such a quiet girl. Miss Annabelle, catching the diamond of the ring Sir Peel B. had given her in the chiffon, tore the sleeve. And Mrs. P., already beside herself with all she had done and must do, rated and railed, "Well, Belle, how will you be married now?" Miss Mettishaw, needing, she said, a needle of fine white silk to catch the tear up, withdrew. She came over with palpitations. She ran to the street door.

Everyone had gone home, to await the storm. In another minute there would be big drops, and the street was unnatural.[10] Nothing would drive off Rose: she had stopped the officer, set on him, held him, was not letting him by. The two stood. Rose saw Miss Mettishaw, but did not see her: it was the officer turned his head.

So Miss Mettishaw looked in the face that spelled her ruin. That face was human, and she did not forget it after her humanity was gone. She carried the face with her into the room in our house: at it her words stopped, but we saw what she saw. She had never considered or noticed gentlemen, being a dressmaker for ladies: she did not then, at that moment, consider the gentleman, only considered ruin. She saw the hawk of her sky – and how could the establishment, and all ladies' things, hope, when skies could be open to such a hawk? She looked on the doom of her cascade fern and the beautiful table, of the cheval mirror, the curtain and greased rod, of propriety, of the establishment. Miss Annabelle's bolting and Rose's choking death were still, at that moment, to come; but in that moment Miss Mettishaw died of them – they had only to come, they came, and by the time they did come she no longer felt any more.

With no thoughts, she saw that fire-raising face. She could only tell us that the officer who ruined the establishment was handsome – as handsome as the establishment deserved. He had a wild bright glancing and reckless eye, whose laughter pity could not stop. A destroying smile – and indeed now it was as though Rose hoped to hold a hawk by the wing. And how indeed was Miss Annabelle, who next day bolted, ever to hope more? Miss Mettishaw, no longer there to care, never heard the end. It was all the same to him – his bad name (he was quitting the Regiment), debts all over the town. No fire, scorching the fern and sending up in a flare the delicate stuffs, could have consumed the establishment more wholly than did that starting from the officer's eye. Foreseeing everything to be said, how the establishment was no better than a house of assignation, Miss Mettishaw put herself out of business and left the town before that week was up. If the establishment could not be what it had been, it could not be. No, the establishment never decayed: it fell.

Miss Mettishaw, who no longer cared for anything, did not care enough for us even to warn us against love. Talking above the machine in her toneless voice, she used to tell us how she once used to have an establishment of her own. The dresses she made for us, in which we never felt very happy, are worn out; and we have out-lived the mood of those past years during which she came to our house to work. But by dying, she left the establishment to us: from time to time it makes us remember her.

So Much Depends

"People grow duller as they grow older," young Ellen wrote in the diary that was her confidant. "They care less. One way or the other, nothing matters to them."

This was, she decided, today's Great Thought. She underlined it, added some exclamation marks, then slammed the book shut – with a bang so loud that two ladies seated at the far end of the room turned to look at her with concern. This was by no means the first time she had disturbed them; in fact, of a long, wet morning in a small guesthouse drawing-room, a less ideal companion than Ellen would have been hard to find. Had it been a half-grown leopard who sprawled on the window seat, Mrs. Ordeyne and Miss Kerry – who, in their two armchairs, were respectively knitting and trying to read a novel – hardly could have been less at ease. This seventeen-year-old girl – with her long legs, shock of curls thrust on end, ever-jingling bangles, rumpled grey-flannel skirt – seemed to be making a point of not settling down; nor, if others succeeded in doing so, would it be her fault. To start with, she had prowled round the centre table, listlessly but at the same time loudly turning over the pages of magazines. Next, she had made an inexpert attempt to smoke, striking many matches and then coughing. When at last she produced her diary and began to write, her two fellow guests had hoped for some minutes' peace. Clearly, however, this was not to be.

Mrs. Ordeyne and Miss Kerry, all unaware of the drastic comment upon them Ellen had just indited, did their best to remain – or appear – calm. Mrs. Ordeyne, reaching into her knitting bag for yet another ball of angora wool, told herself that one must make every allowance; it was hard on a girl being cooped up indoors like this, for day after day of precious holiday. Yes, it was miserable for her. But what, on the other hand, had induced her to do such a silly thing as to come all alone to this guesthouse, where she knew no one and where there were no young people for her to get to know? The clientele of The Myrtles, at Seale-on-Sea, consisted of elderly, quiet folk, plus one or two married couples with young children. Had Ellen friends staying elsewhere at Seale-on-Sea? If so, they must be letting her down.

Alas, thought the plump, kindly lady over her knitting, there it was: Ellen, unhappy during these days indoors, had become the admitted scourge of the guesthouse. Her woebegone air and aggressive moodiness were not to be ignored. Should not someone advise her to make the best of things? Look at Miss Kerry, for instance, giving her whole mind to that no doubt very interesting book. Mrs. Ordeyne, who practically never read, had the highest respect for those who did so.

Miss Kerry, if the truth were to be known, kept her eyes glued to the printed pages only by the strongest effort of will. Concentration became impossible; she had reached a stage when she could neither read nor fall back on her own thoughts. Younger by fifteen years than Mrs. Ordeyne, and by temperament much less patient, Miss Kerry was more on edge than she cared to show. It was second nature with her to conceal feeling – the fact that, for good or ill, her entire future was to decide itself within the next few days was suspected, here at The Myrtles, by not a soul. Her habit of carrying round a book – which she read at mealtimes, even, at her solitary table – earned her the reputation of being clever; in fact, the volume chiefly served as a barricade against people's attempts to make conversation; behind it, she could remain, as she wished, alone. Mrs. Ordeyne had perceived, and at once respected, her fellow guest's wish to keep herself to herself: the two had drifted, during these past few days, into one of those friendships that are the result of circumstances. Mrs. Ordeyne was happy to knit in silence; Miss Kerry, in her odd state of suspense, felt soothed by this easy companionship. She had no idea how intriguing, how mysterious she appeared sometimes, or how strong a curb Mrs. Ordeyne, who loved to know people's stories, often had to keep on her curiosity.

Ellen, of course, wrote Miss Kerry off as a thin and no doubt frustrated spinster. It was for Mrs. Ordeyne, with a homely woman's generous love of grace, to see that here was distinction – and, often, beauty. Erica Kerry's blue-white hair framed a somewhat remote, fine-featured face, which youthfulness sometimes crossed like a flash of sunshine. Her eyes were a changing, intense blue. The unusual, subtle, though inexpensive elegance of her dress set off her slender figure; nor could one fail to admire her feet and hands. As a rule, Erica Kerry wore a mask of irony and reserve: though the former might wear off, the latter did not. Mrs. Ordeyne, in general, got the impression that here, somewhere, was ice on the point of thawing; yet, at the same time, ice which dreaded to thaw. The few exterior facts that had been let drop were as follows: Miss Kerry worked in a London office, supported her mother, was here for her annual holiday, and expected a friend to join her – she did not say who or when.

Mrs. Ordeyne, having long been happily married, was now a widow. She had raised satisfactory sons and daughters, who were now giving her grandchildren: contented, she nowadays asked no more of life.

These were the two who – when Ellen, having done with her diary, proceeded to fling it violently to the floor – once again turned round; this time not in silence.

"What is the matter?" exclaimed Miss Kerry.

"My dear, is anything wrong?" supplemented Mrs. Ordeyne.

The girl on the window seat, stretched at full length, rolled over onto one elbow to eye them blankly. "'Wrong!'" she repeated in a dumbfounded voice. "'Matter?'" Words seemed to fail. Having reared herself up, shaking back her hair, she went on to direct a fierce, single, eloquent nod toward the outdoor scene. "What about that?" she asked.

It was depressing enough. Rain hung in a chilling, sombre, steadily falling veil over the garden's sodden greenery, smoke-dark trees, beaten-down borders, and spoiled roses. Beyond, where there should have been a smiling view of the sea, a sullen grey-brown smudge could be just perceived. And the worst of this was, it was nothing new: today was the fourth wet day in succession. What an obliteration of summer hopes – was this not July, a holiday month, on the so-called sunny south coast of England? Nor would the weather, even, be kept out: gloom from it, entering through large windows, overcast the shabby-elegant, pretty drawing-room. From the washed-out cretonnes of the armchairs and sofa, all colour finally stole away; on the parquet flooring the faded rugs looked bleak. The facts that The Myrtles had once been a private house and that its owner, Miss Plackman, still preferred to keep it much as it was in her father's and mother's time proclaimed themselves by gilt-framed watercolours, mirrored brackets, and Oriental and other knickknacks – but these, too, looked mournful and blotted out. In the elaborate turquoise-blue tiled grate, a fire, lighted by Miss Plackman's orders, tried but failed to burn in the damp air. Mrs. Ordeyne and Miss Kerry sat over it because the idea was cheerful, at any rate: little heat was sent out by the reality. Trees soughed and dripped; a heavy, uneven trickle splashed past the windows from an upstairs balcony.

"It certainly isn't nice," Mrs. Ordeyne agreed, with a slight shiver. "Just give the fire the weeniest little poke, dear," she went on, to Miss Kerry, "then we shall see what happens. It hardly could be worse. Poor Miss Plackman, always so kind and thoughtful! Now, she's a person I really am sorry for. Between ourselves, this year she's having a shocking season. We are not by any means up to full numbers, and on top of that, there've been several cancellations. People lose heart, this weather; they'd just as soon stay at home. I hate to think of that poor, brave little creature fighting a losing game – and look how she works, never off her feet! It would be worry enough to own a place like this when it's going badly – all her savings are in it, I understand – without being manageress as well. How plucky she is, when one comes to think that she was not brought up to this sort of thing. Her father, you know, was a colonel, and her mother had money. They once used to live very comfortably in this house. How queer it must be for Miss Plackman, I sometimes think, to see all these rooms, with their memories, full of strangers."

"I would have rather sold it," Miss Kerry said.

"Well, I don't know. She loved it: it was her home. And last year, for instance, everything went so well – the place was packed out, and we all were so happy. But then last summer was perfect – do you remember? – almost endless wonderful cloudless days. One lived outdoors; by the sea or in some nook in the garden. Yes, how delightful it was," she concluded, with a reminiscent smile. "You should have been here last year."

"Don't," cried Miss Kerry, "please!" Abruptly, she shook her head, as though to dispel a tormenting dream. "If only last summer could have been this! Blue skies, pink roses, dazzling days by the sea, long, lovely evenings under these trees. Do you suppose I don't see it all? The ideal summer. That was what I had pictured, what I had hoped." She broke off, caught a breath, and resumed. "All that was what I'd been counting on. One should never count on anything that is too important. In fact, one should never count on anything, should one?"

Mrs. Ordeyne, after a rapid and searching glance, said, discreetly, nothing. The intensity, passion even, in Miss Kerry's voice had confirmed, more than the speaker knew, Mrs. Ordeyne's suspicions that her friend had "a story" – and, still more, an unfinished one. Never till this moment had Miss Kerry so nearly broken the silence in which she enclosed her life. What more might have come if the wretched Ellen had not been present? Mrs. Ordeyne longed for a *tête-à-tête*. She reproached herself for her wish to probe. At the same time, might it not do Erica good to talk?

Over her spectacles, the good lady fixed on the window seat a kind, thoughtful stare. "It's very dull for you in here," she said to Ellen. "Do you know what I should do if I were your age? I should put on my mackintosh and some nice thick shoes, and take myself out."

"I don't care to walk by myself."

"Do you know nobody here?"

"It's not so much that." Ellen paused and darkly seemed to reflect. "I haven't got a mackintosh," she said finally, "or – " with the air of scoring a point – "thick shoes."

"What a rash way to come away on a holiday," Mrs. Ordeyne felt it right to observe.

"What a beast of a holiday to have come away on," returned

Ellen. She yawned, to show that in her view that was that. She then looked contritely at her diary, now lying face down with rumpled pages on the floor. Why had she been so rough with it? It was her only friend. It shared her secret, known to nobody else – her private reason for coming to Seale-on-Sea. Those early entries which held the clue were, for that very reason, tormenting reading.

The first was dated last May: "Have this evening met only man I shall ever love, called Peter Manfrey. I feel certain we are each other's Fate. I could see he found me quite different from other girls. He is older than me, and quite a man of the world. From now on I shall be thinking of nothing else but Peter, and how to see him as much as I can."

Then, a fortnight later: "The only trouble with Peter is, he is too good-natured. He lets all these other people keep hanging onto him. At all these parties and at the tennis club it is always the same. What is the good of him and me living in the same place if we are never to be Alone? Much of the best hope would be for us to be right away in some exquisite and romantic spot. I wonder where he is going for his holidays. Owing to all this constant interruption, I have not even so far had a chance to ask him."

June: "Oh, I am so happy! Everything has worked out as though by magic! Not only are his holidays in the same month as mine, but I have managed to get a room at the same place he is going to, Seale-on-Sea. He is to be with his parents (because they have not seen much of him since he came out of the Army) in a hotel on the front. Even if I could afford a hotel and if they were not all certainly booked up now, I know Dad and Auntie, being so old-fashioned, would fuss at my going to one alone. But by good luck – Fate again! – I have heard of this guesthouse, also at Seale-on-Sea. It is much cheaper and I daresay pretty awfully dim, but as I shall be out all the time with Peter, I shall not care. Dad and Auntie are much puzzled as to what I intend to do there all by myself. 'All by myself' – little do they know! Poor Auntie keeps on at me about why won't I go with the Robinsons to Cornwall!!!

"I must now tell Peter. How his face will light up! This will be just the chance he must have been always wanting as much as I have."

If little Miss Plackman, sore-tried proprietress of the guesthouse, could have been afforded a glimpse of Ellen's diary, she would have murmured, "Ah, yes, I see. I thought so." Of Miss Plackman's wet-weather troubles, Ellen was not the least. It had been an extra trial, these past few days, that the only telephone at The Myrtles was on the desk in Miss Plackman's office. As a rule, the instrument was not used much: most of her guests came here to be quiet, and showed no wish to communicate with the outside world. Since Ellen's arrival, however, all that had altered: from time to time the girl had been rung up; almost incessantly she put through calls. It was Ellen's wont to come crashing in and out of the office as though the place were a public phone box. Not only was it far from being that; it was the only place the poor lady had to herself. Here it was Miss Plackman's habit to seek refuge for occasional breathing space, however short, in the course of her ceaselessly busy days. In one corner, loomed over by the large desk, was a little old armchair that had been her mother's; into this she from time to time collapsed – kicking her shoes from her aching feet, closing her eyes, allowing her bright, professional smile to fade. Here she could be alone with her thoughts.

This week, her thoughts had been poor company. Miss Plackman could not fail to be aware of the depression, more than meteorological, that had settled over her establishment. Everybody, it seemed, was in low spirits. The remorseless rain showed up all the deficiencies of The Myrtles – deficiencies which in fine weather never appeared. The place, far too large nowadays for a private house, began, with everyone kept indoors, to seem far too small, inadequate for its present purpose – there were not enough sitting rooms; there was no soundproof playroom in which the pent-up children could rampage; there was no elbowroom for those indoor games by which adult energy could have found release. Boredom, together with loss of appetite, was making people criticise the food. Several of the ladies had taken to remaining upstairs till lunchtime; this obstructed the work of the staff, who grumbled. It had been in the hope of luring her guests down that Miss Plackman had had that fire lighted in the drawing-room. However, one peep, just now, had been enough to show her that the device had failed – no one had been there but the ever-dependable Mrs. Ordeyne and her well-mannered friend. And, of course, Ellen. One had to face the fact: no one stayed with that girl.

Poor child! There existed in Miss Plackman an incurable friend-liness to youth, an inexhaustible sympathy with the wish for happiness. But then, did not all these summer guests who came to The Myrtles bring with them dreams and longings? How much it meant to everybody, a holiday! She could guess how people depended for strength and courage, throughout the year to come, on memories to be stored in a few weeks – so short a time!

Bright hours, the gay, carefree, timeless sense of enchantment – what fuel to life they were! Officially, when after her father's death Miss Plackman decided to turn the old home into a guesthouse, she had been embarking on a commercial venture. At the same time, shyly and secretly, she had hoped to add in some way to the good of the world.

Now, having retreated into her office after her anxious glance round the drawing-room door, she sat, hearing rain drum on a glass roof, thinking, How unkind weather can be! Her eyes instinctively turned, for encouragement, to the martial family photographs on the wall. Not for nothing was she a soldier's daughter. Fight on she would – but oh, dear! Piled on her desk were those ledgers with their disheartening story, and this was the day on which she did accounts. Miss Plackman, setting her teeth, forced herself to rise from the dear armchair and face up to the business. Then the telephone rang.

"Hullo?" said a pleasant young man's voice, by now familiar. "Oh, hullo, that you, Miss Plackman? How are you, this sweet morning? Rain coming through the roof yet?" This joke was a shade too near the bone for Miss Plackman's taste. "Listen," he went on, "could I ask you to give a message to Ellen?"

"Unless," said Miss Plackman, "you'd rather speak to her? I happen to know she's in the drawing-room."

"I don't think I'll do that, thank you. I'm in a bit of a rush." As to that, she perfectly saw his point: those conversations with Ellen, so clearly dissatisfying at Ellen's end, had never seemed able to terminate under fifteen minutes. "Just tell her," he went on, "that I wish she'd come round this morning to our hotel. We've got a table tennis going, and we're a cheery crowd here. It would do her good. Do get her to come."

"Well, I'll do my best, but – "

"I know," he said. "'But, but, but.' I've had nothing but 'but' from her. Something's eating her, and I wish you could tell me what. She won't join us and go to a movie, won't come and play rummy, won't even go for a tramp in the rain."

"I don't think she's got a mackintosh," hazarded Miss Plackman.

"Heavens," he said, "hasn't she? The girl must be nuts. Listen, I dote on Ellen. I hate to have her feel low, but in this weather what can one plan? The best hope, as far as I can see, is for as many as possible of us to get together, all be as merry as possible, and keep going. That's what I keep telling her, but she just won't cooperate."

"I'll do my best," repeated Miss Plackman, not hopefully.

"Do," he implored. "I'd come for her in the car, but it's the family car. Dad and Mother naturally have first call on it, and this morning he's running her in to the hairdresser's. And after all, it's less than ten minutes' walk over here to the hotel. Could you, by chance, fix her up with a mack?"

"I've already tried," said Miss Plackman. "But I'm afraid she said there wasn't one in this house she'd be seen dead in."

"Well, simply give her the message. It's up to her." He rang off.

Miss Plackman, sitting down at her desk, reread the two letters of cancellation before tearing them up. That would leave how many rooms empty? Three – no, four next week, when the Begbies left. If the weather changed, the Begbies just might stay on. If it did not change, the Thompsons might go back to London a week earlier. Was it only the rain, she asked herself, that was gradually emptying The Myrtles? Or was it some infectious bad morale? Together, I'm sure, she thought, we could face this. It can't go on forever. Cooperate, that was what he'd said, cooperate. If only everyone would. This seemed to her a campaign, with a crucial battle ahead. St. Swithin's Day[1] – now, when was St. Swithin's Day? Tomorrow.

Ellen had spent her holiday shopping money on beachwear of the most dazzling kind – supplemented by sunglasses on the Hollywood model, oils that guaranteed a deep, even tan, and a rainbow range of polishes for her toenails. She had bought a smart-looking, second-hand evening dress from a friend who had grown too fat to wear it. Two pairs of sandals, a chalk-white light-woollen coat, and a water-proof lipstick completed her purchases. She had, it is true, tried on one rather glamorous coral-pink hooded raincoat, with the idea of donning this during a sunshine-shower; but, at this point, she had discovered her purse was empty. Well, let it go; she had shown forethought enough by including one cardigan and the flannel skirt. Her outfit, when she reviewed and packed it, seemed to her quite ideally planned. Was she not going to meet Romance, on the hot gold sands, by a whispering deep-blue sea? Three whole weeks, day after day, of that. By night, moonlight, dance music – finally, kisses.

She'd let drop, to Peter, quite offhand, the fact that she would be going to Seale-on-Sea. For the fraction of a second, one might have thought, Peter's reaction had been somewhat negative. Then, "Why, that's where we'll be going," he had pointed out. "What an amazing coincidence! How extraordinary! Now, whatever brings you there?

It's an awfully nice little place, but it's pretty quiet. You going with friends?"

"No," she said shortly.

He had seemed surprised; for, so far, Ellen had shown an impassioned ardour for society: she was inclined to crash parties or tag onto older groups, who did not always want her. "Anyway, it's splendid that you'll be there," he had added, with rising enthusiasm. "We must see a lot of each other. You'll certainly like the crowd."

"What crowd?" Ellen had asked, with sinking heart. "I thought you said you were going with your parents."

"So I am, but you know how people collect – old friends of theirs, old friends of mine, and so on. However," he had said quickly, for he had sensed a drop in the atmosphere, "if you'd rather, we can always pull out – go swimming, dancing, or take the car off somewhere. Round there it's very attractive country – woods, and inns where they let you eat outdoors, and best of all, there are the downs, of course. It's wonderful up there on a summer night. Don't know what it is," he had said, waxing lyrical, "but there are places that seem to belong to another world. One feels anything might happen."

Anything might happen. On those magic words, Ellen had pinned her hopes.

Peter, at twenty-two, combined the most winning bonhomie and high spirits with a so far apparently quite disengaged heart. Everyone liked him, and he liked everyone: he had something warmer, more genuine than mere charm. Moreover, he had an attractive way of giving his whole attention to whomever he happened to be talking to: this built people up in their own eyes, making them feel more interesting than they did normally. That this, when a girl was in question, could be misleading, Peter had no idea: his simple wish was that everyone should be happy and feel good. Unlike many popular men, he was quite unspoiled; he worked hard, got on well at the office, and was a devoted son.

Yes, Ellen, in the bestowal of her affections, had made an excellent choice. All that now remained was to get him all to herself – away.

The worst, unforeseen, had happened – rain, spelling frustration. Indoors, no place to be alone; nowhere to go, sit, be. Would she go to his hotel, to hang around, making just one more of the crowd? Ellen shook her head stonily. She would not.

After tea, on the eve of St. Swithin's, the rain stopped. This event, so important to many, was not dramatic: the downpour simply thinned, wavered, lightened, and slowly ceased. Clouds, as though still undecided, still hung low; a heavy drip-drop from trees was to be heard through The Myrtles' garden, across whose humid air stole the scent of sweet William, syringa, flowering privet. A moist gleam, not yet sunshine, began to filter through from the west; in the distance the sea first paled, then brightened. One by one, the guest-house people opened their windows and drew in deep, incredulous, happy breaths. Soon, then, there began a movement outdoors – children were buttoned into their jackets and hurried out for a blow on the sea front; elderly couples set off two by two.

Mrs. Ordeyne, having put on her hat and coat, paused on her way downstairs to tap on Miss Kerry's door. "Anything I can do for you in town?" she called. "Or would you care to come, too?"

No answer: either Miss Kerry was not there or she was sleeping off the fatigue of a day indoors. Mrs. Ordeyne, philosophical, went her way.

Miss Kerry was in her room: at the sound of the knock and voice she sat frozen; not, till her friend's footsteps were out of hearing, daring to breathe. Though her heart smote her, she could not, simply could not at this moment bear to face anyone. In the act of slipping the letter she had just written into an envelope, her hand shook; she felt knocked to pieces by what had been an agonising decision. Before sticking down the envelope, she paused – had she, in her desperation, expressed herself clumsily? Had she not made herself clear? Might she give unnecessary pain? She must make sure. Once more unfolding her letter, she scanned its last pages with eyes burning with unshed tears.

"So don't," she had written, "don't, after all, come here. This terrible weather, now, on top of the strain of all these years we have lived apart, has unnerved me. It is a bad omen. If things between us were to go wrong again, after all this waiting, all we went through before, it would be unbearable, wouldn't it? As for this place – well, if you could see it, you'd understand: there would be nowhere for us, literally nowhere. The last straw, for me, has been a miserable, disappointed girl in this house, lashing and throwing herself about; she's to me a sort of parody of my inside self. I remember, it was my lack of calm that for both of us ruined things, long ago.

"You may say, if we don't meet again now, then better not meet again at all. I've a feeling you will say that: if you do, I must accept it. I have lived in my thoughts of you all these years; I shall live in them every day till I die."

Yes, there it was: said. She was sadly, coldly certain that she was right. To hesitate, at this last moment, to reconsider, would that not only be to drag out the pain? Swiftly she closed, addressed, and stamped the letter, then crossed the room to put on her raincoat. Passing the window, she noticed for the first time that the rain had stopped. "What of that?" she told herself fiercely. "It will begin again!" Taking gloves from a drawer, she saw herself, suddenly, in the mirror – the blue of the raincoat brought out the vivid blue of her eyes. I could have been beautiful, she thought.

The stairs and the hall of The Myrtles were deserted. Slipping out through the porch, pushing open the shabby, damp white gate, Miss Kerry crossed the roadway to the postbox. In went the letter; nothing could now recall it; this was the end. Rapidly, in flight from her own solitude, she walked on, under dripping trees, past endless garden walls – residential outskirts of a small coastal town. Then, swerving sharply, she took the turn to the sea.

Gratefully taking advantage of their emptiness, Miss Plackman was making a tour of the downstairs rooms. To begin with, she gave them a thorough airing; she then tipped out the ashtrays, smoothed down wrinkled slipcovers, plumped up cushions, dusted table tops, straightened rugs, pushed chairs back into place, and sorted magazines. The results were encouraging: quickly the rooms took on the stylish air they had worn in her parents' day. Her spirits rose accordingly. "We'll pull through," she said to herself and the house. "You'll see!" Only one thing was still bothering her – the emptiness of the bowls and vases. Dared she dash down the garden to cut and bring in flowers, wet though they could but be? If she did, might she not run head on into the new arrival – who had so firmly, though so courteously, indicated his wish to be left alone?

The tall gentleman, hair lightly flecked with grey, had, five minutes ago, marched in at The Myrtles' front door with a singular, imperious lack of ceremony. Dumping down a bag, he had at once inquired for Miss Kerry. While Miss Plackman went to look for her, he had paced the hall. On being told that Miss Kerry must have gone out, he cast around him, spotted the drawing-room door, and forthwith made off again, straight through the drawing-room into the garden, via a French window. Miss Plackman, left breathless, had watched him disappear down the path to the summerhouse flanked by a privet hedge. This only could, she supposed, be Miss Kerry's friend; but in that case, he was not expected for two days more. What a strange, high-powered, headstrong friend he seemed for that fragile, somewhat withdrawn creature.

How she wanted, how badly she wanted, to bring in some flowers! Not only did she yearn for them for their own sakes; but the sight of them back in those rooms again might give everyone's spirits an upward turn. While she stood, torn by this indecision, she heard the porch door open behind her, and then a light, somehow listless step in the hall. She cried, "Is that you, Miss Kerry? Oh, I'm so glad you've come. You have a visitor."

"You – you must be mistaken," Miss Kerry said, standing there like a ghost.

"On the contrary. He's gone down the garden. You'll find it still very wet."

Out there, birds twittered and fluted in the damp, sweet silence; the last few drops hanging on sprays and branches glittered in the twilight before they fell. Rosebushes run to briar drooped over to meet the privet hedge, whose waxy blossoms brushed on Miss Kerry's raincoat. Ahead of her, drifts of petals gleamed on the long, long path. Now, from the summerhouse, tangled in honeysuckle, came curling the smoke and the smell of a cigarette. In the half-dark between the pillars, somebody stood.

Miss Kerry came to a halt. "It's not you?" she said.

"Why not?"

"But – "

"I know. I've come two days early. I couldn't wait. Do you know, I thought you might run away?"

It was later, with his arms round her, her forehead leaning against his shoulder, that she said, "Shall I tell you why I was out? I was posting a letter telling you not to come."

"Perfectly foolish!" he exclaimed. "Foolishly perfect! When shall we start teaching each other good sense – today, tomorrow?"

"Tomorrow's St. Swithin's."

"Could there be a better day?"

They both looked up at the sky. The clouds, dissolving, lifting, had thinned to vapour, which was in its turn now being softly drawn like a veil from the evening clearness above; by tonight, one would see the stars. "Just in time," said she.

That evening, at supper, there were flowers on all the tables – damp but gay – but there was no Miss Kerry; and, for the matter of that, no Ellen. The former's absence was so far unexplained; but it was generally known, and to universal relief, that the girl, that night, had been swept away to a dance. Her radiant departure, in fact, had been watched by many. Ellen, in her charming evening dress, hair brushed into a burnish, eyes shining, silver sandals twinkling as she dashed downstairs to the waiting car, hardly was to be recognised as the morose young girl of this morning. She bounced like a happy puppy; she was a pretty thing. Her fellow guests at The Myrtles saw her off with genuine sympathy and benevolence: in fact, so forgiving is human nature that they said to each other, when she had gone, it did one good having young life around the house.

So she set off, with Peter. How was she to return?

Ellen woke, the morning after the dance, to a long-unfamiliar sense of sheer lightheartedness. Could this be, only, the sunshine? Sunshine indeed there was: slipping between the half-drawn curtains, it floated her bed and the whole of her room in light. Hands under her head, she lay basking, blinking: slowly and – how amazingly – without pain, there returned those memories of the night before.

When she got into the car with Peter, she'd realised something was in the air. He had been in a mood she'd never seen before – sometimes singing as he drove, sometimes falling silent, with an intent smile, sometimes taking one hand from the wheel to, in an affectionate but abstracted manner, pat her knee. "Happy?" he once or twice asked her. "Feeling fine?" Yet, somehow, he had failed to await her answer. This lasted for the greater part of their drive. Then, as they were approaching the large hotel where the dance was to be, he pulled the car to the side of the road, slowed, stopped. He turned to face her. "Ellen," he said, "be extra happy tonight. For my sake. Will you?"

"Why for your sake?" she said.

"Because we're such friends, and something marvellous has

happened. I've got engaged."

Ellen's heart stood still. "To who?" she said. Then, primly, "I mean, to whom?"

"Well, you wouldn't know her. The name's Janetta."

"This is extremely sudden. Someone in your hotel?"

"Oh, it's not sudden – been my idea for years, but I never used to think I had got a hope. Wait till you see Janetta, and you'll see why – she's not just someone, she's something out of this world. Yes, she's been staying at our hotel. I persuaded her and her mother to come along. That was one of the reasons I kept asking you over. I was so keen you and she should meet. You'll be crazy about each other, I'm quite certain. However, you'll meet in a minute or two, tonight. This, you see, is our celebration party."

He started the car and drove on. "Yes," he added, "it's been so odd these last few days, in this awful weather. If I could have fallen more in love with Janetta, the way she's played up through it all would have made me do so. She never got frowsty, the way some girls do indoors; she was always on for a heel-and-toe in the rain – and, my hat, she looks divine in a mackintosh! She'd play with the children, poor little brutes, or cheer up the older types when they felt low. It's not just that she's lovely," he sang out, "she's weatherproof!"

Lights from the hotel porch flowed into the car; already the throb of dance music could be heard. Ellen moved as though in a dream through the next few minutes. When she came to herself, she was on the ballroom floor, dancing a samba with a young man called Gerry. Here I dance, she thought, with a smiling face that covers a broken heart. Then slowly, reluctantly, she realised that she was beginning to enjoy herself. An hour later, she had to face the fact that she was enjoying herself very much indeed – frankly, more than ever before. Max succeeded Gerry; David succeeded Max; Noel claimed her from David; then, here was Gerry again. The great gold room, with its mirrors and glittering chandeliers, rose-red curtains framing the floodlit terrace outside, swirled and melted round her;

rhythm ran through her being; her whole soul seemed to throb with the famous band. How delicious it was to float from partner to partner, smile into face after face – without all the time looking around, jealous, intent, and worried, to wonder where one special person might be.

So much so that when Peter grabbed her, crying, "Hi, faithless, spare an old married man a dance," she was aware of a feeling of anticlimax. Had he ever so slightly, ever so slightly faded? There was something dull, she thought, about people who got engaged. Would she, she wondered, feel this if he'd got engaged to her? Yes, she was sorry to find she would. What she found she wanted was everything, everyone, the whole world! Feeling bad about this, she was specially nice to Peter.

"Janetta is sweet," she said, "I adore her dress. She's quite darling."

"Well, she's mad about you," said Peter. "And so, it seems, are the chaps."

So it seemed. She was driven back to The Myrtles in Gerry's car, supported by David, Noel and Max. They wound down the windows, let in sea air and starlight, began to sing. At some point during the singing, she fell asleep with her head on somebody's shoulder. The rest was silence. Somehow, she'd got in, got upstairs and got to bed. All this, the young men had murmured, on a few glasses of lemonade.

Today, she woke to this clean-washed, sparkling morning. She could not wait to behold this bright world, of which she, Ellen, felt queen and ruler. Springing from bed, she went to stand at the open window, stretching her arms out as though they were wings and she could fly. Green of trees, blue of sea, brilliance of garden – there spread below her the early perfection of a summer day. What a splendid thing, she thought, to be not in love! Yes, one grows wiser as one grows older.

Should she note this down in her diary? She decided not; she had a feeling it had been said before.

Emergency in the Gothic Wing

Anastasia's telegram decided it – there was nothing for it but to re-open the Gothic Wing. For a number of reasons, Lady Cuckoo shrank from this decision; and her children glanced at each other and said: "Good heavens!" The Wing had been added to Sprangsby Hall by an eccentric and, some said, peculiar ancestor round about 1800 – there had been goings-on in it; some not quite the thing. Finally, it had been sealed off by the double-locking of the two doors which connected it with the central part of the Hall – otherwise a most cheerful house. The Georgian block, raised on an ancient Tudor foundation and brightened by Victorian bow windows, was sufficiently roomy without the Wing – that is, for life as one lives nowadays.

Lady Cuckoo's idea of reviving an English old-time Christmas for the benefit of some American friends had, however, created an emergency. The Hall was once again to be overflowing. Till now, all had been well in hand, and preparations went on apace. Some few scarlet berries, spared by the birds, gleamed bravely out of the stacks of holly; the surrounding landscape had obligingly draped itself in a light but sparkling mantle of snow. There was no butler and only half a cook, but two or three allies out of the village had agreed to see her ladyship through Christmas. Log fires, burning never more brightly, roared their ways up the enormous chimneys and took at least the edge off the chill. Lady Cuckoo, passing from room to room in a fur-lined cape, on the eve of her house-party's arrival, was delighted – at least, until the telegram came.

Annoying Merribys down with mumps have now nowhere to go Christmas arriving tomorrow with Sims and Momo all news then fond love.

Lady Cuckoo read the above aloud.

"This *is* the end," said the Sprangsby children.

"Wire back 'full up,'" suggested Arthur, who, engaged to Phyllida, the eldest, already counted as "family," so was here some days ahead of the other guests. He was atop of an unsafe ladder, attaching mistletoe to a chandelier. The two American Blomfields, a sister of Arthur's, two school-friends of Harold's (the elder Sprangsby son) and, not least, Uncle Theodore were to arrive shortly. In view of the fact that also, to begin with, there were six Sprangsbys, Arthur's suggestion seemed realistic. "Be firm," he said.

"It seems unkind," mourned his future mother-in-law. "And anyway she hasn't put an address."

"She knows a thing worth two of that!" said Phyllida, furious, letting go of the ladder Arthur was on, which began to slide. "And so, I daresay, do those wretched Merribys – I don't for an instant believe they've got mumps at all! So she picks on a darling sucker like *you*, Mama."

"I shall have to think," said poor Lady Cuckoo, with the air of one who goes to the last extreme. Setting aside comfort, of which there ceased to be any hope, the distracted lady saw no way of arranging her house-party with, even, propriety. Uncle Theodore, seldom co-operative, would object to so much as sharing a bathroom. And only the Blomfields, alas, were married — single persons take up much more space. The younger Sprangsbys were, of course, doubling up; Arthur's sister would go in the old nursery. But, even so — no, there was not another inch! Into the Wing must Anastasia and Momo go. One must hope for the best! They *might* not notice . . . Sims, she believed and hoped, was a little dog.

The upper door of the Wing was, therefore, that afternoon unlocked: the key grated rustily. Lady Cuckoo, to give face to the thing, personally headed an expedition consisting of three of her children and two of the gardeners' wives: these latter carrying firing, brooms and bed-linen. The explorers filed down the lengthy, shuttered and vaulted corridor: 'Tck!" said one of the women, "isn't it musty!" Winter sunshine, however, soon streamed blandly into the painted rooms — and, outside the pointed windows, the park with its elms and snow reassuringly looked like a Christmas card. 'This, with the stars on the ceiling, ought to do for *her* nicely,' said Lady Cuckoo, displacing whirls of dust with a feather mop. 'The young gentleman," she explained to a gardener's wife, "had better be in the one with those nice carved stags."

"You can't mean *Momo*, Mama?" protested one of her younger daughters. "Actually, he's a beastly little musician."

"Amelia darling, this *is* Christmas. Cousin Anastasia's kind to him; so should you be."

"She's horrible to Americans," said the child, stalwart in support of the U. S. A., where she'd been fêted during the war. "Nothing, now, will be fun for the sweet Blomfields — oh Mama, really, why *must* she come!"

Lady Cuckoo gave an evasive sigh. Poor Anastasia, how she did *not* endear herself – and seldom, frankly, had she been known to try. She adhered grimly to Lady Cuckoo; other supporters had long since faded away. How hard it is to be loyal and fair to all! Anastasia was interested exclusively in the arts, and showed it. She leaned, moreover, to the arts in their most advanced and forbidding forms: nothing did she so much despise as anything anybody had ever heard of. Seldom had Anastasia not in tow a still-to-be-recognised young genius; quite often Central European and too often furiously rude. Of these Momo had been the latest and, one was forced to agree, the worst – one could indeed hardly imagine anything less Christmassy than Momo. Anastasia herself had at one time been on the highbrow stage; though, as the Sprangsby children pointed out, soon off even that again. She had once played Mélisande.[1]

Lady Cuckoo reproached herself for these hard thoughts. And, oh, dear, what a reek of ancient damp arose from the Wing's cavernous fourposters! Giving orders that her own upper mattress should be moved in to be slept on by Anastasia, and Amelia's only mattress (to teach her charity) for Momo, the hostess pensively left the scene. In the corridor, she was at pains to skirt the somewhat dangerous head of the spiral staircase, connecting this floor of the Wing with the one below. For under the bedroom suite was a vault-like ballroom – vast, and in décor not unlike the surroundings for a Black Mass. Not in living memory had it been gaily danced in – you only had to glance at it to see why. The Sprangsby children had at one time used it for roller-skating, till vibrations all but brought the ceiling down.[2] Since then it, like the suite above, had been locked off. And all for the best, too . . .

Lady Cuckoo was glad to find herself back in the cheerful, blameless, Christmassy main block of her home, the Hall.

Next day, Christmas Eve, the expected party began arriving, from teatime on. Car after car drew up, with a scrunch on the snow; each time the hall door, flung joyously open, emitted glowing lights and the Sprangsbys peltering out, in a troop, in welcome. Not less was the enthusiasm of the darling Blomfields, who emerged from the comparative warmth of a hired Daimler into the beautiful draughtiness of the teatime hall without anything so dim as a sneeze or blink. If Mrs. Blomfield tightened her furs around her, it was with a gesture which well became her. The Blomfields' delighted and noble faces shone.

"And for Harry," declared Carrie (or Mrs.) Blomfield, "there's been just the final touch of perfection! We observed your antique Wing as we drove past it; and Harry's ever so interested in the occult."

"Our nice old faithful ghost," said Phyllida, "is usually sitting in the kitchen – I don't think he's ever missed a Christmas. The kitchen, you see, *is* Tudor. The Wing is simply a fake."

"Still, it's got *something*," said Mr. Blomfield, happily glittering with his pince-nez. "I unfailingly sensed that as we drove by. Tell me this – is it now inhabited?"

"Not normally," said the girl, passing crumpets to Mr. and Mrs. Blomfield. Mrs. Blomfield said: "All the same, Harry'll never rest since he's had this strange intimation. He's taken some remarkable spirit photographs."[3]

"I'd *advise* the kitchen," said Lady Cuckoo. for a moment looking distraught. "Our dear ghost in there wears such a nice ruff; and altogether it's far more cosy."

Round the candlelit tea-table, all was high spirits and good cheer – firelight dancing on the Georgian silver; family portraits beaming a welcome down at the newcomers out of their dim-gold, hollywreathed frames. The youthful British reserve of Arthur's sister and Harold's school-friends, who entered next all but immediately melted – how could it not? And distinction was added by Uncle Theodore, who took his place with a courteous though melancholy smile. He, however, was unable to look for long at anybody other than Lady Cuckoo. And, to crown all, there was a stir on the snow outside – after preliminary coughing and shuffling, the village carol singers burst into song. Noel, Noel . . .

They were interrupted. Hollow hammering beat upon the Hall door – Lady Cuckoo blinked and put down her cup. She was too right: it *was* Anastasia and Momo. And Sims, who (truly a little dog) yapped, squirming, under his mistress's arm. They had had, it appeared, to walk from the station – not a taxi, owing to dreadful Christmas. "I am feeling terrible, thank you," said Anastasia, rolling round her haunted eyes in their sockets. "But, how could I not? What a dreary farce this all is." She pushed her way to a chair beside Lady Cuckoo's, darkly ignoring all others there. As for Momo, his contempt for the whole occasion was, as he indicated, unspeakable.

Phyllida Sprangsby, having withdrawn with Arthur to put the finishing touches to tomorrow's Christmas tree, said: "That wicked Mama never broke it to Uncle Theodore."

"What, that Anastasia & Co. were coming?"

"Yes. She hadn't got the nerve, I suppose. So *did* you see his poor darling face?"

"He wasn't in tearing form from the start, I thought."

"You see, Mama refuses to marry him." (Lady Cuckoo had been a widow for ten years.)

"But how could she, angel, if he's your uncle?"

"Oh, we just call him 'uncle' to cheer him up. *Wasn't* Anastasia vile to the Blomfields? Ha-ha, though: she's got to go in the Wing!"

"Honestly, Phyllida," asked Arthur, "what is all this about the Wing?"

"*Aha!*" said the girl with an awful look. "Perhaps if I ever told you, you'd never marry me. Or your poor hair might go bright white overnight! . . . Idiot, you've put that top star on crooked. No, don't dare kiss me again till you've got it straight."

Anastasia, dressed like a snake, was as usual last to come down to dinner. "The fire in that room of mine doesn't burn," she announced at once. "Are there jackdaws' nests in the chimney? And what am I to do about a bath? I could share yours," she added, turning to Uncle Theodore.

Uncle Theodore all but dropped his glass – the highball fixed for him by kind Mr. Blomfield. Outrage rendered him speechless for some time. "You would not know where to find it," he said defiantly. "*Oh* yes I would," said Anastasia smugly. "I've made inquiries. It's the green one – a becoming colour to me."

"That has always been MY bath," said Uncle Theodore in his most ominous tone. The rest of the party stood round, helpless – Anastasia tossed her head of hair, which, but for being a tarnished red, might itself have been one of the jackdaws' nests. "You're far too set," she declared, "in bachelor ways! Anyone would imagine that you lived here . . ." Fortunately, dinner was announced.

After dinner they played idiotic games. Amelia disguised herself in a bear-skin and chased Momo – who, it turned out, rather enjoyed himself: he leaped up on the back of a sofa and let off an imaginary gun, shouting: "Bang, bang, bang!" He then seized Mrs. Blomfield around the waist and whirled her away with him to dance a polka – "My!" she happily panted. Arthur, of a more serious turn of mind, suggested now was the moment for playing Murder – to which Anastasia replied that *she*, for one, disapproved of blood sports.

"I revere your principles, my dear lady; I revere your principles," murmured Mr. Blomfield, plying her with a highball, for she looked lonely. "Yet, as the poet says, Christmas comes but once a year. And to me that's a heartening, beautiful thought."

"You're easily pleased, Mr. What's-your-name," sneered Anastasia, and in a tone which detestably echoed around the drawing-room. "This is, I suppose, your first view of civilised life? One can hardly wonder your head is turned. Do *all* American ladies," she went on to ask, eyeing Mrs. Blomfield, who was once again wrapping herself in furs as she cooled off after the polka-dancing, "dress like Esquimaux the whole time?"

The furious Sprangsbys did not know where to look. "Let's *play* Murder," implored Lady Cuckoo, earnestly. So they did; it was followed by Sardines, then hide-and-seek. Momo was the life and soul of the party: all were in form, however – shrieks of rapture rang through the Hall; pursued and pursuers tore up and down stairs, and someone (perhaps Arthur's sister) in search of further terrain, unlocked the door of the Gothic ballroom and hilariously was followed into its darkness by several others. Subdued, some time later, they all filed out again – in order to regain breath, they played racing demon.

Uncle Theodore subtracted Lady Cuckoo from the merriment and led her to a sofa in a corner. He felt it devolved upon him to point out that what she needed was a protector. "Terrible people prey on you," he said, frowning at Anastasia across the room. Lady Cuckoo, serene in a pink brocade not less lovely for being ancient, replied that her children all did their best. "And now," she fondly said, "there'll be Arthur, too."

"When are he and Phyllida to be married?"

"Quite soon. Won't that be lovely!"

Uncle Theodore manfully cleared his throat. "And when, my dear," he inquired, "are we to be?"

"Oh please don't, Theodore – *not* at Christmas!" Lady Cuckoo glanced at the clock and rose. "Time for bed, I think!" she called to them all. "Poor Santa Claus will be waiting to do the stockings."

A count of heads, preparatory to the move upstairs, found one or two of the party to be missing – Mr. Blomfield, for instance, was not on hand. It could be taken that he, Arthur and Uncle Theodore were either assisting Santa Claus or taking a nightcap in the library. "Or maybe," said the comfortable Carrie Blomfield, "they even went for an outdoor stroll – I'd say this Hall should look wonderful in the moonlight." Up, therefore, trooped the women and children.

The night *was* lovely; ancestral elms cast shadows over the moon-blue landscape; here and there a late light gleamed on the snow –

away in the distance, a clock struck twelve. Lady Cuckoo, leaning
for a moment out of her window, felt at Christmas peace with the
world; and she thought with love of all those gathered under her
roof. *Did* the Gothic Wing count as her roof also? – by leaning out,
she could just see its silhouette projecting blackly into some laurels
. . . "Oh dear," she thought. "Anastasia did succeed in mortifying the
Blomfields! . . . Well, I wonder how she will sleep tonight. I *almost*
hope . . . Oh dear, what a wicked thought!"

In the Wing itself, Anastasia sat tensely up in her fourposter,
nursing her knees with her bony arms. Candles, which provided the
only light (the Wing had not been wired for electricity), rendered
Gothic shadows the more intense – somewhere away in them
crouched Sims, petrified by extreme nervousness: from time to time
he let out a whimper. "Sims, don't be neurotic!" raged Anastasia – she
had made a nest for her pet on the quilt beside her, but in vain. She
felt deserted by all – and, indeed, was not Momo the worst? Never
had she had such a disillusionment: his behaviour tonight had been
almost *ordinary* – she had come on him, paper cap on his head,
sliding down the banisters with Arthur's sister! And to think that,
only a week hence, he was to make his début (sponsored by her) as
a totally incomprehensible solo flautist at the Utopian Hall.

Momo, scuttling ahead of Anastasia into the Wing, had no doubt
sensed her disapproval – for now, two doors away from her, he had
penitently returned to Art. Note by note, in a minor key, he was
picking out upon his flute the perhaps most incomprehensible of his
melodies up to date – and never had any artistic sound struck less
pleasingly upon his patron's ear. "Stop it, Momo!" she shrieked, but
without result. She leaped from bed, wound herself into a pallid and
flowing robe, and set off to tell Momo what she thought of him.

A charnel draught, danker than mere cold, met her as she opened
her bedroom door. Only vaguely now did she recollect that she *had*
heard some sort of nonsense about this Wing. Sims, who rather than
stay alone had come jittering after her, uttered a canine shriek and

again fled – as well he might. For the vaulted corridor was not, as it should have been, in darkness – up the shaft of the staircase there wavered a blue and, it seemed, phosphorescent glow. *"Momo,"* moaned Anastasia, "come out! Where are you?" The flute stopped dead – but Momo did not appear. Anastasia (who, give her her due, had nerve) drew a deep breath, approached the head of the staircase and peered down.

Someone, or still worse, Something, was at the bottom.

That blood-freezing pause – would it ever terminate?

Then – "Peace, troubled spirit!" said Mr. Blomfield, tremblingly waving upward his blue torch. Faint was the glimmer of his pince-nez as he peered up the spiral at Anastasia.

Never yet had his interest in the occult brought him within actual range of it. To enter the dreadful ballroom, while it was open, and to be there at midnight had been his plan – armed with psychic notebook and spirit camera Mr. Blomfield had taken up his position during the game of hide-and-seek. But, alas, what appeared to have happened was that someone (probably Arthur, in one of his fits of zeal) had locked the ballroom again, on his way to bed – and, of course, done so from the outside. Here, therefore, was Mr. Blomfield, incarcerated with who knew what? The good man, loth to cause a disturbance, aware of having taken an undue liberty, had endured his plight for as long as possible – would not somebody come to find him – would not loving Carrie raise an alarm? Midnight struck; doomed silence girt round the ballroom – he dithered the small blue spotlight of his torch around the malignant interior. Windows? – they were high-set and out of reach; for Mr. Blomfield was not a tall man. Far, now, from him was any thought of further tampering with the spirit world; his sole hope was that it might leave *him* alone . . .

Hours seemed to pass: now, he could but envisage what must have happened – Carrie had dropped asleep, as she often did, the moment her good head had touched the pillow; and so, as she always did, she would sleep till morning. And a no less blameless slumber, no doubt, had claimed the Sprangsbys . . . His morale had reached its lowest ebb when unearthly flute-notes began to curdle the air. This, no doubt, was the overture to the Worst.

And now, from out the darkness above, glared down the unholy Queen of the Revels.

"Why, Mr. *Blomfield!*" complained Anastasia, recognising the pince-nez.

"Why, my *dear* lady," said Mr. Blomfield, recognising the toothiness. 'This," he added sincerely, "is a great pleasure! I was – er – taking a peep around."

"You quite frightened my little dog."

"Could I," ventured Mr. Blomfield, "come up, I wonder?" Anastasia, clutching her robe to her, asked: 'What *do* you mean?" in a chaste and forbidding tone.

"Madam, it seems I cannot get out any other way."

"How extremely peculiar," grumbled the lady – modestly vanishing back into her room. She did, however, allow Mr. Blomfield transit. But in vain. For Uncle Theodore, on *his* way to bed, had guaranteed the sanctity of his bathroom – it was found that the upstairs door of the Wing was no less firmly locked on the outside. And, as Phyllida had more than once pointed out, once inside the Wing one was out of earshot. In vain had many been known to scream.

"It really is sometimes wonderful," Lady Cuckoo beamed, on Christmas morning, "the way everything works out for the best. Once they all three knew what had happened, they were quite happy. Momo dragged in his mattress, and they made a little camp around Anastasia's bedroom fire. Dear Harry's accustomed to camping (people do, you know, by choice in America) so he was able to show them how. And he poked the jackdaws' nests out of the chimney.

"Then he told Anastasia about Red Indian art; and as nobody else in this old-world country seems to know anything about that, of course, she was absolutely delighted. As for Momo, he started composing illustrative Red Indian music on his flute; and Harry Blomfield got so excited he's going to sponsor Momo all round America . . .

"Anastasia's a different woman this morning – of course she knows *we* still don't know about Art; but, darlings, she even said, 'Happy Christmas!' . . . Poor Carrie *was* a little worried, of course, when her tea came and she woke to find Harry not there; but Amelia traced him almost immediately . . . All the same, it was naughty of you, Theodore – you must *not* be such a selfish bachelor!"

"Well, my dear, there's always one cure for that."

"Oh, don't, please – oh dear, there go the bells: where *are* they all? We must start for church."

The Claimant

It began, out of the blue, with Arthur's getting the letter from Australia. "Why, look," I said, looking through the post, "I didn't know we knew anybody *there!*"

"Nor we do," said Arthur, turning it over

"Well, go on, dear" (I remember saying) "open it. It won't bite you."

Those used to be sunny mornings. The house faced east, over the estuary, and I used to open the windows early in order to air out the smell of paint. We'd moved in the day the workmen went out, and everywhere was as fresh – lovely! The house, though ancient, felt new to us – sometimes we had to laugh, Arthur and I. Look at us, married thirty-five years and setting up all anew like a boy and girl! It *had* been a step to take, leaving Wimbledon Park: I know there were many who thought us crazy. "Whatever will you do with your-selves," I was asked, "right away off by yourselves down there?" As they should know, Arthur was cracked on sailing, and asked no better than gardening when ashore. "No doubt, but how will *you* pass the time?" they would go on.

Since I first knew Arthur, he'd dreamed of the West Country. We'd departed there for our honeymoon, also holidays. So the day came when he sold his business, and sold it well – having himself built it up, he deserved to. So, having no one to come after us, we took what was now our capital and moved West. Compensation for our having had no family was, we felt free to realise our long dream.

I don't think I ever saw such a happy man. I make myself always remember that.

We'd been in the house three weeks when the letter came. July. It was drowsy weather, dulling over sometimes in the afternoons but again bright throughout those evenings. Time passed itself – how, I need not tell you. I know I had not yet got the curtains up. But what matter? We went to bed before dark. And outdoors, nothing but the water, and across that nothing else but woods going steep up, as they did also behind our house. Few from the village came that way. No one to look in on us – so we thought!

By that same post, I got a letter from Mary. Forgetting Australia for the moment, I was deep in her everlasting news when I heard Arthur sharply exclaim. And when he told me, I did not wonder.

For what the man wrote to say was, that the house had had no business to be disposed of. It was his, he claimed, under his uncle's will – his uncle being the last P. St. J. Hobart. Of that, of course, we could not make head or tail. Arthur'd gone into everything most thoroughly before signing. True, old Mr. Hobart had been the owner of the house, as had his ancestors before him – he'd indeed died there. But died what is called intestate. His lawyers (whom Arthur dealt with over the purchase) were altogether satisfied as to that. The old fellow *had* made a will, which was in their keeping, but then one day he came round, asked for it back and destroyed it under their very noses. They asked him, should they draw up another, but all he did was stride out. He returned no more – having shortly afterwards passed away. As he no doubt knew, he had nothing to leave but debts: all the lawyers found, when making their search, was bills. So the house had to be sold to pay off those – mainly local people. (Fancy their letting credit run on like that! He traded on their good feeling, did Mr. Hobart – also, I've no doubt, on his ancient name.) Sad, it seemed, as a story, but straightforward. By all accounts old Mr. Hobart was the last of his line. No word as to any nephew arose.

"What does he call himself?" I wondered.

"He signs himself 'P. St. J. Hobart.'"

"Arthur, those lawyers *can't* have made a mistake?"

"Not they," said Arthur. (And a man knows.) "No, this chap hasn't a leg to stand on."

"You mean," I said, "he's simply trying it on? Or else he's an impostor, I shouldn't wonder."

"Whoever he is," said Arthur, passing me the letter, "he knows this place. Seems to know it like the palm of his hand."

So the man did. It was a peculiar letter, partly insulting (he spoke of "a pack of robbers"), partly aiming to play upon our feelings. The place, he told us, was the scene of his boyhood. He'd lived his life, he said, his miserable life, with one hope only – to return. He wrote, "It's my fate, my passion and my inheritance. MINE. And no one shall cheat me of it."

I said: "Well, my goodness. I mean, really . . ."

Arthur said nothing.

"In fairness," I said, "his uncle ought to have told him."

"Maybe they fell out," said Arthur. "You never know. There's a lot goes on in those old families."

"Arthur, you ought to send this on to the lawyers," I said. "Let them write him – what else are they for? In the first place, he should have written to them, instead of attempting to play *us* up."

Arthur once more said: "Hasn't a leg to stand on."

I said: "Look, dear, this has nothing to say to us. So do kindly put it out of your mind." (For I saw he couldn't.)

"Can't but pity the chap."

"Stop it, do!" I cried.

"He hasn't a hope," said Arthur. Later, I saw him go down the lawn. He stood there and looked up then down the water, then around at the trees. He always went off by himself when he felt badly.

You never know the whole of a man's mind. Now, too late, I can see what upset Arthur. He was taking on on behalf of this Hobart heir because of the way *he* cared for the place, himself. Arthur almost cared for the place past reason – strange, to feel that way so late in life. You never come to the end of knowing a man – at one time, I should not have thought Arthur had it in him. From the moment we first set eyes on the place, it got him.

It may have been partly the situation. You came on it round a turn of the valley, suddenly – just the house, the water and the trees going up. The lawn sloped to the estuary, and there was a jetty – high-and-dry that day, for the tide was out. "Well," I said, "I'm glad that mud doesn't smell." For something told me this was to be our home. I read our future in Arthur's face.

To return to that letter. Arthur did what I said – that is, sent it on to the lawyers. What I was not to know was, that Arthur also wrote to the man himself. Oh, he would have done better to keep out of it! Not that he intended to give encouragement. No, he meant only (he later said) to assure the man that the old home was at any rate in good hands. But Arthur could never express himself on paper – therefore, the nephew took him to be gloating. By return air mail from Australia, Arthur received what read like the work of an angry maniac – had it not been I who took in the post, Arthur'd I'm sure have hidden *that* letter from me. As it was, share and share alike. I asked, "Think he'll go for us with a gun?"

For the nephew was to be with us, shortly. Yes, he was coming flying back from Australia in order to thresh the whole matter out. He expected, he wrote, to be taking the next plane after the one bearing us his letter . . . We turned, of course, to the lawyers. *They* weren't much help – they hummed and hawed, fidgeted and looked sideways. Nor were the village people better. A close lot – smugglers, I shouldn't wonder. They'd been all right so far (they got our custom), but old neighbourhoods are apt to be queer to new-comers. Up to then, I and Arthur had never noticed. But of course that village was in league with the Hobarts. How they knew that nephew was coming I could not tell you – but *they* knew all right. We read that in every eye.

So there we were, left with this hanging over us.

Now it was to come to a fight, Arthur rightly hardened. "While and if that fellow continues his present attitude," he told me, "not a word will I hear. I am never walking out, and I'm never selling out. And that's final."

And when Arthur says so, it is.

Then another morning, we ceased to worry.

Arthur picked up the newspaper – then half put it down again, shaken. I looked – there'd been one of those dreadful air crashes, somewhere halfway across the world. On the route home from Australia. All lives lost. Arthur took back the paper and ran his thumbnail down the passenger list. Among those listed was P. St. J. Hobart.

Arthur and I were ashamed to voice our relief. Later, he walked away down the lawn. The lawyers came on the telephone. "Yes, *I* know," I said, "don't tell me."

That evening, our floorboards started to be torn up. A clock was moved from in front of a sliding panel. Thrown out in heaps were our clothes and papers, from drawers and cupboards, during the crazy search. Night and day it went on. I heard him, Arthur heard him, but neither of us ever caught him at it. Seldom did we enter into a room which was not disturbed, seldom a room he had not just left. How could we doubt for a minute who it was?

"Maybe if we aided him, Arthur, it might stop this?" I once said. Arthur would have no truck. Myself, it came to the point where I spent hours, secretly, looking for that will – only to make certain it was not there. "It's no GOOD!" I found myself standing shouting, at the bottom of the stairs, so's to make myself heard in every part of the house.

But P. St. J. Hobart was not yet ready to give over.

I had the idea of summoning the vicar. Though not a church-goer, I hear the clergy have powers. However, his wife sent word he was on holiday.

At the start, we remained outdoors as much as we could, leaving the premises to P. St. J. Hobart on chance he might weary and be still. We now seldom saw the sun; it was sultry weather. The trees became dark as though full of smoke. To distract my mind, Arthur would take me boating, up river out of sight of the house. Or with sandwiches we would make off into the further woods – sitting our backs up against some tree, Arthur would take my hand in his, then one after the other we'd doze off: we had sleep to catch up with. Nothing but the humming of the insects – till a bird would scream, off away down there. Soon, I could see, our absences chafed Arthur: he could not agree to them on principle. He was right – a man should stay by his own home.

The first *sight* I had of P. St. J. Hobart was in the distance.

Coming back one of those evenings from the woods, we saw him standing there in the doorway, as might the owner. He was tall, bald and wore a curious smile. As we approached, he vanished inside. Though he continued for some time to fight shy of us, we from then on saw him go past the windows.

Then came the evening when he took a long look in at us. The window was closed, for the dusk was damp, due to sea mist coming up the estuary. He put one hand flat against the pane – through the glass I beheld his teeth and his eyeballs. Not only that but I saw him laugh. "Arthur," I said as quietly as possible, "dear, let's shut the shutters, shall we?"

Somehow I'm never comfortable being laughed at. Also, his manner reflected upon Arthur.

Yet you could pity him, there alone.

I should explain that what Arthur never considered, for one moment, was our quitting the house. He was not for our yielding an inch. He took this trouble up as he might a challenge, saying, "No, what's good enough for him is good enough for me." The night Hobart gave me a fright in bed, Arthur did ask if I'd care to go for a change to Mary's. "What," I said, "and leave you? No, I know where *my* place is!"

Giving up looking for the will, P. St. J. Hobart turned his attention upon us. Nothing we did escaped him. Finding we did not go away, he commenced studying us for his own reasons. Wanting, was he, in some way to come to terms? I put it to Arthur, whether we could not? Arthur replied, "Not while he continues his present attitude." I pointed out that P. St. J. Hobart had all but given up sneering: he'd remain quite quiet in the corners of rooms or rove through our woodlands quite inoffensively, or stand by the water much as did Arthur. He knew his way in the dark. He was back home.

For my part, I should not have objected to having a bachelor in the house – had he been a living one.

That was what was the matter. That was what put out Arthur. Arthur could never tolerate what was not aboveboard. "I'd deal fair-and-square," he said, "with any living man." Such had been his rule throughout his business days: to do otherwise would not have been himself. "All I ask," he said, "is a *living* man. As it is, I call this a dirty trick." He felt himself taken advantage of by P. St. J. Hobart.

"Well, you can't blame *him*, Arthur. Blame that air-crash!"

But with Arthur, it was the principle of the thing. Till he'd had this out, he could not enjoy his home. Could not settle to anything till he'd cleared this up. He was hit, you understand, right in his sense of property. He said: "I'll have this out with him, if I die." So it was Arthur, from that day on, who took to going after P. St. J. Hobart. *Arthur* would creep and look suddenly through a window to see whether P. St. J. Hobart was in a room. *Arthur* would stand hour-long in our doorway, watching to see who'd come out of our woods. Or bang down his teacup and dart out – in vain: he'd come back ever so crestfallen.

"Never mind," I'd say, "he's just a Slippery Sam."

For P. St. J. Hobart would never face Arthur squarely. No sort of satisfaction would he give. Wherever Arthur was not, Hobart would be – all the place was queer with that smile of his.[1] Get us out? – no, he'd done better than that. May have been his revenge, may have been his fun.

Looking back, one thing's strange: no such word as "ghost" ever passed Arthur's or my own lips. No, not even when we all but quarrelled.

Only all but quarrelled. P. St. J. Hobart brought about no rift between my dear Arthur and me. I trust I shall always remember that. After thirty-five years – no it wasn't possible. It was just that Arthur was such an upright man, who could not sit down under what seemed wrong, whereas I am the easy-going sort – live and let live.

So the thing preyed on Arthur.

THE CLAIMANT

The end came suddenly.

I don't care to speak of it, so I'll tell you shortly. All that day, it was gathering up for thunder. Stifling and awful. So dark indoors that to get through in the kitchen took all my morning – I don't know when it was that I dished up dinner. Arthur barely spoke and had little appetite: he sat as usual in the master's chair we'd bought with other furniture in the house – and now and then behind Arthur's shoulder I caught a glimpse of P. St. J. Hobart. After, for some hours I don't remember: I put my feet up on the livingroom sofa to snatch a nap, but went deep asleep. The storm breaking woke me. P. St. J. Hobart sat on the end of my sofa, tipping towards me his bald head. He never had come so near before.

He came nearer, showing me his white eyes.

Well, I knew evil when I saw it. I cried out, but the thunder was like great guns. Right overhead. Then I could not see for the lightning – I don't know therefore for how long Arthur'd been planted there in the door. Down, down the dark rain came, smacking on the water of the estuary: it was full tide.

Hobart gave such a laugh as I never heard, but backed off the sofa. "You needn't go," said Arthur, "I want a word with you" – he spread his arms, barred the one way out of the room. At last he'd got Hobart into a corner.

P. St. J. Hobart did not so much as trouble to laugh again. He walked straight through Arthur, out of that door. Arthur made a grab at his own chest, almost unbelievingly. Then he turned, with no word to me, and went after Hobart. I'm so stout, I stumbled as I ran to the window. Hobart, shimmering in the lightning, waited for Arthur to come up with him – through the downpour I watched them come face to face. Like that they stood, as they never had. What began to pass, I shall never know. Hobart broke it off, moved away. Arthur always after him. Arthur again overtook him near the lawn's edge, raised his fist and struck out – battling at air.

P. St. J. Hobart strolled off away down the jetty. Lightning flashed a white sheet on to the water, over which Hobart walked forward, on. Arthur, however, fell where the jetty ended. What remained was the roaring storm and the racing water into which my dear had gone like a stone.

Not till the following day did they bring home Arthur.

More than peaceful his face was, satisfied. Nothing more on his mind, he had said his say. He had had it out.

I suppose I got through on the telephone to the village. I know I was not left alone long. A death finds you friends, wherever you are. Somebody wired Mary and she came, and it was with her that I went away. Never to return.

So there is that place, for whoever wants it. Once again for sale, for I need the money. Empty or not empty, I cannot say. Who is in possession, I do not ask.

Candles in the Window

Aunt Kay came to us every Christmas, arriving at always the same hour, in the winter dusk of the day before. Unfailingly as our grandfather clock chimed, we heard her cab draw up, then her voice in the hall. Children love repetition, and ceremonial. Each time, her coming added solemnity to the pre-Christmas excitement in our home. We four stood crowded at the head of the staircase, waiting for Mother to summon us one by one: Aunt Kay never cared to be crowded, or in any way rushed. Tall in her fur-lined cloak, her dark veil thrown back, she stooped as many times as there were children, to imprint a kiss on each upturned forehead;

and with the kiss went a moment of searching gaze, though the gaze seemed to be coming from far off. Then, drawing off her fine, shabby French gloves, she would sweep ahead of Mother into the parlour, where, under the mantle now wreathed in holly, the same chair by the fire was always hers.

Likewise, her trunk with the studded top always preceded her to the same bedroom: at the back, for she did not care to look at the sea. (Married, as a girl, to a sea captain, she had early been widowed by a gale: nothing had ever been heard of the lost ship.) "Aunt Kay's room" was a little darkened by the hill of so many houses rising behind it, tall sedate old weathered houses like ours, with grey-slated fronts and white-sashed windows. Our town was a small but anciently famous port on an estuary in the south of Ireland: here the sea crooked deep inland between sheltering hills.[1] Quays, less busy now than they were once, made a foreground for climbing buildings, one or two mansions raised on maritime wealth, the old lovely church, the Queen Anne courthouse. And, though major shipping trade had withdrawn, adventurous little trawlers from France and Spain still docked here, unloading exotic cargoes. Also, our town flourished as a market centre; it was the bourn of farmers and countryfolk out of lonely miles extending between the coast and the mountains. Down the narrow streets were little bow-fronted shops. These, at Christmas, glittered like jewel boxes.

Christmas Eve drew everyone into town. There was great festivity: doffing of wide-brimmed hats, merry accordion playing by a blind beggar, greetings shouted from one to another of the jostling ass carts, on whose back shafts perched small boys, swinging their legs. Mothers of families grave in their hooded black cloaks, gazed through the misted panes at festoons of tinsel, gilded crockery, pyramids of oranges, spiced black sausages, holy images, gaudy neckerchiefs, couples of china dogs, debating how to lay out the final shilling, while in their wake their more skittish daughters were ogled by dark-eyed sailors seeking romance. Out through doorways travelled a tempting spiciness from sugar-baked apples, pigs' trotters in jelly. There was coming and going out of the lamplit archways, the echoing courtyards, the twisting alleyways. We children loved our late-evening run through the town; we made last-minute penny purchases, we delivered gifts. Our father was doctor here; we knew everyone. Best of all was the climax, when, finally, we made our ways to the quayside, then looked up, for the whole hill had become like a Christmas tree! A gigantic candle, pink, scarlet, turquoise or amber was alight in a window of every home. These would burn on until the Feast of Epiphany. What a night for a ship to come in from sea. And *this*, surely, should welcome Aunt Kay, we thought.

Aunt Kay, however, remained indoors. The shutters were shut, we knew, and curtains drawn between her and that ceaseless though distant sound, the wintry moaning of the Atlantic at the harbour's mouth. If, as might happen at Christmas, there were a storm, Mother would hasten to the piano and begin to play, for we all felt we could not shelter Aunt Kay enough. Her visits to us (living where we did) were a brave concession. At no other time of year would she stir from the midland city where she lived, by herself, frugally, in back-street lodgings. Aunt Kay was too regal to seem poor. She bestowed herself upon us, for these days each Christmas, with the simplicity of an accepted beauty, ageless but for the silver of her hair and shadowy remoteness behind her eyes. Her carriage was upright, her movements measured; it was an event when slowly she turned her head. Childless, she was drawn to us as a family by her love for our father, her special nephew: he and she had been linked since he was a boy. I, Katherine, the eldest of his children, was named after her. After me had come Barbara, Linda, Frederick. We four, forever upon the margin of her spell, were a little constrained, perhaps, by her lack of chatter. In no way did she resemble the lively great-aunts or rosy, plump and loquacious grandmammas who from time to time visited our friends. (It cannot have been easy, I see now, for Aunt Kay to break out those year-long silences attendant on her very solitary life.)

Yet she distinguished between us. How she noted our characters was shown by the miraculous rightness of her gifts. How could mortal woman perceive, so almost uncannily, the unspoken desires of each one of us? These marvels, did she conjure them into being, or did she spend all year, between Christmas and Christmas, stitching at fineries for us elder girls, or searching dusty trays in curio shops for treasure trove for Linda and Frederick, dinted Roman coins, jointed silver fish? Children take genius for granted, as they take lovingness. I, however, Katherine, the firstborn, was soonest to be fated to cross the threshold. There arrived the Christmas when I was fourteen.

That, too, was the Christmas the snow fell. Snow is rare in Ireland; it was preceded by an unfamiliar, curious, tawny hush. Onto Aunt Kay's cab, as it pulled up, the first of the big flakes came twirling down. Later, they danced between the lights of the shops, glistened on the cloaks of the countrywomen, silvered the backs of the patient donkeys. They veiled with gauze the candles lit on the hill, and looked wraithlike over the dark estuary. In the air, the taste of snow mingled with the tang of the peat smoke and the perpetual brininess from the sea; we shouted aloud with surprised delight, breathing it in. Five-year-old Frederick, buttoned into his reefer, ran with his tongue out. By Christmas morning, the wonder had been perfected: yesterday's grey town, transformed and dazzling, had overnight entered the world of fairy tale! Linda shouted: "The Christmas cards have come true!" The church bells, over the streets with their soundless footfalls, enchanted our ears as never before. And to crown everything I, Katherine, tonight would go to a ball!

Or, as a ball *I* thought of it. It was Christmas dancing in a big house overlooking the harbour. Other years, I had longingly heard the music, pulsing toward us over the water; but this year, oh, joy, I was "old enough." Sympathetic, my fanciful younger sisters helped me build up a fiction of chandeliers, beaux, bouquets, Viennese waltzes. Hanging, new as a pin, in my attic bedroom, my flouncey white dress with the coral ribbons held a day-long reception of its own; one by one my juniors stole in, admiring. Not the least of the awe was mine. Could it be truly *I*, bouncing boyish Katherine, who would sail the floor in the snowy nimbus, tonight? This Christmas's gift from Aunt Kay to me had been a filigree bracelet inset with coral. How had she known? But that, I found, was not to be Aunt Kay's all. When Christmas Day came on to six o'clock, we gathered, by custom, round Mother at the piano, to sing carols. Our great-aunt, standing behind my shoulder, lightly touched my auburn, unkempt mane. "Before you dress," she said, "I'll brush your hair. One must be shining all over, for a ball. Remember! I'll wait for you in my room."

So, at once elated and timid, aglow from a rain-water tub but with an uncertain flutter around my heart, I presented myself in my petticoat at her door.

Our old house, those days, had no electricity. Flanking Aunt Kay's mirror, a pair of candles deepened, by contrast, the shadows in which she stood. From the mahogany wardrobe, not quite closed, there travelled a scent of orris.[2] By her own austere wish, no fire burned in the grate: *she* lived, I think, in a climate quite of her own, which neither summer melted nor winter chilled. However, seeing me shiver, she draped my shoulders, before motioning me to the waiting chair. Then, gathering my hair softly in her hands, she spread it over the wrapper and began brushing, smoothly, evenly, slowly. I could watch her reflection, over mine, in the looking glass. "So, Katherine," she said, "you are growing up."

"Does it take long, Aunt Kay?"

"The rest of your life."

"*Oh*," I said, puzzled and disconcerted. "To me, it seems long enough till I'm seventeen!"

She paused. "You must not be in a hurry. *I* was; I wanted everything all at once." She was using her own yellowed ivory brushes;

she put one down, as though to give it a rest, and took up the other. On their backs were monograms, all but rubbed out by time. These somehow brought home to me, with a shock, the fact of Aunt Kay's being of great age. I ventured: "Did you – ?"

She bowed her head. "I *had* everything all at once; and it was too much. All these years since – shall I tell you how they've been spent? I have spent them reliving that one year I did *not* know how to live, at the time! Happiness is a matter of understanding, Katherine. Had it come later, I should have been more ready. As it was, it went by me all in a flash. I was widowed at nineteen. Did your father tell you?"

"He told us it was all a long time ago."

"Not to me," she said. "To me it is still today." With a comb she drew a gentle line from my forehead backward, down to the nape of my neck. She began to brush between the divided hair. "I did not completely believe them, when they told me; and sometimes, though, Katherine, this you must never tell! though I *know* he is lost, I still can't accept it. If he came back, I should be ready. I *should* be ready! How to love, and how to be loved, is a long, slow lesson. Now, at last, too late, I have learned it. But what's the good?" For a moment, Aunt Kay turned away her head.

Confusedly, pressing my hands together, I sought to express the truth I suddenly saw. I cried: "The good is, your loving *us!*"

"How could I not? You are dear children. But you have each other, your home, your father and mother. What can I give you, more?"

Still shy, but with a vision beyond my years, I asserted: "But it's the *way* you love us, Aunt Kay. The way *you* love us! Nothing else is like that. It's like your having some extra, beautiful power! Like Christmas," I added, by inspiration.

"No, Katherine, no," she faltered.

"I mean it, truly."

For what seemed an endless minute, Aunt Kay's reflective,

faraway eyes searched mine, till ultimately she drew a deep, tranquil breath. "Then perhaps, at long last, that may be the answer? Not in vain, after all, *not* in vain!" Afterwards, with a sudden lightening of tone, she asked: "How shall you wear your hair?"

"Oh, up, don't you think? Right on top of my head."

She swept it up from my nape, started pinning deftly. Watching clusters of ringlets begin to flower, I laughed with surprise, delight. I looked truly *mondaine*! This reassured her. "Katherine, I thought I had made you sad. Simply, seeing you go to your first ball made me think of somebody leaving a safe harbour."

"Aunt Kay," I confessed, reluctantly truthful, "it *is* really only a little party!"

"Nevertheless, I see lights in your eyes, candles in the windows! Take care, take care!"

"I'm still too young, I'm afraid," I said, though unhopefully, eyeing myself at all angles – I looked all of sixteen! Aunt Kay, with hardly less satisfaction, surveyed her handiwork. I stood up. But, "Just a minute," she cried, "I have something for you." She brought from the wardrobe, undid from its tissue wrappings, a little purse – or, more exactly, reticule: it had a silver drawstring, and silver embroidery outlined the floral scrolls of the pale brocade. The lining was of delicate sea-blue taffeta. "*Oh!*" I cried, overcome. "It's not new," she pointed out. And indeed as I held it nearer the candles, I saw the silk was faded, the silver tarnished. "No, old – how could it not be? It has a story. Mine."

"*Your* first ball, Aunt Kay?"

She inclined her head. "Dear, let it be a talisman, *and* a warning!"

While I wormed my way into my party dress (always with care for my head of curls), I heard the others still carolling, down in the parlour. Would Linda remember her promise to come and "fasten" me? I went to the stairhead and peered down, into the holly-strung shadowed well of the hall. Up, now more strongly, mounted the chorus voices. "*Hark, the Herald Angels.*" Our hard-worked piano gave out vibrating notes, like a harpsichord's. Then, first one by one, then in peals and tangles, began the town's church bells, ringing Christmas out. The reverberations now heard through the darkened air, somehow were more disturbing than Christmas morning's. The longed-for, beloved Day was nearing its close! Chilled by the look of the snow on the outer sill of the staircase's lofty uncurtained window, I thought of our town blotted out by its drapes of white. All bells paused, for a second, in which I heard, from the harbour's mouth, the insatiable roar of ocean. My young thoughts shrank timidly from that waste of waters. Inside the ruffled breast of my young girl's ball gown, my child's heart quavered. I gripped the stair rail, crying out: "Oh, no, no!"

At once, below me, the singing stopped. Out hastened Linda, my sturdy ten-year-old sister. "Katherine?" she shouted. "Was that you calling? You needn't have. I'm coming!" Breathless, she hurled herself up the stairs.

The dancing party was but five minutes away. To it, I'd have had to walk, in my heavy topcoat, school hood and overshoes, but now, because of the snow, I was to be "grand": the cab we thought of as Aunt Kay's had been ordered for me. Ah, I was nervous! I dawdled up in my attic, retied a ribbon, sat on my bed and crushed my back flounces, shook them out again, yawned. "Why, my goodness," Linda complained, "they're all *waiting* for you!" So I swept downstairs. Now came the enormous moment when I must show myself, mute as a portrait, framed in the parlour doorway.

So here I stood. Why was it that in that moment I saw the red lamplit walls, the assembled faces, with intensified vision, as though for the first and last time? Over me, like a wave, broke an all but overpowering sense of *home*. I looked, with a sort of wonder, from one to another of those familiar forms. Frederick kneeling on the hearthrug, absorbed in parading his new toys; Barbara, with her long braids and coltlike legs, curled into a corner of the big sofa; Mother still seated on the piano stool, sorting out tattered old sheets of Christmas music, her velvet skirts flowing round her into a bell. Linda, having dodged into the room behind me, picked up our cat and waltzed with it in her arms. Father stood, as so often, with his back to the fire. "Why, my girl," he declared, "one would hardly know you!" He accorded me a teasing, though lordly, bow. Then, as though moved by some instinct, he went across and put his hand on the back of Aunt Kay's chair. "You're a miracle worker," he told her, softly. She, erect in her black dress, smiled from him to me. Then her eyes, more than ever luminous, came to rest on the small, old reticule at my side.

Mother spun round slowly on the piano stool. "Come here," she said, and resettled my back flounces. "Now, stand back." Her gaze took a loving inventory of me, from top to toe. "Yes, you'll do," she said. "You look nice." Why did she sigh?

"She looks odd to me," remarked Frederick, somewhat severely.

"She has fifteen hooks down her back," gave out Linda, knowingly. She dropped the cat, plump, on the sofa, from whence it, too, fixed upon me an unblinking stare.

Father took out his watch, which became the signal for all the rest to turn and look at the clock. He listened. "Yes," he said, "here we are!" The cab was heard, crunching cautiously up the driveway. Everyone rose. I looked round, like a hunted thing, at the row of china dogs topping the bookcase, the faded woodwork view of Killarney over the mantle, the Turkey carpet worn by our many feet, the friendly troughs in capacious chairs. The centre circular table, under the lamp, glittered with sugary crumbs from the Christmas cake. "Please, no!" I suddenly wailed aloud.

Mother, alarmed, said: "Katherine, aren't you well?"

Father merely said: "Nonsense. Frederick, fetch Katherine's coat, cloak, jacket, or whatever she wears. Not fair to make the cab wait: it's busy tonight."

"I don't want to go."

Father bawled, with exasperation: "Then you want *what?*"

"To stay *here*, stay home with all of you!"

"She's shy," said Frederick. Reprieved, he felt, of his errand, he returned to the hearthrug and his tin soldiers.

"Shy!" cried Mother. "She's never been shy before. Come, now, Katherine, be a big girl! Why, there won't be a soul there, tonight, whom you don't know! Not a face, my darling, you haven't almost grown up with."

"But I haven't *grown* up!" I cried. "I *haven't* grown up!"

"The Patterson boys, the O'Sheas, the Gormans, the Lovells," Mother went on, as though repeating a soothing rune.

Barbara, next-in-age of my sisters, had stayed coiled up, cool as a mermaid, among the cretonne cushions. "*No* fascinating strangers," she now said, mockingly.[3]

At those words, what made my heart sink? No wild open seas, ahead, of romance? No beautiful dangers? "No," I agreed deflatedly, "I suppose not."

Aunt Kay had returned to her high-backed chair, composedly as though not a thing were happening. Her face was turned to the fire, away from us. She seemed withdrawn, wishful to be forgotten. What ancient scene did she see, in the dancing flames? Suddenly, vibrant and certain, her voice spoke out: "There's a stranger in everyone, at moments. Life would be a finished story, if there were not. Mysteries, surprises, and revelations, *those* keep our wits awake and our love glowing. Tonight, you're seeming to see a new Katherine, children. But she's not *another* Katherine; she's still yours – yours, with beauty added, or let's say the early dawn of it."

Linda cried: "Oh, make her *go* to the ball!"

Out there, we heard the cab horse stamp in the snow. "Of course she will go," said Aunt Kay. "And she'll dance for all of you. I am very proud of her." She turned to me. "Come, kiss me good night, and start!"

They wrapped me up, and swept me into the cab. Inside, it was cavernous and smelled musty. Father shut the door; Mother gave a last, eloquent tap on the glass. Outlined against the glow of the hall within, I saw my grouped family. They waved; I drove away. Round me, where were the familiar landmarks? At this hour, seen by the wobbling light of the dim carriage lamps, our streets appeared to be those of an unknown city. Past me went unidentified archways, snowdrifted porches and blinded shopfronts. It was slippery going, downhill, till we reached the quay. There, we whipped up and went jouncing over the cobbles. Ahead beamed the festive house; on our flank, below, lay the water, silent and dark.

I did not know how I felt: I was in a turmoil. Through the tight-closed window I sent a glance up the crowded face of our town. Then, all was well. Yes, above me still burned the sentinel candles! Steadily, tier on tier, gleamed those points of light; each flame, on its coloured wax stem, a symbolic heart shape. Each stood for a home! It was still Christmas, going with me encircling me. Nothing *was* left behind.

Happiness

Our home is an old farm, in orchard country. Overnight there had been a light fall of snow, on to which, as we neared the end of our journey, the moon cast shadows of apple trees. Silvery stretched the landscape, here a big barn, there a small steepled church, alike hushed in midwinter peace. Streams, not yet frozen, tinkled under the bridges. In the back of the family car, Carol and I sat wedged among endless packages: resourceful Louise, my married sister, having combined meeting us at the station with a last-minute burst of shopping all around the village. In front, to the slow-down of her driving, three of her children surged, singing loudly, "Carols for Carol." Above the noise, their mother flung back news items over her shoulder. "Alec brought the tree: it's as fine as ever we had – Poor Cissie came in on the bus this morning – You should see the cake; Mother let Frankie frost it, didn't she, Frankie? – Uncle Willard's in one of his regular Christmas moods, cross as a bear." We laughed, yet, as the car turned into our lane, something began to tighten round my heart. How could it not, this time? As never before, grief, loss impinged on a Christmas homecoming. Quickly, Carol, as though our feelings were one, gave my hand a reassuring squeeze. Close together, we watched those familiar windows come, glowing, nearer. Soon, out burst a flood of light onto the snow: framed in the door stood Mother, arms wide open.

Indoors, holly wreathed round the hall lantern made the air pungent with hot berries. Warmth quivered from the kind crimson walls: not large, the hall seemed smaller than ever, overflowing with the entire family. One small new face darted around: Charlie, my solid ten-year-old brother, had as guest a boy of his age, Blinks, a high-strung child with goggle spectacles. Down the stairs came Alec, Louise's tall handsome husband, their baby chuckling on his shoulder. On the outskirts fluttered Cissie Potter, and from the living-room arch glowered Uncle Willard.

Not to speak unkindly of Uncle Willard we could have done without him. This ancient bachelor was noted for thinking of nobody but himself. Deafness alternated, in Uncle Willard, with a hearing that could be inconveniently sharp. Principally of course, he was Mother's burden. He'd moved in not long after Father died, on pretext of giving Mother "support." I suspect we suited him, though he declined to show it. Mother claimed Uncle Willard needed affection; we children did our best, though we doubted it.

"Where," he loudly asked, "is this gal with the broken heart, this miss we keep hearing so much about?"

What had happened to Carol had hit us all. No hint of anything wrong till Jim called Mother (who is his aunt) long distance. "I'm sorry," he announced, she told us later, "but I won't be coming for Christmas." Mother flared up: "Not come, when Carol's coming? When you two've been parted for half a year?" From planets away came his curt rejoinder: "That's just it." The line then seemed to go dead, leaving Mother demanding: "Jim, what's the matter?" Finally he told her: "Better ask Carol." He then hung up.

She could conclude but one thing, rightly. The engagement was broken.

Head awhirl with Christmas, frantic with preparations, Mother stared at the telephone, then rapidly asked for a city number. Yes, there *was* Carol; moreover, with the letter still in her hand. Mother's was the first voice to come through since the girl had read Jim's shattering words. "He's right to be honest; I'd hate him not to be honest," Carol kept piteously repeating, adding: "You mustn't blame him!" Then, though, a sob tore its way through her. That sound was more than Mother could stand, being helpless to comfort from where she was: our home, miles away in the country. She called me, Liz (also there in the city), saying, "Go straight to Carol!" and told me why. Though this hit our entire family, Mother realised I would be hurt doubly. Jim had been always my hero cousin; Carol was my dearest-beloved friend.

Soon I was in her apartment, she in my arms. Speechless for minutes, we sat on her studio bed. All round, in heart-breaking contrast, the small room was bright with pre-Christmas litter. She'd been in the midst of packing when the mail came. It was I who burst out: "I *can't* understand Jim! To do this to you, and to do it *now!*"

She protested: "No, Liz – think! How could he go through with a Christmas of 'acting up'? With me, in front of *you* all, who know him so well? See for yourself!" She gave me the letter.

She had been right: these few lines of Jim's left little margin for doubt or hope. I winced. Now I am older, now I know more about psychology, I can see why Jim, by nature kind and protective, said nothing to lessen the shock, soften the blow. And what had forced him to this? The same old story: a "someone else." Separated from Carol by his work, in a distant country, Jim had fallen prey to such loneliness as unsteadies a man.

The end of Jim's letter startled me. "I have no right," he concluded, "to ask you anything, now. Yet I do ask this: will you go to them, all the same? This can wreck their Christmas; you could still save it. Happiness goes where you are. Goodbye, Carol."

I handed the letter back. "Carol," I said timidly, "*is* it too much to ask?"

She stood before me, pushing her fair hair back. "It isn't that, Liz. Wouldn't I make you sad?"

"Imagine our sadness to feel we'd lost you!" For a minute I felt an inner struggle go on. Then our eyes met. Calmly she said, "I should like to come."

Now, here she was in our midst.

Head high, radiant under the lantern, Carol, unbuttoning her coat, stood smiling around her. "Good to see you, Carol," Alec remarked, taking her coat, in his easy brotherly way. She returned, "It's wonderful to be back."

Meanwhile, no quieting Uncle Willard! "Eh? *Where?*" he grumbled. "Where's she hiding herself, this Miss Broken-heart?"

I helplessly shook my head.

"A-*ha!*" he cackled, "last minute, you brought Miss Pretty instead. Better fun, eh? What's the proverb? 'Weep and you weep alone.' Can't pretend I'm sorry: damp tears catch *me* right in the bones!" He uttered a snort. "If there's one thing I can't abide, it's a whiny woman." Uncle Willard gave point to his last remark by aiming a baleful look at poor Cissie Potter, in "upset" retreat from the rest of us. "One's enough in *this* house," declared Uncle Willard. "The older, the sillier!"

"Uncle!" I protested.

It inclined to be a theory of Cissie Potter's that nobody else's sorrows went truly deep. This girlhood friend of Mother's had succeeded in pickling herself in romantic grief. She modelled herself, in spite of advancing years, on a Victorian lovelorn maiden. Her moist-violet eyes were given to rolling, her figure was ultra-willowy and her voice plaintive. Immune, through spinsterhood, from domestic cares, Cissie had leisure for brooding. Genuinely, she liked to be called "Poor Cissie." As to what had dealt the death-blow to her heart, Mother remained evasive. Cissie herself favoured a veil of mystery. "She needs taking out of herself," Mother would say; for which reason, we had her for every Christmas. Our home is old-fashioned.

This Christmas, our outstanding family trouble banished lesser concerns. Before the blow dealt by Jim to Carol, Mother'd wondered if Cissie would choose to be "overcome" by being under one roof with two blissful lovers. What did not occur to us was that she still might play a big emotional scene, the reverse way. I scented the danger the minute I observed the eager blue bobbing of Cissie's hair bow: she could hardly wait to get going, intrude, and probe. *We* honoured Carol's reserve; loving her for her desperate youthful courage. To Cissie both were incomprehensible. Her eyes already were fixed upon my friend, morbidly, indeed, avidly. *That* must be stopped, I thought!

This evening, early to bed. Carol and I shared a raftered attic, faintly smelling of apples. Away in a crib under the sloping ceiling slumbered Louise's Frankie: cheeks pink still with the contentment left by her happy day. Tucked in the crook of one plump elbow, my niece held, tonight, all her heart desired: a battered blue velvet monkey. How possible to be *satisfied*, when one's six! I asked myself, does one grow harder to please? Nineteen we both were, Carol and I. Already, life involved one in desperate risks. Yet would that be helped? If one *were* a woman, be a woman one must! Frankie would find that, someday.

I put out the lamp. Below, we heard the grandfather clock strike nine: for *me*, after that, nothing more.

What woke me, I could not at first tell. *"Carol?"* Her bed though still warm was empty. Utterly still was the house, with its many sleepers, till I heard, again, that insistent, bewildered crying. Tugging on my robe, I investigated. Across the head of the staircase a door stood open: I looked into the other attic which moonlight filled. In here was Charlie's kingdom, fiercely guarded; stark as a mountain hut. Tonight, two beds were in here.

One bed was jerked by restrained sobbing. On it, twisted into a knot, Blinks lay, fists crammed into his eyes. On the edge sat Carol in a white wrapper. Tousled, in his nightshirt, my young brother hovered anxiously round. "Blinks feels badly," he pointed out, in a hoarse whisper.

"I'm sorry. Sick?"

"No, but he couldn't settle. Keeps jumping out, and now he's trod on his spectacles. He can't see."

"Tomorrow, we'll – "

Carol said: "I don't think it's only that."

"No, it's not," said Charlie. "It's this first Christmas without his mother."

"Where is she?"

"She – she isn't there any more."

Leaning over, Carol eased open one of the tight-clenched fists. "Blinks," she said, "I don't exactly know how it is for you, but I do almost. Both of us losing someone: it's awful. No good pretending it's not."

He let fall the other fist, rolled his head around. "K-keeps coming back on me, when I don't expect."

"I know," she said.

"You do?" he asked.

"So I'm glad you're here," Carol declared, "and I'm glad I am. That's company, isn't it? Let's plan something."

"What'll we plan?"

"Build us a hut. Invent a surprise together. We'll see, or you or I might happen to dream some idea."

He thought that over. "Want me to go to sleep?"

"Well, it would help." She rose, but only to straighten the twisted blanket. Quieter every minute under her touch, Blinks let out his breath in a great sigh. "Wish I could properly see you," he murmured, "I just see *white*. Don't, anyway, go," he demanded. "Sing. Sing, 'Silent Night, Holy Night.'" So she sang.

Christmas Eve it was, when we woke next morning. The boys were off in the woods. Mother, busy in the kitchen, made frequent sorties; Alec chopped; Louise made yet another dash to the village; Frankie shifted armfuls of kittens or dangling puppies from scene to scene. Hum concentrated around the parlour, where the Christmas tree was being arrayed. The baby tottered delightedly in. A ladder stood by the tree. All other years, it was Jim who fixed the tree's lighting. Connection was apt to be tricky: tangles of cord, dully jewelled with unlit bulbs, messed the floor. Cissie's entrance was spoilt, she all but tripped up.

Uncle Willard scowled, crouching over the game of chess at which he was beating himself. Cissie in a flash took in the lighting predicament. Her earrings, like crystallised tears, swayed as she cried: "How one misses a man!"

Carol scaled the ladder rapidly to the top, where she busied herself.

I declared: "I could *perfectly* do it, if I knew how to."

"No one could ever, like Jim! It scarcely feels like Christmas without him. Though of course," Cissie went on, with a glance at Carol, "under the *circumstances*, he could hardly come! It's a dreadful loss to us all!" Stepping back, she placed her heel on a bulb, which exploded.[1]

"Oh, for the Lord's sake!" yelled Uncle Willard, shoving the chessboard from him. "What's this all about?" He sneered at the cord. "Any fool could do that. Show me!"

Uncle Willard's dexterity was unknown to us. In a trice, he had done a neat job.

"There!" he spat out, having made a successful test. Cissie, bored, meanwhile drifted away. I looked up to laugh with Carol, and was shocked to see her turn very white. "Cissie may be mean," she said, "but she's far from wrong. I *have* deprived you of Jim. If *I* hadn't come – "

"Carol, *he* couldn't have, anyway."

"You can't mean, he'd feel you're angry with him? Liz, you're *not*, are you?"

"I guess we're willing to understand," I said, after a pause, "but we need time."

"Let's get on with the tree," she said quickly. Twirling a gilt-glass bell, she admitted: "I can't help wondering where he is, where he's going to go."

("With *'her,'*" I bitterly thought.) Uncle Willard, now halfway back to his game, had a spasm of perfect hearing.

"What, Jim?" he exclaimed, "faugh, there *is* a fool! Write him right off, Miss Pretty, and serve him right! You're one in a thousand, miss. A splendid gal."

Not a hope for the spectacles, this side Christmas. "Poor kid, it's hard to know what to do for him, barely knows where he is," lamented Louise. "And on top of everything! You don't mean Charlie took him off in the woods, half-blind? Why?"

"They were cutting boughs."

"Whatever for?" my sister said.

"These were for Carol, special. Their plan or something. Those two came home dragging half the woods!"

"Heavens! Whatever's doing out there in the barn, so late? Or did Frankie or somebody leave the lights on?"

"In there's where they're building."

"Christmas Eve's one big secret!" Balancing the baby on one knee, Louise blew through the fluffy curls on its pate. Outside the living-room window, the last pink dusk lay over the snow. The telephone rang. "That's probably Alec's mother," she said, sliding the baby to me. Whoever it was, it didn't take long: back came Louise. "Of all the mystification!"

"Well?"

"Somebody wanted to know whether Carol's here. 'Why yes, of course,' I said. *Then*, whoever-it-was hung up!"

"Louise – the voice?"

She looked at me strangely. "Liz, I couldn't be *sure*."

"Well, I never!" cried Cissie Potter. Still with her pearl kid gloves on, she delicately opened the invitation. All of us, this minute, were back from church: in our ears a joyous confusion of bells and music, we assembled to see what the matter was. She went on: "I don't think I ever *knew* such a crowded day!" Unwilling to let the missive out of her hands, she also could not resist passing it around.

It ran: "Miss C. Potter's company is much desired at a Reception for her at our Castle, the Barn, Christmas afternoon. Three o'clock, which should not interfere with her taking her Nap before Christmas dinner. P. S. Better dress warm."

"They thought of everything," Mother remarked. "Cissie, I call that flattering."

"Are *you* asked?"

Mother shook a tactful head. She'd been told she might peep, but was not invited. Nor, we let Cissie know, were any of us. She drew a tremendous breath. "Then – I'm singled out?" She was in a whirl.

Hardly could Cissie wait for the stroke of three. We watched her pick her way to the barn. The door opened, then closed.

Undecided whether to peep or not, Mother was influenced by our curiosity. She found her coat, and followed. Returning, she vanished into the kitchen to see to dinner. We know, of old, when something has been too much. When she *did* tell us, she used these curious words: "It was the most innocent sight I ever saw." Candlelit, at the far end of the dark barn, "Our Castle" consisted of frail boughs, leaning together. Only faith and trust, out of which it was built, can have kept "Our Castle" from falling down. Open in front, it was something between an arbour and a fragile cave. The two keeping house in it, Blinks and Carol, using scarlet quilts as mantles for the occasion, were engaged in doing honour to Cissie, who sat between and above them, enthroned on pillows. Cissie, Mother recounted, was transformed. She revealed a responsive lovely face, from which piteous sillinesses were all gone.

Mother had never realised Cissie's simplicity. What a drear fate, how it brings out the worst, year after year, to be nothing more than "put up with!" Standing back in the darkness of the barn, Mother was smitten to the heart. Taught by their own desolation, these two children had headed straight to this other desolate soul. Their understanding had pierced the poor, foolish mask. Not for themselves only was "Our Castle." They threw it open: all it was, as they were, that they had to offer. They had sensed the fathomless need of the unloved.

Our Christmas tree made the room larger, mysterious and dazzling. One never remembers a tree quite as it is; there is always more, each year. It reflected itself in the uncurtained glass of the parlour windows. We like to think of its shining far out over the dark country.

Round it we moved, under the spell of its treasure. Mother called the names, Frankie bestowed the gifts. There was a clasping-on of necklaces, a bouncing of woolly balls, a whirling of clockwork toys set going. When kisses of gratitude had subsided, there was still, however, an unaccountable feeling of expectancy. What more *ought* there to be?

Mother invited Cissie to play the piano Obligingly, Cissie slid off her bangles and struck one or two sprightly chords, only to pause, hands in the air. Carol, in her shimmering party dress, walked straight across to one the windows: face pressed close to a pane, shielding her eyes, she stayed looking out.

"What is it, Carol?" asked Mother.

"I think it's Jim," she said.

The inevitable happens so very calmly. She left the room to meet him, leaving us waiting. All that agony of trouble to be unravelled, in a few minutes? Why did it have to be? The children absorbed in their new toys, old Uncle comatose in his rigid chair, were not to ask; we others might never know. Closer to one another as we wondered, we sat silently in the light of the tree, reliving these last strange days, moment by moment. What victories, all the same! *Could* a Christmas have been more beautiful than this one, lit by her courage? Soon, midnight would strike: this Christmas of ours would be over. Let us forever remember its dear happiness!

UNPUBLISHED
AND UNFINISHED
SHORT STORIES

The Bazaar

$\mathbf{M}$rs. Bude was depressed, when she woke, by a dark sky; she heard heavy rain falling. She parted the muslin modesty-blinds to look out – the whole row of back gardens with their arbours and aerials[1] wore the same sad air of subjection to circumstance. Mrs. Bude, however, consoled herself with the thought that as it must have been raining since before sunrise it was likely to clear by eleven. Mr. Bude also got up, very silent and red, shaved in the bathroom, dressed, had breakfast and left for the office. He was not interested in the bazaar. Mrs. Bude looked through him intensely, as though he did not exist. "You've got a wet day," he said, more kindly but as though he had always warned her, wheeling out his bicycle.

Mrs. Bude set out soon after ten, leaving preparations for Mr. Bude's midday dinner to the girl, who was becoming dependable. On her way, she called in at the carriers, as she had promised, to make sure the hired china would be delivered. Two or three residential roads converged at this end of the village; black laburnum pods drooping over the pavement stirred and swished in the rain. Gates clicked open and Mrs. Bude, glancing behind, saw other bazaar helpers, also in mackintoshes, hurrying urgently and all slung over with parcels. Mrs. Bude, however, did not wait for the others. She had a sense of high pressure, and was anxious also for a few words alone with Lady Potter.

In the village, people were standing alert in the shop doorways, asking each other in happy detachment what would become of the bazaar in all this rain, and where Lady Potter was proposing to put the band. There never had been a band before; it was an innovation and seemed to have tempted providence. Mrs. Bude, looking neither to left nor to right, herself wondered if wet drums were audible, also what happened if rain got down a bassoon. Her wet red mackintosh creaked with her haste; in spite of the ventilation holes she began to feel stuffy inside it, for this was July. Rain blurred her glasses and streamed down her kind pink face with its perpetual half-smile of diffidence and astonishment. In addition to everything else she carried two trays that kept slipping and some long rolls of Denniston's crêpe paper that it was important to keep dry.

At the gate of the Hall she met Miss Singleton in a sou'wester, with an expression of resolute optimism. "Oh Mrs. Bude," she cried, "here you are! Well, *well*," she added, looking up at the sky.

"Well, *well*," said Mrs. Bude piously.

"I must tell you – of course this is confidential – Lady Potter is very much put out: Mrs. Space has resigned from the Sports Committee!"

"Gracious!" exclaimed Mrs. Bude, almost dropping a tray. But she had quite a distinct sense of pleasurable excitement. "When did it happen?"

"Last night. The committee met in the grounds to make last arrangements, and — well feeling had been running rather high you know, for some time, about the clock golf. Perhaps it was mentioned to you? Several helpers mentioned the matter to me in confidence. So last night at committee Mrs. Armitage happened to speak rather hastily: it seems she had not been consulted. So Mrs. Space said that things being as they were, and owing to the attitude of certain people who should not be named, she did not see that she could be of further use, and left the committee. She seemed very much upset — "

Mrs. Bude plucked at Miss Singleton's sleeve and they stepped quickly sideways into the rhododendrons, for down the avenue came Mrs. Space, very fast, with a set expression. She had felt it her duty to tell Lady Potter that though she was the last to consider a personal matter, her feelings had been very much hurt. She swished past within an inch of the rhododendrons.

Mrs. Bude and Miss Singleton turned the bend of the avenue; the tents came into view. The bazaar was to be held in the Hall paddock. Three pence extra was to be charged at the further gate for a view of the Italian terraces and the walled garden. Though this week's rain might have squashed the flowers, you could admire the cucumbers in the frames and see Lady Potter's peas growing — they said she had peas at the Hall from May to November — and, on the terraces, wind in and out of the *fleurs-de-lys* neatly edged with box. "I do not consider three pence too much to charge," the Vicar had said, and though Lady Potter looked modest the General Purposes Committee had agreed.

The three marquees were up, with their sides hooked open, also the little tent for the fortune teller, with Captain Winch, who was to be disguised as Wise Meg the Gypsy this afternoon, walking critically round and round it. He had brought some Hungarian hangings to drape inside, but nobody would give him any pins.

"Paula," he said, "I'm sure *you* could find me some pins." But Paula Potter, walking rapidly past in Wellington boots, took no notice.

Paula Potter had no heart for the bazaar. She had, it is true, looked forward to walking about in the sun in a chiffon frock, taking Lady Hottenham, who was to open this bazaar, from stall to stall. Lady Hottenham spent ten pounds at every bazaar she opened, and Paula had promised to divide her equally among the stall holders. But yesterday Paula had written to break off her engagement with a young man.[2] She had not found the young man sufficiently ardent; he wrote dull letters and was too economical to telephone from London every day. But today, crossing hers, there had arrived a letter from the young man really full of ardour and suggesting Portugal for the honeymoon. Paula sent off three telegrams and did not see how she could be expected to attend to the bazaar. She darted restlessly in and out of the tents but was most disobliging. She was a nice girl with four freckles and a mouth like a raspberry.

Lady Potter in a Burberry went picking her way from tent to tent. She smiled sympathetically, hoping they would not ask her for anything more. She would rather not know if the tea urns had not arrived or the trestles were unsatisfactory. She avoided groups in dispute; when anything was referred to her, her eyes distended with apprehension, like a rabbit's. "I'm sure that would do excellently," she frequently said, and "I quite agree with you: that would be delightful." In one hand she carried a pair of garden scissors, from her arm hung a basket containing a note-book and a ball of string. She swerved[3] whenever she saw Captain Winch, for fear he might ask her for pins again. Powder, displaced by the rain, lay in clots at the side of her nose. She felt in some way responsible for the weather; this agitated her very much. She saw Mrs. Bude coming but had no time to retreat, so she smiled anxiously.

Mrs. Bude said she particularly wanted a few words with Lady Potter because she feared there had been some slight misunderstanding about the position of the flower stall. "I should like to feel," she said, after twenty minutes' discussion, "that I had acted for the best."

"I think you were quite right," said Lady Potter.

"I should not like to feel," Mrs. Bude continued, "that any feeling might arise – "

"I am sure there will be nothing of that sort," said Lady Potter, longing to go in and lie down.

"I am sorry to hear, Lady Potter," said Mrs. Bude, coming a little closer and lowering her voice, "that there has been this little mis-understanding between Mrs. Space and Mrs. Armitage. I always feel myself that one should not let personal feeling come in when one is working for charity. For instance, yesterday evening I was inclined to be quite upset over this little misunderstanding about the flower stall. It quite upset me; I could hardly take my tea. But as I said to Mr. Bude, we must all work together. I remember saying to Mr. Bude at the time, 'I always feel it is a mistake to let any personal feeling – '"

But at this point Captain Winch came up to ask Mrs. Bude, as a new arrival, if she could let him have any pins. "I'm sure ladies always have pins about them," he said intimately.

Lady Potter, replying to an imaginary signal, moved quickly away.

Lady Potter was a widow; her son, Sir Harold, had arrived yesterday with a Cambridge friend. The young men had understood they were to be the Sports Committee; finding that they were not,[4] they had returned to the smoking-room, taking the Vicar's youngest daughter with them to play the gramophone. The girl, anxious and with a strong sense of impropriety, talked heroically at the under-graduates, saying, "That's rather jolly," and asking for records they had not heard of and did not wish to own. Miss Singleton, who had not been long at a loss to account for her disappearance, walked several times past the smoking-room windows and at last put her face to the glass, saying, "I'm so sorry, Betty, but when you have finished I should be glad of your advice about draping the stall." Miss Singleton had been asking Harold to tea ever since he was five and considered herself an old friend of the family's, whereas the Vicar was quite new.

When Betty returned to the tent, very cross, Miss Singleton was kneeling down on a mackintosh, draping the front of the tea stall with loops of pink muslin. She seemed to be getting on nicely, her sou'wester was pushed right back in creative excitement and Betty knew she had disturbed her from nothing but spite. Betty was glad when Captain Winch, who had been waiting behind Miss Singleton, sly as a magpie, slipped quietly off with her box of pins.

Now that the little matter had been put right, Mrs. Bude spent a wonderful morning. She had the stall to herself; the others would not arrive till this afternoon. Hers was not a very good head,[5] she was over-susceptible to colour; as more and more flowers were carried in, her manner, Paula observed, became really foolish. You would have thought this a private festival. Shaking her sweet-pea into jugs she hummed, she sang; she sorted her roses out into shades, contrasted them, massed them. With a sense of delicious guilt[6] she touched their petals – she knew now, but could not explain, why women went wrong – "They're so sweet, they're so dark," she said – no, they were pale too: it was not that. She thought, "I should make quite a florist," dipping her face into the sweet-pea. The flowers filled the warm, damp air of the tent; they curved yet had wide wings. She flushed and her hands tingled – "I wish I were like you; I wish I were you." Here were the delphiniums with no nonsense about them – Mrs. Bude collected herself and put the delphiniums in Norman[7] jugs – and carnations she thought of wiring into sprays: she pictured pearls and a bare shoulder. She hummed, she sang, she had her own pins: no one interrupted her. She covered the front of the stall with Denniston's green crêpe paper and pinned on pink letters she had cut out at home with "Buy my Pretty Posies."

Lady Potter, passing, thought the idea charming, but frowned: she could not help feeling annoyed with Harold and Paula. Every time the telephone rang Paula sprang in through a window and could be heard pounding across the library. And Harold certainly needed a father's guidance. Already he had offended Captain Winch, and now from some misdirected idea of hospitality he kept coming out to offer the Vicar whiskey when the Vicar was busy pegging down tapes for the potato races. "What about clock golf?" Harold's friend kept saying tactlessly, standing by. The Vicar was already very much upset about Mrs. Space and had had a long talk with Lady Potter about her, wondering whether anything could be done.

Mrs. Bude fetched a Mrs. Bird and a Miss Brown to look at her flower stall. Mrs. Bird said, "You really have great taste," and Miss Brown said that she was artistic. So Mrs. Bude went back with them to admire the fancy stall. A nightdress case covered with pink bows was arranged in the centre, for Lady Hottenham to buy.[8] If Lady Hottenham did not buy the nightdress case[9] it would have to be raffled. "But her daughter is engaged to be married," said Miss Brown optimistically.

Meanwhile, the sky had lightened, the rain stopped. Lady Potter went in to lie down for an hour before lunch. Mrs. Bude, plucking shreds of fern from her dress, went home to dinner.

The sun came out a little way; only this was needed, the tents began to steam. Soon steam seemed to be going up from the whole garden; passing between the rhododendrons up the avenue, in a dull glitter, you would have thought you were in the tropics. To the empty paddock, trampled already as though it had been the scene of a rodeo, luncheon sounds came out from the diningroom, where Lady Potter, economising her forces, ate with her mouth shut but Harold's friend laughed loudly.

Mrs. Bude, in sprigged crêpe de chine, was the first to appear again. She walked in and out of the tents, inordinately happy. She was not a vain woman, but only her reluctance to miss Lady Hottenham's arrival tore her from her looking glass. Mr. Bude[10] had not noticed her appearance, but she was, as a matter of fact, very smart. She wore a lace hat, she had exchanged her spectacles for a pair of rimless pince-nez and touched up her nose with white *papiers poudrés*. She wore white kid gloves, though she knew she would have to take them off. She was forty-two, but excitement filled her and a kind of holiness, as though this were a wedding day. Her look, craning a little, ready for admiration, went from stall to stall: round the empty tents her goodness of heart went with her like a companion.

Mrs. Armitage came in; they smiled gaily and glanced at each other's dresses. Then all the other helpers began to come up the avenue. Soon the band was playing selections from *The Mikado*.[11] "It is very loud," said Mrs. Armitage, "we shall hardly hear ourselves speak." But she smiled with gratification. At the first of the Hall steps they could see Sir Harold helping Lady Hottenham out of her car. She was warm and rather crushed-looking, in a good deal of lace, as though she had not been properly packed. Paula came out in a chiffon dress, without the least air of pleasurable anticipation. Lady Potter, upstairs, thought it was too bad of Lady Hottenham to be so punctual.

Lady Hottenham declared the bazaar open on some duck-boards covered with a red rug under a plane tree at the corner of the paddock. The crowd[12] was, naturally, silent and a large number of people stood round in a semi-circle. Gentlemen, with an idea that the ceremony was religious, bared their heads. The bazaar was in aid of the cottage hospital. "It often seems to me," said Lady Hottenham, "that health is happiness . . . I often think this is very true. Lives of great men all remind us that we should do something for the unfortunate. The unfortunate are in our midst: your beautiful cottage hospital is not a mile from here. I passed it on my drive here this afternoon and thought how gay it looked with those nice geraniums, and yet how helpful to the unfortunate. I see that besides the stalls with their artistic needlework and tempting array of, er, of cakes and all sorts of needlework, which I hope to visit, there are many sideshows and entertainments provided. Even cokernut shies: I am sure we all love to shy a cocoanut.[13] I am sure we shall all spend a very gay afternoon, while keeping in mind the dear cottage hospital. I have much pleasure in declaring the bazaar open."

They all clapped; tears came to Mrs. Bude's eyes and she split the sides of her white kid gloves. Gertie Lewis, in a pink sash, stepped forward to present a bouquet. She ducked, and Lady Hottenham kissed the brim of her bonnet. The band played *Samson and Delilah*[14] and they all streamed back to the tents.

Lady Hottenham admired the nightdress case but bought two dozen guest towels. "It is all so tempting," she said, and bought some white net squares to put over milk-jugs, that were already bespoke. Paula Potter accompanied her, carrying a basket; they moved on to the flower stall. Here trade was not very brisk; Mrs. Bude had sent the two Miss Gibbses away because it embarrassed her to stand all three in a row, looking out for customers." I should like to take this whole stall home as it stands!" exclaimed Lady Hottenham rapturously. "Buy my Pretty Posies," Lady Hottenham read aloud. "How nice," she added, and asked if they sold vegetables. She bought two bulb bowls and trailed off, murmuring. Hot brown light came through the canvas roof of the tent; Mrs. Bude's patent leather shoes began to pinch: she sat down on a chair behind the stall, her face on a level with the sweet-pea. Her thoughts took coral pink wings and began to fly far away. She had a half-crown and a florin in one saucer, seven pence halfpenny in the other.[15] How odd, she thought, if this were my livelihood.

Paula Potter made over Lady Hottenham to Harold, quite unscrupulously, and ran away by herself behind the tents. "It's absurd," she muttered. She tripped over a tent peg and swore; when she looked up there stood her young man, crimson, opening and shutting his mouth at her like a fish.

"I have nothing to say," said Paula icily.

"I know," agreed the young man. "But look here – "

"This is a bazaar. I believe I did once mention we were going to have a bazaar. Not of course that you could be expected to read a letter. But still I believe I did once happen to mention a bazaar. This is the bazaar now; it's going on: these are the tents."

"I know. But look here – "

"I expect you just thought we were going to live in tents. I expect if I had happened to mention we were going to live in tents you wouldn't – "

The young man, raising his voice, said: "But I came down – "

"We can't brawl here," said Paula. It was now ridiculous to reflect that she had spent, this morning, seven and six on telegrams. She turned and walked[16] quickly away, tripping over more tent pegs, feeling wonderfully cheerful. "I shall always," she thought, "remember the bazaar with affection."

The young man, after a glance at her disappearing green heels, walked placidly in the other direction. He had the afternoon before him. It was now ridiculous to reflect he had just spent twenty-five shillings on a train fare. He found Harold's friend and asked him to give him a drink.[17]

Miss Jolley Has No Plans for the Future

"I have no idea," she said. "I haven't had time to think yet. The experience has been awful, but has showed me what true friends I have. Yes, that was Miss Kisby I left the ccurt with. She is a sweet girl, we were friends at school . . . Well you might, of course, but she's rather shy. She came out in all the photographs with her arm up . . . Well, I am rather. I could hardly expect to be otherwise, I suppose. I don't get knocked up easily, but of course there are limits . . . No I suppose I oughtn't, that's what they've all been saying. But at the moment, though it may sound funny, I don't seem to notice if I'm alore or not."

She got up and straightened a pleated parchment lampshade. "Things seem to get to look all wrong," she said, "while one's away . . . Oh thanks. Yes,[1] perhaps I will," she said, accepting a cigarette. "There ought to be some in the flat, but I don't know." Laughing with a good deal of bravado, she added: "To tell you the truth, I'd got out of the way of it lately . . . Yes, I *would* rather not. I'm sure you see how I feel. I might feel I could talk to you if you were just a friend, but I don't want any more to go into the Press. I must simply put all thought of him out of my mind . . . No, my feelings are *not* unchanged. They are very much changed. I don't know who got hold of the idea that they were unchanged. I never said so and when Miss Kisby showed me the bit in the paper I was very much annoyed. At a time like this it seems to me that people rout[2] round in the most unscrupulous way, and put down all sorts of things that have never been said. I *never* said that my feelings for Mr. Wallace were unchanged, and I'm quite certain Miss Kisby didn't either. Unless she was so shy that I[3] misunderstood what she meant.

"Well, I'm sorry if the other would look better in your paper, but I simply cannot pretend. I'm not that sort of girl. I would have been prepared to stand by Mr. Wallace to the end, but he betrayed my trust and upset me very much. So that naturally my feelings have changed. If you must bring in Mr. Wallace's name in connection with mine in your paper, which I should prefer you not to, I should prefer you to say that I would be returning Mr. Wallace's ring immediately if he were allowed to receive parcels in – where he is. As it is, I shall lodge it with the bank till he – till he *is* allowed to receive parcels . . . Yes, it was a nice ring, pearl and amethyst . . . Yes, we bought it together . . . Yes, he was free with money. Of course I had no idea – [4]

"Yes, I have got some. I haven't had time yet to – Anyhow, there isn't an open fireplace in this flat. I must take them round to Miss Kisby's: her flat's more old-fashioned . . . No, that's out of the question. No, I simply couldn't possibly really. No matter for how much . . . No, not even for twice that. Yes, I know girls do, but I do think there are limits. I never have been able to see how they could. Besides – No, please don't go on; you really will upset me . . . No, I suppose there *was* no harm in your just asking. I know many women do . . . No, not for five *thousand*.

"Well, if you care just to *see* an envelope. Or I may have a quite social note or two, when we first met, you see . . . How sticky this lock's got. I wonder if damp affects locks. This flat's been shut up, you see . . . No, I can really, thank you . . . Yes, it is a remarkable writing. I always have thought so. Yes, writing does make a differ-ence, doesn't it. A difference to how you feel when you get a letter. But I remember a friend of mine who knows about handwriting said I ought to be careful. She didn't like the g's. But nothing anyone says makes any difference, does it. I mean, when you feel like I did.

"Oh, are you putting down that about the g's? . . . Photograph an *envelope?* Oh all right, if you want to. All right, I suppose if you want to . . . Here's one when I was in⁵ Brighton. George Street, Brighton. That's three g's. That was one of the first . . . No, I shan't want it back: that'll make one less to burn. I don't know why I always kept the envelopes too . . . I'll put the rest away . . . No, please *don't* start that again. It really does upset me. You see, I *couldn't*, possibly.

"No, I had *no* idea. I thought it was the Stock Exchange. It was all very well for that beast to say in court that he didn't see how a business girl could be so stupid. But I've always worked for publishers; I didn't know about the Stock Exchange. *Did* I look a fool in court? No one will tell me. I did think it was unfair to say that, I did think it was unfair . . .

"Oh, thanks; it's very nice of you to say so. I knew I had to keep calm. And of course clothes *are* important. Miss Kisby lent me the fur. I'm glad you thought it looked well . . . Oh, now you are being personal! . . . No, I never have used much make-up; I suppose my skin's my best point. Do you know, I once saw Mr. Wallace looking at the fur. He must have been surprised, because he thought he knew all my clothes and wondered where I'd got it – Yes, that's one thing I *can* tell you about my future: I shall be buying a number of new clothes. I've rather taken against all the clothes I've got now. I suppose it's natural, really . . .

"Yes, I know I could. But I *won't make money that way*. Please don't re-open the subject. It's really not in good taste –

" – Oh the telephone! (I'm so jumpy!) Excuse me a minute, won't you . . . Hullo? Hullo, dear? . . . No I'm not, just now; someone's here . . . Yes . . . Yes it is as a matter of fact. But this really is the last. I can't bear any more . . . Yes, I know I said I wouldn't but I forgot and went to the door myself . . . No, not a word . . . No, of course I wouldn't . . . No, certainly not . . . My dear, don't you *know* I wouldn't . . . Oh . . . Oh, aren't you . . . Well, of course if your mother says not. I know she thinks you've been doing too much anyhow . . . No, I'm *not* hurt: don't be so silly . . . No, I'll be all *right*, I tell you. I like being alone. Yes, I've got everything . . . Yes, I've got aspirin . . . Yes, I could, but I don't *want* to . . . Don't be so nervy, dear. Your mother's right, you ought to go off to bed . . . Yes, do. About nine. No, ten: I may sleep it out . . . Yes, I'm all *right*, dear . . . I will . . . Nightie-night.

"That was Miss Kisby. She's so unselfish, she worries. I'm afraid all this has got her really upset. Her mother's sent her to bed. It's funny the way people can't understand that you *want* to be alone . . . Yes, quite my best friend. Of course, working, as I have always been, one doesn't have much chance to make many *new* friends. Few but true has always been my motto. I often think people who know a great many people don't discriminate much. Mr. Wallace used to tell me I was unsociable. I don't think I am really. And when I was knowing him there wasn't very much time.

"Of course, what came out in court about my character – I mean, my character with regard to Mr. Wallace – well, you must know what I mean – was a shock to a good many people, such as Mrs. Kisby. You see, no one had any idea I was that sort of girl. I'd always been so particular what I did. It must have been quite a shock. I suppose it needn't have come out really (I hadn't realised it would) if it hadn't been for one thing Mr. Wallace said, and then the Counsel's taking it up like that. That is the sort of thing – I mean about me and Mr. Wallace – that a good many people I know such as Mrs. Kisby would take very hard. She[6] has stood by me very well and encouraged Miss Kisby to, but I suppose it must naturally make a difference to her now . . . Yes, I suppose people ought to have a more modern outlook. But I can't blame them really; I hadn't a modern outlook myself till just recently. Knowing Mr. Wallace made me much more modern.

"However, if I take a[7] holiday now, as I am thinking of doing (yes, I *can* tell you that; I am going to take a holiday), I daresay I may make some new friends. That is said to be half the object of a holiday, isn't it. I should like a cruise, but I don't think I can afford – Yes, I *know*, but please *don't* bring up that again. I'd rather stay where I am than get the money like that. I've given you one envelope.

"Yes, he *was* a great lover. But that's my affair. If people want to read love-letters they should get themselves lovers – Oh dear, what am I saying? You see, this does upset me . . .

"No, I know you didn't mean to. You've really been most considerate. I always did like the *Sunday News* . . . Oh, well . . . It's funny how one likes one paper more than another, isn't it. I mean the news is the same . . . I suppose it's the feature articles. You know, I used to wonder how people who got all over the papers felt. The times I've spread the *Sunday News* on this floor. Mr. Wallace used to laugh; he said I crawled on the news . . . Yes, he liked this flat quite a lot. That's his chair you're sitting in, as a matter of fact. Yes, it really is a nice flat: I'm glad to be back, naturally, apart from everything else."

The Man and the Boy

The hotel terrace was a small restless place, where people sitting stiffly at iron tables waited for other people who did not come. Grey spear-top railings shut it off from the street, and the bay-trees dotted about in tubs were white with July dust. The hotel bus with three commercial travellers had just started downhill to the morning Paris train; it was eleven o'clock; the freshness of morning had spent itself. Tom sat at one table, Benjie sat at another: a bulldog left chained by a French lady to the foot of a third table slavered patiently, looking up whenever the swing door swung.

Benjie, a sullen, masculine-looking little boy with a falling forelock and unbuttoned grey shirt, leant on doubled elbows on the table gouging the gravel under his chair with one heel. Tom, a sullen, masculine-looking young man, sat with his legs crossed, frowning into his pocket book, pretending to do calculations. When his eye lit on his stepson the frown deepened: Benjie's naïve stupor of uselessness showed them both up. There were twelve years in age between them; they had the same dark good looks and were often taken for brothers. Few people they met in hotels thought Tom and Antonia were married: in her presence Tom had the glum nervy air of a young lover not sure of his footing yet. He and Benjie now made a picture of men waiting about. They were both active and dumb and did not mark time gracefully: they were not women's men.

The bulldog got up and walked heavily round the table yanking its chain once more round the iron leg. The swing door let out Theodore, in a panama hat, *Le Matin*[1] precisely folded under his arm – a dapper, highly intelligent Frenchified Englishman of sixty or so. Benjie and Tom both made a point of not seeing him. Since Theodore joined the party ten days ago at Tours,[2] they had got very good at this. Theodore, ignoring not being seen,[3] looked amiably round the terrace, lighted a cigarette, strolled across and stood midway between Tom's and Benjie's chairs.

"Good morning," he said. "Antonia is awake; in fact she's just finished breakfast. She'd like a word with you both – about plans, I fancy."

Tom frowned at his calculations for just three seconds more. Then he looked up and said, "There aren't any, that I know. We're staying on till tomorrow."

"This morning, she seems to think[4] perhaps not," Theodore said with his lucid kindliness. "The tummy's better this morning and she's all for moving on. I must say, I don't think much of this place myself."

"Well, we can't," said Tom. "I'm having things done to the car."

Theodore raised his eyebrows. "That, my dear Tom," he said, "will be for you to explain . . . Morning, Benjie. Life not too good today?"

"Life how much?" said Benjie rudely.

"At your age," said Theodore, "I suffered unpleasant people who said 'Come, come, little chap, can't you find something to *do*?' And too well can I remember how totally it unnerved me – "

"Do mad dogs?" said Benjie.[5] "Because that dog's frothing. I shouldn't wonder if it got hydrophobia soon."

"Dear me," said Theodore. "Well, don't let me keep you both. She wanted to see you both. I think I shouldn't – er – bump about much. The nerves are still not too good." He sat down and opened *Le Matin* comfortably, by this possessing the terrace so completely that Tom and Benjie got up in sullen silence and filed through the swing door.

Antonia lay like lovely carved brown ivory against the blue-white pillows; the jalousies of her room standing[6] ajar against the outside glare. As they came in she turned with a vague voluptuous movement and held out her thin brown arms to Tom. Benjie walked stolidly past the bed to the window: his manner said: "Rather you than me." Tom looked at the arms with a sort of animal irony, but sat down within their reach on the edge of Antonia's bed. She drew his head down, knotting her hands at the nape of his neck. Meanwhile, she studied his face with great dark eyes that had a heroic wildness. She was a lovely young woman at thirty-three, the lines of her face and body still excitingly pure.

"Still cross?" she said.

"No," said Tom stubbornly.

"Well, you were. But I was a pig last night – Theodore says so. But, you know, my tummy felt awful – full of tin rats." She looked at Tom's eyelids and added: "Darling."

"Better?" Tom said.

"Much. I thought we might move on – But, oh look, the post has come and I've got all sorts of letters – Oh, Benjie: I've had a letter from Godfather. He's got a bicycle for you."

"What's the good of that here?"

"Don't shout," said Antonia, "come and talk to me properly. Oh, he isn't sending it out to here naturally. It will be there when we get back. Now aren't you glad? I thought you'd be so pleased."

"If we ever do get back."

"We must get your hair cut," Antonia said, frowning thoughtfully at her son. "Anybody would think you were an Italian, really."

"Oh gosh, I don't care."

"Don't say gosh, and read Godfather's letter. Here – Darlings, I think we might[7] move on today, don't you? I don't mind where; just the next place."

She had let Tom's neck go so he now sat upright on the edge of the bed with his arms folded. "We can't move today," he said. "I'm having the car decarbonised."

"Good heavens: what ever made you do that?"

"You know it had to be done."

"But it was, before we started."

"No, it wasn't: I had everything fixed up, then you said you[8] couldn't spare it and then there wasn't another day."

"So you simply went out this morning and fixed this up? It is my car, after all."

"You said last night you must stay in bed all today."

"Yes, you did say that," said Benjie. "Mother, I heard you."[9]

"Go out and stop them."

"I can't now; they started at eight o'clock."

"They're on it now," said Benjie.

"Shut up, Benjie, you horrible little boy. And your shirt smells, that's the fourth day you have worn it."

"God knows," Tom said, "I don't want to stop on here."

"Why? What's the matter with here?"

"Oh, it's no worse than any other place."

Benjie, back at the window, clicked the latch of the shutter. "All places are holes," he said.

'Tom, how can you bear to hear Benjie speaking to me like that!
– Benjie, go straight off and put on a clean shirt and don't come near
me again till you don't smell. You know I'm one mass of nerves. It
simply horrifies Theodore – "

Benjie pressed one eye to the shutter. "It may interest you to
know," he said, "that Theodore's sitting on the terrace with a mad
dog."

"Shut up," said Tom. "Shut up and for God's sake get out." When
Benjie had gone he said: "How much further is Theodore coming
with us?"

"Oh, miles, I hope: he knows so much about churches."

"I give him three days," said Tom. "After that I go back to England
and Theodore can damn well look after the car."

"No, you won't do that," she said kindly. "My lovely stupid, you
won't."

This town sat on a rock rising out of one of those plains of immense
France. A river doubles glinting past the foot of the rock: over the
river there is a steep drop. One flank shelves, with grey jumbled
roofs, yards, an embanked road for motors zigzagging down
between. Down where the road flattens there is a dusty faubourg,[10]
across the river, linked to town by a bridge. A boulevard dark with
trees runs round the top of the rock, broadening out at the river side
into municipal gardens. A cathedral church of flamboyant gothic
gives the town interest: it is without charm – that quickness and air
of secret pleasure many little French towns have it quite lacks. It has
a limestone greyness and with the end of summer grows sluggish
and sinister: glare beats on its restless slate-grey trees; wind creeps
under the heavily dropping sky; straws blow about the cafés; dust
hardens one's lips. Michelin gives three gables to the hotel – so here,
yesterday, Theodore, amateur of late gothic, directed Antonia's party
across the plain from the more smiling, peach-coloured town of
Albi.[11] He collected, he indexed aesthetic experience, though

rapture had never flowered in his precise mind.

Benjie saw no reason to change his shirt: how much simpler it was
to avoid his mother. He left the hotel and made for the market
square, where he stared at objects aggressively. He was twelve, man
enough to feel an angry vacuity: he hoped never to cross the English
Channel again. Kicking an apple drearily past the stalls till it rolled
under an old Renault parked by the kerb, he missed Tom's company.
He sidled into a garage yard and stood silently watching two silent
mechanics: here his contempt for the French lifted a little. With an
obscure feeling of outrage he saw his mother, her pink nightdress
slipping off her shoulder, running her hand up Tom's stiff arm,
saying: "You won't." The voluptuous delicacy of women, embodied
in her, antagonised him: he would rather have had a grim aunt who
scrubbed his ears. Wait till I am in the army, Benjie thought.

Two nuns streamed past with a sanctimonious bustle. Avoiding
their stuffy skirts, Benjie walked head on into Theodore, coming
from the cathedral, eupeptic,[12] bland.

"Hullo," Theodore said. "Do you know what's been decided?"

"The car won't be ready," Benjie said, with some triumph.

"Tut," Theodore said. "However . . ." They unwillingly turned,
together, up a cobbled side street.

"You're pretty bored, are you?" said Theodore.

"Well, there's nothing to do, much."

Theodore expanded a quick smile that Benjie, walking with eyes
on the cobbles, doggedly, felt. "Cricket?" said Theodore. "Trains?
Other chaps? Or what? Why not have left you behind? She likes
having you round, what?"

"She thinks because it's my holidays . . ."

"She's very devoted."

Benjie, striding with his fists in his pockets, wriggled his
shoulders and shook his forelock back. Theodore with the smile in
his tone went on: "And Tom quite a father too, in his way."

"I dunno," said Benjie, "I've never had one."

"Still, you've a lot in common."

"He hasn't got much time, much . . . Gosh," Benjie said, "these nuns here. What they must sweep up."

"Still, you're a lucky boy."

Benjie was one of the dumb, for whom there is no escape. Striking his heels heavily on the cobbles, he looked from side to side, like someone under arrest. But the street was all doors and walls with no alley to escape up: it ran into the *grande rue* opposite the hotel. The cathedral bell rang for noon with iron insistence, drumming dull echoes through the air, while smells of cooking curled out of the doors. "One thing, there is always lunch," said Theodore. "Which breaks the day up, doesn't it . . ." He went on: "Another thing about being my age: you don't bore me as much as I bore you . . . I think now I'll go and find an aperitif. There won't be lunch, I think, till your mother's down."

"Gosh," said Benjie, "I've got to get a shirt."

The day got really sultry before lunch was over. They had the nearest window in the restaurant opened: what air there was came through and fanned Antonia's arms. She[13]

Story Scene

When Leonard Osten got home, about half-past six, the whole place looked unnaturally tidied up. To start with, his old mackintosh and his knapsack were gone from the hall rack — he missed their smell before he saw they were gone. The old dog's lead — there was no dog now — and the golf balls were also gone from the brass tray; the entrance lobby smelled of nothing but wax. Len hung his hat on its peg and went thoughtfully in.[1]

In the livingroom, the coalite[2] fire quivered in a full glare of electric light. All Rene's picture papers were stacked on the window seat: work basket, generally gulping open, was latched primly. The chintz covers on the armchairs and the settee had been tucked in so tight, without a wrinkle, that it did not seem proper to sit down. The circular oak table shone like a polish advertisement: on it had appeared a pottery bowl with flame tulips growing out of a bed of moss – Rene must have been out for these, for she did not raise bulbs. Len touched the tip of a tulip with the tip of his finger to make certain this was a real flower, not wax. Then he looked round for his pipe. But the things he liked to find at his elbow had been tidied away. He went round the room, and was just opening his mouth to shout to know where the pipe was when his nose led him to it, on a corner shelf.

So he lit up, pacific. Now he'd come on the pipe, he had time to be struck by these preparations for Flora. Flora was his cousin. Rene must have been killing herself, getting the house so pretty – "at" Flora, no doubt, but for Flora as well. Seeing what an event was being made of Flora, he kicked himself for having brought nothing back – olives, chocolates, a pineapple. Rene would think nothing of him. He must see what the local shops could put up.

Len did not sit down; he hitched one heel on the brick kerb of the fire and looked round – liking to think that Flora would soon be here. She would think they had got a nice place – and so they had.

Rene had been perfectly civil but not warm to Len's family. He had not many relations, and she had put up coolly with those he had. She had been a little sniffy about the sound of Flora – an unmarried cousin, in business, did not sound to her much. But that evening the Ostens met Flora in London, Rene must have been more impressed then she showed. Flora was, now, a highly successful woman, with plenty of style and with money to spend: her manner with waiters when she ordered the cocktails had made Rene at least flicker an eye. On the short train journey home, after that first meeting, Rene had said: "Len, she seems years older than you." Then: "She's not a bit like the rest of your family." Then, lastly, with her slow provocative smile: "If you and she really did grow up together, I wonder Flora didn't teach you more."

In fact, over the second round of cocktails in the Louis Seize lounge of Flora's London hotel, Rene had gone so far as to ask Flora to come on a visit – or rather, she had asked Flora to ask herself. Any move from Rene to another girl was so rare, Len did hope Flora would follow up. She did: she wrote and asked herself for this weekend. Len had seen too little of Flora since his marriage; now he felt old times were beginning again. Rene said: "She'll find it quiet down here."

"Flora lives at top speed; she'll like taking it easy."

They lived twenty miles from London, one of those spreading places round an old village, on a main line. Trains emptied the men into London every morning – except such men as Alec, lucky enough to have local businesses. Len had added: "Flora likes anything. And we'll have Alec round – he and she get on like houses; they always did."

To this Rene had said nothing; she had seemed to be having one of her silent fits. Len, taken down a little, came to form the idea that Rene was "off" the idea of Flora's coming.[3] So it touched and cheered him, now he got home this evening, to find the place en fête for Flora. What a good girl Rene was, for all she did not say. Where was she? Changing her dress? She must be pretty tired. He was starting upstairs to find her when it struck him that now would be the time to give Alec a ring. They ought to fix something up for tomorrow evening and, quite likely, Sunday afternoon. Apart from this question of entertaining Flora, it was high time Alec *did* look in again. If Alec had not been such an old friend, Len's best friend (he had been best man at the wedding), you might have thought he had started giving the house a miss. Len had already commented once or twice that it seemed an age since Alec had dropped in, but Rene said the[4] garage kept Alec busy.[5]

The telephone was at the foot of the stairs. Just as Len got to it, he heard Rene run quickly across her room; she pulled her door open and called down rather sharply: "Len? What's the matter?"

"Matter? I thought I'd give Alec a ring."

"No, don't," Rene said. She came downstairs, put her hand on his chest and pushed him away from the telephone. While Len, startled, looked down at her hand on his chest, she withdrew it as though he were a jellyfish. She smiled oddly, not raising her eyes, then walked ahead of him into the livingroom. "Oh, all right, then," Len said. He always made slow adjustments; when he had to think, he thought with a slow cautious intensity that brought his thick dark eyebrows gradually down. In his mind he would drag a matter kindly about till he grew familiar with it. His face, with the long upper lip, was open, quizzical, pleasant. Flora had told him once he had button eyes, like a bear. He said, as he followed Rene into the livingroom: "You've got everything looking very nice."

Slight and straight in her red dress,[6] Rene was standing away back near the recessed curtains – as though she wanted nobody in this room.[7] She looked tensed up – she *had* overdone herself. She was a small pale woman with an Undine face – a face that for all its delicate curves and shadows could be stubborn and cryptic. She had a broad forehead, soft hair, rather heavy eyelids; her eyebrows rose at the outer tips, like wings. Something humble in Len, rare in his type, made him not try to break her mystery down. She was serene and teasing; she made very few friends. They had been married three years. Her compliance (whatever she thought) with his way of life, and her dependence, made her satisfy him. Till he fell in love with Rene, Len had never thought about marriage; his life (except for Flora) had been among other men, so what he and Rene married were, he now took marriage to be.[8] In the evenings, he came home to her with a rapture that nothing in his stolid slowness expressed.

"It looks fine," he said. "Flora'll be – "

"Oh, you did notice?"

"It hit me in the eye."

"Things have to do that," she said, "or you never notice at all."

"Sorry. Look here, take it easy: you're tired."

She put a hand on the wireless cabinet, as though to steady herself: she licked her lips before any word came out. "I wonder," she said, "if you ever have any notion what I get tired *of*. For months I've – please listen: no, don't just stare at me, *listen* – this can't go on, Len. I can't go on any more."

Her voice stopped. Len felt his face change, as though it knew more than he did. He stooped quickly and knocked his pipe out into the fire. "You'll feel better after supper," he said.

"You don't understand. Don't you really know what I mean?"

"No, I must say I don't," he said with a touch of sharpness. "You make this sort of fuss whenever you get tired. Why don't we have supper?"

"When you don't notice and don't notice," she said, "you sometimes make me feel I shall go mad. Why, Alec – "

"What do you mean, Alec?"

"That's what I'm trying to tell you. I and Alec – "

"Look, leave Alec out of this."

"But that's what I mean. It's Alec I'm going to."

Len frowned; he frowned slowly down at his wristwatch, then turned to compare his wristwatch with the clock. He saw the door was ajar, walked slowly across the room and shut it. Rene's hand was still resting on the wireless cabinet: he saw the cabinet shake. "Look out, you'll have that thing over," he said. After that he began to refill his pipe. An idiot immovability gripped his face and his mind. With a jerk he pulled his lower lip, which with his jaw was hanging heavily down. At last he heard himself say: "I don't know what you are saying. It doesn't mean anything." He paused, puzzled, to rub the pad of his thumb against the brick edge of the chimneypiece. "If it did mean anything," he said with more decision, "you would not be saying it *now*."

"It's got to be said sometime."

"But Flora's coming to stay."

Rene left the wireless cabinet: she put up a hand slowly, and slowly raised from her forehead a wave of mouse-coloured hair. *"Are you mad?"* she said. "Are you not, not normal, really? I nearly kill myself, trying to tell you: all you say then is, 'Flora's coming to stay.'"

His face lit up with obstinacy. *"You* know Flora's coming: you got the house nice." Pipe in hand, he made a gesture and said: "You got those tulips."

"Yes. But that was this morning."

He repeated loudly: "I don't know what you're saying. Where do you get this from? We've not *seen* Alec for weeks."

She said: *"You* haven't seen him . . ."

While this sank in[9] Len's silence, she walked down the room, past him: she gave him a strange veiled altered look as she passed. She went and leaned with her back to another wall, as though she had to have something behind her. He said: "You can't mean Alec . . ."

"Things like this do happen."

"Not to us."

"You wouldn't notice," she said. "It's been awful lately, keeping on here with you. I don't mean I've got it in on you, Len: you've been good to me. But it can't go on any more."

The heat of the coalite fire got insupportable. Len pulled open a curtain, unscrewed[10] a casement window and thrust out his head and shoulders into the dark. Lights from houses back to back with his garden shone through the trees. The village clock struck seven; he heard a train come roaring out of the cutting. The lawns and orchards gave off their familiar wintry smell. He had been born, and grown up, in this place: from birth he had heard those distant trains, that clock. He heaved himself back into the room and said: "I don't believe about Alec."

She said: "I can't help what you don't believe." She added: "You *said* it was funny he'd stopped coming."

Len's eyes, without a glitter, looked dark and sunk further in. "You don't mean, he comes when I'm not – "

"No, he won't do that. We go out in his car; we – " Rene stopped.[11]

Len suddenly shouted: "Shut up: I'm not asking you anything!"

"I'm not telling you," she said, equally angrily.

"You are, you're trying to tell me that, that – "

"Yes, that I'm going to Alec."

"Why?" Len said, suddenly facing round, in a voice as though he had not spoken before.

"Why am I going, or why am I telling you?"

"I just said, why?"

"I've just got back from seeing Alec," she said.

"You mean, you'd got the house nice for Flora and got those tulips before you saw Alec?"

"Yes, Len, *yes*, Len: that's what I keep saying." Rene hardly ever wept: with hysterical quietness she now ran her right hand fingers up her temple and lifted her hair. "He telephoned me just at tea-time," she said. "He brought the car up to Wood End for us to talk. Since – since we knew we must go, he's been trying to sell the garage: he's got an offer today. So it's now or never, he says."

"I've got to see Alec."

"No, no, *no*."[12]

Flora stepped smartly down the station incline beside Len, who carried her cowhide case. It was three o'clock on Saturday afternoon; she had just got out of the London train. The wet weak February sunshine fell on the white palings: Flora, who had spent holidays here as a girl, said the place had not changed at all, so far. "It's grown," Len said.

"It would do that, naturally. Where you live will be new on me."

"Yes, it's where Bent's Farm was."

"Pity that farm went."

"Our garden's got a bit of the old orchard . . . You look fine,

Flora."

"Oh, I'm feeling fine, thank you." Flora shot at Len one of her sharp but calm looks. "You don't look much: how's business?"

"Business is all right."

"Oh well, life doesn't get any easier, does it. How's Rene?"

"Rene's all right." They passed under the railway bridge, walked uphill, turned to the right again. Len shifted Flora's substantial case from one hand to the other.

"How's your car?" Flora said.

"Oh, it's all right; I thought you might like the walk."

"Oh, *I* do," she said. "But I ought to have packed lighter. Talking of cars, how's Alec?"

"Oh, Alec's all right."

Flowers Will Do

Mrs. Simonez and her daughter Doris occupied the top flat in one of those London houses that have ornate frontages and high steps. Mrs. Simonez called the neighbourhood Chelsea, but it was really Fulham, as Doris knew. The house had not been made over, simply leased out in floors. Up where they lived, the Simonez had a room each, and a bathroom blocked by a dresser. By day, their divan beds were got up with fancy cushions; they cooked on the landing and ate off a folding table in Mrs. Simonez' room. The mother was hard put to it, keeping these close quarters at once "artistic" and fresh. Their furniture dated from better days; it was too large for the flat and they bumped into it constantly, when they were not bumping into each other, but it showed they had been accustomed to live in style. They kept themselves to themselves and never spoke to anyone on the stairs. Mrs. Simonez prided herself on keeping this little home for Doris – who worked in an office. They had a few, but not very many, friends.

At half-past ten one muggy February evening, Doris sat on her divan side by side with Sydney – her first at all serious young man. The hanging light, through its shade, shed an orange glow. Nothing showed that this was where Doris slept: the wall cupboard was latched on her shoes and dresses; frilled shelves concealed her brushes and pots. Sydney, whose evening calls had become regular, no longer took notice of anything. He leaned back, one elbow stuck in the cushions, his head propped on the wall. Doris now sat upright on the edge of the divan: they had been holding hands but had just let go – one more of those disturbing currents of feeling had made her sharply disconnect from his touch. An aluminium coffee pot on the gas ring still sent out a smell of hot metal and coffee; on an Indian table pulled close to the divan stood cups, a messy ashtray and a saucer in which two chocolate biscuits still were. The packet of Gold Flake Doris had bought for Sydney was wedged down in the cushions; smoke thickened the air. Doris had got up once to open the window, a second time to turn down the gasfire.

"How you fidget," he said. "You're like a cat on hot bricks."

She combed back the wing of hair from her forehead. "It gets close in here," she said. "It's the stuffy night."

"Well, it would get close; there's not much room to turn round. I don't know how you manage, you *and* your mother."

"We like it all right," she said touchily.

"Oh, you've got it all very nice; I don't say you haven't," said Sydney, rolling his head on the wall. "But with all these new inexpensive flats going up, I'd have thought you might have done better, for the money."

"If you don't like it here, you don't have to come."

"Well, you don't have to bite off my head, do you? I can't help taking an interest, can I?"

"Can't you?" said Doris, immovably.

"You know I can't," Sydney said, on a deep note. He smacked the springs of the divan between her back and his body, to make her lean back close beside him again. But that made her spine stiffen; she dug her heels in the carpet; her rather frozen face continued to loom forward into the air. She was handsome, heavy, naturally pale, twenty-six and more than ready to marry; her big limbs showed through her black afternoon dress. The more her manner became cautious and rigid, the more her whole being said: "What next?" Her hopes of Sydney were, by evenings and evenings, being warped into contempt for him. Humiliation and anger stood in her voice as she said: "Well, I don't see why you come."

"I see why I come," he said, giving her shoulder an equivocal look that she, slightingly, did not trouble to see. The jerry-built house shook as the street door shut, down below. She said: "That'll be mother."

"She's popping back early."

"Doesn't much matter, does it?"

Sydney, however, got up from the divan and primly settled himself in the armchair. She brushed ash out of the trough he left in the cushions, then had time to give him one expressionless look – they heard her mother on the last flight of stairs. Mrs. Simonez coughed, then nosed brightly into the room.[1] "Why, hullo, Sydney," she said. She was a foxy-faced, dressy little woman, letting out sparkles from three marquisite clips.[2] A velvet tricorne with rather rubbed corners was set forward correctly on her waved white hair.[3] The glass eyes of her fox fur glittered some way under her own with an air of complicity. She glanced round the room as though looking for something, then sat down beside Doris, where Sydney had been. Mother and daughter could not have been more unlike. Mrs.

Simonez removed from the divan cushions the almost empty packet of cigarettes. Having loosened her fur, she glanced in her sharp, marked way at the two chocolate biscuits left in the saucer; then she put her veil up, took one and nibbled it. "Well, here I am back," she said. "They put the big picture early, and Mrs. Lewis and I didn't care to stay for the comic."

"Nice picture?" said Sydney.

"Clark Gable," said Mrs. Simonez. "There's too much nonsense about him. But he's a manly man, and one doesn't see many now."

Sydney glanced at his wristwatch, started moving his feet. He said: "Well, I must be getting along."

"Oh, don't let *me* drive you out."

"No, I must be getting along."

Mrs. Simonez gave a faintly insulting smile. Doris went out to the landing to look for Sydney's hat. Sydney rose and shook hands with Mrs. Simonez. "Well, if you're in really *such* a hurry . . ." she said. Doris saw him to the top of the stairs, then came back into her room, shutting the door. With heavy movements, suffering and defensive, she emptied the ashtray into a screw of paper, then started to clear up the coffee cups. She disposed of the last biscuit by swallowing it. Mrs. Simonez sat on the divan, watching. She put up her hand to her head, and then took her tricorne off; she said: "My goodness, it's close in here. It's not right for you to sleep in. You ought to air the place out." As Doris pulled back the curtains, opened the windows wider, Mrs. Simonez said: "Well, did you and Sydney have a nice time?"

"Oh, it was all right," said Doris, shifting her bust and shoulders inside her tight silk dress.

"I daresay," said Mrs. Simonez, "it was all right for Sydney. Oh, Sydney knows where he's well off. Sydney knows where he gets something for nothing – lounging round like a lord, with you running round after him."

"Shut up, mother," said Doris. She kicked her high-heeled shoes off, opened the cupboard, got her felt slippers out.

"And what did he bring you this time?" said Mrs. Simonez. "My goodness," she said, pointing round into space, "one simply can't see the place for chocolates and flowers. Did he ever bring you so much as the evening paper he'd read on the bus? No, Sydney thinks he's conferring a big favour by dropping in and guzzling biscuits and coffee and smoking your cigarettes and messing your divan up — don't tell *me* he spent all his time in that chair: why, he took half your distemper downstairs on his back." Mrs. Simonez screwed her head round and looked hard and bitterly at the wall over the bed. "Look at that greasy patch his head's starting to make," she said. "This is going too far, Doris. It's not nice."

"We just sit," Doris said.

"Oh, *I* know you're a good girl. As for Sydney — well, I'd really think better of him if he *were* more of a man. Oh, Sydney's careful, all right. Oh, Sydney knows where he is — just because he's only got a pair of women to deal with, he thinks he's free to lounge in and out as he likes. My goodness, Doris, your father'd soon have shown him the door. As it is, though, Sydney's got me to reckon with — and I think he felt it this evening, shooting off out like that. Well, I have enough[4] of this, Doris: if you haven't, I have. I've got my pride, if you haven't. What *is* all this leading to?"

"Boys are slow these days; boys have got to think," said Doris. "You've got to give them time."

"Well, you waited round long enough. It's a year since he started coming. He's never once taken you out."

"He's saving up," said Doris. "Sydney'd have to save up, if — "

"Yes, *if* — " said Mrs. Simonez. "But has that ever been mentioned? *Has* Sydney said one word to you about . . . that?"

"Not straight out. But — "

"He's getting good money, you say. He's in a position to — he's got prospects, I mean — "

"Oh yes, they think well of him."

"Oh, they do?" Mrs. Simonez said, with infinite bitterness. "Well, then that's more than I do. Sydney's not half one man.[5] He should be ashamed of himself – yes, and so should you be, Doris. If you can't do better, at your age – dressing yourself up for him, evening after evening, turning out your own mother, wet or fine, spending money we skimp for for him to smoke the place out with dirty smoke. Oh, it makes me mad!" cried Mrs. Simonez, smartly striking at the head of the fur on her knee as though she meant to decapitate the fox. "Why, when I was a girl I had men down on their knees. If I'd had to go like that after your father – well, *you* wouldn't be here – "

While all this was being said, Doris had gone on like someone shut up with an electric drill. She defended her nerves with a screen of movements – stolidly getting out her face cream pots and her brushes, unzipping her dress, and peeling her stocking off. She dragged herself out of her clothes with a weary immodesty, not like a girl undressing before her mother. When she had tied the sash of her dressing gown, she wheeled round to the divan: the taut contemptuous mother and stolid suffering daughter faced each other at last. "Would you mind moving, mother, I want to strip my bed." Mrs. Simonez picked up her fur and got up: Doris, with a series of strong-armed movements, stripped off the divan-cover and flung the taffeta cushions in a pile on the rug. She worked like someone digging their own grave. "You keeping on like that, you always watching," she said, "won't make Sydney more likely to marry me."

"You're all nerves," her mother said. "You're all over the place."

"Yes, I get fed up, all right," Doris confessed.

"I don't want to upset you, dear, but I can't help worrying, can I?"

"I'm tired," said Doris. "I just want to get to sleep."

Mrs. Simonez went out and lit the ring on the landing to heat up her glass of milk. Mother and daughter, in their alike kimonos, their hair in setting caps for the night, jostled each other in and out of the bathroom. At last the two doors shut; the last light was snapped out.

Through the thin[6] dividing wall, Doris could hear her mother rustling round in her bed with brisk canine movements. Doris herself lay like a bar of iron, with her hands knotted under her head. She heard traffic drag past the end of their hollow street. Light from a street lamp made a square on the dark. Through the floor there came up, intermittently, voices – Mrs. Benger,[7] below, had someone with her again.

Mrs. Simonez was not on good terms with Mrs. Benger, the woman below. Mrs. Benger did not behave like a lady; there had been unpleasantness ever since she moved in. Mrs. Simonez sent down a series of notes, about late-night noise on the stairs, about landing lights left burning – for wasted light on that landing Mrs. Simonez had to pay *her* share. In return, she got only one note up; Mrs. Benger complained of the smell of cooking. Out on her landing, where her gas cooker stood, Mrs. Simonez simmered the stews and hashes that were to nourish Doris on her return. The skylight over the cooker would not open – it was the landlord's business to see to this – so the fumes, naturally, found their way downstairs. Mrs. Benger's objection was anti-human – how was the mother to make Doris a home? She referred Mrs. Benger to the landlord. and went on with the stews. She would have liked, of course, to have a tiled kitchenette.

Not only was Mrs. Benger no lady, but one really would not like to say what she *was*. Her landing smelled of cosmetics and cigarette smoke; she ate out, or had her meals delivered from the delicatessen.[8] Almost every evening, over the supper table, Doris heard complaints about Mrs. Benger. Doris, herself, could not help feeling curious – she had been disloyal enough to play up to one or two of those overtures on the stairs. When the Benger flat door was left open, Doris could just see a lamp with a tilted shade, in front of a mirror, spikes of dyed lilac, a wrinkled skin rug. Mrs. Benger went out, in almost all weathers, in a fur coat of antique smart cut. Often she wore no hat, always her cherry gauntlets. Under her parchment make-up she looked about forty. There was no doubt she knew a number of men. Doris thought: She could tell one a thing or two. Mrs. Benger, coming up the stairs with her latchkey, had been obliging enough to let Sydney in one night. He said he had no doubt she was rather a one. "Mother certainly thinks so," replied Doris: at once, Sydney softened to Mrs. Benger. He used to lag on the stairs, on his way down from the Simonez', wondering if she might come to her door.

Doris and Sydney worked in the same office. Since they had started courting, they fought shy of each other, anywhere round the office, because they did not want to start any talk. "We don't want them to think there's anything up," he said – she, actually, could not see why. Secretiveness was part of her policy; but, on the other hand, this was her first boy. About once in ten days they nipped off in the lunch hour to an A.B.C.[9] a good way along the Strand, and in the evenings he sometimes waited for her. At lunch they never said much, because you are four to a table, and after work they had to fight for their buses. Nothing would have got started between them if it had not been for a staff dance.

That night Doris did not sleep; that stuffy night after Mrs. Simonez had said her say about Sydney was a turning point. She went to the office next morning heavy lidded and tight lipped. Some new energy or passion stood behind her impassive face like a threat, and made people look at her. One does not injure a nature like hers for nothing. The day, balmy, too fine, with the lassitude and sweetness of spring in it, declined slowly over her typewriter: at half-past five she stepped out into clear light. As she waited for Sydney at their corner, all round her the buildings stood up, blue-pink and brittle; a shadowy brightness drowned the street. Sydney, who had not expected to see Doris, started when she put her hand on his arm.

"Oh, hullo," he said.

She said: "You in a hurry? I thought we might walk a bit."

"I don't mind," he said. They struck up a bye-street. Sydney whistled under his breath and Doris, by him, walked with her eyes down. When she kept on not speaking he said: "What's up?"

She said in a dead voice: "Oh, one thing and another. No, it's just mother, really: she's been on about you."

"Why, me?" he said. "What's she been on about?"

"You always coming, and – She's old fashioned, you know."

"Oh, she's old fashioned, is she? And what have I done?"

"It's what you've not done she's been on at me about. What she wants to know is, what's going to come of it."

"Well, I must say – " he said. "You really have got a nerve."

"Yes, I have got a nerve," said Doris. "I am fed up."

"What, with your mother?"

"No, with you. You don't know what you want."

"Oh, I know what I want all right."

"Well – "

He stopped dead and looked at her, between gratification and panic. "You've rushed me all right," he said. "Do I get you a ring, or what?"

She said: "Flowers will do for a start."

"Flowers?" he said. "What do you want, *flowers?*"

"Just to show – " she said, not raising her eyelids. [. . .][10]

"Well, that's not so very funny," she said.

Doris came home, late, with a bunch of tinted lilac. The plumes nodded over the paper sheath – she brushed them past her mother and went into the bathroom to fill a vase at the tap. "Gracious!" said Mrs. Simonez, following her, "wherever did that come from?"

"Off a barrow," said Doris, rather brutally breaking the stems of the lilac – the stems were too long.

"What, you brought that home off a barrow?"

"Sydney got it for me."

"That's not a natural colour," said Mrs. Simonez. "They dye it." She added: "Whatever made him to do *that?*"

"We got engaged," said Doris. She carried the vase from the bathroom into her room, moved her father's photo and put the vase on the bureau, under her mirror. Mrs. Simonez had kept following her, like someone attracted by a horrible sight. "You did what?" she said sharply.

"We got engaged," said Doris. She sent a challenging look into the mirror, over the lilac heads. Mrs. Simonez put her knuckles up to her mouth and sat down on the divan without saying a word. Doris put her gloves away in the bureau drawer and said: "We're ever so happy, mother."

Silence. She said steadily: "Don't you be upset."

"It's all very well," said Mrs. Simonez. "It's all very well . . ." Then a smell of burning came from the landing oven: as her mother sat on there without moving, Doris went to rescue the shepherd's pie . . . The evening was dreadful, altogether; Mrs. Simonez could not look at her supper; Doris ate with stolid voracity. Now and then she raised her slow dark eyes and looked across at her mother's face. Mrs. Simonez had poured out a glass of water; she sat upright, sipping at it like a bird. The elbow she rested on the folding table made it shake on its frail legs. When Doris got up to change the dishes she said: "After all, mother, you married, yourself."

"It's *how* you marry," Mrs. Simonez said.

Yes, it was as though Doris had just revealed to her some shocking disgrace. The thin lips of the mother shut tightly over unsayable things. Her liquid-glass eyes, with a burning look behind them, moved in every direction, as though she had not the strength, yet, to look her abased daughter straight in the eye. "*You* know what I think of Sydney!" – the exclamation was all she had, so far, allowed herself. As she continued to sit there at the table her face, under its cap of hard white waved hair, took on a mauvish tinge. When Doris got up to fetch the coffee, Mrs. Simonez cried: "What would your father have said!"

Doris simply fetched the coffee. Her heavy composed movements had taken on a new sort of majesty. Mrs. Simonez detected something male, obtuse and cold in Doris's attitude; it was as though the girl had moved into another sphere. Doris said: "You'll learn to like Sydney, mother: it's been ever so difficult, till now."

"You've been after him," now burst out Mrs. Simonez. "He's never been after you. Oh, I've noticed how things were."

"Well, that's been my affair, hasn't it."

"It's all dreadful," Mrs. Simonez said. She met the unmoving gaze of Doris; she flinched and her tone changed to the close-up tone of a beggar. "Then you'll find a place for the three of us, somewhere, all three?" she said.

"You surely never would want to live with Sydney, mother."

"You mean, you'd go off and leave me to live alone?"

That was the root of it;[11] that had been said, now. Doris could only get up and clear the dishes.

As she went out with the tray to the landing sink, a man in a camelhair overcoat crashed up the stairs to their flat, three steps at a time "Could one of you ladies come down?" he said. "Mrs. Benger, below, has been taken terribly ill."

"Right," said Doris. She lodged the tray on the cooker and went downstairs, through the open door, to the moaning. In Mrs. Benger's front room, between hoops of apricot lamplight, the woman's face was bent up by the end of the couch – she lay rigid, sweating, twisting her wrists round. Now and then, inside the folds of her house-coat, she thrust a knee up. "It's my inside," she said.

"You'll be all right," said Doris. "Where's a hot water bottle?"

"I am awful. It's my inside. Leo knows where the brandy – "

"Quick!" said Doris to Leo. He looked quite knocked out. Doris knelt to plug in the electric kettle. "Who's your doctor?" she said, bringing the hot bottle.

"I haven't got a doctor."

"Then better get ours." Doris sent Leo down to telephone from the hall.

"Oh," said Mrs. Benger, biting her lip, smiling, "I've given Leo a fright – " Something flung her body sideways: she started moaning again. [. . .][12] Going into the back room, Doris stripped off the eiderdown from the bed. A sheaf of flowers in waxed paper lay where Leo had dropped them.

"Where's Leo?"

"He's telephoning."

"I got sick the very moment he came . . . He ought to go," Mrs. Benger said, looking up with the eyes of a sick monkey as Doris slipped the hot water bottle under the eiderdown.

"I'll tell him," said Doris. "He won't go, I'm afraid."

"There's not much he can do, really.[13] You are good, Miss Simonez. I'm ever so sorry. It's just my inside."

It was just on midnight when Doris got back to her own flat. Mrs. Simonez, not even undressed, sat in a chair with her door shut in front of her gasfire; her eyes were jellies from weeping. When Doris came in she unbendingly looked at her, but did not say one word. "She's all right now," said Doris. "The doctor's made her comfortable for the night."

"Who's comfortable?"

"Mrs. Benger; she had an attack. They sent for me down. I thought you'd hear all the fuss."

"Oh . . . I took it you were with Sydney."

"As if I would run out without saying a word!"

"Things are so changed now," said the mother, "I don't know what to expect . . . So she had an attack? Why didn't you send for me?"

"Oh, I and her friend managed."

"I wouldn't want to intrude."

"Do go off to bed, mother. Why do you sit up and worry?"

"I've been thinking things over," said Mrs. Simonez. "You haven't got any father, so Sydney properly should come and ask me."

"Sydney's ready to do whatever you think right."

Sydney found he was glad they had got everything fixed. He thought proudly of Doris; he liked her better for having got him in hand. The tiresome phase of courtship, for a man like Sydney, is the phase at which he has to be dominating, and Doris had let him out of this. The day after the evening when she made him buy her the lilac, he found that he looked forward to leaving his uncle's and setting up a little place of his own. He remembered how comfortable Doris made him, those evenings round at her[14] mother's flat – his thoughts only took an at all unpleasant colour when he recollected, also, Mrs. Simonez . . . Doris was content to avoid Sydney till he had settled to the idea of marriage: at the lunch hour she was not to be found, and that evening she came out in a hurry – she had to get back to her sick friend. "Well, look here, when am I to see you?"

"Oh, *we've* got time enough," she said.

He was beginning to say: "But, what's the use of our being – " when she swung herself on to her bus, in which she sailed slowly out of his disappointed gaze. All the ride home, Doris's lips were set in something just less and more lasting than a smile.

Mrs. Benger had left her door on the latch: Doris walked through the front room and tapped on the bedroom door. "Righto," said Mrs. Benger in her husky, intimate voice – for a moment she reared up among her pillows and looked at Doris with an intent expression, as though expecting her to be someone else. "Why, you are good," she said, dropping down in her bed again.

"I thought you might want something."

"Well, I don't know what, really," Mrs. Benger said, and turned round the room her consuming dark gaze. Through the window, behind the big mirror, last light died drearily in the sky. The gasfire was turned down to a bead. Light from the dwarf lamp at Mrs. Benger's[15] elbow crossed the tumbled surface of the bed,[16] showed the book dropped face down, tray with the scummy tea dregs, the mirror clouded with face powder. Leo's freesias, flopping[17] out of a carafe, waxy-sweetened the air. Smoke blurred the room and the ashtray was full of stumps. "Perhaps," Mrs. Benger said, "you'd tidy about a bit?"

"You ought to have someone with you."

"No, that fidgets me, really. My woman came in this morning, and she settled me up. I'll be all right tomorrow – for a bit, that is. Did you know, Miss Simonez, that your doctor's at me to go into hospital?"

"Goodness – an operation?"

"Oh well, don't let's bother," said Mrs. Benger with nervy lightness. She fumbled about the bed for a cigarette, lit one and pushed the box over to Doris. "You see, I can't *be* sick," she said. "It doesn't do. People hate to have to stick round and be sorry. Or they don't stick round then they feel bad, so they forget. – Look, dear, let's have a drink: it's all in the front room."

"Not for me, thanks ever so much."

"Oh, well . . . I suppose *I'm* better without it, just for today . . . There wasn't anything for me down in the rack, was there – no letter or telephone message or anything. It's awful having the telephone down in the hall, isn't it – makes you feel so cut off when you can't go down. I heard the telephone going all afternoon, but if it *was* for[18] me they never came up and said. It was quite likely Leo; he'll have been wondering – I wonder, dear, if you'd just give Leo a ring? Tell him I'm fine this evening, say I'll be up tomorrow."

Mrs. Benger scrawled a number on the back of a bill; Doris went down with it and telephoned. In three minutes she had to come up again and say there was no answer from Leo's end.

"He probably wouldn't be there," said Mrs. Benger quickly. "There *was* no note or anything in the rack?"

"I'll try another ring later."

"No, don't do that, dear, please." Mrs. Benger grinned and said ruefully: "I did give him a fright – one must never do that, you know. Still, I daresay that *was* him this afternoon all the time that bell kept ringing away . . . Don't *you* ever go sick on a boy friend – oh well, girls don't; you wouldn't. You look ever so strong."

"Yes, I'm strong all right."

Mrs. Benger rolled round on her pillows and eyed Doris with her kind cavernous monkey eyes. "Is that your boy I see going in and out?"

"Who, Sydney?" said Doris, nonchalant. "Yes, that's my *fiancé*." She went across and began to straighten the dressing table. "All this powder," she said, in a slightly bullying tone. "Where can I get a duster?"

"In the front room drawer, somewhere. Oh, so you're getting married? Well, I do think that's nice! You been engaged long?"

"Just since yesterday evening, as a matter of fact."

"Oh, that does make me feel bad!" exclaimed Mrs. Benger.[19] "You two'd just fixed everything up, then Leo dragged you down here – "

"I was only up there with mother."

Mrs. Benger said, with ever so slight a flicker: "Mother taking it well?"

"Well . . ." said Doris, "you see, I'm all she's got."

"Well, you can't help that, can you, my dear."

"Still, it's hard on mother . . ."

"Nonsense," said Mrs. Benger. "She'll think twice as much of you now you've got off."

It was true that Mrs. Simonez started to treat Doris with a kind of gloomy respect. She was no longer half so free in her comments on what Doris said and did. All Mrs. Simonez did was to purse up her lips and suffer. She never did cease to disparage Sydney, but she disparaged by innuendo, not openly. She even allowed to pass, with an icy lack of comment, Doris's popping in at Mrs. Benger's, below. To be intimate like this with Mrs. Benger (and there was nothing between not knowing Mrs. Benger and being, at once, extremely intimate with her) was, of course, an act of disloyalty. Apropos of nothing, Mrs. Simonez repeated: "Of course, things are so changed now: I don't know what to expect." Her manner to Sydney showed an icy correctness.

"What does keep on eating your mother?" he said. "*I* understood that we'd put everything right."

Soon Doris acquired a small pearl ring – and every Friday, when they had left the office, she reminded Sydney to buy her flowers. Those evenings she brought her sheaf home, she almost always looked in on Mrs. Benger. Mrs. Benger had got up with her face thinner; she put higher colour under her eyes; her monkey smiles, her hollow bold looks,[20] her melancholic gaiety all seemed to be tautened up from within. But Leo had started coming again: his sports car was once more outside the door. "Why don't[21] you two come in one evening, Doris," she said, "and have a drink with us both?"

"Sydney'd like that."

"You bring Sydney along."

So Doris fixed up with Sydney: two evenings later they went downstairs, about nine, to the Benger flat. Mrs. Benger came to the door to meet them; Leo sprawled all disjointed across the divan – a young man who had just had his head pushed off someone's lap.[22] Flattening his back hair he got up, with his tom-cat grace. Sydney's head turned stiffly above his collar: he took his drink, sat down and looked round the room. The intimacy between the two women was a little frozen by the presence of the young men: Mrs. Benger, at first, moved about with a more conventional smile than Doris had ever seen on her face, the hem of her brocade house-coat stiffly brushing the floor. Doris took just a dash of lime in her gin, looked round and placed herself with a matronly firmness on the arm of

Sydney's chair. Leo fell back on the divan, put a hand up and pulled Mrs. Benger down beside him.

"Gorgeous carnations," Leo said to Doris, across a few feet of room, with his bold smile. She looked down at the shoulder of her afternoon frock – the fern round the carnations tickled her jaw.

"Oh, she is ever so lucky," said Mrs. Benger, pulling at Leo's fingers – his hand was back in her lap.

"Doris spots the bouquets," said Sydney. "Girls know what they like, don't they. I only pay up."

Leo grinned as he sprawled there alongside of Mrs. Benger, but went on looking abstracted and sensual. Leo's unseeing dark eyes, fixed on the engaged couple, made Sydney put his arm round Doris's waist. Talk warmed up as it got more desultory; peaceful darkness crept back to Mrs. Benger's face. "They cheer me up," she said, nodding across the hearthrug. "When are you going to get married, you two?"

"August."

"Oh dear – that really is a long time."

"Sydney's holiday doesn't come till then. And mother'll have to fix up somewhere, you see."

"She'd rather like to come to us," Sydney said. "But I tell Doris that that would never do."

"I don't need telling," said Doris, "I know perfectly well."

"What's it feel like, getting married?" Leo said, half waking up.

"You'll know, one day, dear boy," said Mrs. Benger. Across his inert body she reached for a cigarette. Sydney, pressing Doris's waist, said: "Ah, we all come to it."

From under the crooked tilted lampshades light came at face-height across the room. Above the ceiling Doris could hear footsteps – Mrs. Simonez kept walking about with a tireless but complaining energy that was instinct in every creak of the floor. "Your mother's ever so active," Mrs. Benger said. "I wonder she doesn't wear herself out." Petals fell off a spike of almond blossom as

Mrs. Simonez lunged at the bathroom door.

"Mother likes to keep busy when she's alone."

"I daresay it's lonely for her up there . . . Maybe I should invite her down?" said Mrs. Benger. "But I thought we'd be nicer just we four."

At these words, the final spell fell on the room; the two pairs of lovers sat and looked at each other. Doris thought of those voices she used to hear, from down here, when she lay up there, racked, those evenings when Sydney had said nothing and gone. The recent opening of her senses (that she used to keep shut, to avoid pain) made her eye Leo with a curious eye. She had never considered a man's beauty before. She looked at the hand he had let drop on his chest, while the other hand lay on[23] his lover's knee. "Yes, he's awake really," said Mrs. Benger. "He's learnt to talk, really – come over and talk to him." She got up and gave Sydney another drink, gave herself one more, than amiably elbowed Doris off the arm of his chair. "I'd like Sydney, a bit," she said. "You go and wake Leo up." She pulled a square pouffe alongside of Sydney's chair, and Sydney took a long pull at his drink then turned round at her, ready for anything. Infected by the spirit of friendly looseness, Doris crossed the rug and sat down there beside Leo.

"Oh, hullo Doris," he said, opening his eyes wider, "you've brought your lovely carnations over here." He pushed himself a little up on his elbows and began to talk about that night Polly passed out. His looks, with their indifferent air of closeness, stole from under his eyelids into Doris's eyes, and her heart shook as though she were being touched.

"I lost my head," he said. "But I had got a nerve, really – considering I'd never seen you before."

"I'd seen your car, often."

"Come a run in it someday. You're not getting married right off?"

"August," Doris repeated.

"Well, that's lots of time to come a run in my car . . . Listen to *them,*" said Leo. "Hark at Sydney and Polly. What do you and I think they're laughing at?"

"Some joke, I daresay."

"Let's us have a joke – let's think some sort of joke up," he said, confidentially slipping hold of her hand. She looked down at the long brown spatulate fingers reposefully pressing between hers. There was a pause. "You and I are dumb," said Leo. "There surely ought to be something to laugh at?" His eyes wandered thoughtfully over Doris. "I'm such a slow starter," he said.

She frowned over this, as though he had said something deep. "Well, we don't have to keep laughing," she said. All at once, she knew she needed a rock – dumb habit made her look over at Sydney. Now, though, she saw Sydney for the first time.[24] Her whole being started. There he sat, flushed and twisted, tilting his drink at Polly – she only saw a stranger whom she did not love. Why, I couldn't . . . she thought. Why, how ever could I? . . . What a shocking thing. Imperiously, she freed her hand from Leo's as though he were just a child: her cheeks burred, she got up, holding her glass. "I'd like a spot more lime and soda," she said.[25]

"Goodness," laughed Mrs. Benger, brushing ash off her house-coat. "Whatever's Leo been doing to you?"

Sydney saw Doris upstairs as far as the Simonez' landing. They stood about a bit by the gas cooker, but she did not ask him to come in. "It's late," she said.

"Oh, right-o." Sydney looked cautiously down the staircase. "Phew," he said in a low voice, "Polly's a one! She and I got on like houses. See she colours her toenails? . . . I don't take to her boy friend – he's a gigolo type."

"You needn't," she said, trembling, "have told them I buy my flowers myself."

"Well, I like that. When I fork out."

"You wouldn't see . . ." she said. "However . . . Hop off, Sydney;

it's late."

"Oh, all right, all right, all right – what do I get?"

At the top of the stairs, she offered her cold cheek. Then: "Shut up," she said. "Get *out*! You've been drinking too much."

On these words, Mrs. Simonez, in her Japanese wrapper, opened and appeared in the flat door. Like a puppy frightened out of the larder, Sydney made a quick bolt for the stairs.

The Last Bus

The moon was full and the heavens themselves were clear, but a ground mist curdled over the landscape. The two people waiting at the bus stop on the high ridge looked down on a whitish, semi-transparent sea, through which contours of the lower downland, like those of a submerged continent, were just visible. Without the mist, the view could have been startling – you could see for miles in any direction; you should have been able to note the island-like knolls of trees, the lonely and self-sufficient farms and cottages, the villages that, lightless and battened down, seemed to huddle like primitive settlements; and, most of all, the lovely erratic pattern of the downland roads that, hedgeless, surmounted ridges, dipped out of sight, reappeared, crossed one another and rippled on, each with a destination that, somehow, you could not doubt.

As it was, all this open country, less than half seen, could be strongly felt. Its effect on the man and woman waiting for the bus was, if anything, oppressive. Both had urgent reasons to wish to be somewhere else by a fixed hour; and their principal feeling was, at the moment, that of being too far from anywhere. Their total dependence upon the bus made them nervous. Anxiously they heard a church clock strike ten, somewhere down there right off in the mist. Now and then stamping their chilling feet – for this was only two evenings before Christmas – they stared in the direction from which the bus should come.

They had been strangers to one another, and had even eyed one another a shade suspiciously, until they had realised that they were both waiting for the same bus. Then – partly because it seemed idiotic that two human beings should ignore one another in this inhuman silence, partly as an outlet for their nerves – they had begun to talk: intermittently, stopping to strain their ears. She was a youngish countrywoman; he, in his dark overcoat with the collar up, looked urban, a civil servant; his nipped features were spare; now and then his glasses caught the diffused moonlight. She, laden with bulging string bags, satchels, parcels (she was carrying country produce back to town), stood, unaware of their weight and her numbing fingers, in an attitude at once stocky and statuesque. Whereas he who had with him nothing but a despatch case kept nervously shifting his grip on that.

"It *cannot* have passed before we got here?" said he – and he had said this before.

"No; it's just late. It's never before its time."

"You are quite sure what its time *is*?"

"Why, of course I am," she said conclusively. "It's the last bus."

"My heavens," he almost raved, "*that* I do know, only too well! –

What do you think has happened?"

She considered, then said: "Well, it's Christmas, for one thing."

"In that case, we may be left here to see the New Year in?"

"Well, I hope not," she said. "I'm in a hurry, too."

" – Stop, listen!" He put up his hand sharply. "Or is that simply one more of those damned lorries?" (For lorries had been playing them up already.)[1]

She listened, critically, to the vibration gathering in the distance, then pronounced: "No, that would not be a lorry. That's the bus all right. But – " again she listened – "it sounds to me sort of funny. Does it to you?"

It did. The sound was a sick sound – uncertain, jerky, rasping. The dimmed lights which, like pinpoints, now appeared in view shook and blinked with the efforts the bus was making. The bus traversed, in a series of these convulsions, the saucer of land above which the watchers stood. "Sounds to me," said the woman impartially, "like it's conking out." Her companion, for his part, was beyond words. The bus attempted to breast the hill towards them: change of gear tore a final screech from its vitals – it stopped dead. Triumphantly, silence fell.

The woman hitched up her parcels, the man regripped his despatch case: the two of them started downhill, as though in expostulation, towards the hulk, in whose dimmed blue inside the passengers were astir like uneasy ghosts. One by one the passengers got out, following the driver and the conductor: a despondent crowd began to form round the bonnet. The driver played his torch into the engine, shrugged, glanced at the conductor and said nothing.

"Surely," exclaimed a lady, "there must be *something* that can be done?"

"I dessay you're right, lady," replied the driver,[2] who, however, confined himself to shrugging again, stepping back and lighting a cigarette.

"But look here," asserted another voice, "I'm on important business!"

"*All* our business is very important," added somebody else. As for the civil servant, he turned to the countrywoman and emitted a long, bitter, expressive laugh.

"So they think," he said. "But if they knew about *me* – !"

"Well, whoever we are," she said, "we've all got to get to *some-where.*"

There had not been so many passengers in this last bus: in the course of exchanging looks of despair they took stock of each other, there in the misty moonlight, and automatically counted each other up – a lady in a fur coat, a small boy attached to the lady, an American soldier, a corporal in the A.T.S.,[3] an elderly clergyman, a commercial gentleman, a capable spinster type, a couple of students who looked foreign, a couple of lovers and a lean dark man in mufti who singled out the despatch-bearing civil servant for an address in rapid, emphatic French. To which the Englishman answered: "*Je ne sais pas.*"

"What does he want?" asked the countrywoman, sorry for any-body for being foreign.

The Englishman said: "He is asking what one had better do."

"That won't get him far," said she, shaking her head.

What they did all do was, get back into the bus. And even our two disappointed ones took their places, as at least some satisfaction for their long wait. The conductor, they were informed, was setting out on foot for the nearest village – by which one must understand, the least distant one – to telephone for a relief bus: it was much to be hoped he could flag a ride . . . At first, the passengers could not help sitting up alertly, as though this in itself might help them to continue their journey at any minute. And at first, their combined mood created a sort of psychological whirring, almost audible, in the unearthly blue gloom of the static bus.

The fur-coated lady then said: "We must try to imagine that time is no object."

"We must employ philosophy," said the clergyman.

"Why, sure," said the American, "show me some."

One student added, in broken English, that science would revolutionise the idea of time.

"No more revolutions for me, if you please," said the commercial gentleman, who, under a blue lamp, had been busily totting something up.

"Coo," murmured the little boy, from the lee of the lady's fur coat, "I bet *I* could make this old bus go!"

The spinster, with a good-natured laugh, indicated the lovers who, both wrapped in his overcoat, occupied, cheek to cheek, a dark front seat. "Here at least," she said, "we have two young people lucky enough not to care *where* they are!"

The girl only nestled her head lower, but the man raised his slightly, aroused to thought. "Yes, but we've got married," he said. "We've got to know where we're going."

At this, the corporal in the A.T.S. paused in the act of lighting a cigarette to give the spinster an informative smile: "Love's all right, but it won't take you all the way."

The Frenchman sighed and said in his own language: "Yet there was a time once – long ago, it is true – when I should have been happy to travel no further than that."

Only the newcomers, so far, had not spoken: the civil servant now glanced across at the countrywoman, as though he felt it was time *they* should set to partners. She sat feeling over her bags and parcels, to make certain nothing had fallen out: through a tear in her knitted glove gleamed a wedding ring. "And you," he said, "have urgent reasons to travel?"

She replied simply but fully: "I ought to be getting back."

"We must face the fact," said the spinster, "that we are not getting anywhere. It is extraordinary that our combined wills should be insufficient to move this bus. One could almost think that, between us, we could generate something. Our intelligence level" – she glanced round her fellow passengers – "is, on the whole, high. We represent several nationalities – "

"Ma'am," interposed the American, "we've kinda gotta stick here, so we've kinda gotta like it."

"One could always," said one of the students, "descend and walk."

"In that case," said his friend, "either this bus or its fellow, being in motion, would pass one; one would be left behind by oneself, travelling slowly, and, still worse, without any certainty of one's direction."

"Well, I must say," exclaimed the corporal, "this makes me sick! If you know what I mean, it's so like life – sitting there on your bottom wondering what will happen!"

"My dear child, my dear girl," said the clergyman, unable to hide his distress.

"Well, I'm sorry, I'm sure," said the corporal, "but I and all the girls I know don't intend to stand for it."

As she spoke, the little boy extricated himself from the lady's fur coat and began to tramp loudly up and down the bus. "*I'm* moving," he shouted triumphantly, "whichever way I'm going, I'm going somewhere!"

"Ah," said one of the students, "but you do not progress."

"At least," said the Frenchman, following the little boy sombrely, impersonally with his dark eyes, "what is essential is there – power, fire, energy. See him resist stillness: how right he is. Acquiescence is fatal: it is decay."

The civil servant opened his case an inch or two and looked, almost secretively, eagerly, at the papers inside. "If the light weren't so bad," he murmured, "I could always be getting on with something."

"In which case," asked the clergyman, courteously turning round in the seat in front, "you would have the illusion that you were getting somewhere? A help to you, my dear sir, but no help to the rest of us."

"Then do you, *my* dear sir," returned the civil servant, "propose to help by reminding us that faith moves mountains?"

"It is not a question of mountains," said the clergyman mildly. "And where this or any bus, or the course of the world, is concerned, I cannot claim to believe in *un*intelligent faith."

"Yes,' said the spinster, "and there is another thing – suppose we could all, by combined power, move this bus, should we all, do you think, agree on its destination? Tonight, it is true, it *would* happen to suit us all to arrive at the same place. But suppose we set out on a wider, long-term trip?"

The American stared at her ruminatively; the young husband shifted his beloved's head on his shoulder in order to listen better; the Frenchman, in a fidget of half-understanding, asked that the question be asked again; the students excitedly stamped out their cigarettes; the A.T.S. corporal eyed the spinster with at least a gleam of thoughtful respect; the clergyman cried: "Now, come; let us talk this out!" and the lady in the fur coat said: "Harold, stop trampling, dear; people want to hear what they're saying."

The countrywoman, intercepting Harold in mid-bus, said: "My big boy is a fidget, just like you," and allowed him to poke about in her string bag. "Well, at any rate," she observed to the civil servant, "we've come to be quite a party: we were such a pack of strangers."

As for him, he resignedly snapped his despatch case to. "Our thoughtful lady's question," he said, "has delusive simplicity of the kind that will no doubt keep us talking all night."[4] It was, in fact, about two o'clock in the morning when "the relief's" approaching headlights, melting in mist and moonshine, made the passengers realise, with some surprise, that, in point of fact, their bus *was* still standing still.

Fairies at the Christening

Nona Julia having been born exactly five weeks before Christmas Day, her christening could be combined with a Christmas party. This delighted her parents, who were young, handsome, happy and rich. It was not the economy which appealed to them – no, indeed, the young Claybees gave parties on the slightest excuse. Rather, they envisaged the sort of enchanted party they would be able to have, with their first child's great day lit by a Christmas tree. The tree would be crowned by a gilded cradle, topped by a star; white and silver ribbons would be threaded through wreaths of holly. Long before Mrs. Claybee was out of bed, she had been at

---

work on the lists of guests and godparents – sucking her pencil, frowning, ruffling her hair, tearing sheet after sheet off her writing-pad.

"This is by no means going to be so simple as we thought, my girl!" she exclaimed, from time to time, to Nona Julia.[1] The baby also frowned slightly and looked wise. "Take my advice," her mother went on, "and don't make too many best friends: I know what that lands one up in!" It always ended, of course, by Mrs. Claybee's tossing away the lists in order to concentrate, rapturously, on Nona Julia. In this dalliance, time rolled on, no less observed by the baby than by her mother. Tom Claybee, who in the first flush of father-hood had begun by saying that *nothing* mattered – why worry, darling? – began to worry himself. They really must soon get organised as to the christening party. "Perhaps we should put our minds to this?" he suggested, the first evening Angela (looking beautiful) came downstairs.

"Well, it's all so *difficult*, darling. You've no idea."

"Still, we ought to face it."

"Oh, it's not the guests," she moaned, "it's the godparents. As far as the *party* goes, there's no reason why we shouldn't ask everybody: we always have. Though of course, by this time many of them may have made other plans for Christmas. – Not that I shouldn't be sorry if they had," she added. "Nona Julia rather expects a crowd, and I certainly wouldn't like her to feel we'd muffed things. Still, it's not the party that's difficult: no, it's these fearful godparents!"

"Ought one to speak of godparents like that?"

"Oh, I wouldn't if they existed," she said hastily. "What is fearful about them is that they, so far, don't."

Tom stubbed one cigarette out, then lit another. He felt himself plunged into deep waters.[2] "I suppose most people decide these things in advance," he said. "As a matter of fact, I thought we had got the godfathers sorted out? – your brother Gervase and good old Andy. I believe, strictly, a girl's only allowed one godfather, but – "

" – There!" exclaimed Angela, beating the palms of her hands on the arms of her enormous brocade chair. "I *knew* you really wished she had been a boy!"

To clear up this misunderstanding took time, and tenderness. Tom, on returning to his own side of the fire, paused another moment, then felt it safe to go on: "All I'd meant to say was, what's the harm in stretching a point? She can perfectly well have two godfathers: there's no law against it."

"No; why should there be?" said Angela, slightly bored. "In fact, I've been taking it for granted that Gervase and Andy *would* be standing by. I thought at least that had been settled," she said reproachfully. "Do just ring them both up and make certain, this evening, darling, when I've gone back to bed. If they've made other plans for Christmas, they'll have to break them. – No, *godfathers* are quite simple."

"I see," said Tom.

"What really causes a headache are these appalling godmothers.[3] I suppose even you will agree she can't have about fifteen?"

This was too much. "Look," he said, "Angela, either you calm down, or go to bed. Fifteen godmothers! – are you running a temperature?"

"There *are* fifteen expectant ones – at least. Oh, what a mess! I shall have to tell you my past . . ."

She did. From the point of view of a young wife it was blameless, from that of[4] a young mother, extremely awkward. The whole story came out – Angela, it appeared, had been accumulating godmothers for her first child ever since she had been a child herself. All her life, she'd been sweet as she had been thoughtless. At her first school, for instance, she had sworn eternal friendship with another little girl called Boofie – Boofie's being godmother, to the first child Angela ever would have, had, naturally, gone along with that. At her second school, she had signed on Eileen, and then Carmel (she could not, now, remember their other names). Her Paris "finishing" year had been signalised by a riot of lifelong friendships, each one sealed by the same promise – in fact, if Angela kept her word, a Bolivian, an American from the Middle West, an exiled Romanian aristocrat and a West Indian heiress were all, shortly, due to be standing beside the font. During her time round London, she had acquired several more heart-to-hearts, all of whom, she'd been given to understand, had since then been steadily laying in gifts for their godchild. She'd also worked at an art school, where she became intimate with a sculptress – (such an artistic influence upon future offspring had been, of course, too good to be missed) – and had put in evenings helping at an East End girls' club: *there* she'd procured a godmother of a quite different type – a selfless, inspiring social worker. Finally, three or four women had been particularly sweet to her when she got engaged – advising and helping her (she had no mother). She had shown affection and gratitude in the good old way . . . For all she knew, *all* these expectant godmothers remained lined up, waiting for Nona Julia.

"I must have been mad," moaned Angela, at the end of her story.

Tom tried not to look thunderstruck, but failed. "Do you still know where all of them are?" he said.

"More the point is, do all of them know where I am? Now I think of it, I do wish I hadn't let you put that announcement of Nona Julia in *The Times*. Oh, how I hate breaking promises! I can't bear Nona Julia's having a mother who does that."

"One could stretch a point, I suppose – " Tom again began.

" – But not *past* a point," Angela cut in sharply. "No, she can have three godmothers; just exactly three. What she cannot possibly do is to have so many that the rest of the party can't get into the church. What would the Vicar say? He might stop the christening. And Nona Julia'd never forgive us, never: she'd feel we'd made her ridiculous at the very start. Oh, how I blame myself! – Tom, we shall have to think."

Tom, who had been thinking, fully agreed. He stared, waiting for inspiration, at the golden tip of Angela's shoe, shining in the dance of the firelight. She, made sleepy by the very idea of thinking, languidly stretched her arms above her head: the chiffon sleeves of the *négligée* fell away. They both heard the log fire flutter, the little gold clock tick. The Claybees' Queen Anne house was deep in the country: tonight, a soft dark wintry pre-Christmas silence wrapped it round. Along the chimneypiece a whole parade of Christmas cards was on view already. These *should* have reminded Angela of the portentous imminence of the Christmas christening: instead, she thought, "Why, cards get prettier every year! What a scrap-screen these will make, for Nona Julia's nursery!"

To celebrate young Mrs. Claybee's first evening down, the long low white-panelled drawing-room had been filled with flowers: chrysanthemums, violets and hot-house crimson roses glowed and curled in the light of the many lamps, their scent drawn out deliciously by the heat. She longed to have Nona Julia here to enjoy it all. At the thought of her daughter, Angela became lost in pride and bliss. So completely had she forgotten the godmother problem (now, like all other troubles, safely shelved on to Tom) that she looked blank when he, clapping his hands to his head, shouted triumphantly: "I've got it!"

"Oh yes, darling?"

"You write all their names down on little pieces of paper, I'll shake them up in a hat, then you shut your eyes and draw three."

"Oh, but . . ."

"I daresay it sounds mad," said Tom. "But whatever are we to do, in a mess like this? There's no way but allowing Fate to decide."

"What I mean is, you don't think it seems irreverent? After all, godmothers ought to be *good* women."

"These must all have seemed to you good, at one or another time," said Tom firmly, brooking no more discussion. Having fetched her a pencil and yet another writing-pad, he disappeared in search of one of his hats. He came back to find Angela scribbling, and tearing strips. She looked up and said: "Somehow this makes me nervous. Heaven knows who or what we may not be letting in! Oh Tom, only think what some godmothers do and are. Look at fairy tales – how do we know those are *not* true? Godmothers bring gifts, they spin spells, they put wishes on little girls. Darling, we're risking bringing out of the past three people I may have completely forgotten. Who knows what they mayn't have turned into? Life does queer things to people. Who knows what we're letting loose on to Nona Julia?"

Tom set his jaw and said nothing, simply held out the hat. She, with a shiver, dropped in the twists of paper; he shook; she shut her eyes and drew. She unfolded the three she had drawn, silently read them, and, still in silence, passed them across to Tom.

"Well, that's that," he said, having read. The three names conveyed nothing at all to *him*. "Do you know if they've, meantime, got married? Do you know their addresses?"

"The first and second, I can find." She paused, then stonily said: "Not the third – I've lost sight of *her*, absolutely and completely."

"In that case, we drop her out. – Like to draw again?" He once more held out the hat.

She recoiled from it. "No!" she protested. "This has been quite enough. A girl *is* only supposed to have two godmothers."

"Two let it be," said Tom.

That year, it was a white Christmas. Angela carried her daughter to the window, to look out at snow for the first time; but the baby only blinked, puckered up her face and rolled her head inwards towards her mother's breast. Perhaps the glare from the lawn, from the fields, from the whole expanse of blue-whiteness glistening in the sunshine, was too much? So Angela was enchanted all alone. Across the snow ran tiny prints of birds' feet; the boughs of the cedar were draped with frosted lace; cherry-trees gave the illusion of having come out in flower. Bending down her face over Nona Julia, she murmured: "Oh, treasure, my treasure, what a christening morning! The world is dressed up in white for you!" The air outside the window was crystal, silent: silence seemed to be spangled with echoes of carols, promise of Christmas bells.

Yes, this was Christmas Eve, and the christening day. The Claybees had sent chrysanthemums for the church font – on *that*, they implored the Vicar, let there be no prickly holly! They had sent a sack of coal for the church furnace, so that the old stone building might be warm right through. "We shall have to wrap up, wrap up well," Nurse muttered, bustling about all morning, airing Nona Julia's trousseau of fleecy shawls. The christening was to be at three o'clock; the godparents had been bidden to a family lunch; the rest of the party ("everyone") was expected in church. Celebrations would open upon the return home.

Everything was ready. On trays in the butler's pantry waited rows upon rows of polished champagne-glasses. Beyond yet another baize door, yards of fresh butter-muslin stretched over plates of dainties, sweet or savoury, everything from marzipan to caviare. The majestic Christmas-christening cake stood apart, with a veil to itself. Best of all, at the alcove end of the drawing-room soared Nona Julia's first Christmas tree – festooned with pink and silver, crowned by the gilded cradle, topped by a star, slung all over with glittery horse-shoes, cupids. Tier upon tier poised its candles, eager to be lit.

In good time for lunch that morning, the godfathers' car swept up to the Claybees' door. Of those two large, steady and cheerful men, Gervase and Andy, it need only be said that they were so perfectly appropriate to their roles, so outstandingly the ideal godfathers, as to need no description. They were all drinking sherry in front of the drawing-room fire when a second car hummed round the bend of the drive: in a moment more, Lady Panderwaite was announced. A tall, voluptuous brunette in a leopard-skin coat swam into the room and threw herself upon Angela, whom she kissed thrice on both cheeks, murmuring many things. Angela, once disentangled from

the embrace, threw an anxious glance over this first of the godmothers, and was, on the whole, reassured – Lady Panderwaite, if a
trifle flamboyant, should not do badly. Romanian-exile school-friend
of Angela's Paris days, she had since then married a wealthy British
explorer. Today she sparkled all over with jewellery, vivacity and
emotion: indeed, her gazelle eyes, set off by make-up, were at the
moment swimming with tender tears. "After all these years," she
cried, "all these years!" Angela glanced at Tom, Gervase and Andy,
wondering how this would go down with them. She was glad to see
that, after a minute of being overpowered, they adjusted to Lady
Panderwaite, and soon liked her well.

"I cannot say," added the lady, peeling out of her leopard to reveal
a clinging creation of *crème-de-menthe* green, "how much Angela's
remembering of our solemn pact has meant to me. I would have
come to this christening from the end of the world, if necessary – as
it was, I have had to fly only five hundred miles. Yes, a broken
promise would be a terrible thing; it would somehow destroy one's
illusions and break one's heart!"

Angela, recollecting how many, many names had been left to be
tipped out of Tom's hat into the fire (and, still worse, how each
name had stood for an ancient promise) avoided meeting Tom's eye:
she could only suffer and blush. She said hastily: "I wonder where
dear Miss Hingham can be? I do wish we *had* insisted on sending the
car to meet her. – We have three different stations," she told Lady
Panderwaite, "and she refused to tell us which one she'd be coming
to, or by what train. She has almost a mania about making her own
arrangements, being independent, not giving trouble. So often,
exactly that sort of thing *does* give trouble – supposing she never
turns up? Oh Tom, where can she be?"

As though by magic, the question answered itself – as, into view
of the windows came a lean, sturdy figure, footing it over the snowy
lawn. Miss Hingham, having taken a bus from one of the stations
part of the way, and a somewhat over-ingenious shortcut the rest,

was soon shown in, and removed her rabbit-fur stole. She was a social worker best friend, from the East End club. She beamed around at the company with her shy, kind, good face. "Bless you," she said to Angela, "and this dear, happy day! I'm so touched," she added, refusing a glass of sherry, "by your having kept your promise. And, dear child, not only touched but pleased. So long as we stand by our promises there will, I know, be always good in the world."

All four godparents being assembled, lunch was announced.

When they set out for the christening, a few more snowflakes came floating down vaguely through violet air. The three cars, cautiously driven, crept in file through the lanes between the house and the church. Sealed up in the leading car, in warmth and a swirl of fur rugs, travelled Nona Julia, Angela and Nurse: Tom, trusting no one else with these precious passengers, drove. Snowflakes melted like kisses against the windows; white-powdered hedgerows slipped by softly. Now and then the baby, contented, stirred in her shawls, or opened unfocussed eyes in which were reflected the gleams of the afternoon. Nurse held her, Angela pressing up close. For Angela, all this was like a deep, sweet dream – a dream cut short by the halt, by the car's door's opening,[5] by the scurry, umbrella-guarded, up the short path from the church gate to the porch.

Inside the porch, nightmare set in, without warning. For, *who* was this who stood in the shadows, waiting – and waiting with such a fateful air?

A voice inside Angela told her. The Third Godmother . . .

Bright-coloured Lady Panderwaite, pale Miss Hingham, each escorted by one of the two godfathers, stepped from their cars, were ushered into the church, and made straight for their places beside the font. It was here that the Unknown joined them. The wrong-looking little figure – beret pulled down over wisps of brittle blonde hair; "loud," shabby tartan overcoat; preposterous scarlet bootees, mock-fur gauntlets – edged its way into the forefront of the group round the font, and there stood firm. Impossible to account for, utterly impossible to displace by stares, frowns, murmurs or courteous nudges, this cuckoo among the godparents held her ground. Her small, pale, rather puffy face, mute of any expression, looked ageless: she seemed neither young nor old. She greeted no one, keeping her eyes cast down, till the moment when Nurse uncovered Nona Julia's head – then, she started forward, as though expecting to take the baby into her own arms. Tom made an anxious movement; Angela caught a breath. The Vicar glanced once over his glasses, then shook back the sleeves of his surplice, opened his book, raised his voice. The christening began. As though brought to a halt by the holy words, the intruder stood with a frozen smile. Her look, however, stayed fixed upon Nona Julia.

Above, the arches, the vaulted roof of the church soared up into dusk. Beyond the font, the perspective of aisles was lamplit: far off, the chancel brasses shone. Now and then from swags of holly a berry dropped. There was a smell of evergreens, ancient stone, musty hassocks, woodwork polished for Christmas. Here and there lamplight caught the head of a cherub, or a line of gilt lettering in an old memorial; back on their tombs in the shadows crusaders sternly slept. Day faded slowly out of the coloured windows. In the foreground Angela saw, through a blur, what should have been reassuring rows of faces – friends, bound for the party, had come to the church, had packed themselves into the pews nearest the font, and all stood looking towards the baby. She could but feel how perplexed or marvelling eyes returned, again and again, to the Third Godmother. Trembling a little, she slipped her arm through Tom's. The Vicar's voice rose and fell, and she tried to pray.

Tom whispered: "Steady, darling."

"I'm scared."

"I know. *Who* is she – any idea?"

"She must be Boofie. The third name out of the hat."

They were back at the house: the party was in full swing. Indeed, the candles of the Christmas tree were by now beginning to burn low – though a low-lit, amber effect of candle-light magically persisted in all the rooms. In the same way, a sort of electrical, hushed excitement seemed to flow through the nearly two hundred guests. Something mysterious and disturbing was afoot this evening. The current, whatever it might be, made a circuit through the ground floor of the house; for, everywhere, wide folding-doors stood open – guests could move where and as they chose. On the whole, they were showing a tendency to cluster – in or around sofas, in curtained window-embrasures or before the roaring fires. There was a vibrant, almost tense, hum of talk; and, from group to group, greetings, calls and laughter, all pitched just slightly out of the normal key. Certainly the party was not flat; seldom had any party had more "atmosphere."[6]

Nona Julia, princess of the occasion, had made a serene, swift progress, in Nurse's arms, throughout the company: she had now been carried upstairs and was no longer on view. Since then, in default of her presence they had all drunk her health. Yes, the champagne had gone round, and came round again – yet, even while raising their glasses to their lips, it might be noted that friends exchanged glances, as though wondering whether these golden bubbles might not be, also, under some spell?[7] And it indeed seemed that the champagne, drunk in any amount, rather tuned down than tuned up the noise of the party, by intensifying a sort of unearthly intimacy between the guests. Talkers closed in; the centres of floors cleared. Still, no one spoke directly of what was in the air – either from fearing to be the first to do so, or from lacking words in which to say what they felt – which was as peculiar as it was inexpressible. Soon, each of the thronged rooms, linked by their open doors, held no more than a sighing, shell-like murmur.

Nor did the murmur peter out: it broke off sharply. Within a split second, there fell a complete hush.

The three godmothers came walking down the drawing-room.

Side by side, looking neither to left nor right, the three passed straight down the centre of the long, shining floor, to disappear through the archway giving upon the stairs.

This was the first, and last, time the three were seen together – by the outside world.

Up to now, the first and second godmothers had been holding stately, separate little courts, hovered over by one or the other godfather. Lady Panderwaite, upon the return from church, had taken up her position beside the Christmas tree, which she all but outshone. In the blaze from the dozens of little candles, she had enthroned herself on a golden Florentine chair – her jewellery sparkled with every movement; her exotic gown shimmered like green flame. Turning those eyes from face to face, she had discoursed brilliantly (if with the faintest air of preoccupation) on almost every subject under the sun. She held, but did not drink, a glass of champagne; which, while she talked, she at intervals held aloft, nto a fuller radiance from the tree. It was noted that the champagne in her glass held more, and more lively, bubbles than any other. She fascinated but faintly alarmed her listeners – whenever these showed signs of melting away, either Gervase or Andy, watchful, would round up others. Between Lady Panderwaite's circle and the rest of the party there had been, it must be admitted, always a slight gulf. Several of those who refused to cross it explained that the heat from the candles was overpowering.

Miss Hingham had, on the other hand, shown every wish to remain obscure. She had made immediately for an upright chair at the less frequented end of the diningroom, from which neither Tom nor the godfathers could budge her. She had been brought what she asked for, a cup of tea, and from time to time she nibbled a finger biscuit, pausing to brush crumbs from her threadbare skirt. She gazed with remote kindness upon the festive scene, enjoyed a chat with the waiters in charge of the buffet, and smiled at such guests as happened to come her way. She was not for long allowed to remain alone; in fact, it began to be odd how the Claybees' smart young friends instinctively gravitated towards her. Yearning, somehow, to tell all their troubles and ask her advice or help, they swarmed like flies round the honey-pot of Miss Hingham; having soon to be driven off by the godfathers rather than led up. This thin lady in the old-fashioned hat had, decidedly, the air of belonging elsewhere. What *could* she be carrying round with her in that crammed, worn handbag – of such antique style that it more rightly should have been called a "reticule"?

It was recollected, later, that away down there, at Miss Hingham's end of the diningroom, the electric tenseness hanging over the rest of the party was not felt. It was replaced, in her ambience, by something *as* strange – but good. It was ironical that those who had hung upon her words could not, by next day, remember a single one of them. What did remain was an indefinable something which, from then on, altered and sweetened life.

The person thought to be Boofie had held no court. Still in the bad little thrust-down beret, she had sauntered, aggressively solitary, from room to room. From wherever she came to a halt, people moved away. Sometimes, arms folded, she leaned against the panelling, turning that intent, unseeing stare of hers this way, that way. Steered clear of by the waiters, she made a dart at champagne left standing in any glass; and, in the same way, mopped up the last dishevelled eatables left on plates. On whichever room she entered, she had the same effect – it was as though a window, letting in dead-cold air, had been surreptitiously opened behind a curtain.

She had melted from view when the party moved from the church: the Claybees had dared to hope that might be the last of her. But alas, far from it: here again she was – this time, at large in their home! *How* she had got in, how she'd made her way from the church, no one seemed to know. Tom, Gervase and Andy had, at the outset, gone into hasty conference: it would be better, they had decided, to take with this so-called Boofie one or another definite line – in short, either bid her welcome or run her out. But the dementing thing was that, though there and everywhere, she was never "here." Perpetually to be sighted in the distance, she never was to be cornered, face to face. In vain did Tom and Andy – working in opposite directions, so that they met halfway – between them fine-comb the crowded rooms.[8] Somehow, some way, she still slipped through their fingers. Her smallness helped, of course. She remained everywhere, nowhere. It *was* uncanny.

Andy shrugged and said: "I don't see what more we can do."

"All the same, something's got to be done, old man. Angela's worrying herself sick."

Angela, actually, had had the good idea of retreating to a sofa in her sanctum, in company with a promising new best friend, who was soothing her. Thanks to this, she began to feel better – till, through the open door, they both heard that sudden, icelike fall of the hush.

"My heavens!" she said, "what's *that*? Have they all dropped dead?"

The obliging new friend offered to go and see. Angela lay back with her eyes shut.

The friend, coming back, reported: "That was the godmothers. They have gone upstairs to say goodnight to the baby."

"Who says?" cried Angela, starting up.

"Everyone says."

"How many have gone up?"

"Three."

How, where and when had the three godmothers made contact? So far as anyone knew, they had hardly so much as spoken to one another the whole day. At lunch, Lady Panderwaite and Miss Hingham – who had not, one might say,[9] anyhow much in common – had been placed at opposite sides of the table. They had gone to the christening in different cars; throughout the party they had stayed in different rooms. Also, neither of these two godmothers had taken the slightest notice of the third – at least, *visibly*. Neither had batted an eyelid when she appeared in church. Perhaps, now, one came to think of it, that had not surprised them? Had these three, who had never met till today (and, indeed, how should they: they were so fantastically unalike) been acting in accord with some pact or plan? If so, it was a pact outside mortal ken.

Not a sign or a glance had passed between them. Evidently, they had communicated by other means – in a manner known to their kind only. All through the party, they had been maintaining touch: when once their moment arrived, they knew it. They rose and met. They had foregathered, and been for the first time three. Possibly nothing could happen until they *were* three. Strangest of all, no one had seen them going to meet each other. Conspicuous Lady Panderwaite had unnoticed been able to rise from her golden chair. No one could tell how Miss Hingham had slipped past the crowded buffet, or by what invisible route she had made her way to that doorway at the distant end of the drawing-room. As for the hitherto skulking little Third, with what forbidding grandeur she had invested herself, as, with the others, she made the grand exit!

And, from what arose the impression that they had gone upstairs? Everyone *said* they had done so: no actual witnesses to their ascent of the staircase could be found. Had there, then, been nobody in the hall when they swept through it? Yes, there must have been: guests were all over the house. But the groups round the foot of the staircase, now being interrogated by Angela, all explained, they had not been there at the time. Other people had been in the hall then – why not ask them? But those other people no longer seemed to exist.

She made a start by herself up the empty stairs. This took courage. She attempted to master those wild forebodings, those throat-gripping terrors known to mother-love. Her one thought was, Nona Julia. She must keep calm – she did.

Up here, the soft-carpeted corridors were empty, cryptic, silent.

She hurried in the direction of the nursery then, for a moment, faltered outside the beloved, familiar door. What utterly *shut*, almost sealed-up look it had! She fingered the door-handle – how if it refused to turn? However, turn it did, and she crossed the threshold . . . Nona Julia's domain was in semi-darkness: a glow came from the fire inside the high fender; from a table away in a corner a pygmy lamp, shaded to imitate a toadstool, cast shadows up the walls, to the ceiling. For an instant, it seemed that the shadows round Nona Julia formed into the outline of three gigantic heads. But, no – that was an illusion: no one stood round the cradle.

"*Nurse* – are you there?"

"Why, yes, madam," Nurse replied – but not altogether promptly, and in a drowsy voice. Of course she was there: in the dim red from the fire, the starch of her apron gleamed. There she sat, on duty, correctly stiff in her chair; but, nevertheless, nodding – before she could speak again, she had to bite off a yawn. "To tell you the truth," she admitted, "I've been taking forty winks. Baby's asleep so nicely, and it's been quite a day."

"*Have* any people been in here?"

"Why, nobody comes in my nursery without permission," said Nurse, trying to bridle – but, drowsily.

"I daresay; but you've just told me you dropped off. Would you have known if anyone *had* come in?"

Without awaiting the answer, Angela rushed to the cradle. Nona Julia slept. On her silk quilted counterpane reposed three objects, foreign-looking and queer. Angela, having swept these up, took them over to the lamp in the corner[10] to examine them. One was a diamond bracelet, wrought in the shape of a series of linked hearts: to it was attached yet another, pink paper, heart, on which, in a foreign script, were indited the words, "*In this life, there can never be too many.*" The next was a small account book, in a black shiny cover, with a silver pencil tied to it by a cord.[11] Inside the cover was written: "*Dear child, of all matters keep careful account. One day, you may be asked what the total is. Work hard, think of others, and love truly."*

The third was a letter, addressed to Nona Julia. Boofie's hand-writing (Angela thought, as she read) had not changed much since she was ten years old.

The letter ran thus: –

"YOU will not remember, Nona Julia, but never let them forget to tell you that I came. The godmother they forgot to ask is always the one who brings bad luck and bad wishes, and I meant to. I would have known how, because I have gone to the bad, they say. Anyway, I am an inconvenient person. Your mother's wise, she knows that – there never was any place in her life for inconvenient people. But I was not inconvenient to her when we were both ten. That was when she made me your first godmother. What one has once been made to be, one is, always. That is why I am here.

This is what I am wishing you, Nona Julia – a life in which there can always be some place for inconvenient people. Make them tell you how my name came out of the hat. I WAS to come here. Dear godchild, I have been waiting for you for years and years, and once I hoped to be good for you, but I lost my way somehow. The world is full of people with no places, flittering around like bats, and someone must be good to them: that is what I wish you. I came here ugly and full of spite. But from the moment your nurse took the shawl off your face, I knew you had something for me and I had something for you, though we are never to meet again.

The two others have wished you Happiness in Love and Truthfulness.[12] *They are allowing me to wish you the final thing necessary, if you are to be a person.*

After this, we are going. All three of us must be out of here long before the hour of midnight strikes and Christmas Eve is over. You have been christened on the one magic day. Remember there is always magic in the world.

Sleep sweet, Nona Julia, and wake happy. You are at the beginning of what I wish you – Life."

The last of the guests had gone. When the last of the cars had driven away, the village carol singers came and took up their stand on the snowy lawn and sang "Noel." The air was already milder: through opened windows night was allowed to blow through the littered, now empty party rooms. Before they went to bed, Tom and Angela Claybee went into the nursery to kiss Nona Julia, who slept sweetly on, with Boofie's letter where Angela had slipped it, under her pillow.

Angela, through her sleep, heard the clocks strike twelve. The day of magic was over; the greater Day had begun.[13] She thought of the world, and said "Happy Christmas."

Christmas Games

Phyllida turned, at last, into Market Square. Gasping with breathlessness and anxiety she looked across it – yes, there, outside the Red Lion, were lined up the country buses, half a dozen of them: lights full on, packed up inside with people and showing every sign of being ready to start. "Oh, wait!" she called, to the world in general, and, only pausing to shift from one to the other hand her suitcase, which by now weighed like lead, she put on a last spurt of speed and dashed over the cobbled space. "Plenty of time, miss, plenty of time!" shouted one or two of the onlookers, but she could not believe them. Since she had started out on this Christmas journey, everything, everything possible, seemed to have gone wrong.

She had stayed too long in London, doing belated shopping, and thereby missed the train she'd been told to take; she had lost her ticket and had to pay for another; and she had, just now, emerged from Brindford station to find (as she knew she deserved) no car to meet her, and the last of the taxis whirling away. A porter, on learning her destination, told her there was still a bus to there, but she'd have to run for it – a late-evening, extra service, laid on for Christmas Eve. Run she did, often losing her bearings: she had never been here in Brindford before. This was, in fact, her first Christmas in England – as things were, which was sad, the charm of the old-fashioned town at this festive season was being totally lost on her. Peals of bells being rung from an ancient steeple mingled with the throbbing inside her head; she was dazzled by the many lights of small shops – windows a-shimmer with tinsel, slung with paper chains, cast their reflections on to the damp pavements, till she felt herself lost in a mirror maze. Good-humoured townsfolk, gathering late to talk, formed an obstruction at every corner – nobody else in Brindford was in a hurry. *If* she were to miss this last bus, there would be nothing for it but to hire a car for the whole of the fifteen miles. Had she the money to pay one? – she was pretty sure not. What a way to arrive at an unknown house; if, indeed, she ever arrived at all!

Phyllida surged up and down the line of buses, crying, "Oh, which one for Little Birdover?" She found herself being hoisted by willing hands onto the one for Mockington-under-Wyck, pulled off it again, thrust firmly into another; which, she was told, put Little Birdover[1] passengers down at a nearby corner called Gallows Cross. Someone seized her suitcase and swung it on the rack; and men standing up passed her from hand to hand to the back seat; upon which five stout women cleared for her six inches or so of space. Gratefully, slim little Phyllida wedged herself in between them –

lapfuls of parcels, bunches of mistletoe, babies, extended into the distance on either side.

"Goodness," remarked her placid right-hand neighbour, "you ran it fine! However, all's well that ends well."

"Yes," agreed Phyllida, wishing that the end were in sight.

"Excuse me, but aren't you strange to these parts?"

Phyllida nodded. "I've come from London." All heads, at that, turned to look at her, somewhat dubiously, and someone suggested: "You'll be finding it quiet here, then."

"Oh, but that's what I'll like! I grew up with the prairie all round me – I'm a Canadian."

That set them all off talking. What, then, was she doing in London? She was a student. Didn't she miss her family? Yes, that *was* sometimes bad. Was she not young to have come so far, alone? She was (she said proudly) twenty. Did she know two Canadians, ever such nice young lads, who'd spent their leaves at Great Grogsby during the war? Alas, not – Canada is so big. Did she – but at this point the bus started: having been throbbing for some time, it heaved, with a grind of gears, into forward motion, to nose its way out through the small streets into open country. All round Phyllida flowed dark, hidden England, to be excitedly sensed by her, not seen. The bus lights ran over tree trunks, hedgerows, here and there a gate; each, picked out for a moment, slipped back to be lost to view. From now on, it was hard to talk without shouting, but her companions were in excellent voice: the five, while she stared at the windows, continued their questionnaire.

"You don't, then, know many in this country?"

"So far, almost no one. – I've only been here two months."

"Tck-tck – lonely for you, at Christmas! Not got any relatives on this side?"

"One of my aunts lived in England; but she's dead."

"Tck-tck. – Then what brings you into these parts? Going to friends?"

"I hope so. – That's to say, I haven't met them yet."

"Little Birdover people, I shouldn't wonder? Birdover people are friendly – that is, mostly."

Phyllida saw no reason not to reveal her plans. "I'm going to Mrs. Throcksby's – Ravenswood Hall."

This news produced an immediate hush, an uneasy blend of constraint, condolence, suspicion. Significant glances and nudges were exchanged; it seemed to Phyllida that the women seated on either side of her drew away a little. Another, at the end of the line, said: "Ah, well," in a forlorn attempt to remain hopeful. What remained unsaid, by the others, spoke volumes more. After an awkward interval, her good neighbours turned to each other, to speak of their own affairs; for the rest of the journey Phyllida felt ruled out.

Misgiving gripped the young traveller by the throat; the apprehensions which had hung over her all day surged up and began to reach fever-pitch. Why, oh why, had she ever accepted this invitation? Mrs. Throcksby's letter arriving out of the blue, had seemed, at the time, the solution of her whole Christmas problem – growing more and more homesick, as the season approached, she had dreaded spending those days alone in a semi-deserted London hostel. Mrs. Throcksby, introducing herself, had written that she had been a dear friend, a very close friend, of Phyllida's late Aunt Beattie,[2] the one who had died in England. As Aunt Beattie, after sailing from Canada, had ceased to keep in touch with the rest of the family, there was no way of checking up on this information; however, the whole thing sounded likely enough. Mrs. Throcksby, she said, took an interest in girls' hostels; and, on scanning the books of the one at which Phyllida lived, had been delighted to see a familiar name. Dear Beattie had spoken of her niece Phyllida Haughton – who had been no more than an infant when she, Beattie Haughton, left home. It would therefore give Mrs. Throcksby the greatest pleasure if Phyllida would spend Christmas at Ravenswood,

Little Birdover.

"I have lived very secludedly," she had added, "since my poor husband's death; but we still keep a typical English Christmas, and shall be glad to show you something of our old-fashioned ways. Two of my nephews, and my invalid uncle, will be at Ravenswood; in addition to my companion, a sensitive, cultured person, and myself."

It had, in fact, all sounded pretty good. Why, then, as Christmas Eve approached, had Phyllida fallen into a state of conflict? Several times she had considered sending a telegram saying that she was ill and could not leave town – but, besides being unwilling to tell a lie, she had, each time it came to the point, lost her nerve when she went to despatch the message. Reluctance (for which she could not account) to embark on the journey to Ravenswood had mingled with the most odd compulsion to do so – as though Mrs. Throcksby's letter had cast a spell on her! The lady's handwriting, topped by the heavy black gothic lettering of the note-paper, had, each time she looked again at it, seemed ominous. Why, though? Was it not Phyllida's policy to stand no nonsense from herself? What was she, indeed, but a thoroughly lucky girl, having this chance to enjoy a Dickens-y Christmas, in a traditional English country home?

Every time she leaned forward to look out of a window, she met the reflection of her own small, fair, anxious face, with the beret pushed back, against the outside flying darkness. Now, however, the bus lurched downhill into a belt of white mist, on which the lights fell chunkily: Phyllida's image vanished. The passengers, to cheer their way through this blinded scene, broke out into singing carols or cracking jokes with each other; and with this Phyllida's spirits rose – there *was* something warming about this jovial, close-packed, human rush through the night! Stops began to be made, and people got off or on. All at once the conductor yelled: "Gallows Cross – this is you, miss!"

Nobody else, it turned out, descended here. Phyllida's suitcase was dropped down to her, and, armed with directions and good wishes (in some of which she detected a pessimistic note) she set out on her tramp to Ravenswood Hall – first gate on the left, they'd said, on this side of Little Birdover. Looking back, she watched the bus disappear – then, slowly, the road ahead of her glimmered out into view, under faint, cloud-muffled gleams of moonlight. This was not a "white Christmas": snowlessness still surprised her – from the dark woods she drank in damp, mysterious smells; and she could hear somewhere, magnified by the winter silence, the tinkle of an English, unfrozen brook. Something august, but a little frightening, brooded over this breathless night.

She had had enough of the sound of her own footsteps by the time she came to the spiked gate, set in still higher walls. This, from all accounts, was the entrance to Ravenswood. She pushed at the gate, which creakingly yielded: inside, the drive was pitch-black, tunnelled through arching evergreens. She felt in her overcoat pocket for her torch – blessing the last-moment instinct which had made her bring it! – and kept its small, bright beam probing ahead of her. Round a bend, the drive broadened into a gravel sweep; at the far side massively loomed a house – high, narrow, and without a light showing. Ravenswood gave, in fact, every impression of having been bolted and barred up for the night. She at last located the entrance porch, its nail-studded door and iron bell-pull.[3] She rang: the lugubrious jangling set up inside the house produced, for quite a long time, no sign of life, and she was about to attack again when, without warning, bolts were pulled back inside. A key grated round in a lock and the door opened – opened just wide enough to allow someone, dimly outlined by lamplight, to peer round it. "What d'you want?" asked the man, in an edgy, harsh voice. "I say," he repeated, "what do you *want*?"

"To come in, please. – This is Ravenswood, isn't it?"

"Well, and what if it is?"

"I'm Phyllida Haughton – Mrs. Throcksby's expecting me."

"She may once have been: by now, she's given you up."

"Well, I'm sorry; but would you tell her I'm here?"

He hesitated, then, with marked reluctance, said: "All right, then, you can come in and wait. I'll ask."

Stumbling over the threshold with her suitcase, Phyllida found herself in a pine-panelled hall. A lamp stood on a table, but gloom poured down from above, from a number of echoing galleries. The place – which to a more calm or more knowing eye would have revealed itself as a neo-Gothic monstrosity, built about 1880 – smelled of musty woodwork and tiles; and from somewhere back away in the shadows an old clock gave out a dragging tick. She, chafing her hands together – for it was colder in here than it had been outdoors – stood anxiously, while the man who had let her in shambled off through an archway and poked his head round a door, to announce: "Well, here *is* your girl: she's arrived."

At once, a voice let out a triumphant "*Ah!*" A female form came gliding into the hall, and both Phyllida's hands were seized in a clawlike grip. "I told them you wouldn't fail us!" cried Mrs. Throcksby.

"I missed my train, I – "

"Oh, never mind, never mind, dear!" cut in her hostess, peering at her intently. "The important thing is that *here* you are, just in time!" She divested Phyllida of her overcoat, and removed her gloves and even her bag from her, with the air of making quite certain she should now remain. "Now," she said, "come along, come along."

In the drawing-room into which Phyllida was propelled, three more people sat, tensely, round the smouldering fire. The atmosphere was so charged with expectation that the girl almost turned and ran out again – for why *should* such importance attach itself to the late arrival of a young, unknown, quite insignificant Christmas guest? An inscrutable, aged gentleman in a wheeled chair continued to sit like an image, but darted a snake-like look: Mrs. Throcksby introduced him as her Uncle Ben. A very thin, long-faced lady, knitting away beside him, proved to be Miss Battiter – the cultured companion referred to in Mrs. Throcksby's letter.[4] Miss Battiter swift y eyed Phyllida, up and down, gave a slight nod, exchanged a glance with her patron, but said nothing. A nice-looking fair young man – till now engaged in frowning down at the carpet, whistling soundlessly – shot up, when Phyllida entered, to his full height and stood staring towards her. Admiration, quick interest, but something more – one might have said, foreboding – were in his eyes: he appeared to be trying to signal an urgent warning.

"And that," explained Mrs. Throcksby, indicating the youth, "is my great-nephew, Felix – Why, wake up, Felix: shake hands! Where are your wits?" Felix held out his right hand, awkwardly. "And my other nephew, Claud," the hostess went on, "you've already met: he welcomed you at our door. – Come, Claud, dear, come and sit down again.' Claud took his place, morosely, in the family circle. He looked like a clever, crossgrained, middle-aged schoolboy – one with something dire upon his mind.[5] Phyllida wondered whatever made Claud so hostile.[6]

It struck her, too, that ever since she had entered, no one but Mrs. Throcksby had uttered a single word. Tongue-tied herself, she sat and looked round the drawing-room – which was enlarged by cavernous tarnished mirrors around its walls, and lit by lamps whose reflections bleakly faded away. Against the mirrors, on tables, stood transparent cases of stuffed night-birds, some posed with beaks open, others with outstretched wings. A set of ebony chairs, carved in strange designs, all faced the same way and seemed to stand at alert: small tables were dotted about between them, and on one of these stood objects draped in a sheet – possibly, she thought, glancing that way again, those might be some of the presents for to-morrow? So far, she admitted with sinking heart, Ravenswood failed to resemble Dingley Dell. On the chimneypiece, below a sombre engraving representing a scene from *Macbeth*, vases held a few sprigs of berry-less holly – stuck in, she guessed, for her benefit, at the last moment. This was, however, the room's sole Christmassy touch.

"Are you looking for anything, dear?" asked Mrs. Throcksby.

"Why, no!" said Phyllida, giving a violent start.

"You're beginning to feel at home, I hope, already? How pleased she would be, your poor Aunt Beattie Haughton, to think of you safe here under my roof at last!" Mrs. Throcksby rapidly licked her lips, then added, "and after all your adventures. Tell us about them, do."[7]

A ripple of impatience, at this, seemed to run through the others – Miss Battiter looked up anxiously at the clock; Uncle Ben let out a frustrated bleat and began, like a baby, to slap the arms of his chair. Mrs. Throcksby quelled them all with a glance. "Plenty of time," she told them. "Pussy hasn't been found yet. – Go on, dear, about your dreadful journey." Phyllida, turning to face her hostess, began her tale of lost trains and confused arrival, but, somehow, made little headway with it – she was put off by something avid in those glittering eyes. What did they make her think of? – the Wolf Grandmother. Mrs. Throcksby, draped in blackish-purple, wore her hair in a frizzed fringe over her bony forehead: her somewhat peculiar smile darted in and out, overshadowed by a long, beaklike nose. Though concentrated, overpoweringly, upon Phyllida, she seemed to be hardly listening to her story, till it came to a certain point – she then interrupted: "Bus? – Oh, I hope you did not get into talk with those country people? An inquisitive, ignorant, super-stitious lot! I do hope you did not mention this house?"

"Of course she chattered," Claud put in. "Girls always do."

Mrs. Throcksby looked blackly put out: silence once more fell. Outdoors, in the distance, a villager crossing the fields could be heard whistling a Christmas carol; elsewhere a late train whistled, a dog barked. Those sane sounds called straight to Phyllida's heart – *Oh* to be out of Ravenswood, free again, in the kindly country! How ever was she to live through this pent-up visit? Instinctively she turned and looked round for Felix – who, still in that state of agitation, hovered always not far from her chair. Hunching his shoulders in his nice tan tweed coat, he kept tensely driving his fists down into the pockets. Was he, in spite of his refreshingly normal looks, just one more of those "cases" one heard of? Or, was this love at first sight,[8] slightly out of control? Nonsense, thought Phyllida briskly. Nonsense apart, however, she had been about enough to know that romance did tend to surround her path; or, to put the matter more modestly, that she was not so bad. She was, in point of fact, strikingly pretty – sitting buttoned up to the throat in her cherry-red suit, bright tips of hair curling cut from under her beret, small feet in their fur-lined bootees tucked back under her chair, she shone like a lamplit flower in this grim drawing-room. She sent a smile, with just a hint of inquiry, in the direction of Felix. Here – she hoped – was a friend!

Miss Battiter, at a sign from Mrs. Throcksby, skewered her knitting, got up and hurried out of the room. Phyllida's hostess, her brow clearing with the same alarming suddenness as it had darkened, said: "We've been keeping a little something warm for you, dear; we thought you'd need it, after travelling so far. You'll enjoy it – one of our special home-made brews." Phyllida, who had subsisted since leaving London on nothing but buns and sandwiches out of paper bags, murmured thanks. "And you, Claud," his aunt said, "go out and look again!" Claud also rose, to pad out after Miss Battiter. The others sat with eyes fixed on the clock – Uncle Ben's frustrated excitement became quite painful.

"It's very kind of you," Phyllida repeated.

"Not at all: you'll do well to keep up your strength. This being Christmas Eve, we all sit up late. In a minute, we are going to play some games."

"Ah!" squeaked the uncle, showing his toothless gums and jubilantly rubbing his hands together.

"Games?" echoed Phyllida, faintly. The yawn she smothered ran away in a shudder all down her spine.

"Yes, indeed. We've been only waiting for you."

"But your nephew, Claud, just now, said you'd given me up."

'That was only Claud's fun, dear. He doesn't care for girls; but, as I said to him, 'This year, we cannot get on without one.'"

"Cannot get on with what?"

"Why, our games," explained Mrs. Throcksby, licking her lips.

Claud reappeared, with a black cat under his arm – he dropped the beast on the hearthrug and said: "Here's pussy." The cat, swaying its bristling tail, turned its head and looked slowly at those around it with an at once conspiratorial and malignant air. Miss Battiter, having re-entered on Claud's heels, meanwhile advanced towards Phyllida with a large cup and saucer on a small tray.[9] Felix shot forward, seized the tray from Miss Battiter, swayed in his tracks a moment, appeared to stumble, dropped it. Of the steaming liquid soaking into the carpet, no small part had splashed on Phyllida's skirt, and objects which must have been floating in the brew lay around on all sides, among the broken china – one, at least, looked oddly like a toad's leg.

Felix, going down on one knee by the arm of Phyllida's chair, went through the motions of clearing up the mess – she, at the same time, leaned forward to mop her skirt. Swiftly, wildly, he whispered into her ear: "You're in *danger! Must* have a word with you – get out of here *somehow!*"

She never quite knew, later, how she achieved that hysterical dash out into the hall – she called out something (she dimly recollected about looking for water to sponge her best, new suit, and was at and out of the door before they could stop her. From the hall, she fled to the exit porch, to be confronted by bolts, bars, chains and turned keys. Steps could be heard behind her; she moaned with fear – but it was Felix who stole up and seized her wrist. "*Not* that way," he muttered, "not enough time!" and, pulling her with him, made off down a stone-flagged passage. Through yet another doorway, she caught a glimpse of a kitchen – ordinary-looking enough but for a large black cauldron placed on the centre table, with the air of being in transit to somewhere else. At the end of this passage, lit by a glowering oil lamp, the way out was also barred and bolted, but Felix, with Phyllida still in tow, took a sharp turn and began to mount twisting back-stairs. The boy and girl crept and stumbled. At the first landing he pulled up, and, cautiously, eased open a stiff sash window. They crawled out through it on to a flat-topped roof, and he pushed down the window behind them, silently as before.

Breathless, they sat leaning shoulder to shoulder. Below them, down in the black-dark courtyard, something rattled its chain; far above, steep gables, clusters of chimney-stacks took form slowly against the clotted night sky.[10] Phyllida's nervous system raced like a little engine – coatless, she shivered, partly from reaction. Then, comfort stole in from the warmth of Felix's frame; and, relaxing, wholly yielding herself to the sheer and blessed sensation of escape, she allowed his hand to brush lightly over hers. "Gosh," he sighed, "you've been wonderful. – Cigarette?"

That, for some reason, unhappily broke the spell: she withdrew her hand and said sharply: "Well? – What *are* we doing up here?"

"Lying low, till the hue-and-cry has died down."

"But I can't say I hear any hue-and-cry." This was true: nothing stirred indoors in the house behind them; Ravenswood seemed to be locked in astounded silence – as it might well be, for how had its guest behaved? How if her fears in the drawing-room had been some mad delusion? Mrs. Throcksby's family party might, after all, have been nothing more than slightly stiff and eccentric – had she not heard, at home, that the best English ancient families were like this? This was, after all, her first visit to such a house; many more might be like it – how was she to tell? *Oh*, how she had blotted her copy book – what would they think of Canada? So kindly received in the drawing-room, so quickly offered refreshment – then, tearing out on to the roof like a hunted cat! "Cat," it was true, immediately brought to mind that ominous animal on the hearthrug; but might not that be no more than an ancient and honoured pet? Who was this young man, this Felix, to play such tricks on her nerves?

"If this is your fun," she said, "I don't think it's funny. Cigarette, indeed! Have we simply come here to smoke?"

"Later," admitted Felix, "I'd love to kiss you. But I suppose you're wanting some explanation first?"

"I wouldn't mind one," she said, exceedingly drily. "As I see it now, you've put me in bad with your aunt,[11] after all her kindness asking me here for Christmas – a stray girl, with no friends in this country and no other place to go."

"*That* was what so exactly suited her book. – Who was to know if you vanished?"

"You're just setting out to scare me."

"You were already scared stiff, when you first came in at the door – and rightly. Didn't anything warn you?"

"Warn me what of?"

"My aunt has taken up witchcraft."

She pressed both hands flat on the roof, as though it suddenly heaved; then heard her own voice dither: "Say that again."

"You heard me."

"But – your aunt was a friend of my aunt's: she *must* be respectable!"

"Witches frequently are. – What was your own aunt up to, for the matter of that?"

Phyllida failed to answer: she could but recollect that for years they'd hear nothing either from or of Aunt Beattie. "Then, the rest of them?" she asked faintly. "Uncle Ben, Claud, so on?"

"All in the same boiling," said Felix bitterly. "Uncle Ben's a proficient warlock, Claud's coming along, and Miss Battiter's under instruction from Aunt Eugenia. Old Claud, I think, was a bit off his stroke tonight – he rather funked this new project, involving you, on the grounds that it could possibly lead to trouble. I'd hate to upset you, but like to know *what* they'd planned – ?"

He broke off, suddenly staring down at the far side of the roof, into the garden. Her eyes followed his: a long faint ray of bluish light wavered over gravel, a bush, an edge of the lawn. In the trees, somewhere, a bird gave a croak of terror. Phyllida's teeth chattered; she pressed her hand to her mouth lest she be betrayed by the very sound. Felix, meanwhile, had whisked round to face the window behind them – his eyeballs shone out, unearthly: a candle was creeping upstairs. As one, the two fugitives flung themselves flat, face down – blotted out, they dared hope, on the roof's leaded blackness. The candle hesitated, inside the window, but then went on up: soon its trail of gleams could be traced through the attic skylights. "That was old Claud's step," Felix muttered. "Must have been sent to look for us. But just as glad not to find us, if you ask me. He . . . Oh my gosh, darling, hold on – !"

They held on. Below, the silence was rent by the prolonged, demonic shriek of a cat. Hell seemed to jag through the air at them – where would it ever stop?

"Get me out of this . . ." Phyllida moaned at last. "Can we climb down, shin down a pipe, jump? Dead or living, I won't go back through that house!"

They found themselves in the garden, with nothing worse than scraped hands, bruised knees and elbows and, on Phyllida's part, torn nylons. (Not for nothing had Felix mountaineered over the roofs of Ravenswood, as a child.) From the lawn, the unnatural blue ray had faded out: now, however, a sort of fulvous[12] glow pulsed from between the cracks of the drawing-room shutters; and, as they watched the silhouette of the house, sulphur-pale smoke, luminous in the surrounding night, began to come puff by puff from the drawing-room chimney. Within, a monstrous bellows must be at work.

"My . . ." breathed Phyllida.

"Yes, they're going strong," said Felix, staring with bitter face. He added, almost harshly: "Come on, let's get going. Seen enough? Then what are we waiting for?"

They stepped back – and none too soon. For the hall door burst open, swinging wide on its hinges, and Miss Battiter, long hair streaming, uttering a shrill whinny, bounded over the threshold, with Uncle Ben in his chair giving close chase. The chair lurched down the porch steps, swayed back again into balance and resumed, at top speed, its malevolent course. Felix pulled trembling Phyllida into a bank of shrubs, just in time – pursued and pursuer were headed their way, and, a split second later, came whistling past. A scorched smell remained, to hang on the air. The desperate scutter of flat feet, the crash of branches, the rubber-shod bouncing and swish of the flying chair-wheels died out, at last, far away in the grounds.

"So, what?" said Phyllida.

"Battiter's nerves have cracked. Hope she does make a getaway, but I doubt it. I somehow thought that would happen, one of these evenings. – All clear, I think – for the moment. Come on, come *on*!"

"But where to, where to?"

"I've got friends in a farmhouse; they'll take us in, I know."

Serpentine, the sheltering line of shrubs led through to the stygian gloom of the drive; down which, pausing to listen, not daring to speak, they groped. At the end, the spiked gates were locked: interminably, they edged their way along the inside of the wall, till their fingers happened, with joy, upon strong-stemmed ivy. To climb, to drop down on the other side on to the cushiony grass verge of the road, was the work of minutes which seemed blessedly few. There they stood, smelling the woods, hearing the brook – Phyllida drew her first free breath, and Felix kissed her. Hand in hand, they set off towards Little Birdover.

"All the same," she said, "how did *you* get into this?"

"You may well ask. I must seem a weak, blind fool! From the start I've never liked Aunt Eugenia, but to come to believing *this* of her was another matter. I don't really know when I first smelled a rat; and it was only last year, I had to face the worst. Since I've been a boy she's kept me hanging around; handing me fat cheques every Christmas and on my birthdays – either as bribes or hush-money, as I see it now. For some time I've felt bad about taking her tips, when I didn't like her, but to tell you the truth, I've sometimes hardly known where to turn. A succession of jobs packed up on me – I swear, through no fault of mine: possibly Auntie put the evil eye on them – my mother's an invalid, with no one but me in the world; she needs comfort and care, and I'd hate to see her go short. That's, at least, how things have been up to lately. However, just this last month I've landed up in work with a good big firm which cannot but stay the course: it offers me a pretty solid future. So, I came to Ravenswood *this* year just for the pleasure of tearing Auntie's cheque up, saying I'd repay others, and warning her I'd got wise to her little games. I didn't just want to fade out; I wanted to snap her hold on me – though, frankly, easier said than done.'

"What did she want *you* for, though? Also for witchcraft?"

"Some idea, I daresay, of passing it down through the family, to the next generation – not enough to have roped in that wretched Claud. But also she kept on hoping I'd bring a girl here to stay – 'Have you *no* nice, pretty friend?' she'd keep on and on at me. She and Uncle Ben have reached a point in their rites when they cannot get further without a girl to work on: and no one from round here, of course, would come next or near the place – you know how quickly rumours get round the country . . . What was my horror, when I arrived this morning, to hear they'd succeeded in trapping somebody – *you*! I at once tore back into Brindford, to meet that train you were thought to be coming on, with the idea that, by *some* means, I'd head you off. When you weren't on it, I like a fool decided you'd somehow got wind of the matter, or simply changed your mind. So I trundled back here to stage my big scene with Auntie. Why I didn't wait for that later train, I can't think."

"I might, of course, have simply thought you were mad."

"You don't think so *now*, Phyllida?" he said soberly. Their hand-clasp tightened; Phyllida shook her head.

"Nothing at all to say?" asked Felix softly.

"Not yet, I don't think."

"Neither have I, then – yet. One day, I'm going to say, 'I love you.'"

Ahead of them, the village church clock struck midnight. This, at last, was tomorrow – and Christmas Day.

At the farmhouse, the good people asked few questions. Tea was made and drunk in the cheerful kitchen; while, upstairs, an extra truckle bed was being got ready for Phyllida, in the children's attic. Her last waking sight was of two small cherubic forms tucked up in cots, from whose ends hung bulging stockings: Santa Claus, apparently, had already called. Cheek, then, upon her own pillow, she blissfully knew no more.

She was not to know, for instance, that, soon after, the attic ceiling was lit by a distant fiery glow, or that the yard outside, together with all the village, rang with movement, echoed with urgent calls and the clink of buckets hurriedly drawn from wells. Dreamlessly, Phyllida slept on: she thereby missed the excitement which kept all Little Birdover up and about that night. Ravenswood Hall – who knew quite at what hour? – had burst into flames, to become a blazing furnace long before help arrived. So great had been the heat that it cracked the walls: they fell, leaving nothing, this Christmas morning, but fuming rubble. Unaccountable rings of footprints, it was reported, remained on the ashes which blackened and strewed the earth.[13]

Home for Christmas

Millie at once saw, from the light on their bedroom ceiling, that snow must have fallen during the night. As though someone had spoken, she woke from a deep, plausible dream to the unreality of this unknown spare room silently glared into by the snow. The satin pattern on the blue wallpaper glimmered, and the white door through to the dressingroom, the white mantlepiece seemed to be carved out of something solidly bright. Someone must have been in and gone out (with a glance at them both sleeping) for the curtains had been drawn right back, the gas fire lit, and an oval tea-tray stood on the commode between the two beds. At the far side of the commode, the tray and the lamp, Tom lay like a papoose, rigidly sleeping, rolled in his eiderdown. His profile was thrust into the pillow. The Edwardian white ends of the two beds cut off most of the room.

Millie lay enjoying the silence. Their voyage home had been long: she was still glad not to waken to the dragging sound of the sea, the straining sounds of the ship.

They had arrived last night – Tom, in his agitation, running the car on to the edge of the lawn. Tom must have driven thousands of times through his father's gate, yet (because she was there?) he seemed not to know the way: he had swerved too wide at every turn of the drive, so that their lights veered madly over the evergreens. In fact, he had given Millie every reason to fear that this important night of bringing his bride home might coincide with one of his "queernesses." But once they were inside, in the red hall, with his family lined up, smiling, everything had gone better. Millie was just that bride all young men's families hope to welcome some day – she was small but not silly-looking, her smile was composed but eager; she lifted her golden-brown eyes, beaming, to each face. For their parts, Tom's family had been almost effusively kind – in fact, it all went off with immense smoothness as though the arrival had been rehearsed. So much so that Millie said to herself, how is it that important things in one's life seem always to have happened before? Even Tom played his role with a weary exactitude. *Had* it all been hollow? . . . She had just wondered enough to be glad of the snow this morning – it should keep the first day here pitched on a merry plane.

Tom so often woke up tense and silent that Millie, though disappointed, thought little of it when he[3] said nothing about the snow. He got up as soon as he woke and stood in the bow window, looking out in a queer, rather caged way. In fact, you would think from the way he looked at the lawn, that an enemy had followed him to the door. "It will make such a Christmassy Christmas," Millie ventured. "Have you often had a white Christmas here before?"

"Once. Last time," said Tom. He walked off to his dressingroom.

Millie had an equable temperament. While she was dressing, she looked out at blackbirds making prints or the lawn. She hummed, and merrily clattered her jade-backed brushes. She got down a little late, though before Tom: the family – Mr. and Mrs. Brosset, Aunt Shandie and Tom's two sisters Olivia and Wendie – smiled from the breakfast table as she came in. The mantlepiece was crowded with Christmas cards, also depicting snow-scenes. The solid diningroom was stuck over with holly and mistletoe. Millie thought some talk had stopped when she came in, but now she sat down it all started again.

"I do like a white Christmas," said Millie, unfolding her napkin and looking down happily at her sausage. "Tom says you had snow last time he was here for Christmas."

"Why, yes," said Mrs. Brosset, with just a glance at the others. "I believe we did. Why, yes; we certainly did."

Then Tom came down, and once more they were all smiling. But while they smiled constraint fell on the room.

It was twelve o'clock in the morning: Tom and his sister Olivia stood in the window of the morningroom. Millie had gone to the town with her mother-in-law and Wendie; they all had to do that last-minute shopping that nearly always crops up on Christmas Eve. Aunt Shandie had taken holly round to the church. But though the house sounded empty, Olivia had carefully shut the morningroom door, and she and Tom talked in stealthily lowered voices. She said: "You don't think she's noticing anything?"

"Why should she? She's new to everything here. You don't know Millie," said Tom. "She's easy-going; she never bothers much about anything. If she weren't like that I could never go through with – *this*."

"Do *you* really know Millie?" said Olivia sternly, fixing on Tom her direct, reflective stare. "She might notice a hundred things and not tell you. The fact is, she is pretty frightened of you."

Tom returned Olivia's look – then he jerked away and looked out, so that the white reflection froze his face. "*Why* bring this all up?" he said. "The others have got more feeling – they haven't as much as looked crooked at me."

"But you and I know more than the others, Tom."

"If there just wasn't *snow*," he said. "Snow, of all things! Snow *now*, of all times. Snow waiting for me . . ." He got out his cigarette case, but this was a mistake, for his hands shook. Tom said: "I could swear *she* sent the snow."

The fall had not been heavy: snow just powdered the trees, glittering as the sun crept through a film. The dark brick gabled house looked almost plum-colour as Millie, with her mother-in-law and Wendie, scrunched gaily round the bend of the avenue. They were all three chattering – after weeks of honeymoon Millie was glad to be back in women's society. Parcels filled their baskets or twirled from their fingers on string loops. "Why, look," cried Wendie, "there's Tom at the window, watching for us." She gave Millie a sly, flattering smile.

"He doesn't see us," said Millie, impassively.

"Well, he must be looking at *something*. People don't just stand there *looking*."

"Tom does," said Millie unguardedly. She said: "How many Christmases since you had Tom home? Four? Funny, in a warm wet country like England that he should have had snow both times. He doesn't care for it, either."

Wendie and Mrs. Brosset, with a glance across Millie, agreed: "No, Tom never cared much for snow." They walked, with rather ironly happy steps, up to the homey house. But in the morningroom window they saw Tom see them, spin round and bolt away.

In the cloakroom, taking off their galoshes, when Mrs. Brosset had gone off for a word with the cook, Wendie looked at Millie with sudden boldness and said: "Millie, there's one thing I do think you ought to know. It's quite evident that Tom hasn't told you – that's not *my* business, of course – but if you don't know you may say the wrong thing and bring some awkwardness up. The last Christmas Tom was back here with us wasn't much of a Christmas for anyone. A girl who was here got ill – she got *so* ill that she had to be taken away."

"Appendicitis?" said Millie.

Wendie glanced round, then she shut the cloakroom door. Then she got out a comb and tugged at her hair, at the mirror, not looking at Millie. "No, much worse," she said. "She went right off her head."

"Without warning? Oh dear."

"Well, we had never seen her before she came to stay here, so if she *was* feeling funny, how were we to know? When she'd been taken away of course we blamed ourselves fearfully, but as mother said, how ever were we to know?"

"What made you ask her for Christmas, if you had never seen her?"

"Tom had asked us to ask her. She'd been a friend of his."

Millie, filling the marble cloakroom basin, methodically started to wash her hands. "Did she get better?" she asked, in her kind calm little voice.

Wendie said: "Well, no. She got worse – I suppose that was being shut up. So we were almost glad – if you know what I mean, Millie – when we heard she had died. That was only three months ago."

Millie, drying her hands on the roller, looked at the fourth finger of her left hand. Her engagement ring sat at the plump base of the finger, pressed down by the platinum wedding ring. "Three months ago," she said. "Three months ago, just fancy. Three months ago was when Tom proposed to me. What a sad story. But thank you for telling me, Wendie."

"Don't tell anyone. *Don't* tell Tom. I suppose I oughtn't to have."

'This is a simple lunch," said Mrs. Brosset, carving the excellent slab of cold corned beef. "But we must save our insides up for Christmas, you know. Also, Millie, this afternoon will be active; we want you to help us trim up the Christmas tree."

Aunt Shandie, who did not cease to devour Millie with an interested eye, said: "Yes, a Christmas tree feels funny without children, but it's a family custom we've never broken, you know. I say, Christmas makes us all children at heart. And, who knows, there may be some real children again!"

"Stranger things have happened," said Olivia, taking salad, looking down her nose. Of all the Brossets, Olivia had seemed least friendly to Tom's bride. Olivia was a forbidding-looking dark girl, whose manner suggested muffled anger, or strain. In appearance, she was so like Tom, she might have been his twin, and it was clear to Millie coming in from the outside, that since childhood there had been a bond between them. Tom went on eating corned beef impassively, while Millie watched Olivia watching his face.

Aunt Shandie, disturbed by the uneasiness as a bird is by a sudden change in the weather, went on sending tinkling remarks across. "We keep the same Christmas pleasures year after year," she said. "Except, of course – " She broke off and dabbed her mouth with her napkin, looking round with her little bright flustered eyes.

"Except of course what?" said Millie, tranquil as ever.

"Except, of course, we don't care to play hide-and-seek."

"I'd love to help with the tree in half an hour," said Millie over her shoulder as she and Tom, arm in arm, left the diningroom. She had taken Tom's arm; she was insisting that Tom should walk her over his old home. "Show me it all," she insisted, "take me upstairs and downstairs. I want to see the old schoolroom, the back stair, the attics, everywhere where you played. Why, I think this house must have been just grand to grow up in, Tom. It must be full of memories. It's such a nice spreading house. Anyone could get lost in it easily."

Tom did his best to enter into the mood. The house, though not more than forty years old, had a respectable air of reaching into the past. Two wings ran out from the main block; the passages were cut off from the central landings by sound-proof baize doors. A quite perplexing number of doors down the passages quite often led, as Millie discovered, to cistern cupboards or housemaids' cubby-holes. Stretches of waxed oilcloth reflected the piercing light let in by skylights or windows. They looked into the sisters' rooms, the room that had always been Tom's (properly hung ship prints and school groups) and into the old night nursery, now a sewing room. Moderate central heating took the edge of the chill off, and though Millie, with her fingers on Tom's arm, could feel his inner tension increasing, there seemed no physical reason to feel fear.

He stood still and said: "Well, I think that's about it. The girls will be waiting for you – wouldn't you run along?"

"But what's up there, Tom? What's up that flight of stairs? – Listen, your old schoolroom: we haven't seen that yet."

"Why not let that keep for another day? Get your coat and let's go into the garden while it's still light."

"But what *is* up there?" She stood pulling his elbow till he went with her up the cord-carpeted stairs.

The room at the top, the schoolroom, had a window at each end. Bentwood chairs were pulled in to the bare, square table, that had been carved and dug in and stained with ink. School books and juvenile books in the big bookcase gave out, in spite of the heating, a dead smell. Under one window stood a strong deal chest, hasped with iron: it stood the height of a table and was about five foot long. This room had not been decorated for Christmas; you could see that nobody came in here – and from here the snowy landscapes outside the windows looked metallic and threatening. The room seemed to stand in a frightened trance from this light. Millie, detaching her arm from Tom's, said: "No, I don't like this room so much." She added: "It feels quite cut off from everywhere."

"It is," he said. She whisked round to look at his face – but dared not look long; she said in an uncontrolled voice: "Let's go down, Tom; let's go down to the girls – *What's the matter?* Have I done anything?"

"You?" said Tom. "Not that I know." He walked past her to the far window to kick the chest, with his most curious smile. "That's all right," he said. "It's perfectly empty now. Come and look at it, Millie: it's very strong."

"What was it for?"

"Well, it was once used to hide in."

"Come downstairs," she said suddenly, desperately.

"Well, you brought me up here. I thought you were after memories? This is the Mistletoe Bough chest: a girl got shut up in here. Come here, Millie, I'd like to show it to you. Would you like to get inside and see how it feels?"

"*I'm* going down," she repeated.

"No, you mustn't leave me alone . . . This is why we don't play hide-and-seek anymore."

Millie stood with a box of painted glass fruit in her hand; she kept passing brittle pears and oranges to Olivia who, standing up on a ladder, wired them to the spikes of the Christmas tree. Wendie was clipping the candle-holders on. "I say, Millie, you do look white," she said.

Looking down from the ladder, impassive as ever, Olivia only said: "Where's Tom?"

"He went off to write a letter in our room."[2] Millie added: "We were up in the schoolroom: it looks very deserted."

Olivia reached out for another trailer of tinsel. "We none of us ever cared for that room much."

The tree was done: its unlit candles and jewel ornaments gleamed in the last afternoon light. Then the drawing-room in which it stood was discreetly shut up till tomorrow. After tea, Millie fetched down her fancy work; she was alone in the drawing-room with Aunt Shandie, who sat with her board of patience the other side of the fire. Aunt Shandie's impatient sighing and the slippery sounds of cards drawn off the pack distracted Millie, who could not help listening: she wondered where all the others had slipped away to. Tom had not appeared at tea. Whenever she felt Aunt Shandie looking across the fire, Millie bent over her work: she did not like being watched. Then, cocking her head like an old parrot, the aunt said: "*This* will be a brighter Christmas for Tom."

"I hope so," said Millie, stitching away.

"That poor creature. I could have told from the first, we were bound for trouble. But nobody listens to me. Chasing about like that – up and down stairs, in and out in the snow. They turned the lights out and ran about in the dark. On top of the engagement and everything. It was a big party, too big a party, and I never did like excitable games. This was the only room where they left lights. I stayed here by the fire, and I remember I said to her: 'You stay quiet with me.' But oh no, she must be off after him. He came in and pulled her out and they went off to hide together. And what happened then? Well, well, he knows better now. No more silly games. Oh no, you've got him quiet. He and she would have soon come to no good – "

She stiffened and went quickly back to her cards, for Olivia looked in to say: "Millie, come here a minute: we just want to ask you something." They shut themselves into the room with the Christmas tree, where Wendie and Mrs. Bosset already stood, looking frightened and tightly holding each other's hands.

"We don't think Tom's well," they said. "We think you should go to him, Millie. He's sitting up in your bedroom, with all the lights on, and he won't come down or speak to us; we've all tried. He keeps asking for you. He seems to think you have quarrelled. Do make it up with him, Millie: nervous excitements are so bad for Tom."

Millie said: "I don't understand. But you none of you want me to. If I'd known what had happened that other Christmas I'd never have let Tom come back here at all. I should have been told when we married. What *did* happen?"

Mrs. Bosset said: "The poor girl he'd got engaged to shut herself into[3] that box and could not get out again."

"I did not even know he had been engaged."

"I expect he did not want to distress you, dear."

Millie's look held the nearest thing to contempt. She went up to Tom: he was sitting in an armchair pulled up to the unlit gas fire; he had wrapped round his shoulders the eiderdown from her bed, but he still shivered. She saw he was at the height of one of his "queer" fits, to which their honeymoon had accustomed her. The nullity of the pale blue spare room surrounded him, in the glare of electric light. "Leave me alone," he said, as she came in. "This is the only room I can stay in."

"Why?"

"It's the only room in this house that is not damned by the past. It's a room I only came into when I married you. But you should never have made me come back here again."

"I didn't know about the girl in the box. We could never have come back here if you'd told me that."

"I could only live[4] with someone who didn't know. They've all told you now, I suppose. But no one knows but Olivia. She let her out: I put her in. It was the day we had announced our engagement, so there was a party here: we were all playing hide-and-seek in the dark. She and I went up to hide in the old schoolroom; she told me she did not really want to marry me. She said she had changed her mind and wanted to go away. I was mad with her; we had a fight in the dark, knocking about among the furniture. I said she would be making a fool of me in front of all my friends and my family – but really I was so much in love with her that I did not care what I did. I knew she was terrified of being shut up. – So I opened that chest under the window, and picked her up and put her in – she was small – and put down the lid and sat on it. She hammered about inside. I lighted a cigarette and sat where I was and took no notice of her. I said once: 'I'll let you out when you're sorry.' I don't know how long I sat. She started to be quite quiet, but I thought she was trying to frighten me. Somebody who was in the seeking party felt their way into the room and found me by my cigarette. They put their hand on my arm and said: 'Caught.' It was Olivia. She said: 'Oh, it's you.' When I did not speak she suddenly turned the lights on and stared at me. She said: 'Who else is here?' and I said, 'Look for yourself.' She pulled me off the chest and opened the lid. *She* lay there, with her knees doubled up, not looking at us, not moving, not saying a word. Olivia got her out. She stood and began to moan, then she ran off down the passage, still moaning away.[5] Olivia guessed: she said to me, 'Now what have you done?' I said: 'She wasn't in there long,' and Olivia said: 'It must have been long enough.'

"When we both went after her, she had gone. The others were all there in the hall, frightened; they said: 'What's the matter with her?' She had run right past them, out of the front door; it was still open and the snow was outside. Aunt Shandie came out of the drawing-room and said: 'I told you so.' None of the others moved; they all looked at me."[6]

Ghost Story

H olly, no doubt brought in by the butler, was stuck in the Sèvres vases each side of the clock. The oppressiveness of the gilded and crowded drawing-room was increased by the glare from the chandelier, and by the steadily roaring fire, which slowly baked the unused air. The door stood ajar – it was no one's business to shut it – and a loud, halting tic-tac came from the hall clock. The high hall and the gallery gave out a dull echo: except for this there was not a sound in the house. The two guests stood by the fire; their hostess had not appeared yet, and gave no sign.

These two cousins, who met for the first time, already eyed one another with a certain good faith. The inclemency of their arrival drew them together. Oswald had driven down from London; Verena had come by train and had been met by the car. Overawed by the drawing-room – this was their first visit – they had not yet sat down. They were second cousins: any family likeness betrayed itself in their less imposing traits – both were smallish, both wore spectacles, both showed an innocent nervousness.

But Verena had the composed, rather challenging little manner of a girl who has to go about by herself. She said: "But you've travelled; you've been in Canada."

"I was most of the time in an office in Ottawa.[1] I did not trap or lumberjack, I'm afraid. I've never," Oswald said, with his rather feminine titter, "felt the call of the wild."

"Then you're like me," said Verena. "I don't like alarming experiences. Let's admit we should both rather not be here – though of course it's nice to have met. Poor Patrick, killing himself at Brooklands, has put us both in this rather awful position. I was brought up to expect – and I daresay you were too – that Cousin Meta would ignore my existence, always. I had never thought of her money; not because I don't like money but because there seemed no reason why it should ever be mine. Now, Patrick's awful death in that car has left me all unsettled. And I understand that, quite apart from her grief, Cousin Meta is very much put out. It really must be annoying, at her age, to have to go into the family highways and hedges to look for another heir."

"Did you ever meet Patrick?"

"No," said Verena, colouring slightly. "Though, for some reason, I always hoped that I might. Though I can't feel that much would have come of it: I would not have been his type; he was very handsome and dashing. I don't know that he had a nice character, but I daresay that was Cousin Meta's fault. She spoilt him. They say that pigheaded old maids always set their hearts on that type of young man . . . Considering that he and I never met, his death was a quite ridiculous blow to me."

"I must confess," said Oswald, "that when I heard of the smash I did for a moment think, now what does this mean for me? Then I made myself put the matter out of my mind, till Cousin Meta's invitation for Christmas came. Without being too mercenary, Verena, we've got to face her motive in asking us here."

"She may just be feeling lonely, poor old thing. This is her first Christmas with no one at all left . . . It's extraordinary that all those brothers and sisters should have died off, without marrying anyone."

"And they had a great deal of vitality. My father came here once and said it was really dreadful. He said he could hardly see how any one house could hold them. The thing was, they were greatly taken up with each other."

"With each other?"

"Yes, greatly taken up."

"I wonder how Patrick stood it."

"Oh, they were all dead when he started to come here. Cousin Meta sent him a telegram the night her last brother died, and Patrick walked straight in and more or less took possession." Oswald, conscious of being not handsome or dashing, added: "He knew which side his bread was buttered, I daresay."

"Well, so do we, Oswald," said Verena frankly. "What else made you and me give up our other Christmas plans?"

Oswald paused, then said: "Is your morale good?"

"No. I've felt like death since the car turned in at this gate."

It was Oswald's turn to say: "I *do* wonder how Patrick stood it."

"But they were all dead."

"That is just what I mean. You don't suppose, do you, that they died willingly?"

Verena, who had taken her gloves off, rolled the gloves up into a tight ball and looked down at them with a slightly quivering chin. She said: "I suppose we shall be meeting Cousin Meta at dinner. I suppose we may feel more human when we have met her."

The ageless butler, coming into the room, inserted between them a tray of dark brown sherry.

In his lofty bedroom, dressing for dinner, Oswald felt the sherry evaporate. Across a chasm of silence,[2] in the opposite gallery, he had heard Verena uncertainly shut her door. Was she already as loth to be alone as he was? He could have wished that he and she were married . . . But, good heavens, thought Oswald, there's hardly room in here for *one* person to move. Except for the height above, there seemed to be no space: from round the walls bureaux, brackets, locked presses rode darkly into the room; a great scrolled couch was pulled, diagonally, across a mirror. The mantlepiece, the bureaux, the brackets were crowded with objects of a highly personal kind: there were small pictures, trophies and curios, all suggesting the exercise of some sinister taste. A row of bootjacks stood under the dressing table. This was not like a spare room: all these things round[3] seemed to Oswald so much in possession, so much to forbid disturbance that he was given the very strong impression that he'd been put in someone else's room.

Oswald once more tweaked the lapels of his dinner jacket. As he opened his door, Verena, also in evening dress, appeared on the opposite gallery. After exchanging an apprehensive look, they went round to meet at the head of the stairs.

But Cousin Meta did not appear at dinner.

The cousins' places were set side by side at one end of a table that, otherwise empty, stretched on into the distance like a damask canal. "Quite a family table," Verena said. Half-lights crossed on the damask curiously, for the lighting system was focused on the portraits: straight into every oily masterpiece light[4] was bent with such violence that the faces seemed to start forward into the room. The reassuring[5] coarseness of the family features – these people seemed to be popping out of their ruddy skins – was undone by the pressure behind[6] the mouths and eyes: each brother and sister seemed to be sealed up in an inferno of haunted egotism. The women were told[7] by their bosoms, men by their colours: sex left no other differentiating mark. Not one of these was a face that one cared to regard twice, and Verena and Oswald, after one look round, ate with their eyes on their plates, or sipped claret like anxious birds.[8] A long rich dinner was served. Just once, Verena said: "They were all great eaters." But the butler, by his continuous silent presence made further allusions impossible.

Verena withdrew gladly, but Oswald did not sit long over the port. He got up to go after her to the drawing-room, but found her out in the hall, looking upstairs, clutching tightly about her shoulders her white rabbit-skin[9] wrap. At a height over the pitched-pine galleries, above the hanging electric lights, the glass roof admitted the black night. A Christmas Eve silence, made thick by the mist of the Thames Valley, bound up the listening house. Oswald said: "What's the matter?"

"I heard somebody call me. Do you think she expects us to go up? This is not my idea of a Christmas with relations."

"That depends how you look at it. Come where no one is listening: I don't like this," said Oswald, looking about.

"No – there's one door open up there."

In the drawing-room Verena looked about her, and finally drew up a beaded stool – unlike the other chairs in the room, this did not already seem to be occupied. Oswald walked round; he also opened a box of dominoes, but glanced at the heavy albums on the piano. "There are possibly more pictures in there," he said. "Might not Cousin Meta like us to look at them?"

"Not tonight. Do you think Cousin Meta's ill?"

"The butler did not say so – but then I couldn't ask him; he's stone deaf – did you notice? He just delivered that note of Cousin Meta's about not being at dinner, then went away."

"Or perhaps they cut his tongue out."

"My dear Verena, control yourself. – No, I think Cousin Meta is just waiting a little, to see how much we can stand. Or she may simply be feeling moody; Christmas makes some people a little depressed, you know. After all, we're still strangers to her."[10]

"You know we are not, Oswald. If we were, we should not be feeling like this. Should we know so well that this house was dreadful if it were nothing to do with us? No, we've got off light so far because we're only collaterals: poor Patrick stood between us and all this . . . A maid came in when I was dressing for dinner; I said: 'Whose room is this?' She said: 'Miss Janet's room.' Cousin Janet was a bit of a naturalist; she often used to skin mice and stick moths on pins. My room is full of glass cases. What have you got in yours?"

"Bootjacks," said Oswald after a moment.

"Then that would be Cousin Henry's room."

"You seem well up in all this."

"It all comes back – what I've heard. Cousin Mabel used to walk in[11] her sleep; she weighed sixteen stone and fell down the turret stairs. Cousin Sibella adopted a dumb child; it used to sleep in her room but it got smothered one night: she thought someone had done it and was so angry that she smothered herself. Cousin Aubrey and Cousin Demeter were twins and used to make secret signs at one another at meals. When they were sixty-five they went out in their pony trap, which[12] bolted into a steam roller. Your Cousin Henry had a stroke from which he never recovered when he was trying on one of his tight boots. Cousin Janet – my Cousin Janet – died of a rat-bite. Cousin Aloysius was the practical joker; he lived on with Cousin Meta for[13] some years after the others, till one night he let himself down from the gallery on a pulley, hoping to make her think he was a vampire bat. But something went wrong with a rope, and so he was hanged: Cousin Meta wired for Patrick then."

"So then Patrick crashed at Brooklands."

"Yes," Verena sadly said. "He didn't deserve to. Suppose, Oswald, *they* had a thing against him?"

"For being – ?"

"For being alive." She stopped: the cousins exchanged a long queasy evasive look. Verena got up and looked for the dominoes. "We're not half so alive as Patrick," Oswald hurriedly said. "We are not alive in a way *they'd* notice at all."

"Then Cousin Meta will not think much of us." The butler brought in a tray of drinks. He bowed and handed Oswald another note, which Oswald read and passed across to Verena. "Goodnight to you," their unseen relation had written. "We hope that you have everything that you want."

On Christmas morning, a thick white mist from the river surrounded the house. Ornamental shrubs near the windows could just be seen through it; the mist threw[14] indoors a sort of glare, like snow. In the diningroom, gleams came from the gilt frames of the portraits, the gilt scrolls on the embossed wallpaper. Oswald, coming down a few minutes after Verena, opened the envelope that he found on his plate: his Christmas card from Cousin Meta depicted a robin sitting on a plum pudding. He shook the envelope; nothing else came out; he gave a slight gulp and put the card away. "You haven't opened yours," he said.

"Nor I have," said Verena. She looked, in a sort of daze, at a coach and four. "I think this is sweet of Cousin Meta," she said. Oswald, who had been tapping the top of his boiled egg, put his spoon down and looked at her in amazement – her good faith was, apparently, absolute. "How did you sleep?" he said. "Or rather, did you sleep?"

"Well, it *was* rather odd . . ."

"Well, I'm through," said Oswald. "I'm quitting. I'm getting out before lunch, and I strongly advise you to come too. There are some things – "

Verena's face fell; she said: "What happened?"

"I would really rather not tell you."

"Cousin Henry?"

Oswald changed colour: he pushed his uneaten egg away, poured himself out some coffee, then said: "This is no house for a girl."

Verena said: "I am not sure that it isn't." Sitting facing the window she looked, in the thick milky glare from the mist, quite nearly handsome, elated, mysterious. She eyed Oswald once or twice, then said, with a small smile: "I met Patrick, as a matter of fact."

"Yes, he'd be due to turn up for Christmas, too."

"Now Oswald, don't speak in that horrd voice. Patrick's not like the others; he's sympathetic. He came because we were here."

"When he might be racing round hell in his motor car."

She only gave Oswald a tolerant smile. "I admit that I couldn't sleep," she said. "All Cousin Janet's moths kept me awake: their wings made such a flutter behind the glass, till I had to get up and take them off their pins. But after that I still couldn't stay in her room, so I put my fur coat on and stood in the gallery. Then I admit I remembered all about Cousin Aloysius and the pulley. I wondered what you'd think if I went and knocked at your door; after a few more minutes I didn't care what you did think, so I started off round the gallery. Then, at the top of the staircase, I met Patrick. He looked so nonchalant. He gave me a sort of jolly slap on the shoulder, and – "

"And said?"

Verena looked suddenly scared, and suddenly flat. She said: "I can't remember; I can't remember a thing. – We, he – I don't know. I think we sat on the stairs . . . I remember waking in Cousin Janet's bed and seeing the housemaid pulling the curtains back. I said 'Merry Christmas'; she did not take any notice."

"And the moths?"

"The poor moths were all back again on their pins."

When Oswald shrugged, pursed his mouth up and did not say anything, Verena threw him an agonised look of doubt. "I did *not* dream Patrick," she rather too quickly said.

"At any rate, you were lucky to sleep at all . . I take it, however, that you mean to stay on? Do do so, by all means; I leave the whole field to you."

"Oh, you make me feel so awkward. I'd forgotten the money."

"I shouldn't do that, Verena. Patrick kept it in mind."

"Oswald, how *dare* you! Oh, I am disappointed.[15] I thought last night we were getting on so well . . . It's dreadful to fight at breakfast on Christmas morning – especially with *them* looking at us. And you can't bolt off like this; it's going to look so funny. What will Cousin Meta say?"

"I shall never know," said Oswald, getting up and pushing away his chair. "As a matter of fact," he said – he stopped and stared at his cousin – "I doubt whether Cousin Meta *will* ever say anything, because I increasingly doubt whether Cousin Meta exists at all."

Verena shot up and wildly put her hand on his arm. "Then who wrote to invite us? Who keeps on sending those notes down? Who sent these Christmas cards?"

"Ask the servants."

"They would think we were mad. Or what do they think?"

"They never speak: we don't know."

Though Oswald kept speaking of going up to pack, he lingered on in the morningroom with Verena. Irritated though he had been at breakfast by the thought of this modest, trim, little woman having a dream lover – and that a rip and a sponge who had killed himself in a race – the touch of feminine softness she had acquired this morning appealed to him. He even toyed with the idea that Cousin Meta – if indeed she *were* living – might be throwing two young people, to be her co-heirs, together with some romantic design. She might wish them to continue the family . . . In the rich and un-prepossessing morningroom – in which the family smell, now familiar, came from the curtains, and pomade-patches showed on the backs of the armchairs – Oswald gave his cousin a series of close looks. The unspeakable night he had passed made her living presence, this morning, most unexpectedly grateful;[16] the rational irritation he'd felt at her talk of Patrick was, moreover, enhanced by real prickings of jealousy. "Verena," he said, sitting down by her armchair, "we either see Cousin Meta, or we both clear out."

"Oswald – but I – "

"I shall take you along with me," Oswald said in his firmest masculine tone.

Women in Love

J oanna's decision to sell the cottage came hard. Weekend cottage in principle, it stood for the inner, warm continuity of her life. The place was old; it stood in a pocket of unspoilt country, not much more than an hour away from London – set in a rambling garden, in part orchard. Ramshackle when she had taken it over, it showed, by now, Joanna's improvements – result of carefully saved-up money, sensible "planning" and loving thought. The few rooms were full of her treasures – favourite books wedged into the one or two shelves, antiqued ornaments picked up one by one (some chipped or cracked, so, low-priced, but the dearer for that).

Few who encountered Joanna during the working week might have realised her life had this secret core. In the city office, where she held a responsible position, she would have struck one chiefly as efficient – equable in her dealings with others, reserved in manner. She was thirty-five, in a quiet, strong way goodlooking. Friends outside the office, who knew her better, had at least some idea what the cottage meant to her – some of them had visited the place, for she would have felt it wrong not to share this pleasure. There was no doubt, however, that, at weekends, her happiest hours were spent alone. Here, solitude satisfied her completely. The parlour, with its outlook on to the garden, had the atmosphere taken on by a room which is in an intense relationship with its owner.

Each Friday evening, when she unlocked the door, came in, lit the oil lamp and knelt down to put a match to the fire, a beloved reality resumed for her.

She put the cottage down on house-agents' books. The first Friday evening after she had done so was one in April. Now, kneeling by the hearth, watching flames crackle up among the twigs, she heard herself wonder (thinking aloud), "How many evenings more?"

The telephone rang. It was a friend, Margaret, who, only just back from a holiday, had only today heard Joanna's sad news. *Was* it true? Yes, said Joanna, it was. The ensuing flood of condolence was of the kind she found least easy to bear. – "Please, Margaret, don't: I'm trying to toughen up!" But *why* was this necessary? the friend wailed. Joanna explained: her father's sudden death had, it was found, left her mother exceedingly badly off. Money must be found. Joanna's brother and sister, both married, were hard put to it raising families – they would want to help, but it wouldn't be fair to let them. Joanna's only capital was the cottage: it *must* be sold.[1]

Yes, there had been some enquiries already. Tomorrow, Saturday afternoon, the first "order to view" people would be coming. Wouldn't Joanna find that painful – showing them round – the friend wanted to know. "Well, one's got to go through with a thing," said Joanna briskly. She ended the telephone conversation as soon as might be.

In through the open door from the kitchen wandered a big tabby, guardian of the place in Joanna's absences. "*You*'ll stay, I suppose," said Joanna, picking him up. "And be nice to 'them' . . . I hope they'll be nice to you."

Never had a Saturday April afternoon been sunnier.

The mantleshelf clock stood at half-past three when Joanna heard a car draw up at the gate. Through the window she saw it – an open sports car, this year's model. The couple who got out came eagerly up the path to the cottage, looking round them. Joanna, squaring her shoulders, went out to bring them in.

Three became a crowd, filling the parlour. The girl, about twenty-three, was slender, pretty, sophisticatedly at ease, delightful in somewhat "London-y" country clothes. The tall man seemed about ten years older: there was something simple, serious, at the same time striking about his face. He was somewhat diffident – as though, once face-to-face with Joanna, and in what was (to him) so much *her* ambience – he disliked his role of possible purchaser. The girl, on the other hand, showed an almost electrified vivacity – "Oh, weren't they really *heaven*, the garden daffodils!" Joanna sized the two of them up (rightly) as an engaged couple. The girl's name, it transpired, was Tonia, the man's, Andie.

Tonia roved round the parlour, assessing everything – *no* fear of "making free" inhibited her! "What a find!" she exclaimed, taking an old china jug from a shelf in an alcove, turning it over – "though, of course, it has got a crack!" She glanced up at the ceiling: "Awfully *low*," she said, "though I do quite see, that's part of the charm." She knocked her fist against a partition wall – "I suppose one could knock this through? What's next door? We'd need *one* big room."

"I don't call this small," said Andie.

"Oh but, darling, think – we'll give heaps of parties!"

"*You*'ve rather liked to be quiet here, I should think?" the man said suddenly to Joanna. Standing, arms folded, impassive, she briefly nodded. "I should think," he said – betraying in tone and manner more wistfulness than he probably realised – "this was an ideal place to be quiet *in*?" His eye followed Tonia's flittings with a blend of love and exasperation.[2]

The girl fiddled open the latch of the kitchen door, said "May I?" – and, not awaiting an answer, disappeared through it. From off-stage, her voice continued to come. "Andie – *the* most olde-worlde brick-floored kitchen! . . . Oh, here's the bathroom, off it – *rather* peculiar? . . . Here's where the stairs begin. *I*'m going up: I must see! I can't, simply, wait!"

Her steps could be heard, click-click, up the small bare stairs. "Come on – what are you doing?" she called back.

The man made no movement to follow. Remaining with Joanna in the parlour, he offered her a cigarette, lit it for her. Now, at the sound of Tonia's[3] step in the bedroom above them, his eyebrows twitched. "I'm afraid," he said, "Tonia's making a bit free? Patience is never her strong point. Hope you don't mind?"

"On the contrary," said Joanna, "I'd much rather you looked round the place, as you like, as though I weren't here."

"In ways, I expect you'd as soon not be?"

Touched by his understanding, she bit her lip. "I thought," she explained, "I probably *should* be, to answer questions."

"I see. Well, thank you." He half-laughed. "What ought I to ask?"

"I've got a list of *answers*, here," she smilingly said, "if that's any help to you?" She produced the list – which had been waiting, folded, under the clock – and ran her eye down it. Her voice took on an "armoured," businesslike tone. "The price I'm asking, I take it the agents told you?" He nodded: she ticked *that* off . . . Next – if you *did* want the cottage – when would you want 'possession'?"

He said: "We're getting married next month."

"Good," she said with a nod.[4] "Then, that would mean 'at once'?"

"But what about you?"

Turning her face away, she said, gruffly: "The sooner I'm out, the better."

Diffidently he said: "You have *got* to go?"

"Mm-mm."

"Then I see, in a way. No point in dragging things out." Fumbling his hands together, inter-knitting his fingers, staring at them, he said: "Though I'm sorry, somehow." He glanced at the row of books, the bowl of primroses on the table. "You seem the one who *ought* to be here."

She kept her eyes, implacably, on the list. "Rates . . ." she continued. "Water . . . Transport – as you've got a car, that probably won't concern you. *I* go and come on the bus: it stops at the corner . . ." Her voice trailed off.

Tonia, down again from upstairs, could be heard crossing the kitchen, whistling. She stood in the doorway. "There's a vast great cat asleep on your bed," she said to Joanna, "I suppose *you* don't mind?"

"Bobbin?" said Joanna. "He's not supposed to."

The girl cried, to Andie: "Up there, it *could* be made rather lovely! Attic ceilings, and wee little diamond windows. We could have an enormous four-poster, *yards* of chintz. – I expect birds twitter around like anything, in the mornings, don't they?" she asked Joanna – "and sing, and everything?" To Andie she said: "You and I'd love waking up to that!" She seated herself, as she spoke, on the arm of the big chair in which he was sitting – she slid an arm round his neck, leaned her cheek on the top of his head, let her hair fall over his face. "And one sees," she told him, "the top of that marvellous flowering apple tree."

"Pear," said Joanna. "Apple trees blossom later."

"Go up and look, you lout!" Tonia lovingly said to Andie, pulling one of his ears. "See for yourself. Our nest – that is, it possibly could be. My heavens, one would imagine you didn't care!"

He heaved himself out of the restful depths of the chair – if chiefly (or so he gave the impression) in order to disengage himself from her. He walked away into the kitchen; but not upstairs – instead, he made his way out into the garden. Through the parlour window, Joanna and Tonia saw him, pottering aimlessly, placidly, hands in his pockets.

"*Why* do I love him so madly, when so often he's such a disobliging pig?" Tonia cried out suddenly to Joanna.[5] "We're supposed to be going to be married – I suppose he told you?"

"So I had assumed," said Joanna coldly. "He did, as a matter of fact, say so just now. Why?"

"Why are we going to be married? – you well may ask me! It's a thing I've started to ask myself."

"I did not mean that," said Joanna sharply. "I meant, merely, what's that to do with me?"

But the girl was in a race of her own thoughts. "Nothing I ever want does he ever do! And there really seem to be times when I don't exist for him! For instance, *now* he's gone off with the cigarettes – what am *I* to smoke?" Joanna supplied her with one. "Thanks," said the girl. She inhaled, then slowly turned her eyes on Joanna, studying her as though for the first time. "Or do *you*," she asked, "wonder why he loves me?"

"Why in the world should I? It's not my business."

"I agree, it's not," said the girl. "But I thought you might. A number of people do."

Joanna crossed the room, to the kitchen door.

"Where are you going?" the girl cried, instantly.

"To put the kettle on. This is tea-time."

"I implore you, not! *Tea*, to me, is the end."

"I'm sorry, but this *is*, still, my house."

"I asked you a question. I wish you'd answer."

Joanna paused, and turned round. "Listen," she said, "I look on this afternoon as a business occasion, simply and purely. You and your *fiancé* are here, by formal appointment, to view my property. I require to sell; you may be[6] thinking of buying. Should you find you want – that is, that both of you want – to go further into the matter, we'll talk further – but, please, *about that only*. All and everything else – and this I think you *should* see – is outside my province."

"You're not very human, are you?"

"I'm not inclined to be human, just at present . . . And *I* want tea, whether you do or not." Joanna disappeared through the kitchen door. The girl was left to gaze after her – not abashed, but a little stricken, and wholly mystified. After a moment, she crushed out her cigarette, and followed Joanna – as far as the kitchen threshold: from there she continued talking, propped in the doorway.

"If you mean, being human hurts," she said, "I know that. It's a mistake to love, I'm inclined to think. It upsets you fearfully, does it, leaving this cottage? In that case, why on earth do you? – why do you *have* to? Have you got yourself into some hideous financial mess?"

"No," Joanna said (from within) shortly. She was to be heard filling the kettle from a tap – later, setting china out on a tray.

"You don't *look* like that type – but one never knows." The girl paused, thought, then asked: "I say – do you hate us?"

Unhearing, Joanna appeared in the kitchen doorway, bearing the tray with cups, loaf, jampot. She steered her way past the girl and put the tray down on the parlour table, beside the primroses. Having done so, she turned, asking vaguely: "*What* did you say?"

"*Do* you hate us?"

"'Hate' you? – but what an idea! Why?"

"The idea of us. The fact that we *can* be here – that is, if we choose to – and you have to go? The fact that we *have* the power to buy you out? The idea of *us* here – doing what we like here – instead of you? I once read some story, somewhere, about an outgoing owner putting a curse on a place – because she loathed the idea of having successors. You wouldn't" – the girl looked dubiously at Joanna – "*you* wouldn't do that, would you?"

Joanna started, quite dumbfounded. "Goodness," she exclaimed, "what a morbid story! I couldn't imagine anyone having *that* mentality – that is, if they truly cared for a place. Where I'm concerned, certainly, quite the contrary. Whoever comes after me here will have my goodwill – for this reason – " She glanced around the beloved room. "What I could *not* bear would be, thinking of this cottage with people in it who were not extremely happy . . . That's what it's used to," she added, tenderly laying her hand against the chimneypiece as though touching a living thing.

Tonia, looking at Joanna broodingly, said: "*You*'ve been so[7] happy here – all alone?"

Joanna nodded. "But that," she added, "is how I happen to be."

"I'm beginning to wonder," Tonia said, "whether it isn't easier for one person to be happy, than for two."

"Surely not – I'd be sorry to think so. Two are more . . . natural."

"So one might hope – but look at Andie and me. We're in love, all right; but look how we're both on edge! You're shrewd, you know – I can see. You've had quite a fair sample of us this afternoon. What I wanted to ask just now, when you slapped me down, was – whether anybody *could* think we had got a hope? Many people who see us together don't. We've so little in common but *love*, it does sometimes seem to me. And sometimes, when he goes silent – he often does – or stares at me in that thoughtful and broody way, I suspect that that's how it seems to *him*. We have awfully different outlooks, on several things, and I more and more see we have different tastes. The attraction of opposites, I suppose. At the start, marvellous. But how about when we're married?"

Joanna, in her austere and distant way, said: "I understand, marriage solves many things."

The girl did not heed. She went on: "For instance, I get him under the skin. I know I've behaved like nothing on earth today – poking about your house, shouting brash remarks. The devil got into me, but I'll tell you why – "

From the kitchen sounded the whistle of a "whistling" kettle. Frustrated, the girl broke off. "There's that *kettle* of yours boiling," she said drearily.

Joanna had already made for the kitchen. Once again, Tonia followed her to the threshold; where, again, she propped herself, to continue talking. "I don't want to be mean," she went on, " – don't think I am! But no sooner were we out of the car and into this cottage than Andie was like a cat on hot bricks, all on *your* behalf! Whatever *I* did, it seemed, I put a foot wrong! You and he were instant sympathy, I could see at a glance – and don't think I mind! Or rather, *that's* not what I mind. What I do mind is, being totally written off. You've got your feelings, I know – but how about mine? After all, he and I *are* lovers, and we *are* going to be married, and we *are* looking for[8] a home – surely that's important?"

Joanna, to be heard filling the teapot from the kettle, did not answer. Now, she reappeared – with the teapot and hot water jug – in the kitchen door, and crossed the room to the table. "You don't think," she said, making room for the teapot, "that possibly you've imagined the whole thing?"

"Oh my hat," said the girl, resigned, "how maddening you are!"

Joanna, for an instant, gave her a smile – a smile that said: "I *do* understand, partly – and that 'partly' is slightly more than I want to!" *Aloud*, however, all that Joanna said was: "Would *he* – would your *fiancé* – like some tea?"

Tonia, ruefully, said: "That's just what he'd love. He's old-fashioned – that's been one of our troubles. Do you bang on a gong, or anything? – Or I'll find him, shall I?"

"Do – will you?"

"I shouldn't half wonder," said Tonia, "if he'd taken to the woods. Primrosing" – she shrugged her shoulders at the bowl on the table[9] – "and so on." She worked her heels back into her pretty shoes –

late y, half off; as though already the country had made her feet[10] hurt. Leaving the parlour, she was to be heard limping across the uneven floor of the kitchen – next, through the parlour window, she could be seen in the garden (now in a dazzle of late-afternoon sunshine) shading her eyes, looking helplessly this way, that way. Finally she disappeared, to the left.

Joanna seated herself at the table, opposite the teapot, waiting.

The parlour window was darkened by a large shadow: here was Andie, having come from the right. He leaned through the open window into the room. "What, tea?" he said.

"Yes. Come in."

His eyes travelled round the room, again. "Where's Tonia?"

"She's gone off looking for you."

"Then she's lost," he said – with a tender exasperation which in itself bespoke endless, protective love. "No girl ever had less sense of direction! Keep that tea hot – if you can? – while I look for *her*."

Joanna pulled a cosy over the teapot.

Tonia's wanderings had landed her up in the old woodshed. She had snagged a stocking. She was sitting – by no means securely – on a stack of chopped logs near the open door, inspecting the damage to the stocking, when Andie found her. From her manner, she might have broken a leg. "What on earth have you done?" he said in alarm.

"Only my lovely stocking. And where have *you* been?"

"Oh round the place."

"A stroll round 'our' country estate?"

"Well, *I* wish it were. As we know, it could be. For a minute or two, just now, I let myself imagine it really was. Down there, the orchard ends in the woods, and there's a plank bridge over a stream." A blend of vision and longing lit up his face, then were slowly clouded.[11] He sat himself on an ancient carpenter's bench, opposite her. "But the thing is, how do *you* feel, Tonia – Tonia darling?"

She ran her finger, again, down the run in her stocking, and said nothing.

"You don't really like it?" he said. "You *don't* 'see' the two of us living here?"

Instead of answering, she looked, behind and around her, at the dusky woodshed crammed with traditional, ancient, country junk – broken harness, a wheel propped up with a chicken roosting on it. With detachment, she said: "I suppose, this *could* make a garage . . ."

"What's the[12] point of planning?" He shrugged his shoulders. "Come on: we'll say our goodbyes and get back to London."

"She'll be disappointed."

"Oh, she'll *sell* this place, soon enough. *That* needn't worry her. I should think, the next people who see it will snap it up."

"I didn't mean that," said Tonia. "I mean, she's keeping tea for you."

"Yes, I know."

Bobbin, the big tabby, strolled into view in the woodshed door. He stared, for a moment, neutrally at the strangers, then twitched his tail and walked off – lord of the earth.

"We'll never get *that* out," said the girl. "Cats stick to places; they own them. *He*'ll boss us around – you watch!"

"We shan't need to watch," he said in a deadened voice, "we shall not be here." He burst out: "Tonia, are we never to want the same things?"

"*Who* said *I* said there was anything the matter with this cottage? And I'm the one who could tell you, as a matter of fact. You go daydreaming off among the birds and the bees; I at least took the trouble to look at the top floor."

He said: "You *could* have waited, I thought."

"What else are we here for?"

"It's still her house."

"That, she's made *very* clear to me!"

"I don't suppose she intended to. She's been more than . . . civil."

"Oh, she's been marvellous! It's a pity she's not me."

"What on *earth* do you mean?" he said, frowning.

"She suits you," said Tonia, turning away her head. "*I* don't seem to know how to, these days – I merely love you." She put a hand up, to ward off interruption. "It's all right; I realise you do *love* me. But any decision brings a fight to the surface. This afternoon, for instance, *should* have been fun . . ." She stood up, and, twisting her handkerchief miserably, uttered a sob.

He said: "The way we've been living, the pace we've been living at – we haven't given ourselves a chance. Scrappy half-hours and hectic evenings. I'm certain, all we need is time – time together. And peace; we could have *that* here. – Tonia, my love, don't be miserable: I can't bear you to!" He stepped to where she was standing and put his arms round her.

In his arms, already a little comforted, she gave a final sob and said: "I don't know. In a way, this place frightens me – it's so all-or-nothing. For us, it would be either heaven, or – quite the other thing."

"Why should it be 'the other thing'?" he said. He kissed her. For an instant they stayed together; then she raised her head from his shoulder, listening. – "Someone's coming!" They stepped apart. Tonia to appear as disengaged as possible, brought out her compact and went to work on her face.

Joanna, with Bobbin under her arm, composedly appeared in the woodshed door. If she sensed an "atmosphere" in here, she did not show it. "Good," she said, "you've discovered the woodshed. I meant to show you. It's useful; there are no other outbuildings. Most of this junk," she said, with a nod at it, "is not mine; I found it here – it could always go. On the whole, this old roof's wonderfully good – though one or two of the tiles at the far end" (she pointed) "look loose, to me. I expect you noticed?"

Andie said: "No, actually . . ."

"Well, look again, after tea. – Won't you, now, come in?"

"Oh dear," cried Tonia, "I suppose tea's got cold?"

"Let's hope not," said their hostess.

They followed her.

A round, brown teapot. Comfortable, man-size willow pattern cups. Andie sat up to the table, facing Joanna. Over tea as a meal, here in this parlour, hung an air of habitual ceremonial – if, as a rule, a ceremonial for one. Spooning jam from the jar, he spread it carefully over his slice of bread. "Nice . . ." he remarked in a general way.

"The jam?" said Joanna, gratified. "It's not bad."

"You made it?"

"Mm-mm. I do well for fruit, in this garden." She laughed, and added: "That sounds like sales-talk!"

Tonia sat, knees crossed, on an arm of the big chair, a short distance off. Having yielded to the compulsion from Joanna, she *was* (somewhat carelessly) holding a cup and saucer. The cup, she had so far neglected; the saucer she was using as an ashtray – she was chain-smoking. She rose – at this point – ran an exploratory finger round Andie's plate, then went on to lick the jam off the finger. Her expression showed that she did not care for any jam, but that since there must, apparently, *be* jam, she recognised this as the best kind.[13] "Made this?" She gazed at her hostess. "How on earth?"

Joanna said: "Oh, you'd soon learn."

"I didn't only mean the jam," said Andie. He drank to the bottom of his cup, gave a deep sigh. He tipped back his Windsor chair, took a look at the pear tree, out of the window.

"What I can't see is, what you'll do when you're *not* here!" the girl exclaimed, to Joanna. Tonia's directness, this time, was no longer aggressive or impertinent – she sounded concerned, sorrowful.

All the same, Joanna flinched. For a moment she looked like a person at bay, lips pressed together – to gain time, she filled a saucer with milk and put it down for the cat. That done, she steadied herself. "Oh," she said, "I shall grow to like London at weekends: many people do. Concerts, and so on. Art galleries . . . My friends so often tell me how much I miss. I've *got* a one-room flat; I've had it for years. I could make it nice; so far I've rather neglected it – I have so little time, you see, from Mondays to Fridays. There's no reason why *it* shouldn't be a home, if I settle into it properly – as I mean to." She paused, as though to renew her store of conviction; then went on – "In many ways, I expect, it will be a rest for me – here, there's been always so much to see to. *You'*ll find that," she began to say to Tonia,[14] then corrected herself – "Whoever comes after me will find that. In the country, it's endless." Her voice softened; it could stay brusque no longer. "Outdoors – *and* indoors, in a cottage like this. That's what keeps life so full. That's what makes one happy."

"Happy?" queried the girl. (She dwelled on the word partly sceptically, partly satirically, partly longingly.)

"Contented," explained Joanna.

"You think the two are the same?"

"Surely . . . More?" Joanna asked Andie, reaching out her hand for his empty cup.

Watching her pour out, he said with a smile: "You've got everything under wonderfully good control. That all you want?"

"I'm not young any more," said she.

He said: "Don't be too certain."

"She *is* certain," said Tonia – "*I* should say, about everything!" She turned to Joanna: "You know all the answers – but they're *your* answers.' She turned again to Andie: "Though *you* think they're *the* answers, don't you? . . . 'Contented'! – are you and I just to be *that?* Never ask for more? You – you *appal* me!" she told the two at the table.

Neither of the two at the table answered.

Their silence affected Tonia: she thought again – nibbling at the tip of a painted fingernail. "Or don't *I*, perhaps know what contentment means – what it *could* mean?" she asked the woman behind the teapot.

"Possibly," said Joanna – for once, tentative.

"Well then, what *could* it mean? Go on, tell me!"

"I suppose . . . having no longing that isn't satisfied . . . These content me, for instance," said Joanna, somewhat shyly touching the bowl of primroses.

"Yes," said the girl, impatiently, "but – enormous longings? The kind one can't explain, that tear one to bits?"

"There can be enormous contentment – I understand."

"Oh . . . ?" said the girl. Thoughtful, she looked at Andie.

"Though to me," said Joanna – slowly; she was unused to voicing ideas – "contentment is never a small thing. Small things can cause it, but it's a large feeling. I – I've come to know that from living here. Of course, I've been lucky."

"How content shall you feel, *always* there in that pokey flat?"

Joanna said: "Well, there's usually something. – And the flat's not pokey; and there's a tree in the courtyard. – I'm lucky having had this for so many years, lucky to have learned how to make a life – once one has made one, one can make another."

"I wouldn't call that luck," said Andie. "I'd call it courage."

Joanna lowered her eyes. Embarrassed by having spoken of herself, she reached round the table, collecting china, taking the spoon from the jampot, beginning to stack the tray. She said: "I'll just take these into the kitchen, then we'll . . ."

Andie got up, to help her. Constrained to say one thing more, she straightened her back and looked from him to Tonia. "Of course, I can quite see, for me it's simple. Alone, one has only one's own problems."

Tonia said: "You never thought of marrying?"

Joanna (looking the girl straight in the eye, calmly) replied: "I wouldn't say that."

"Then, why . . . ?"

"Two people don't always think of the same thing." A conclusive pause was followed by a change of tone: "Do you," Joanna wanted to know, "know anything about a kitchen range?"

The girl murmured something about an electric grill.

"Then perhaps," said Joanna, "you'd like to look at one? Mine, here, I put in three years ago. It's far from heavy on fuel, and heats the bathwater – also warms up the kitchen, wonderfully quickly. A woman comes in and gets it going for me, on Friday mornings. By the way, she's an excellent caretaker; she looks after Bobbin – I must give you her name." She had started propelling Tonia, by moral force, in the direction of the kitchen – to Andie she turned, and said "You, perhaps, should take a look at it too? My range. Like most things, it does better if it's understood."

"Like most people, also, I should imagine," said Tonia – with a sidelong, kindly-take-note-of-*that* glance at Andie.

Andie said to Joanna: "Show us its ways."

The three went through to the kitchen, leaving the parlour empty. A faint breeze, having sprung up, stirred the muslin curtains over the open window. Tonia's last cigarette, put hastily down, fumed in an ornamental crinkly china dish on the chimneypiece.[15] Through the door to the kitchen, ajar, there could have been overheard – that is, were there anyone in the parlour *to* overhear – the tones of Joanna giving an authoritative talk about the range, of Andie asking relevant questions, of Tonia's dutiful "yes's" and "*I* see's." An oven door was opened and shut, a demonstration in clinker-raking was given . . .

Andie came back into the parlour. He went to the chimneypiece and ground out Tonia's derelict cigarette, to stop it fuming. Off-stage, Joanna could be heard asking if Tonia'd like to take some daffodils back to London? Very well, then good – would she pick as many as she liked? Here was a basket . . . Shortly after, Tonia passed outside the parlour window, swinging a massive basket. Joanna, meantime, had followed Andie back into the parlour – again, now, she brought out her "answer" list, with the evident intention of going on with it.

"Well, thanks very much – that was interesting," he said – with a retrospective nod in the direction of the kitchen.

"It was important," Joanna pointed out, firmly.

He smiled: "Yes, we might, I expect – without that – have blown ourselves up!"

She looked disproportionately startled – indeed, agonised. Her fingers, holding the list, gave such a jerk at it that the paper tore. She blurted out (it seemed, irrepressibly): "What makes you say that?"

He was, naturally, startled by her reaction. "Stupid," he said. "A thing one *does* say. – Why?"

"Only, I know somebody who was blinded."

"By a blow-up?"

"Yes. Right in his face." She drew a hand across her own face, as though the thing had happened to *her*. Then, she collected herself. – "Oh, not a stove like the one in *there!*" (She gestured towards the kitchen.) "Not a modern range: they're as safe as houses. The worst mine could do, if you mishandled it, would be, burn less well, choke up, perhaps go out. No, what exploded was an old oil pressure-stove – a bad, tricky kind, long ago off the market. Don't know where he got it from; I suppose he'd borrowed it. If so, whoever lent it him should have warned him. He was always rather an idiot about those kinds of things – I'd have thought *anyone* knowing him would have known that."

Absently trying to piece together the torn list, she added: "He was out camping."

During what she had said, a note in her voice had caused Andie to fix his eyes on her searchingly. There began to dawn in his face a look of perception. He *said*, however, only: "I'm sorry."

She bowed her head, saying nothing.

He ventured: "This happened lately?"

"Three weeks ago. You remember that freak heat-wave we had in March? Early to go camping, all the same. But he liked that; he liked

catching the early morning light, in the early spring. He is – he *was*
– a painter."

"Of all things, to happen to a painter!" he said, awed.

"Yes . . ." she said.

"Apart from everything else," he said, "what will he *do* now? –
How will he make a living? That *was* his living?"

"Yes. When I first knew him, it wasn't much of one; but lately he'd
been beginning to make a name. In fact, more than that: since last
year he *had* a name. If he was not yet famous, he was about to be.
He had an exhibition – a show, they call it. It was an unexpectedly
great success. People not only came, but they bought the pictures.
Even I had had no idea he would do so well."

"Well, at least," said Andie, "that's *something* – isn't it?"

She no more than looked at him, unseeingly.

"I mean, he's now got a bit of money behind him."

"No," she said.

"*What* . . .?" he asked, puzzled.

"He should have. He thinks he has, but he hasn't. The money's
gone."

"*Without* his knowing? – how could that happen?"

"A man in the art world, a man he trusted, had the idea of starting
a gallery – or, at least, *said* that was the idea he had. Apparently, it
did sound a good proposition. He said he had found the premises,
but needed to raise money to buy the lease. To my friend, it sounded
a reasonable investment – it *could* have been, if the man had been
. . . *bona fide*. He was not. What he did with the money, no one will
ever know. Overnight, he ran out – totally disappeared." (Her voice
shook with anger.) "The news broke – the news of his get-away –
Two days after the accident happened to . . . this friend of mine."

"So *he* hasn't heard – yet?"

"Who tells news like that to a man lying in the dark?"

"Naturally, no. But sooner or later – "

"No," said Joanna calmly.

"But he's bound to hear, when he's better. Or, bound to ask."

"When he does ask – by the time he's well enough to do that – the money will be there. It will be with his sister. He will be told that, before he bolted (bolted for *other* reasons) the man did the decent thing: sent the money back. That won't sound to *him* as incredible as you might fancy. As I told you, he thought well of this man, and anybody he likes seems to him good – or at least *some* good: that is his kind of temperament. Anybody he's trusted, he goes on trusting. After he married, he never had a suspicion of his wife – till the day she left him."

"Oh, he did marry, did he?" asked Andie quickly.

"What do you mean?" said Joanna, sharply.

He frowned down thoughtfully at the carpet. "So his *sister'll* be able – somehow – to raise the money? It's quite an amount – I imagine, from what you tell me?"

Joanna half-turned away from him. She repeated: "It will be there." Her manner, though still firm, was for the first time also evasive. "However," she said, "none of this concerns you: why let it worry you? I'm sorry; I'd simply intended to talk business – *then*, I felt I ought to explain why I couldn't take that harmless joke you made, about an explosion. Why should I have told you all this, though – all the same?"

He looked straight at her. "Look, don't be angry, but – "

"Well?" she said, on the defensive.

"Actually, you've told me more than you realise. I mean to say, now I do know all this, how can I help putting two-and-two together? To me, the link between two things stands out a mile."

"I've no idea what you mean," she said, crushingly – with a look which defied him to say anything more.

But he went on. "One, that stove blowing up, putting your painter friend 'out' for the rest of his life; with, on top of that, a crook making off with his money. Two, your decision to sell this cottage – as quick as can be, provided you get your price. Would it, by any chance, be, that the price you ask is just about the amount of the missing money? . . . I'm not *asking*, mind you – but how can I not wonder."

Turning her face away from him still further, and still more obstinately, she said nothing.

"Yes," he said angrily, "I thought so. I can't say how much I admire you – that's beside the point – but *I* still think you're doing a terribly wrong thing. Wrong to yourself – what business have you to sacrifice this whole world that you've made – " he looked round him – "this *reality* for you, this whole core of your life? And, just as much wrong to him – as a man. If *I* were he, I'd never forgive you!"

"Can't you understand," she impatiently cried, "that he'll never *know*? If one or two people are careful – and I assure you, they *will* be – however can he?"

He said, with deliberate brutality: "I suppose, it *is* fairly easy to trick a blind man."

"Trick" stung, like a whiplash. "That's enough, thank you," she said, quivering.

He was not to be silenced. "I could never – no, I would *not* – do to a person a thing they would not forgive if they *did* know. They may know or not, but one's injured them, all the same. One has no right to!"[16]

Notes

Salon des Dames

"Salon des Dames," Bowen's first published work, appeared in the *Weekly Westminster Gazette* on 7 April 1923 (pages 6–7) under the name "E. D. Bowen." "Dorothea" was her middle name. Set in Switzerland, the story manifests Bowen's fascination for hotels and the continent. The macabre idea that corpses might rot unnoticed in closed rooms, as well as the reference to apprehensive heads bobbing up suddenly, anticipates the winding of the muffler around Monsieur Grigoroff's neck. Although innocent enough in context, the gesture bears implications of strangulation. The American flirt, Miss Villars, owes touches of personality to Henry James's Daisy Miller. Paragraphing has been adjusted for dialogue, which occasionally runs together without breaks. All French expressions, silently corrected whenever faulty, have been italicised, whereas the published text mixes both roman and italic type for French words. When Miss Villars translates her own statements, or where they seem patently self-evident, no translation is given.

    1. "She was a wonderful girl."

    2. The original reads "Mrs. Pym," which is clearly an error. The "was," to create a parallel with the other verbs, is missing after her name as well.

    3. A paragraph break has been added.

    4. "Once, when I was staying in Rome."

    5. "Have you read."

    6. "And once I have returned from Florence."

    7. "And then I am going to go on to Naples."

Moses

"Moses" was published in the *Weekly Westminster Gazette* on 30 June 1923 (page 16). As with "Salon des Dames," Bowen published the story under the name "E. D. Bowen." The story evokes Henry James, noticeably Roman sceres in "Daisy Miller" and *The Portrait of a Lady*. Bowen expresses her passion for Rome most fully in *A Time in Rome* (1960), a travelogue mixed with a history of the city, in which she mentions the Moses statue (173). In "Moses," Fenella is not married to Mr. Thomson, for the narrator conjectures how they would behave were they married.

1. Michelangelo's statue of Moses (1515), originally intended as part of a magnificent tomb for Pope Julius II, is located in the church of San Pietro in Vincoli in Rome.

2. A paragraph break has been added.

"Just Imagine . . ."

"Just Imagine . . ." appeared in the fashionable illustrated magazine, *Eve*, in the October-December 1926 issue (pages 27, 37–9, 72, 74, 78, 80). Over the years, *Eve* published stories by D. H. Lawrence, Edith Wharton, and other luminaries. Whereas Noel appears never to leave England, and hardly budges from London, Nancy comes and goes from the Argentine. The story, for its adherence to the uncanny, owes a debt to Edgar Allan Poe's supernatural tales.

1. There is a zoo in Regent's Park, which Bowen mentions in *The Death of the Heart* and her essay "Regent's Park and St. John's Wood."

2. Hyde Park is adjacent to Knightsbridge.

3. A paragraph break has been added.

The Pink Biscuit

"The Pink Biscuit" was published in the 22 November 1928 issue of *Eve* (pages 34–5, 76, 78, 80). Although it focuses on Sibella's crisis of conscience about stealing a biscuit, the story recalls other women's narratives about shopping written in the 1920s: Miss Kilman and Elizabeth Dalloway go to the Army and Navy stores in Virginia Woolf's *Mrs. Dalloway*, and Miriam wanders London streets and window-shops in Dorothy Richardson's *Pilgrimage*. The seaside location anticipates the interlude at Waikiki in *The Death of the Heart*, as well as Bowen's many other essays and stories with littoral settings. Capitalisation in this story is sometimes erratic; I have lower-cased "colonel," for instance, as well as "titan." The woman who comes in to help, the "temporary," sometimes appears with quotation marks and sometimes without, so, for consistency, I have removed them all after

Mrs. Willyard-Lester's initial reference to her.

1. The original reads "glowed on," which does not suit the context.

2. A paragraph break has been added.

3. The verb is mistakenly in the present tense in the original: "become."

4. The names and pronouns cause some confusion. Sibella is alone in the scene, except for the couples who turn to look at her. The "she" has no clear referent, and, in context, it makes no sense that Sibella is unconscious of her own appearance.

5. In the published text, the word is misspelt, "ascetism."

Flavia

Bowen wrote "Flavia" for *The Fothergill Omnibus*, edited by John Fothergill and published in November 1931 by Eyre & Spottiswoode in London (pages 57–70). Fothergill concocted a basic plot around which seventeen different authors crafted a story:

> A man gets into correspondence with a woman whom he doesn't know and he finds romance in it. Then he sees a girl, falls in love with her in the ordinary way, marries her and drops the academic correspondence. Happiness, then friction. He writes again to the unknown woman and finds consolation till by an accident it is discovered that the married couple are writing to one another. (v)

Other contributors included G. K. Chesterton, A. E. Coppard, L. P. Hartley, Storm Jameson, Margaret Kennedy, and Rebecca West.

1. The original reads "were," a grammatical error, for the verb agrees with "Caroline."

2. Wengen: a village in Switzerland known for its ski slopes.

3. *The Athenaeum*: a literary journal that ran from 1828 to 1921, at which time it was incorporated into the *Nation*. In turn the *Nation* merged with the *New Statesman*, for which Bowen wrote reviews.

4. Kruschen salts: a proprietary aperient (medicinal, laxative). The advertising slogan, "that Kruschen feeling," was popular in the 1920s.

5. The original reads "all woman," which should be plural.

6. Marcel Boulestin: a writer and chef (1878–1943). Boulestin translated Max Beerbohm's *The Happy Hypocrite* into French, then published his own novel, *Les Fréquentations de Maurice*, in 1911. Having conquered the literary world, he opened the restaurant, Boulestin's, in Covent Garden in 1911,

which introduced London to classic French cooking. He published the
bestselling book, *The Mainstream of the Kitchen*, in 1925.

She Gave Him

"She Gave Him" forms one chapter in *Consequences* (pages 46–51), billed,
according to its subtitle, as "a complete story in the manner of the old
parlour game in nine chapters each by a different author." Published by the
Golden Cockerel Press and edited by the novelist A. E. Coppard,
Consequences appeared on 14 October 1932. The entire book consists of only
sixty-seven pages. Six short chapters precede Bowen's: "The Man" (written
by John van Druten), "The Woman" (G. B. Stern), "Where They Met"
(A. E. Coppard), "He Said to Her" (Seán O'Faoláin), "She Said to Him"
(Norah Hoult), and "He Gave Her" (Hamish Maclaren). After Bowen's
chapter, the book winds up with "The Consequence Was" (Ronald Fraser)
and, lastly, "And the World Said" (Malachi Whitaker). Each chapter
showcases an author's ingenuity rather than narrative continuity. The plot is
awkwardly contrived: a man named Henry Maybird goes to the country
where he meets Magdalen Taylor. Out walking, the couple see a child, also
named Henry, dodging cars on the road – as a game. Not knowing that the
child is playing, Henry Maybird saves him from an oncoming car and
sustains minor injuries by doing so. Whereas her fellow contributors write
expositorily and tend to forget material that others have introduced, Bowen
advances narrative through dialogue and circles back to previous settings
and information, such as Henry's mother having been an accomplished
pianist. At the beginning and end of her chapter, Bowen plays on the notion
of what men and women give each other: looks and shivers. The relatively
harmless car accident in *Consequences* contrasts with the fatal car accident in
To the North, published only four days before *Consequences*, on 10 October
1932. Sporadic ampersands appear in the Cockerel Press printing, which I
have silently changed to "and."

1. At the end of the preceding chapter, Henry has been laid on the
ground and Magdalen, kneeling beside him, grandiloquently states that "he
must be saved at all costs" (*Consequences* 45). Henry, despite his condition,
gives her a "fishy look" (45), for he suspects she has other motives in mind.

2. She became a Woman: in earlier chapters, Magdalen has a sexual
relation with a married man. She moves to Maida Vale with her beau, but
his wife ruins their domestic happiness (*Consequences* 32–4).

3. Kilburn gaslight: in the first chapter of *Consequences*, John van Druten writes that Henry Maybird and his musical mother live in Hampstead, very close to Kilburn (1-2). When Henry sells the house, he claims it is located in Kilburn "as a kind of gesture of defiance at the vanity of things material" (7).

4. The phrase, a modified translation of "Vénus toute entière à sa proie attachée," derives from Racine's *Phèdre* (Act I, scene iii).

Brigands

"Brigands" appeared in *The Silver Ship: New Stories, Poems, and Pictures for Children*, edited by Lady Cynthia Asquith and published by Putnam in London in 1932 (pages 183-200). Lady Asquith identifies both boys and girls as readers of this collection. In the introduction, she gives out her home address and invites children to write and tell her what colour of cover they would like to see and their preference for themes – "Fairy. Adventure. Animal. Everyday Life" (viii) – for subsequent volumes. Other contributors to *The Silver Ship* included Angela Thirkell, L. A. G. Strong, George Moore, Alfred Noyes, G. K. Chesterton, Hugh de Sélincourt, and Lord David Cecil.

1. This punctuation is Bowen's; a semi-colon after "find" would make the sentence grammatical.

2. School-room and schoolroom alternate in the story; the latter spelling has been adopted.

3. The original reads, "Priscilla stuffing with cream puddings." The reflexive pronoun, "herself," has been added.

4. "Vendetta" is in upper case in the original.

5. Wheel-barrow and wheelbarrow alternate in the story; the latter spelling has been adopted.

6. Sal volatile: an aromatic solution – ammonium carbonate – waved under the nose to restore someone who has fainting fits.

7. The original reads "policeman," but the previous sentence mentions two policemen.

8. Bass: twine made from plant fibres. Because he has been tying up hyacinths, Perkins holds the twine in his hands. Bass is also commonly used to make brooms or mats.

The Unromantic Princess

Like other stories that Bowen wrote in the 1930s, "The Unromantic Princess" was a commissioned piece. It appeared in *The Princess Elizabeth Gift Book*, edited by Lady Cynthia Asquith and Eileen Bigland (pages 83–99). Published in 1935 by Hodder & Stoughton, the book was sold in aid of the Princess Elizabeth of York Hospital for Children. Paul Bloomfield illustrated "The Unromantic Princess" with two drawings. As the numerous orphans in her novels attest, Bowen keenly observed the plight of displaced and unhappy children. She characterises children differently in the tales that she wrote in the 1930s. In "The Unromantic Princess," "Brigands," and "The Good Earl," children possess commonsense and bravery. Unlike adults, they are not afflicted by grandiosity. The dismissal of the fairy godmothers in "The Unromantic Princess" implies a rejection of an older generation, in keeping with the privilege generally accorded to youth in the 1930s. The plot reverses "Cinderella": the princess looks for the boy; good sense rather than good looks prevail. The manuscript draft of this story is in the Columbia University archives; cleanly written, it bears few erasures and closely resembles the published version.

1. Poke bonnets: bonnets with a projecting brim, fashionable in the nineteenth century.

2. This sentence does not appear in the manuscript.

3. The situation, and more particularly the quadrille, recall Lewis Carroll's *Alice in Wonderland*.

4. The manuscript has a crossed-out phrase: "looked disdainfully at her green ve vet shoes."

Comfort and Joy

"Comfort and Joy" appeared in a double issue of the literary journal *Modern Reading* in 1945 (pages 10–16). Edited by Reginald Moore, *Modern Reading* included prose by Storm Jameson, F. Scott Fitzgerald, Anaïs Nin, Henry Miller, May Sarton, and others in its 1944 and 1945 issues. In his headnote to the double number published in 1945, Moore notes,

> For reasons comprehensible only to those with a knowledge of the exigencies of wartime publishing, we should not have been able to produce No. 12 as a separate number for three or four months, and we

felt that both our readers and our contributors deserved better than this. Hence our New Year Number, comprising Nos. 11 *and* 12. (7)

Printed in London, this pocket-sized journal was produced "in complete conformity with the authorised economy standards" (4). Bowen does not discuss the war explicitly, but war exerts its pressure. Children are displaced. Flats are shut. Soldiers are billeted on families. Cyril's being jilted on Christmas Eve anticipates the plot of "Happiness."

    1. "Tiding" in the first line has been amended to "tidings."

    2. In the context of the story, the husbands' absence insinuates that they are at war.

    3. The original reads, "Happychristmas." In the exchange between the two girls, paragraphing has been slightly altered to follow alternating speakers.

    4. This sentence was originally included in the preceding paragraph.

    5. "God rest your merry, gentlemen" has been amended to "God rest you, merry gentlemen."

The Good Earl

"The Good Earl" appeared in *Diversion*, a book edited by Hester W. Chapman and Princess Romanovsky-Pavlovsky and published by Collins in 1946 (pages 133–46). Proceeds from the book were meant to benefit the Yugoslav Relief Society. Rebecca West, who had written extensively about Yugoslavia in *Black Lamb and Grey Falcon* (1941), supplied a passionate introduction to *Diversion*. Other contributors included Sacheverell Sitwell, Rose Macaulay, Lord Berners, John Lehmann, Noel Annan, Henry Green, and Edward Sackville-West. Using a "we" narrative voice, Bowen casts this story as a communal commentary on the earl's grand schemes. The narrator more precisely discloses that he is male when he refers to "we young fellows." As internal evidence indicates, this allegory of wastefulness and class pertains to Ireland. Two earlier versions of this story exist: corrections to a typed version on sixteen pages of pink paper are incorporated into a second version on eighteen numbered pages of white carbon paper (HRC 4.6). Bowen made a few further changes to the second version by hand. Where these emendations illuminate something about the process of revision or about the story, I have made a note of them. Capitalisation in the story has been regularised, but Bowen clearly intended an allegorical dimension to the story by capitalising "Earl" and "Lough" and "Steamer," among other nouns.

1. In the typescript, "to" yields to "into." "To" seems more natural, but "into" was the preposition used in the published form.

2. The first three references to the Little Dog are lower case; thereafter they are in upper case. They have all been regularised to upper case.

3. Forenist: Bowen uses a variant of "fornent" or "fornenst," which means "right opposite," "over against," or "facing."

4 Quotation marks are placed around the quoted speech in the carbon typescript version. Occasionally Bowen adds quotation marks throughout the typescript. Omitting the quotation marks, as happens in the published version, enhances the mythic dimension of the fairy tale.

5. The original reads "to raise and maybe sell."

6. Bowen crossed out "not" and substituted "now" in the typescript.

7. I removed a comma after the initial "For."

8. Bowen included a phrase in the typescript that was edited out of the published version: "and from houses that he possessed in Dublin."

9. The original reads "is" but "are" is the logical verb form in context.

10. Bowen adds an "s" to create the plural, "stoopings," in the typescript.

11. The typescript, with handwritten corrections, reads differently: "his eyes looked at you out of his head like lamps."

12. The scene recalls Christ's resurrection.

The Lost Hope

Although Bowen wrote this story in 1945, it did not appear until 29 September 1946 in the *Sunday Times* (pages 3–4). Mr. Russell, literary editor at that newspaper, commissioned and held "The Lost Hope" for a year while accumulating enough material for a series. Meanwhile, Bowen signed a contract with the *New Yorker* in October 1945 granting that magazine the right of first refusal on articles and stories. She explained to her agent at Curtis Brown that, in the circumstances, the publication of "The Lost Hope" in the *Times* did not contravene her contract with the *New Yorker*, which, in any event, turned down all the pieces that she submitted. In a letter dated 15 October 1946, Bowen clarified the situation for the agent who handled magazine sales at Curtis Brown:

Mr. Russell explained that they might not be using the story immediately, but that they wanted to collect some for a proposed series. I had not, however, anticipated that they would be holding it for so long. All this happened prior to my receiving and signing the *New Yorker* contract – which, though it dates from October 18th[,] did not reach me for signature until considerably later. I think this clears the matter. (HRC 10.5)

She let the *New Yorker* contract drop because it proved too confining. The setting of "The Lost Hope" recalls Bowen's essays about seacoasts, including "Folkestone" and "The Idea of France." Moreover, returns – people coming back to residences that they have left because of the war – characterise the short story "Ivy Gripped the Steps" and the essay "Opening up the House," which both date from the same period. James's story, "The Middle Years," has a discernible influence on "The Lost Hope": the seaside, the ageing writer, the younger man.

1. The microfilm of this story being hard to decipher, some of the punctuation is unclear. At this point, the punctuation may be a semi-colon or a comma. I opt for the latter for syntactical reasons.

2. A paragraph break has been added.

3. "His room" might be intended.

4. "Assisting at" derives from the French, *assister à*, which means "to witness," without any sense of "to help."

I Died of Love

"I Died of Love" appeared in 1946 in *Choice: Some New Stories and Prose*, edited by William Sansom, illustrated by Leonard Rosoman, and published by Progress Publishing in London (pages 129–37). In his foreword, Sansom wrote that the editorial principle behind the selection of "modern narrative prose, of creative and not critical work" (vii), emphasised good writing. He added, "There is, however, a tendency away from the toughies, a tendency on the whole to write less as one speaks but rather as one might, given the time and the thought and the sensibility, hope to speak" (vii). The gist of the volume is away from conventional short stories and towards experimental hybridisation. In this vein, William Plomer calls Bowen's "I Died of Love" a "ballad" and a "strange and delicate fragment" in his prefatory comments in *Choice* (viii). Indeed, the story uses the collective "we" as a narrative position, much like "The Good Earl." Also, the story runs in a circle, with Miss Mettishaw presented as storyteller at the beginning and end, as in a ballad. The soldier with the handsome face who leaves debts all over town draws his pattern from Wickham in *Pride and Prejudice*, a novel that Bowen discusses in *The Heritage of British Literature*. She also excerpted sections from *Pride and Prejudice* for a radio dramatisation of Austen's writing life, "New Judgement: Elizabeth Bowen on Jane Austen,' broadcast in 1942. Literary influences aside, one should not forget that Bowen herself was briefly engaged to a British soldier, Lieutenant John Anderson, in 1921 (Glendinning 48). A ten-page typescript with handwritten corrections of "I Died of Love' is extant (HRC 6.3). I have noted some of Bowen's changes in the editorial notes.

1. In the typescript, Bowen concluded this sentence with the phrase, "after the rest it had had from remaining shut.'

2. Bowen crossed out a clause that originally concluded the sentence after a colon: "she could not however forget what it might have been."

3. The typescript reads "faultlessly" rather than "blamelessly."

4. The typescript reads "discard" rather than "refuse."

5. In the typescript, Bowen crossed out a sentence following this: "No lady called without an appointment."

6. The word "would" has been added.

7. In the typescript, another clause added to this sentence clarifies the motives for the marriage: "he was esteemed locally and could have had his pick, but the bride would be called on to bring in money."

8. The typescript more damningly states that "the flounces of her skirt and petticoats were stained green with grass."

9. In the typescript, the sentence ends, "as though protecting something," which is crossed out.

10. In the typescript, the sentence reads, "In another minute there would be big drops, and the trees in the gardens were all rustling."

So Much Depends

"So Much Depends" appeared in the September 1951 issue of *Woman's Day* (pages 72, 149–50, 152–60). While recalling the middle portion of *The Death of the Heart*, set in a house on the English coast, "So Much Depends" also looks forward to Bowen's essay, "The Case for Summer Romance," published in *Glamour* in 1960. Summing up a summertime flirtation in that essay, Bowen wonders whether holiday romances need be serious. In "So Much Depends," disappointed love and broken engagements, mainstays of Bowen's plots, are reconfigured in Ellen's moody self-obsession. Ellen's flightiness contrasts with Erica Kerry's much more anguished, less public love. Space breaks in the published version have not been followed; no manuscript exists to indicate Bowen's intentions for space breaks. Although the layout editor at *Woman's Day* inserted spaces whimsically, I have retained only breaks that indicate shifts in time, space, or perspective.

 1. St. Swithin's: 15 July. Legend in Britain has it that if it rains on St. Swithin's Day, it will rain for the next forty days.

Emergency in the Gothic Wing

"Emergency in the Gothic Wing" appeared in the *Tatler* on 18 November 1954 (pages 18–19, 52). Bowen wrote a weekly book column for the *Tatler* for eight years, from 1945 to 1949, and, after a hiatus, from 1954 to 1958. The goofiness of this Christmas story may partly be explained by its appearance in a magazine devoted lightheartedly to the comings and goings of aristocratic society: balls, hunts, openings, sightings of royalty.

 1. Mélisande: a character in Maurice Maeterlinck's play *Pelléas et Mélisande* (1892), which was the basis for several musical compositions, most notably Claude Debussy's opera of the same name.

 2. In "Bowen's Court," an essay about her house in County Cork, Bowen explains that a "Long Room," intended for balls, took up the entire length of the third floor. Although generations of children played in this room, it was never used for dancing: "Any ball is held, by tradition, down in the drawing room. Why? *The Long Room floor will not stand up to vibration.* So I was told by my father, he by his, his by his father, whom his father had told. No one of us, in consequence, ever tried" (193). The actual layout of Bowen's Court inspires the fictional layout of Sprangsby Hall.

 3. Spirit photographs: manipulated photographs that provided, through double exposure, spurious evidence of the spirit world. Spirit photographs purported to show emanations of dead people. An amateur of the genre, Arthur Conan Doyle published *The Case for Spirit Photography* in 1922.

The Claimant

"The Claimant" appeared in *Vogue* on 15 November 1955 (pages 122–3, 167–8). It was also published in *The Third Ghost Book*, edited by Cynthia Asquith, in 1955, and in the magazine *Argosy* in January 1956. In his introduction to *The Third Ghost Book*, L. P. Hartley comments that traditional ghosts gibber and clank chains. He adds that

> a stylized ghost is much easier to handle, so to speak, than one whose limitations are uncertain. If he can only squeak or clank a chain, we know where we are with him . . . But if the ghost can be so like an ordinary human being that we can scarcely tell the difference, what is the difference to be? Where is the line to be drawn? (ix)

The ghost in "The Claimant," more psychological than chain-clanking, resembles the spectre in Henry James's *The Turn of the Screw*. Bowen was fond of plots about moving in. Her last, unfinished book was tentatively called "The Move-In." In the short story "The Cat Jumps," a couple move into a house where a murder took place. The story "Women in Love" also dwells on inspecting a house with a view to buying it and moving in. These plots, with their recollection of Daphne du Maurier's *Rebecca*, imply that possession, in all senses of the term, supersedes property ownership.

    1. The original reads, "all the place was queer that smile of his." The "with" has been added.

Candles in the Window

"Candles in the Window" appeared in the December 1958 issue of *Woman's Day* (pages 32, 81–3). American spelling has been silently converted to British. Most space breaks have been omitted because a layout editor added them to fit the story into available column inches. This Christmas story recalls James Joyce's "The Dead" (the snowfall) and *A Portrait of the Artist* (the aunt who visits at Christmas). The story has indications of retrospection. Katherine, the narrator, claims, parenthetically, "(It cannot have been easy, I see now, for Aunt Kay to break out those year-long silences attendant on her very solitary life.)" She mentions that the house had no electricity "in those days." Kay is something of a fairy godmother, akin to the other godmothers in Bowen's postwar stories.

    1. The description of the town on the estuary is reminiscent of Cork, although some elements recall Wexford.

    2. Orris: a derivative of irises used in fragrances and medicines. Its smell resembles violets.

    3. A paragraph break has been added.

Happiness

"Happiness" appeared first in *Woman's Day* in December 1959 (pages 58, 122–4). The reconciliation between lovers countervails Bowen's many stories that conclude with the estrangement of lovers. Christmas spirit compensates for blasted hopes and unhappiness. In many of her Christmas stories, including "Emergency in the Gothic Wing" and "Christmas Games," Bowen takes pleasure in representing the curmudgeonly uncle – in this case, Uncle Willard. Space breaks introduced into the magazine layout have been omitted.

    1. A paragraph break has been added.

The Bazaar

Handwritten in a relatively clear hand, "The Bazaar" comprises twenty pages with some corrections (HRC 1.5). The manuscript is undated, but it may have been written between 1925 and 1930. The situation shows evidence of a careful reading of Katherine Mansfield's short stories; the resemblance of "The Bazaar" to "The Garden Party" goes without saying. Virginia Woolf's technique of rapidly passing from character to character, not to mention the singing and the humming women reminiscent of the working women in the central section of *To The Lighthouse*, marks Bowen's own technique. By emphasising the lightness of social comedy, she seems to be thinking through and absorbing Woolf's influence on her writing. Capitalisation has been regularised (so that words such as "bazaar," "providence," and "charity" are in lower case). An ampersand has been converted to "and." Where Bowen forgot quotation marks or commas, I have silently added them.

    1. Bowen spells this word "aeriels" and may have a flower or plant in mind.

    2. I have added "with a young man" because the "engagement" appears, at first reading, to refer to Paula's wanting to shepherd Lady Hottenham around the bazaar.

    3. The handwriting being hard to decipher, this word might be "scurried" or something else altogether.

    4. The comma has been added.

    5. The word "head" may be mistranscribed; the manuscript is hard to decipher.

    6. The manuscript reads "gilt."

7. Possibly "hornam" or "Hornam" or "kcrman" or "Worman" or something else. The initial letter is difficult to decipher.

8. Bowen inserts a phrase here, but her intentions are hard to construe. She may have hoped the sentence to read otherwise: "Arranged in the centre, for Lady Hottenham to buy, was a nightdress case covered with pink bows."

9. I have added "case," although Bowen may have momentarily changed her mind about whether a nightdress or a nightdress case was for sale. Later in the story, Lady Hottenham admires the nightdress case.

10. Mr. Bude is not present. Presumably Mrs. Bude remembers that her husband did not notice her appearance before he left for work.

11. *The Mikado*: Gilbert and Sullivan's operetta premiered at the Savoy Theatre in London in 1885.

12. In the manuscript, the sentence has no subject: "The was silent." Clearly "crowd" or "audience" or "assembly" is intended.

13. Bowen spells cocoanut in two ways – cocoanut and cokernut – with the implication that Lady Hottenham corrects her colloquial diction. To shy a cocoanut is to throw it.

14. *Samson and Delilah*: Saint-Saëns's opera, *Samson and Delilah*, based on the biblical story, premiered in Weimar in 1877, but was banned from the English stage until 1909.

15. Bowen omits "in," because she originally wrote "in another," then crossed it out in favour of "the other." Through inadvertence, she forgot to reinstate the "in."

16. The manuscript reads "walking."

17. The story ends here abruptly.

Miss Jolly Has No Plans for the Future

Handwritten with a fountain pen on ruled paper, "Miss Jolley Has No Plans for the Future" comprises seven pages (HRC 8.4). The style of writing and the use of black ink in the manuscript are characteristic of Bowen's writing habits in the late 1920s and early 1930s. Nevertheless, the monologic technique resembles narratives written in the 1940s – "Oh Madam" (1940), "The Dolt's Tale" (circa 1946), and Stella Rodney's answers to a coroner's inquest in *The Heat of the Day* (1949) – to convey criminal intent or implication in crime by association. Part way through the manuscript, Bowen ceases to use quotation marks around the woman's monologue. She spells "court" sometimes with an upper case, sometimes not; it has been standardised in lower case.

1. Bowen usually puts a comma after an initial "yes" or "no" in a sentence. On several occasions, she does not. I have added several such commas, where appropriate.

2. Rout: to root around or dig up.

3. "I" is missing in the original.

4. In the original, the second page ends here, but Bowen pencils the number 5 at the top of the next page (the third). From this numbering, one could infer that some pages are missing from the manuscript.

5. The word "in" has been added for sense.

6. "She" apparently refers to Miss Kisby's mother.

7. Bowen accidentally writes "I" for "a" here.

The Man and the Boy

"The Man and the Boy" (HRC 8.4) is handwritten on ten sheets of ruled paper, of the same sort as "Miss Jolley Has No Plans for the Future." With its interwar affability, the story may date from the late 1920s. The European setting recalls "Salon des Dames" and *The Hotel* (1927). The reader learns that Benjie, despite his physical similarity to Tom, is Antonia's son from a previous marriage. Spelling and punctuation errors have been silently corrected. The title "The Man and the Boy" is loosely scrawled at the top of the first page in pencil.

1. The chief newspaper in the south of France is *Nice Matin*. Having been ten days earlier in Tours, the travelling party has moved south to Provence.

2. Tours: a small city in the Loire Valley in France. A comma has been added after "Tours."

3. The manuscript reads "sit," but the preceding comment about Benjie's and Tom's deliberate avoidance of Theodore promotes the possibility that "seen" is meant.

4. There is a ditto on "to think" in the manuscript.

5. Benjie, taunting Theodore, means, "do mad dogs unnerve you, too?"

6. Bowen altered "stood" to "standing"; the former is grammatically correct after the semi-colon, while the latter suggests the immobility of the jalousies left ajar.

7. Bowen erased "might," but the sentence makes more sense with that auxiliary verb.

8. Bowen changed the original sentence, "then you couldn't spare the car." Altering it, Bowen left "then you said couldn't spare it," which requires an extra "you."

9. Originally this formed one sentence. Throughout this story, Bowen, drafting hastily, omits quotation marks, full stops, and commas in quoted dialogue.

10. Faubourg: a suburb or district within a city.

11. Albi: a French town near Toulouse.

12. Eupeptic: having good digestion. But I have had to guess. The handwriting being illegible, the word looks like "emphatic" and might be anything at all.

13. The story ends here abruptly.

Story Scene

There are two drafts of this fragment about Leonard Osten and his adulterous wife Rene. The first page bears the pencilled title, "Story Scene," in Bowen's hand (HRC 1.1). Revising, she reworked one draft into another directly on the typewriter. I have transcribed what appears to be the more evolved draft; while resembling the first, the later draft is more elaborate and integrated in terms of plot. Nevertheless, the drafts run together and bear many crossings-out and alterations. In the version that I did not transcribe, Bowen describes Len, age 32, as having "the face but not the temperament of a Pierrot." By contrast, Rene has "a Madonna face – though faintly stubborn and cryptic." In this version, she resembles an Undine rather than a Madonna.

1. The word "on" is omitted after "went" to avoid the double preposition.

2. Coalite: a fuel made by extracting the elements that smoke from coal.

3. The typescript reads, "idea of Flora coming."

4. Bowen substituted "that" for "the," although "the" is more likely in context.

5. Bowen crossed out a sentence that indicates Rene's implication in Alec's life: "Rene (who seemed to know) said, now the garage was growing they were taking a lot of evening work."

6. This opening descriptive clause could fit somewhere else in the sentence (after "Rene," for instance). Bowen added the phrase above the typed text, but does not indicate with a caret exactly where it belongs.

7. A superfluous "in" falls at the end of the sentence; Bowen forgot to cross it out.

8. Bowen crossed out a parenthetical phrase that allies Flora with men: "(for Flora, his cousin, had been one man more)."

9. Originally, Bowen wrote "sank into Len's silence"; revising, she wrote, "sank in, Len's silence." I have removed the comma.

10. The typescript reads, "uncrewed."

11. A paragraph break has been added.

12. A space break is likely: at the bottom of the typescript page, there is an unaccounted for space, as if a line were missing. In the last short section, Bowen accidentally mixes up Len and Alec. It is more probable that Len as the host, not Alec as an old friend, meets Flora at the train station. It would also be odd for Flora to ask Alec about Rene. The error becomes clear when Flora, walking beside "Alec," asks after "Alec." I have adjusted the names accordingly. In the last section, paragraphing has also been added to reflect dialogue; Bowen, usually when writing early drafts, runs dialogue together without paragraph breaks.

Flowers Will Do

This twenty-two-page story exists as a typescript (HRC 4.4). The typist habitually substitutes an "8" for an apostrophe – a typing error clearly – which I have corrected. Letters accidentally disappear from "handome," "cuboard," "cuhion," and so forth; these, too, have been corrected. Commas are missing in some instances of quoted dialogue. Occasionally the dialogue is not paragraphed for alternating speakers, so I take the liberty, following Bowen's usual practice, of starting a new paragraph for each new speaker. In a few instances, lines are cut off at the bottom of the page. Mrs. Benger is first called "Mrs. Belt"; her name changes when Doris begins to pop into her flat for visits. Only latterly is her given name, Polly, revealed by Leo. The story is so nearly complete that it may have been published somewhere with minor corrections. Sellery and Harris do not, however, mention its publication anywhere. With a plot about callous lovers and loose women, the story would appear to have been written in the 1930s. Bowen wrote longhand until the mid-1930s; therefore, this story, written on the typewriter, likely dates from the late 1930s.

1. The sentence begins with a "Then," which chimes awkwardly with the "then" after the comma.

NOTES

2. Marquisite: possibly "marquisette," a machine-made net fabric, or "marcasite," a crystallised form of iron pyrites used for ornaments and jewellery.

3. A misspelling, "while hair," occurs in the typescript.

4. "I have had enough" would be more fluid. but Bowen omits the "had."

5. This phrase is written "half I man" in the typescript. Bowen might have intended "half a man."

6. Although this word is spelled "tin" in the typescript, it seems unlikely that the house, however jerry-built, would have an interior wall made of tin.

7. Bowen originally wrote "the woman below." She replaced this with "Mrs. Belt," who returns as "Mrs. Benger." "Benger's" was the proprietary name of medicinal powder that, mixed with milk, soothed digestion and restored strength.

8. This word is spelt "delikatessen" in the typescript.

9. A.B.C.: Aerated Bread Company, a chain of self-service tea-rooms and bakeries across the British Isles, started as a bread production company in 1862.

10. One or two words are cut off at the bottom edge of the page. It is possible that several lines of dialogue have been lost at this point.

11. Originally there was a comma after "root": "that was the root, of it."

12. Some lines may be cut off at the bottom of the page; the very tops of cut-off letters are visible, but illegible.

13. The sentence, "There's not much he can do, really," is not attributed to either Doris or Mrs. Benger. Yet only these two characters are in the room. Either woman could speak the line, but it makes more sense that Mrs. Benger, who wants Leo to leave, would claim that he cannot do much. Doris Simonez would be less likely to presume so far.

14. The typescript reads "his," which makes ro sense.

15. Mrs. Belt converts into Mrs. Benger at this point.

16. The typescript reads, "the bed's tumbled surface of the bed."

17. The typescript reads, "freezias, flooping."

18. The word "for" has been added.

19. Bowen writes "Mrs. Simonez," an accidental confusion, for she means "Mrs. Benger."

20. Bowen adds the words "the which of" by hand, but the phrase adds nothing to the sentence. I have therefore omitted it.

21. The typescript reads "Why not you two . . ."

22. The word "a" has been added at the start of this phrase. Beneath

Bowen's erasures, one can discern a different sentence: "Leo lay sideways across the divan – young man who had just had his head pushed gently off someone's lap."

23. The typescript reads "in." The preposition is wrong. A hand might lie in her lap, but it cannot easily lie "in her knee."

24. Bowen erased another version: "It was as though she saw Sydney for the first time." Revising, she wrote, "Now, though she saw Sydney for the first time." I have added the second comma.

25. Bowen wrote this paragraph twice over. The first version ends suddenly: "All at once, Doris pulled her hand free. 'Well, we don't have to keep laughing.' She looked across at Sydney, flushed and twisting his head round, tilting his drink at Polly. She did not love Sydney. She thought: Polly's seen, too – oh, what a shocking thing. With her." The dynamic is more complex in this version. Doris, glimpsing her relation with Sydney through Polly Benger's eyes, realises that she does not love Sydney at all.

The Last Bus

The carbon copy of "The Last Bus" is dated "29.11.44." at the end of the eight-page typescript (HRC 6.10). The story is an allegory about Europe and its future directions. It owes something to E. M. Forster's *The Celestial Omnibus* (1911), the title story of that collection being one that Bowen considered teaching at Vassar in 1960 in her class on the short story. Following editorial practice in other stories, I have separated dialogue into paragraphs according to speaker, whereas Bowen, beginning with the conductor's dismissive, "I dessay you're right," lumps together dialogue among several speakers in single paragraphs. The point of doing so may be to indicate the coalition of voices – young, old, male, female, military, civilian, bureaucratic, English, and foreign – that contribute to making the new Europe. Although the story ends inconclusively, Bowen thought it finished, for she drew a line across the page at the end and added the date.

1. A paragraph break has been added.

2. There is a semi-colon, not a comma, in the typescript.

3. A. T. S.: Auxiliary Territorial Service, the women's corps of the British Army. Originally staffed by volunteers during the Second World War, the A. T. S. changed its structure of rank to correspond to full military status as of 9 May 1941.

4. In the typescript, an ellipsis follows the civil servant's remark.

Fairies at the Christening

"Fairies at the Christening" exists as a twenty-one-page typescript with extensive corrections in Bowen's hand (HRC 4.4). Sellery and Harris do not list it as published in any book or magazine, and I cannot trace it to any published source. I have amended obvious spelling mistakes and errors in verb tense. Bowen interchanges periods, em-dashes, colons, and semi-colons. Some rough punctuation has been left unchanged, although Bowen would probably have refined the story in subsequent revisions.

1. The word "nonna," meaning "grandmother" in Italian, connects the child to the three wise women who show up at her christening.

2. Originally Bowen wrote, "He felt he had suddenly plunged into deep waters." Not fully erasing this sentence, the typescript erroneously reads, "He felt he himself plunged into deep waters."

3. The typescript reads, "What are really the headache are these appalling godmothers."

4. The "of" has been added.

5. The typescript reads, "car's door opening."

6. Bowen uses em-dashes after "laughter" and "flat" in the last two sentences in the paragraph. I have altered these to avoid having four consecutive sentences that hinge a clause to the sentence with a dash.

7. Bowen, perhaps accidentally, added the question mark to the typescript by hand.

8. There is a ditto on "crowded" in the typescript.

9. The typescript reads, "not, might say."

10. The original reads, "corner lamp in the corner," with the first "corner" a handwritten change.

11. Bowen uses a colon not a full stop after "cord," which I have changed to reduce the number of colons in the sentence.

12. The typescript reads, "*wished you, Happiness in Love, and Truthfulness.*"

13. Bowen crossed out "holy, most wholly human, day" and replaced it with "greater Day."

Christmas Games

I cannot trace "Christmas Games" to any published text. It exists as an eighteen-page typescript with extensive emendations in Bowen's hand (HRC 2.6). The atmospherics of this story, which is a pastiche of sorts, owe something to Sheridan Le Fanu's *Uncle Silas*. The name of the gloomy country house, "Ravenswood," alludes to Sir Walter Scott's *The Bride of Lammermoor*, whose protagonist is Edgar Ravenswood. At the same time, the destroyed house recalls Edgar Allan Poe's "The Fall of the House of Usher." Other influences are evident. The engraving of a scene from *Macbeth* that hangs on Mrs. Throcksby's chimneypiece could represent the witches' coven in that play. Fairy-tale qualities taken from Rumpelstiltskin (the footprints) and Hansel and Gretel (the two young people lured to the witch's den) also enter the plot. Mrs. Throcksby's lip-licking and avid glances remind Phyllida of the "Wolf Grandmother" in "Little Red Riding-Hood." Because "Christmas Games" resembles "Emergency in the Gothic Wing" and because it shares a Christmas Eve setting with other mid-1950s stories, it may have been written around 1954. Spelling mistakes, such as "boottees," "suddeness," "jublilantly," "siezed," have been corrected. Bowen gives a slightly Gallic quality to the word "invalid" by adding a final "e," which I have omitted.

1. In the typescript, Bowen writes "Birdington," but elsewhere she calls the village Little Birdover. The name has been altered here for consistency.

2. The typescript reads, "Aunt Beattie's."

3. In the typescript, Bowen writes "pull-bell."

4. Correcting the typescript by hand, Bowen left a jumbled phrase: "referred to in Mrs. Throcksby in letter."

5. Before revision, the sentence read, "Bespectacled, saturnine, frowsty, stopping, he looked like an unpleasing kind of professor but more than mere learning seemed to be on his mind."

6. Bowen added the rhetorical question mark at the end of this sentence by hand.

7. Before revision, this phrase read, "then added; 'And after . . .'"

8. The typescript reads, "love first sight."

9. In the typescript, "cup-and-saucer" is hyphenated.

10. "Clotted" is circled in pencil, for no discernible reason, but is not crossed out.

11. The typescript reads, "bad your aunt."

12. Fulvous: reddish-yellow or tawny.

13. Bowen crossed out "on" and tried the phrase "found in the ashes." Restoring "remained," she forgot to restore "on" as well.

NOTES

Home for Christmas

Bowen wrote an essay called "Home for Christmas" for the December 1955 issue of *Mademoiselle*. Despite bearing the same title, "Home for Christmas," the story, has nothing else in common with the essay. It exists as a twelve-page typescript (HRC 5.7). Bowen's compulsion to write Christmas stories in the mid-1950s fixes the date of composition of this particular story at that time. While sharing the spookiness of such stories as "Just Imagine . . ." and "The Claimant," this story has a more sinister quality, for Tom urges Millie to get inside the trunk; he wants her to repeat the action that cost the previous woman her wits. Dialogue has been broken where necessary into separate lines for alternating speakers. Typographical and spelling errors have been corrected. "Gasfire" alternates with "gas fire," so the latter has been adopted. Similarly "hide-and-seek" sometimes does and sometimes does not have hyphens; I have regularised the term with hyphens.

1. A ditto on "he" occurs in the typescript
2. The typescript, amended by hand, reads, "He went off to write a letters in our room."
3. A ditto on "into" occurs in the typescript.
4. A ditto on "live" occurs in the typescript.
5. Originally the phrase was "screaming away." Crossing out "screaming," Bowen may accidentally have let "away" stand.
6. The story ends here abruptly.

Ghost Story

I have added quotation marks that were omitted from the eleven-page, unfinished typescript of "Ghost Story" (HRC 4.6). Bowen made some corrections to the typescript by hand. "Ghost Story" appears at the top of the first page. Because of the Christmas setting and the comic mode, the story was probably written in the mid-1950s, around the time of "Emergency in the Gothic Wing."

1. Mistakenly spelled "Ottowa" in the typescript, although Bowen also tried "Ottoawa."
2. The typescript reads, "Across in chasm of silence."
3. Bowen crossed out "him" after "round."
4. A ditto on "light" occurs in the typescript.

5. The passage is heavily revised. The word "reassuring" may or may not be intended.

6. The amended passage reads, "behind about the mouths and eyes"; only one preposition is required. Because the word "behind" is typed intralineally, as a later addition, it takes precedence over "about."

7. The more intelligible phrase, "could be told," is crossed out.

8. Bowen erased a phrase from the end of the sentence: "contracting their shoulder blades as though blasts came on to them from the walls."

9. There is an unlikely plural, "rabbits-skin," in the typescript.

10. The typescript reads, "we' still strangers strangers to her," with the missing "re" on "we're" and a ditto on "strangers."

11. The word "in" is missing in the typescript: "walk her sleep."

12. The typescript reads, "their pony trap bolted"; the comma and "which" have been added.

13. The typescript displaces a preposition: "he lived with Cousin Meta on for some years." This error is probably due to an addition, "with Cousin Meta," inserted between lines in the wrong spot.

14. "Threw" is a guess, for the original reads "rhew."

15. "I" has been added. Bowen crossed out the phrase, "I'm so disappointed," but she forgot to include the pronoun in her revision.

16. Word order is conjectural because Bowen added some material intralineally. She might have intended, although it is unlikely, "her living presence, this morning, unexpectedly most grateful."

Women in Love

"Women in Love" exists as a twenty-six-page typescript and its carbon copy (HRC 10.1). While typing up the story, the typist inserted carbons backwards; they have left an inky imprint on the verso of pages 4, 7, 9, 11, 13 and 21. Consequently, these pages are missing from the carbon copy. There are, on the other hand, two versions of page 24 in the carbon copy. Bowen made emendations in blue ink to the typescript and added the title, "T.V.? *Women in Love* by Elizabeth Bowen." The title announces Bowen's ongoing engagement with D. H. Lawrence, manifest in *The House in Paris* and short stories such as "Attractive Modern Homes." She lectured on Lawrence's stories "Tickets, Please" and "The Rocking-Horse Winner" in the undergraduate course that she gave on the short story at Vassar College in 1960. In those classes, she emphasised the explosive force in Lawrence's stories and their regional specificity (HRC 7.3). In a review of an anthology of his works, Bowen recuperates the intensity of Lawrence's writing: "what he saw (if not always what he said) sinks itself into the memory, deep down; his vision not only fuses with but permanently affects the vision of his reader" (*Collected Impressions* 157). In the same review, Bowen notes that the characters in Lawrence's novel *Women in Love* "split apart under too great pressure" (*Collected Impressions* 159). Bowen's short story "Women in Love," takes a melodramatic, perhaps Lawrentian, turn when Andie and Joanna, building on sympathetic feeling towards each other, nearly quarrel; Joanna speaks "sharply" and "impatiently," and Andie responds "angrily.' Having known each other for a brief afternoon, they have little reason to speak with so much heat. Tonia's narcissism is somewhat overdrawn; she asserts her presence with the repeated, italicised, first-person pronoun "*I*." The story has an inconsistency: the reason for selling the cottage that Joanna gives to her friend Margaret on the telephone has to be construed retrospectively as a falsehood. The narrator does nothing to contradict the initial assertion that Joanna is selling her country house in order to help her financially strapped mother. Later she intimates that she wishes to sell the cottage to help the blind artist. Andie infers that the man is her brother, building on the evidence that his "sister" will have the money. Joanna neither confirms nor denies this allegation, which raises the possibility that the man is not Joanna's brother but her lover, hence "Women in Love."

In light of the notation, "TV," the story was probably meant for dramatisation. Adverbial indicators for vocal intonation – "glumly," "angrily" – adorn the text, often in the middle of dialogue. Indeed, the story was likely written as a television treatment. In a letter dated 28 May 1959, Spencer Curtis Brown wrote to Bowen in New York:

One of the TV Companies here are [sic] making a series of half-hour television films under the general title of WOMEN IN LOVE. They are for joint English and American release, and they are having different English, American or Continental stars in each film. WOMEN IN LOVE is a broad title, since it can cover not merely women of any age in love with men of any age but women in love with houses, places, relations, or indeed anything else.

If you cared to rough out a short outline of a story for them, they would be prepared to commission this for £200. For this fee they would buy, of course, only television rights, and you would be perfectly free to write the story up later in a form suitable for publication and sell it to any magazines anywhere you wanted or include it in any collection. Consequently the £200 would be sheer extra money.

It would not be necessary to give them a polished story, but merely an outline of a character, and of a dramatic situation into which they get and out of which they get. It must, of course, be a story which is capable of visual presentation, equally a story requiring only four or five sets, and preferably with no more than five or six characters. If you would like to send such a story, then we could collect the £200 immediately since the commission is firm.

The star for whom they would particularly like you to write would be either Wendy Hiller or Margaret Leighton, both of whom you probably know. As an example, they are using MARRIAGE A LA MODE by Katherine Mansfield and THE LEGACY by Virginia Woolf. (HRC 11.3)

Bowen typically wrote stories and novels first, and oversaw their adaptation to the radio or screen subsequently. Hence she may well have written this treatment in the form of a short story as a way of working out the contingencies and exigencies imposed by the film company. I have corrected obvious typographical errors and added missing quotation marks. Certain unhyphenated words, such as "goodlooking" and "mantleshelf," are Bowen's compounds.

1. Joanna later reveals to Andie that "somebody" was blinded and that she hopes to raise money to support him. The sudden death of the father, mentioned only at the beginning of the story, would also be a plausible reason to sell the cottage. That Joanna's side of the telephone conversation is reported, rather than quoted, lends credence to the statement.

2. Paragraph breaks have been added to separate passages of quoted speech attributed to different speakers.

3. Bowen erroneously writes "Joanna's," but Tonia has gone upstairs.

4. The word "irritation" is typed between lines above "with a nod." Or it may have leaked through from another page because of carbon paper badly placed.

5. "To" has been inserted. The sentence originally read, "Tonia suddenly asked Joanna." Bowen forgot to add "to" in her revisions.

6. The word "be" has been inserted.

7. There is a ditto on "so" in the typescript.

8. There is a ditto on "for" in the typescript.

9. The sentence originally read, "she glanced at the bowl on the table," but Bowen crossed out "glanced" and wrote "shrugged her shoulders" above. If "she shrugged her shoulders at the bowl" seems like an odd gesture, it may be due to the fact that Bowen never finished revising the phrase.

10. The typescript reads "feel hurt," but "feet hurt" is more likely.

11. The verb "were" refers, ungrammatically, to "vision and longing." But "was" is more logically the verb that completes "blend" or "face."

12. The word "the" is missing in the typescript.

13. The original sentence is uncharacteristic of Bowen's style: "Her expression showed (a) that she did not care for any jam, (b) that since there must, apparently, *be* jam, she recognised this as the best kind." I have altered the sentence slightly.

14. The typescript reads "Joanna," which is clearly an error.

15. Although Bowen hyphenates "chimney-piece" earlier in the story, the unhyphenated spelling, "chimneypiece," has been adopted to conform with occurrences of the word in other stories.

16. The story ends here abruptly.

Works Cited

The Elizabeth Bowen Archives are held at the Harry Ransom Humanities Research Center at the University of Texas at Austin. Throughout this volume, all archival material, including letters, manuscripts, typescripts, broadcasts, and notebooks, is designated with the acronym "HRC," followed by a box and file number. All HRC designations refer to the Bowen archives unless otherwise indicated.

Bowen, Elizabeth. *Afterthought: Pieces about Writing*. London: Longmans, 1962.

—. "Bowen's Court." *Holiday* 24 (December 1958): 86–7, 190–3.

—. *Collected Impressions*. London: Longmans, 1950.

—. "Comeback of Goldilocks et al." *New York Times Magazine* (26 August 1962): 18–19, 74–5.

—. "Enchanted Centenary of the Brothers Grimm." *New York Times Magazine* (8 September 1963): 28–9, 112–13.

—. "Guy de Maupassant." *Literary Digest* 1.1 (April 1946): 26.

—. "The Idea of France." 1944. HRC 6.3.

—. Introduction. *The King of the Golden River*. By John Ruskin. New York and London: Macmillan, 1962. iii–v.

—. Introduction. *The Observer Prize Stories: 'The Seraph and The Zambesi' and Twenty Others*. London: Heinemann, 1951. vii–xi.

—. *The Mulberry Tree*. Ed. and intro. Hermione Lee. New York: Harcourt, 1986.

—. "A Novelist and His Characters." *Essays by Divers Hands: Being the Transactions of the Royal Society of Literature*. New Series, vol. 26. Ed. Mary Stocks. London: Oxford University Press, 1970. 19–23.

—. Preface. *Early Stories*. New York: Knopf, 1951. v–xvii.

—. "Rx For a Story Worth the Telling." *New York Times Book Review* (31 August 1958): 1, 13.

—. "The Short Story in England." *British Digest* 1.12 (August 1945): 39–43.

—. *A Time in Rome*. New York: Knopf, 1960.

WORKS CITED

Coppard, A. E., ed. *Consequences*. Waltham: Golden Cockerel, 1932.

Fothergill, John, ed. *The Fothergill Omnibus*. London: Eyre & Spottiswoode, 1931.

Glendinning, Victoria. *Elizabeth Bowen*. 1977. New York: Anchor, 2006.

Green, Henry. *Loving*. Intro. by Jeremy Treglown. 1945. London: Harvill, 1996.

Joyce, James. *A Portrait of the Artist as a Young Man*. Ed. Chester G. Anderson. 1916. New York: Penguin, 1977.

Lassner, Phyllis. *Elizabeth Bowen: A Study of the Short Fiction*. New York: Twayne, 1991.

Lee, Hermione. *Elizabeth Bowen*. Rev. ed. London: Vintage, 1999.

MacKay, Marina. *Modernism and World War II*. Cambridge: Cambridge University Press, 2007.

Sellery, J'nan M. and William O. Harris. *Elizabeth Bowen: A Bibliography*. Austin, TX: Humanities Research Center, 1981.

Wilson, Angus. Introduction. *The Collected Stories of Elizabeth Bowen*. 1981. New York: Ecco, 1989.

Yeats, William Butler. *The Autobiography of William Butler Yeats*. New York: Macmillan, 1965.

EU representative:
Easy Access System Europe
Mustamäe tee 50, 10621 Tallinn, Estonia
Gpsr.requests@easproject.com